Tiadath Mage

Grant E. Brazell

National Library of Australia Catalogue-in-Publication entry:

Copyright © 2015 by Grant E. Brazell

Tiadath Mage / written by Grant E. Brazell.

ISBN 978-0-9871115-2-4

Fiction / Fantasy

Artwork © by Grant E. Brazell
Arcane brushes supplied by www.obsidiandawn.com
Cloud brushes supplied by www.amaranthdreams.com
Original Sword artwork by Soojin Mitton

A823.4

Published by Lyshan Press

Printed in the United States of America

First Printing: December 2015

DEDICATION

To those who believed

Though this is a stand-alone novel and can be read on its own merits. It does, however, make assumptions that you have read, Tesania – Trannyth's Keep

By the same Author

Tesania series

Tesania - Trannyth's Keep
Tiadath Mage

www.grantebrazell.wordpress.com

ACKNOWLEDGMENTS

I would like to acknowledge and thank all those people who helped this story become what it could be.

To my wife, Kim, for patiently reading and editing each chapter and rewrite along the way. To my son, Matthew: for his inspiration.

Thank you to my Beta readers; Kim Brazell, Vicki Gardner, Elizabeth Harris, Shere Kahn, Jessica Tanaka, Arthur Wallis, Wanigesekera Maheswani and Michael Lambert. To all of you I owe a debt of gratitude. Your feedback and support of TIADATH MAGE and the characters was a great help and motivation.

Prologue

Soft tendrils of mist curled lazily through the masts of the Lady Tesania's ship, Advance; entwining themselves amongst the rigging and sails slipping silently toward the decks below.

"How goes it?" Captain Wallis asked his first lieutenant as he stepped from his cabin at the rear of the ship.

"The wind's slackened," Lieutenant Chable replied gesturing to the sails. "We're making barely two knots."

"Very well," the captain replied as he scanned the glassy ocean. Only the odd ripple reflected the moon's soft light as he turned back to the lieutenant. "Have the men set more sail," he said while glancing up into the rigging. "I see a mist is setting in."

Peering up curiously, the lieutenant said, "Strange. It was clear a few minutes ago." Shaking his head, he walked forward to the boson's mate. "Send the men up. We'll have all canvas set if you please."

"Aye, aye, sir," the boson's mate replied crisply before hurrying along the deck blowing his shrill whistle and yelling orders to the men.

Surveying the rigging once more, Chable shook his head. The mist was thickening substantially, already it had engulfed the royals and the topgallant sails were now only barely visible. Swirling amongst the yards, it grew and expanded as it traced along the ropes and lines hungrily exploring. "It's coming in fast," he said as he returned to the captain.

"Indeed," the captain replied. "Visibility will soon be down to nothing."

"It's a strange thing," the lieutenant replied as he turned slowly, surveying the ocean. "It seems to be localized on us," he said, frowning. "It's like it's following us."

"Nonsense," the captain scoffed. "The night is cool; the water still warm from the day's sun. I should think I wouldn't have to explain this to you," he growled.

"How do you explain that then?" Chable asked gesturing toward the ocean with his chin.

Moving to the taffrail, the Captain grasped the sun baked wood and leant forward to study the water below. Moonlight reflected brightly off the ship's white, rippling wake while the wisps of mist that had fallen behind the large stern danced and swirled as they dashed to rejoin the clawing mass working its way down the ship's rigging. "There appears to be some—" Midsentence, he whirled about as a chilling scream rent the air from above.

Rushing forward, his attention firmly on the thickening mist above, Chable called out, "You men! What's going on up there! Get those sails set!" Turning on his heel he strode to the boson's mate. "I want the name of that man. The captain will tolerate no tomfoolery aboard this ship."

The mate nodded sourly and spat over the side. "Aye, sir," he gruffly replied.

"Very good," Chable said as he turned away. "This mist is trouble. Mark my words," he muttered as another scream rent the air followed shortly by another and then a cacophonous choir of terrified wails. Chable's head whipped up to the mainmast sails. Churning mist seethed and boiled as it cascaded down the masts at frightening speed. Something caught his eye amongst the whiteness, for a moment he struggled to recognize what it might be until it hurtled out of the mist, cannoning into his left shoulder as it drove him to the deck. Another thud and then another announced sailor after sailor falling dead from the heights above.

Excruciating pain shot from Chable's shoulder to his overwrought brain as he fought to shove the dead weight of the sailor's smashed body off himself. Gingerly he climbed to his feet, dizziness overtaking him as he stumbled to the rail, retching over the side as a finger of mist settled on the rail beside him. Dazed and confused, he watched as it seemed to consciously look about before curling along the rail toward his shaking hand. "This can't be happening," he muttered. Snatching his hand away, he turned and staggered toward the captain. The groans and creaks of tortured masts above thundered over the ship as stays and ropes gave way, blocks and splinters of wood raining down on the men left alive. Chable's pace quickened as he rushed along the deck, dodging falling debris and hurdling bodies. The mist reached out for him as he passed, snatching at him, clawing at his throat, restricting his breathing. Coughing and spluttering he beat it away as he skidded to a halt on the quarter deck, gasping, "Captain. What do we d—?" his question dying in his throat as the captain's face turned slowly toward him, a ball of mist playing in his open mouth while tendrils drifted lazily from his nostrils. Lurching forward, the captain reached out, his eyes pleading as he collapsed forward and thudded heavily into his beloved deck.

Horrified, Chable turned. Desperately, he looked around. Men writhed on the deck as the mist engulfed them. Every fiber of his being screamed at him to rush and help them, but he knew there was nothing he could do. How could he fight such an ethereal foe? In shock, dismayed at the death and carnage around him, he made the last decision he would make as the first lieutenant of the Advance. Stumbling forward, he grasped the coat of a small boy cowering behind a water barrel. "Get off!" he roared. "Abandon ship!" As the shrouds holding the main mast aloft snapped and whipped about the ship he sprinted for the side and threw himself over the rail into the cold grip of the water below.

Fighting to the surface, Chable sucked at the air. Coldness cut at his skin like a thousand knives while the weight of his soaked clothing threatened to drag him back under the unforgiving water. Kicking his legs, he ignored the pain shooting along the torn nerves of his shoulder and struggled to a floating piece of debris. Dragging himself half on, he turned and stared in horror at his once proud ship. The mist obscured it almost completely; the odd glimpse of the side timbers was all he could see. Tortured sounds of the hull being crushed rushed across the still water, each crack hitting him like a blow to the face. A tear came to his eye as the mist slowly began to dissipate, revealing his ship. The hull was splintered and torn, masts gone, railings smashed and hanging at grotesque angles while jets of air hissed from open ports as the unforgiving ocean forced itself into the shattered holds. In disbelief he watched, his jaw working as the Advance settled deeper into the frigid water, gave one last groan and rolled onto her side before slowly slipping beneath the barely perceptible waves.

***

Strange visions came to Chable on his third day adrift on the flotsam of his beloved ship; sails on the horizon bearing directly toward him.

He knew it to be an illusion; days of sun and no water were playing havoc on his mind. Dreamily he lay his head down on his makeshift raft, certain that he would soon join his mates in the great shipyard in the sky.

***

Farmer Jaryd surveyed his land from atop the highest hill on the farm. Reaching down, he stroked his horse's neck as it nickered and trembled underneath him. Squinting against the sun's glare he watched an eagle soaring majestically above the southern fields, scouring the wheat fields for prey. The year had been a good one, the calving had gone well and the crops were nearly ready for harvest. Lady Tesania herself had even visited and praised him deeply on his management of her Orash farm.

"Shh," he whispered as the horse grew more agitated, shuffling its shod hooves on the rocky ground. "We'll be heading home soon."

Skittering forward, the horse almost threw Jaryd from its back. Snatching at the reins he managed to regain his balance. "Whoa there girl," he said gently as he looked about. "What's the matter?" Twisting in the saddle he glimpsed a tendril of mist as it curled along the horse's flank toward him. "What the—" Jaryd exclaimed as the horse reared and bucked, throwing him from the saddle. Arms flailing, he braced himself for the impact, but he never hit the ground.

Struggling as he flew through the air, Jaryd watched in terror as the land dropped farther and farther away while the mist drifted around his face, wandering wistfully up to his eyes. "What are you?" he demanded as he rose higher, even above the soaring eagle in the sky.

Seemingly contemplating him, the mist hovered for a few moments and then withdrew behind him. Throwing his head from side to side he desperately tried to see what it was doing. "Show yourself!"

Floating lazily around to his face once more the mist swirled and pulsated in front of him as it formed a featureless face, the empty sockets staring at him. "Who are y—" Jaryd's head jerked back as a penetrating presence shot from the mist and invaded his mind. Pain hammered through his skull as the invader rampaged through his synapses, searching, probing every memory and thought. Cringing as he fought against the assault, he screamed, "Let me go!"

The mist obliged, the farmer's thrashing arms clawing at the air as he gained momentum. His last thoughts were of his wife and children as the mist exploded past him, its attention now turned to the cattle and fields of wheat below.

1 - Disturbing news

Two stately swans glided peacefully along the slow flowing Wyvern River as the soft morning breeze played wistfully among the swaying reeds. Ripples fled across the water as the bow of a small boat pushed against the current, the rhythmical splash of its oars biting the water echoing lightly off the clover covered river banks on either side.

Tesania twirled a dainty parasol in her hand, watching as it spun above her head. "We'd better head back soon," she suggested to Deavon as he pulled at the oars in the centre of the little boat. "I think we may soon get wet," she said gesturing up at the gathering clouds in the sky.

Nodding, Deavon dug an oar into the water, pulling the boat around. "Ayana will be wondering where we've got to."

Tesania laughed. "I'm sure," she said lightly as she leaned on the rail of the small craft, dipping her fingers in the cool water. "But I do enjoy our little trips upriver. It's so peaceful."

"The last four years have been peaceful," Deavon replied, "since we destroyed Trannyth."

Flicking water at the ranger, Tesania said, "Don't remind me." Frowning, she sat up straight. "I still have nightmares about him."

"Well they have been," Deavon protested. "The kingdom is thriving," he continued, "and your lands are some of the best in Eldanal."

Tesania didn't reply; instead scanning the lush green banks drifting by. She thought of how lucky she'd been when the King and Queen of Eldanal had granted her all the property and lands owned by the disgraced Lord Dalgliesh upon her return from destroying the evil mage and his beasts. It had been too much at the time, overwhelming, beyond her simple village girl's grasp. Yet over the past four years she had come to enjoy the challenges of managing her new estate and holdings. From the simplest task of explaining to the gardeners exactly how she wanted the topiaries to be trimmed along the pathways to visiting her far flung farms and ranches. Her people meant the world to her; she liked to think of them as her extended family. Rarely did she raise her voice to the young maids and never tolerated others doing the same.

"Tes," Deavon said gently, breaking her from her thoughts. "It seems you have a visitor," he advised, nodding over his shoulder as he pulled the boat toward the little pier on the eastern bank of the river.

Tesania peered around the burly ranger in an attempt to see who waited for them. "Oh," she said. "It's my harbor manager."

"Greetings," the manager called as the boat bumped against the pier.

"Reas," Tesania greeted him as Deavon stood and held his hand out to support her. Rising as the boat bobbed up and down, she allowed him to lift her lightly onto the rough, weathered wood of the pier. "Won't you partake in some cider with my friends and I?"

Reas turned, taking in the small tables set out on the manicured grass. "I'm afraid I must admit that the good

Lady Ayana here," he said gesturing, "has already entertained me whilst I awaited your return."

Nodding as she took a seat at the nearest table and motioned for a maid to bring cider for herself and Deavon, Tesania asked, "I presume the reason for your visit involves the Advance?"

Fiddling with the cap in his hand, turning it around and around as he looked down at his feet, Reas eventually ventured, "Your ladyship. We have had news about the missing ship . . . ." Pausing, he refused to raise his eyes to meet hers.

"And?" Tesania questioned. "Has she arrived?"

"My Lady . . ." Reas mumbled shuffling his feet nervously. ". . . the Advance has sunk!" he blurted.

"Sunk!?" Tesania exclaimed rising to her feet sharply. "What do you mean sunk? Where?" she asked. "What of the crew . . . ? Where are they now?"

"Only one survivor was rescued by a passing trader," Reas replied cautiously. "The first lieutenant . . . Chable I believe his name is."

"And Captain Wallis?" Tesania demanded.

"Lost, I'm afraid," Reas replied, shaking his head.

Tesania sank to her seat in shock as Deavon approached and placed his hand on her shoulder. "How?" she asked quietly.

"Lieutenant Chable is not of . . ." The harbor manager paused, thinking how to continue. ". . . Ah, how should I say; sound of mind at the moment," he said sadly.

"Tell me," Tesania pushed.

"He doesn't seem to make much sense."

Standing and stepping toward the man, Tesania demanded, "Tell me what he said, Reas. I want to know what happened to my ship."

Reas stood silently for a few moments before lifting his head and replying. "The lieutenant reports that a mist destroyed the ship," he informed her, shrugging. "He's rambling. I don't think we can take any of what he says into account."

"A cloud of mist destroyed the ship?" Deavon asked.

"So he says." Looking toward a chair, the harbor master asked, "May I take a seat, Your Ladyship?"

"Enough of the ladyships," Tesania insisted as she waived him to sit. "Tell me exactly what the lieutenant had to say." Turning toward Deavon she grimaced. "All of them," she whispered tears welling in the corners of her eyes.

Reaching out, Deavon placed his arm around her trembling shoulders before looking at the harbor master. "We want to know everything," he said to the nervous man. "Leave nothing out."

"Very well," Reas agreed as he shook his head slowly. "But remember. It's the ravings of a madman."

"Get on with it!" Tesania snapped.

Lady Ayana reached over and placed a placating hand on Tesania's. "Let him speak, dear."

Tesania turned to Ayana. "They were my people," she said, voice almost a whisper. "I need to know."

Gripping her hand, Ayana smiled sadly before addressing the harbor manager. "Please continue."

Reas coughed and shuffled in his chair before saying, "The lieutenant reports that two days out from Wyvern harbor they were beset upon by a mist in the early evening."

"Nothing unusual for this time of year," Deavon ventured.

"True enough," Reas agreed. "But Chable insists this mist had a life of its own. That it killed the men." Pausing, he looked to Tesania and sadly continued. "And, it seems, Captain Wallis."

"But the Lieutenant somehow managed to survive?"

"It seems he managed to scramble over the side and take refuge on some wreckage."

"He abandoned his ship?" Tesania asked incredulously.

"He maintains that by this time the ship was in ruins. The masts were gone, rigging and broken timber strewn everywhere."

Lost in thought, Tesania nodded as she struggled to picture the ship in such disarray. "So, he was the only one to make it over the side?" she asked.

Reas nodded. "He says he watched from some wreckage as the mist crushed the ship and it sank."

"And the mist?" Deavon asked.

"Dispersed as quickly as it came."

"It seems an incredible story," Lady Ayana interrupted shaking her head in bemusement. "He must be quite insane."

"Three days adrift at sea with no food or water will do that to a man," Reas observed before saying, "He may recover his senses and tell us the real story when he's had time to recuperate."

"Let's hope so," Tesania replied quietly. Her thoughts raced as she turned to Deavon. "I'll have to let their families know," she said sadly.

"We've already sent dispatches," Reas assured her. "Most of the families would already know."

"Thank you," Tesania whispered. "Please extend my sympathy to Lieutenant Chable. Inform him I'll come to talk to him personally tomorrow."

"As you wish, Your Ladyship," Reas said as he stood pulling his cap onto his head and nodding. "Good day."

"Good day," Tesania mumbled as the harbor master turned and started toward his carriage. Drawing in a deep breath, she turned to a maid. "We'll be returning to the house now. You may pack everything away," she said, waving at the tables and chairs. "And please ask the gardener to draw the boat up and have it stored."

***

Tesania sat quietly as the hard wheels of her carriage crunched along the gravel road leading to the grand entrance of her home. Staring into the distance, she barely noticed the lush, manicured gardens or the butterflies and bees flitting industriously from one vibrant flower to the next. A small cloud in the distant blue sky held her attention as she went through the harbor master's words in her head once more. "How could mist?" she asked eventually, turning in her seat toward Deavon, "sink a ship?"

Deavon took her hand in his. "We don't know that it did, Tes," he said. "The lieutenant may be rambling."

"And if he isn't?" Tesania asked, her eyes searching Deavon's.

"There haven't been any other reports of attacks on ships," Deavon said, shrugging. "I would have heard at the Rangers' Headquarters if there were."

"All those people . . ." Tesania whispered, ". . . lost."

"It happens, Tes," Deavon said gently. "Ships are lost at sea for many reasons. It's a dangerous way to make a living."

Biting at her lower lip, Tesania once again turned her attention to the clouds in the sky. "I have a bad feeling about this," she muttered as the carriage driver pulled the horses to a stop.

Deavon stood and jumped from the carriage, skidding as his feet struggled for purchase on the gravelly ground. Turning, he held his hand up and helped Tesania alight before turning to help Ayana. The head maid approached as Tesania smoothed the folds of her dress. "My Lady," she said curtsying. "You have a visitor awaiting you inside."

"Another visitor," Tesania said, frowning. "Who is it this time?"

"A representative from your farmlands in Orash," the maid replied as the carriage driver led the horses toward the stables.

Tesania brightened. "Jaryd," she said, smiling at Deavon. "I wonder why he's here?" she asked curiously. "It's almost harvest time."

"Only one way to find out," Deavon said laughing as he placed his arm through hers and led her through the stately entrance way. Their footsteps clattered on the marble flagstones as they walked, the sound echoing up to the vaulted ceiling before disappearing among the dozens of tapestries and paintings adorning the whitewashed walls. Pausing before two large doors carved with chubby little angels holding harps and playing amongst a forest of trees, Deavon asked, "Ready?" as he reached for the handle.

Nodding, Tesania moved forward as the door swung open. "It's so good to see you, Jary—" Stopping in midsentence, she looked about the room in confusion. "I'm sorry," she muttered to the young man standing by the fireplace. "I was expecting Jaryd."

Stepping forward, the young man informed her, "I'm his son, Kerin."

Tesania nodded. "It's a pleasure to meet you," she said as Deavon stepped forward and clasped the young man's hand.

"Well met," he said.

"Indeed," mumbled Kerin.

Tesania stepped forward, extending her hand for Kerin to take. "How is your father?" she asked. "I trust he's well?"

Kerin stood quietly for a few moments obviously struggling with his emotions before turning and walking to the fireplace once more. With his back to the room, he said quietly, "My mother asked me to report to you."

"I know your mother well," Tesania said as Kerin turned toward her.

"My father," he said, swallowing as Tesania watched him intently, "is dead."

Hand flying to her mouth, Tesania suppressed a cry of dismay. With eyes wide in disbelief, she asked through her hand, "Dead? How can this be?"

Kerin turned back to the fire as he fought to control himself, the fire cracking and popping as Deavon and Tesania waited for him to continue. Eventually, with his voice breaking, he muttered, "Ten days ago. He went to inspect the fields and never came back."

"What happened?" Deavon asked, voice gentle.

Kerin spun anger in his face. "We don't know," he yelled, voice echoing around the room. "I found him in the fields after the mist destroyed everything."

Tesania's eyes darted to Deavon's as he waved her to silence and walked to the young man placing his hand on his shoulder. "Accidents do happen on farms." he said consolingly. "It can be a dangerous business."

Throwing Deavon's hand from his shoulder Kerin spun about. "It was no accident!" he raged. "He was murdered."

"Murdered?" Tesania asked quickly. "By who?"

"I don't know," Kerin said quietly as he settled back to staring at the fire. "His body was crushed beyond recognition . . . as if he'd fallen from a great height."

"And the mist you mentioned?" Deavon asked gently. "What of that?"

Kerin shrugged. "It disappeared as fast as it arrived." Turning slowly toward Tesania, he said, "It is my duty to inform you that, along with my father, we found all the crops and livestock on your farm killed or destroyed after the mist had lifted."

Reeling, Tesania felt dizziness overtake her as the room spun; stumbling as Deavon reached urgently toward her and helped her to a plush, padded chair, she gasped, "What is happening?"

2 - Tricks of the mind

Tesania gripped Lieutenant Chable's hand as he moaned. She regretted forcing him to recall the sinking of the Advance, but she needed to know, to hear for herself what had happened to so many of her people. "And the mist came from nowhere?" she asked softly.

Chable's haunted eyes regarded her before he answered, "The wind had slackened. We were only making a few knots."

"I understand," Tesania said patiently as she adjusted herself on her chair. "And that's when the mist came?"

Nodding, the lieutenant peered out the window of the hospital room in silence, as if reliving the horrible event, before turning his attention back to Tesania. "The Captain had just come on deck. . . . Everything seemed . . . seemed to be normal. Until . . . ." he said, his voice fading as his attention drifted to the window once more.

"Until?" Tesania pushed gently.

Jumping at her voice, the lieutenant's eyes flicked to Deavon and then Tesania as if seeing them there for the first time. Shifting himself on the bed, he withdrew his hand from Tesania's grasp and turned his attention back to the swaying trees outside before whispering, "At first I thought it was just a cloud of mist," he said. "But the Captain thought it strange that it was localized on our ship." Pausing once more, he gathered himself while Tesania watched him closely. "He was right of course," he continued, his voice growing as he swiveled to face Tesania. "It was following us! We could see it against the wake! Tendrils that had fallen behind us were rushing to rejoin the ship!" Turning away once more, he calmed himself. "It was unnatural I tell you. A thing I've never witnessed before."

Tesania glanced at Deavon, concerned as she wondered if the man was indeed insane. Deavon shrugged toward her, his own face puzzled. Thoughtfully, she turned back to the lieutenant and asked, "This mist sank the ship?"

"It did," Chable answered simply.

Tesania forced herself to remember the many mists she had seen. Conceding that it was sometimes hard to see through, she could only say it was otherwise no more than a low lying cloud of damp air. Shaking her head, she refocused on the lieutenant and asked quietly, "How did something as harmless as a mist . . ." she paused while looking for the right words. ". . . manage to sink a ship the size of the Advance?"

Chable shrugged. "I can't tell you," he said morosely as he glanced toward the ceiling. "It started in the rigging, up near the royals. It was like it was alive, crawling along the ropes and yards, as if searching!"

Tesania watched the man's face as he talked; the obvious horror he had endured was plain to see as he continued his story of the final moments of the Advance, tears rolling down his face. "The last I saw of the ship was when she sank beneath the waves."

Reaching out, Tesania placed her hand consolingly on his shoulder. "I'm sure it was a terrible thing to see."

Nodding, Chable agreed as his eyes flicked to hers. "They think I'm mad," he stated simply, shaking his head. "But I know what I saw. Whether they believe it or not, it was the mist that destroyed my ship. I don't know how," he said, shrugging. "All I know is it did, like it was possessed by some kind of magic."

Tesania's eyes whipped to Deavon who stepped quickly forward. "What makes you think it was magic?" he asked Chable.

"A mist destroyed our ship," Chable declared angrily, sitting forward. "A mist! What more proof do you need?"

"I didn't mean to imply you were wrong," Deavon said as he sat on the end of the bed and considered the lieutenant. "Was there another ship nearby? Were you near land?"

"No. We were alone, out to sea."

"He's right," Tesania said thoughtfully as she stood and walked to the window. "If it was the mist that did this, it must have involved some kind of magic." Spinning on her heel, she asked Deavon, "But who in Eldanal wields that kind of power?"

Deavon shook his head, nonplussed. "We know from past experience that the mage's of Eldanal don't wield that kind of magic."

"Whoever it was," Chable interrupted. "Whether you think I'm mad or not, that kind of magic is exactly what they had."

The room fell quiet as each of them considered the consequences of what had been discussed, Tesania looking out the window, Deavon following her gaze while the lieutenant stared down at the bed sheets. Eventually, Tesania walked to Chable and placed her hand on his shoulder. "We don't think you're mad at all," she assured him. "We," she continued while gesturing toward Deavon, "Have seen first-hand the evil and corruption that magic can do if in the wrong hands." Considering him for a moment, she continued, "I'm sorry for the loss of your Captain and crew. It saddens me deeply that they were lost while in my employ." As Chable looked up at her, she went on, "For now, I want you to rest and recuperate. Do you understand," she asked as his sad eyes once more shed tears. "What happened was not your fault. I for one am pleased you managed to survive."

Chable seemed lost for words, so Tesania went on. "Promise me you will not punish yourself over this," she demanded lightly.

Swallowing deeply, Chable replied, "Lady Tesania. Thank . . . thank you for your understanding."

Nodding bravery." Motioning to Deavon, they said their goodbyes and headed for their carriage outside the hospital's doors.

***

Tesania's stately town carriage trundled along the paving stones of Wyvern City, the click clack of the horses shod hooves echoing in the street. The conversation with Chable worried Tesania as she moved in rhythm with the swaying cab. Far from answering her questions it had only served to create more. "Do you believe him?" she in satisfaction, Tesania said, "Thank you for your

asked Deavon as they bumped along.

Deavon stared out the window, his hand on the sill, steadying himself. "If it were only his account of the Advance's demise, I don't think so," he replied. "But with what has happened at your Orash farm, Jaryd dead, the crops destroyed." Turning toward her, he smiled weakly. "In both cases, witnesses claim that a mist was to blame."

"But mist?" Tesania inquired, frustrated as she clasped at the empty air in front of her eyes. "It's so flimsy, so . . . it's just wet air."

"Deadly wet air, it seems," Deavon replied.

Nodding slowly, Tesania considered what he'd said before saying, "Another mage using the forbidden ways?"

Deavon shrugged. "The evidence would suggest so," he replied.

Tesania sighed and collapsed back against the leather seat. A thought came to her as she contemplated the situation. Sitting forward again, she said, while looking sideways at Deavon, "This mist attacked my ship."

"Yes . . . And?" Deavon eventually asked when she didn't continue.

"Have you heard any reports of other ships being attacked? Or missing?" As Deavon shook his head, she continued. "And then the same mist, or a similar one, attacked my farm in Orash."

"Yes," Deavon agreed, nodding before falling silent.

"Do I have to ask?" Tesania inquired, raising an eyebrow.

Laughing, Deavon answered, "No, Tes, I have heard no other reports of farms being attacked by mist."

"That's what I thought," Tesania said, frowning. "It seems someone's targeting me."

Deavon considered her words for a moment before nodding in agreement. "It would seem so," he replied. "In saying that," he added seriously, "Just because I haven't heard of it, doesn't mean it isn't happening."

Tesania considered his words. He was correct of course. Whilst now a General in the King's Rangers, Deavon was still junior to many other generals and wouldn't have access to all the reports coming in. And then there were the other factions, the Army, the Mages; none of whom would share their information with him. "If it is another mage gone bad," she said eventually. "What can we do about it?"

"Nothing at this stage," Deavon replied. "But I think it's serious enough to convene a meeting with the king."

Nodding, Tesania agreed. "I can't have my people being hurt," she said sadly. "We must do something."

"Agreed," Deavon said. "I'll talk to the king and his advisors as soon as I can."

"They won't like being called in on short notice."

"Something's happening, Tes," Deavon replied. "Something we can't begin to understand." Turning back to the window, he muttered, "Whether they like it or not, they will convene."

3 - Confusion

King Eldine of Eldanal strode purposefully into his palace stateroom, nodding in greeting to the gathered men and women. The meeting had been arranged hastily, interrupting his usual Sunday activities. "It had better be important," he growled as he sank into his ornately carved, throne-like chair.

Clearing his throat, Deavon rose from his chair, its wooden legs squealing on the marble floor as he pushed it back. "My apologies for calling this meeting on such short notice," he said as he looked to each of the gathered dignitaries.

Waving his hand irritably, the king said, "Yes, yes, General. Get on with it."

Walking to the head of the table, Deavon gathered himself and began slowly. "A few days ago, one of Lady Tesania's ships went missing at sea."

"You called us in on a Sunday to tell us this?" General Legana snapped. "Ships go missing all the time."

"Granted," Deavon replied, scowling briefly at his former mentor. "However; I believe this may be an extraordinary case."

"How so, Deavon?" Archmage Peanne asked before Legana could interrupt again.

Turning to the archmage, Deavon smiled deeply at her. "Naisa," he said, nodding in greeting. Aware that Naisa's rise to the coveted position of Archmage of Eldanal had only happened a few weeks earlier and that she would still be finding her place among these austere people, he kept his tone professional while addressing her. "There was only one survivor. A Lieutenant Chable. It is his account of the loss of the Advance that brings me before you today."

"I hardly think one man's tale of a sinking ship warrants convening an urgent meeting," Legana interrupted once more. "Surely it could have waited until—"

"Perhaps, if you let Deavon speak," Naisa's voice cut across the room. "He will enlighten us."

Scowling, Legana rose from his chair before leaning on the table, jutting his chin toward the archmage. "I see you're going to be as obstinate as your predecessor," he said bitterly, looking her up and down. "I had hoped you might show a little more grace than he."

"Grace?" Naisa asked, smiling at the general. "If by grace, you mean letting you ride roughshod over the Mage's Guild, you need to rethink your ideas."

"Enough!" the king demanded as he leant forward, glaring from Legana to Naisa. "Both of you need to work together," he said, "And that goes for the rest of you," he added glaring around the table. "The interest of Eldanal should be uppermost in your minds."

Legana retook his seat, scowling once more at Naisa. "You're quite right," he said, turning to the king. "I will, as always, endeavor to work with all your majesty's services."

"I should think so," the king muttered as he sat back and turned his attention to Deavon. "Please go on."

"As I was saying," Deavon began, cringing inwardly at what he was about to say. "Lieutenant Chable talks of a cloud of mist attacking and sinking his ship."

"Mist?" the king asked confusion on his face. "Sank a ship! You're wasting my time, General," he said, his voice threatening as he began to rise.

"Please, Your Majesty," Deavon said urgently. "If you would just hear me—"

"Sire," General Legana interrupted, frowning as he looked slowly around the table before coming to rest on the king who glared at him expectantly. "Forgive me," Legana apologized. "But this isn't the first I have heard of this cloud of mist."

Deavon watched the general, hope rising that he may now have an ally. Legana looked at him, a half grin on his face. "We have recently had reports of outlying farms being destroyed."

Nodding, Deavon turned to the king. "Lady Tesania's farm in Orash was destroyed, her manager killed," he said quickly. "His son reported that there was a mist involved."

"That farm is one of the ones reported to us," Legana said as he stood and paced along the table. "Others as well," he said, turning back to the king.

"And you didn't see a need to inform me?" the king demanded, his angry eyes boring into Legana from beneath his creased brow.

"We haven't confirmed anything," Legana replied. "I didn't deem it anything to bother you with until we investigated more. Besides," he said. "What would you have said if I came to you and said a cloud of mist had destroyed some crops on an outlying farm?"

"I see your point," the king replied before asking, "And what have your investigations revealed?"

"Not a great deal," Legana replied. "From the few that have been investigated it seems that a cloud of mist was present when the farm was destroyed." Walking to the head of the table, Legana stood beside Deavon. "I'm still awaiting reports from other farms."

"And you believe that clouds of mist are responsible?" the king asked, doubt clouding his eyes as they flicked from Legana to Deavon.

"I thought it fanciful," General Legana replied, shrugging, a half smile on his face. "I mean, we are all adults," he stated while glancing around the table. "Would any of you truly believe a cloud of mist could destroy a whole farm?" he asked. "And I'm not just saying damaged the crops," he added. "I mean destroyed . . . totally flattened!"

"I would," Naisa said flatly.

"I'm sure you would," Legana replied, sneering.

Scowling at the general, Naisa turned from him and addressed the king, "A skilled mage could control the weather in such a way."

"Not any mage I've ever seen," Legana said, laughing loudly.

Naisa turned to him. "You are quite right," she agreed to his surprise. "A mage using the ways as we allow could not do such a thing."

"The forbidden ways?" Deavon asked softly, a sinking feeling in the pit of his stomach as he said the words.

"Another of your people out of control?" Legana accused the archmage.

Ignoring him, Naisa continued, "We all know the powers of the forbidden ways. Trannyth was testament to that. But the Mage's Guild works tirelessly to eradicate it. We have made much headway in the last few years in removing any texts and parchments teaching it."

"Still," the king said as he regarded the archmage. "If one of your people has turned to the forbidden ways again;

could they control the weather? Turn a simple cloud of mist into a weapon?"

Frowning, Naisa she sat back in her chair in thought before shaking her head. "I worked closely with Archmage Edana before his retirement. We have no suspicions of any mages powerful enough to control the weather this way. None even studying the forbidden ways, let alone practicing it."

"An apprentice perhaps?" Legana asked.

Shaking her head, Naisa said, "No. The power required for a spell like that would be incredible. I doubt that even I could do it," she admitted as she turned to the king. "This is not the work of an apprentice," she assured him before adding, "Another problem we have, is the fact that the mage would need to be nearby to control the mist. These attacks are too far apart to be the doing of one person."

The room fell quiet as each of them considered what had been said. Deavon mulled Naisa's words over in his mind. He had no answer but something that the lieutenant had said in the hospital nagged at him, something that didn't seem to fit with her words. Eventually it came to him. Looking to Naisa, he said, "Chable mentioned they were well out to sea when the attack happened, nowhere near land, and there were no other ships nearby."

Naisa considered his words for a moment before replying, "The mage must have been on board the ship."

Shaking his head, Deavon explained, "Chable was the only survivor."

The concern on Naisa's face radiated through the people in the room as she pondered Deavon's words. "To cast magic more than a mile is almost impossible," she said. "But to cast it across the expanse of the ocean is unheard of. Not even the strongest and most highly trained mages of Eldanal could achieve such a feat."

"What are you saying?" the king asked his voice anxious.

"I believe . . ." Naisa said, swallowing, ". . . that there is a mage from another land casting these spells." Looking around the table ominously, she added, "A mage with powers we can only dream of possessing."

"Bah!" General Legana spat. "If Aliaga had mages with such power they would have invaded us centuries ago."

"Not Aliaga," Deavon exclaimed loudly, causing the others to start in surprise. "Sorry," he said, lowering his voice. "But there was an invasion," he insisted. "Just . . . not in Eldanal."

"Where?" the king asked. "Get on with it."

"Aliaga itself was invaded," Deavon continued. "Remember?" he said turning his attention to Naisa. "The abbot's story in Unastine? When we were on our way to Trannyth. He told us about Tesania's sword . . . where it came from . . . why it was forged."

Nodding, Naisa said. "I do remember," before beaming at Deavon. "How could I ever forget that long winded tale?"

Deavon laughed. "He did go on a bit, didn't he?"

"Perhaps you could share this story with us?" the king interrupted irritably.

Sobering, Deavon turned his attention to the king. "My apologies, My Lord."

Waving him on, the king said, "Yes, yes, get on with it will you."

Deavon measured his words before beginning. "When we were travelling to Trannyth's Keep we made a diversion to the monks of Unastine to see if they had found any information on Tesania's sword," he enthused as he remembered the journey. "They had found the Tenule chronicles, a text from centuries ago, that told of the sword."

"Perhaps you would be good enough to tell us," the king said sourly. "The important parts, mind," he added. "I have no desire to hear the whole story."

Deavon adjusted his clothes as he controlled himself. "The Tenule chronicles told of an invasion in Aliaga's past, many generations ago. It spoke of a mage from across the seas, from Ted—"

"Tiadath?" Naisa interjected, "that was the name, wasn't it?'

"Yes," Deavon said, nodding to her in thanks. "A Tiadath mage with an army behind her invaded Aliaga. There was nothing they could do to stop her. Aliaga's mages had no answer to the power she wielded. The royal city was eventually overrun, the nobles locked in the dungeons," he went on as the king adjusted himself uncomfortably in his chair. "It was only when Tesania's forefather forged the sword and defeated the mage on the battlefield that the remnants of Aliaga's forces were able to defeat the invading army and the king was returned to his throne."

King Eldine considered Deavon's story before eventually turning to Naisa. "Do you believe we are dealing with one of these . . . Tiadath Mages?" he asked.

Naisa weighed her answer before saying, "I have no way of knowing that at this moment. But, due to the nature of the magic being used, it would seem plausible that we are dealing with at least one of them."

Clearing his throat and leaning forward, the army representative at the table spoke for the first time. "That it is a mage from this place called Tiadath is only supposition at this stage, I realize," he said. "But perhaps it may shed some light on the situation if we examine possible motives."

"You're quite right, General Ardel," Naisa said, smiling at the ageing man. "Perhaps you have a theory."

"A possible invasion," he replied simply, shrugging. "Destroy our crops so we can't feed our people when they eventually attack."

"They wouldn't dare invade Eldanal," General Legana said as he walked to Ardel and placed his hand on his shoulder. "As always, my friend, you are too quick to battle."

General Ardel turned in his seat and looked up at Legana. "I would rather explore the possibilities and be ready than sit back and be ripe for the plucking."

"Ripe for the plucking," Legana said, laughing uproariously. "A colorful euphemism."

Ardel scoffed at his counterpart. "I trust you have the definitive answer," he said, nodding in mock acceptance of Legana's wisdom. "Perhaps you would share it with us?"

"Indeed," the king grunted.

The smile slipped off Legana's face as the room fell silent. "I don't actually," he said, embarrassed. "But I certainly don't think we should jump to conclusions."

"We shouldn't dismiss them either," Ardel said angrily, slapping his open palm on the table. "We should be ready for anything."

"I don't disagree," Legana said, nodding. "But where will you be ready? Hmm? Where will they land? On the south shore? The west maybe?" Sweeping his arm at the wall, he continued, "Wyvern harbor would be a wonderful place for them to land."

"I see your point," King Eldine said as he waved Ardel to silence. But I am hesitant to commit to this explanation without more proof."

"It may not be an invasion," Deavon said softly while he stared at the floor, deep in thought.

"What was that?" the king asked irritably. "If you have something to say, speak up and say it."

Deavon looked up quickly, as if unaware he had spoken. "I'm sorry," he said quickly, a little abashed. "I was just thinking aloud."

"About?"

"Something Tesania said when we left the hospital yesterday." Nodding his head as what he was about to say made more sense to him; he tapped his finger on the table and said, "Yesterday we assumed that only Tesania's assets were being attacked by this mist." Pausing as he thought more, Deavon became surer about it. "Tesania said she felt she was being targeted by someone."

"Targeted?" Legana scoffed. "Why would anyone go out of their way to target her?"

Deavon stood and began to pace, head bowed as he struggled to find an answer. Eventually he looked up and offered, "Jealously? Someone may be jeal—"

Naisa gasped. "It isn't jealousy," she announced, her eyes darting from one man to another. "Don't you see? It's revenge!"

4 - Reasons

Tesania accepted the hand of a palace page as she stepped lightly from her carriage. The summons she had received was short and didn't give any clues as to what it was all about, but she knew it would concern what Deavon had said to them in the meeting he had called and therefore assumed it would be about the killer mists. *'They must have believed him,'* she thought as the page led her through the towering doors of the palace and into the majestic grand hallway where she had once, what felt like long ago, sat with Deavon waiting to meet the king.

The opulence of the hallway still amazed her even to this day, with its high, vaulted ceilings, extravagant paintings and flagstone floors. She studied the kings and queens of long past as she walked, each seeming to follow her with their eyes as she passed their gilded frames.

Shivering eerily, she focused on the page once more as he stopped by a seemingly blank wall and tapped twice before pushing open a hidden door. Bowing, he ushered Tesania in, announcing, "Her Ladyship, Tesania."

Tesania peered into the dark room, her eyes adjusting after the well-lit hallway. Deavon rose from his chair as she entered and came toward her, offering his arm as he directed her to a seat. Naisa nodded to her, beaming as she said, "Hello, Tes."

"Naisa," Tesania said excited at seeing her friend. "I trust you're well?"

"I am," Naisa replied.

"You will have to come for a meal," Tesania urged as Deavon removed his arm and pulled a chair back for her.

"Yes, yes," the king said irritably. "You can organize your social lives at another time."

"Here, here," Legana mumbled glaring at Tesania before turning to the king. "I suggest we get on with this. We all have much to do today."

King Eldine considered Legana for a short while before replying, "Indeed." Turning to Tesania, he regarded her seriously as she nervously adjusted her clothes. Eventually he spoke, "Deavon here," he said gesturing, "tells us that one of your ships was destroyed by a cloud of mist."

"So I am informed by the only survivor," Tesania replied, aware that Deavon would have already explained all this.

"And you believe the man?"

Tesania measured her answer, looking down at her hand as she rolled a length of lace from her bodice between her finger and thumb before looking up and saying, "At first I would have said it seems far-fetched."

"But you don't think so now?" the king asked, his eyes intense as he watched her.

Tesania shifted uncomfortably under his gaze before looking to Deavon, who smiled lightly at her, but otherwise offered no support. Tesania considered the question before turning back to the king. "I believe," she began slowly. "That something horrendous happened out there. Something unnatural."

"Magic?"

Nodding, Tesania replied, "I wasn't present at the time. But, it would seem as though some kind of magic was involved."

"So you do believe the man?"

Tesania felt trapped. She had no real proof of magic and yet here was the king wanting her to say it was so. "I can only tell you what I have been told," she answered. "Between Chable's account of the sinking and what happened on my farm in Orash, I would say it was some kind of magic."

Deavon cleared his throat. "I think we have all accepted that it was magic," he said as he looked at Tesania apologetically. "I think we need to move on."

"Agreed," the king replied, his eyes still on Tesania. "My apologies, Lady Tesania," he said with a slight nod. "I just wished to know your thoughts on the matter."

Tesania looked to Naisa. "There are people better suited to making judgments on this than me."

General Legana rose from his chair and walked to the far end of the Table. "Well said," he uttered. Stopping, he turned to the gathering before saying, "The purpose of asking you here on such short notice, Lady Tesania, is that we think the Advance was sunk by this cloud of mist your lieutenant talks of."

Tesania nodded and said, "It sounds fanciful, almost insane, I know. But I . . . we," she added as she looked to Naisa and then Deavon apologetically, "have seen powerful magic at work before." As Naisa murmured her agreement, Tesania went on. "Trannyth turned simple Banmoras into his beasts."

"Among other things," Naisa said, scowling. "He was out of control."

"Trannyth is in the past," Legana said dismissively as he waved a hand at Naisa. Looking at Tesania, he said, "You've heard of mages from Tiadath?"

Tesania felt her eyes widen, "You think this is the doing of a Tiadath Mage?"

"Possibly," Legana answered simply.

"Why?" Tesania asked, confused at his suggestion. "Why would they target me?"

"Not only you."

Tesania's head swiveled to Deavon as she gasped, "So there have been other attacks?"

Nodding, Deavon replied, "General Legana here has had reports of other farms being destroyed by clouds of mist."

"Where?"

"It doesn't appear to be in any logical order," Legana answered her, shrugging. "We've had reports of farms in Rilmir, Carella, Orash and a few other places. They're far flung."

"So they're random?"

"Well," Legana replied as he cleared his throat. "The farms belong to either you or His Majesty here," he said while pointing toward the king.

"Which lends credibility to my theory," Naisa said to Tesania. "Someone is targeting you and King Eldine."

"Why me though?" Tesania gasped. "What have I done? Why should innocent people die simply because they happen to work for me?"

Naisa adjusted her position in her chair and looked apologetically at Tesania. "That's why we called you here. To see if we can find that out."

"But why?" Tesania asked, her eyes darting from one person to the next searching for the answer. When all remained quiet, she focused on Legana. "Surely you have some ideas? You must have heard something?"

Eyes downcast, the General replied, "I have heard nothing of why you might be targeted or who may be behind the Tiadath Mages' acts."

"Assuming it is Tiadath Mages," General Ardel said sourly. "It is still supposition."

Deavon cleared his throat and leant forward, arms resting on the table as he said, "Naisa thinks that it may be at least one Tiadath Mage who has been hired by someone to destroy your assets as well as those of the king."

Confused, Tesania turned to Naisa. "Who?" she asked, shaking her head. "I have no enemies? I've done nothing to any—" Stopping abruptly, she spun on Deavon, "Lord Dalgliesh!"

"Dalgliesh," the king erupted, fist slamming onto the table as he stood, the sharp crack echoing through the room. "Of course!"

General Ardel spoke from his chair, his eyes on the table, voice cynical, "We do not have any proof that it is a Tiadath Mage, if indeed any still exist after all these centuries. Nor do we have any proof that Dalgliesh has anything to do with it."

"It seems most likely," Legana said angrily.

"Although Dalgliesh was banished," Ardel said vehemently as he shoved his chair back and rose, "his lands and all his assets removed and given to Lady Tesania here," he said gesturing at Tesania before lifting his hand and pointing at Legana. "You are jumping to conclusions," he accused the general. "You of all people should know the importance of good intelligence and logical decision making."

All eyes in the room went to Legana, expecting his angry reply. Instead he looked abashed as he stared at the army general. "You're quite right," he said eventually.

"Dalgliesh has no money as far as we know," Ardel said as Legana fell quiet. "He couldn't begin to afford to hire this mage you speak of."

"Not so," Legana replied, regaining his usual arrogance as he continued. "Dalgliesh fled to Aliaga after he was banished."

"That explains nothing."

"But it does," Legana said triumphantly. "Dalgliesh had his hand in many ventures. Not just in Eldanal, but in Aliaga as well. Trust me when I tell you, he landed on his feet."

"Where is he now?" the king asked.

Shrugging, Legana replied, "I've no idea, apart from that he was last seen in Estel."

"Regardless," Ardel interrupted. "Money or not, we don't know that Dalgliesh has any involvement in the attacks."

"It seems a reasonable assumption," Naisa said. "He would certainly have the motive, and . . . as General Legana has said, he seemingly has the resources."

Ardel considered her words before looking to King Eldine. "Dalgliesh may very well be behind the attacks. But I'm not convinced."

"Wise words," King Eldine replied. "But it seems the most logical theory we have."

Nodding slowly, Ardel silently agreed before saying, "We have to explore other avenues though. In case Dalgliesh is not involved."

"Agreed," King Eldine said before demanding, "In the mean time, I want you to follow the lead we have. Send your best people. Find out where Dalgliesh is," he said as he looked from Legana to Ardel. "I want you two to work together on this. Do you hear me?" As both men nodded, the king headed for the door. "I want them on a ship tomorrow," he said. "We don't have time to wait. And send a dispatch to the monks of Unastine. I want everything they know about this place called Tiadath." Turning to Naisa, he said, "Find out what you can about their mages, what magic they use, how they use it." As Naisa nodded, the king acknowledged each of the gathered people, turned and left.

Legana turned to Ardel. "I have a man on the ground in Estel. I'll send him instructions immediately."

Ardel stepped from his place at the table and headed for the door. "I have just the two for this mission. Shall we all meet in your office in say, three hours time?"

"Agreed," Legana said to Ardel's back as he left the room. With a glint in his eye, he looked at Deavon. "The game is afoot." As Deavon nodded, he added, "I'd like you in the meeting this afternoon." Starting for the door, he paused and as if as an afterthought said to Tesania, "And you as well, if you wish." Nodding to Naisa, he also left the room, leaving the three former travelling companions alone.

Tesania looked to the new archmage. "What if it's true?" she asked. "What if Lord Dalgliesh has hired a mage from Tiadath?"

Shaking her head, Naisa replied, "I don't know Tes. Truthfully."

"We'll have to stop him," Tesania said sadly as she thought of the crew of the Advance and Jaryd. "I won't let any more of my people die."

Concern on his face, Deavon reached out and took Tesania's hand. "It may not come to that," he said. "If it is Dalgliesh, we may be able to stop him without any need to confront the mage."

'That would be ideal," Naisa agreed. "This mage seems extremely powerful."

"So was Trannyth," Tesania said.

"This mage sounds much more dangerous than Trannyth."

Tesania flared. "My forefathers forged the sword to kill a Tiadath Mage," she stated flatly. "I won't leave it sitting idle while my people bear the brunt of this mage's attacks."

"Dalgliesh is the problem," Deavon assured her gently.

"He isn't the one casting the spells."

"True," Deavon agreed. "Let's wait and see what the soldiers find out."

Tesania wasn't at all happy to wait for the soldiers' reports. It worried her deeply that the attacks on her people would continue while the soldiers tried to find Lord Dalgliesh. As they walked out the palace doors and Naisa said goodbye, Tesania looked determinably up at Deavon. As he regarded her, concern in his eyes, she whispered, "My sword stopped a Tiadath mage once. It will do so again."

5 - A general Summons

General Legana's secretary slipped out the door to his master's office and walked toward the two army generals sitting against the far wall. "He'll see you now," he advised. "Lady Tesania and the others are already inside."

Rising, Giddy looked at Raim. "I wonder if Tes knows it's us?"

"We shall see," Raim said, grinning at her in his usual amiable way. "We haven't seen her in how long?"

"Months now, I would think," Giddy replied as she adjusted her shirt and made for the door.

* * *

Tesania sat at Deavon's side in Legana's office, her chair pulled up to the front of his table, an earthenware goblet of wine sitting untouched on the deep, mahogany wood. Naisa and General Ardel sat on Deavon's other side, their goblets also untouched while Deavon himself sipped sparingly at his own.

Legana sat on the far side of the table, refilling his wine as a knock came at the door. "Enter," he called.

Tesania turned to see who entered, jumping to her feet and rushing to them as they came into view. "Giddy . . . Raim!" she cried as she hugged one then the other. "They didn't tell me it would be you."

Disentangling herself from Tesania's embrace, Giddy re-adjusted her shirt as she smiled at her friend, saying, "We wondered if you knew."

"I haven't seen you in so long. We'll have to catch up."

"You won't have time for that," Legana assured them. "Please take a seat," he said gesturing to two empty chairs on the left side of his desk. "We have much to discuss and little time." As the two soldiers sat, Legana offered them wine, both eagerly agreeing as he reached for fresh goblets.

"Why am I not surprised," Deavon sighed rolling his eyes.

"It's past noon," Giddy assured him, grinning as she raised her hand to her throat. "You wouldn't want us parched during the meeting would you?"

"No, Giddy," Deavon replied laughing as he said to the General, "I hope you have more than the one bottle."

Looking to the bottle and then to the two soldiers, Legana placed it on the far side of his desk, well away from the them and said, "Shall we begin?" As Giddy sipped her wine and no one else at the table objected, he considered the two soldiers for a moment before continuing, "General Ardel here," he said motioning to the ageing man in front of him, "has chosen you for a mission of great importance."

Placing her goblet down, Giddy looked from him to Deavon and then Tesania, the smile slipping from her face as she saw the seriousness in theirs. "Go on," she said soberly.

General Legana stood and began pacing the room before saying, "In the past few weeks many strange events have taken place. Events we cannot begin to explain." Stopping at his window, he looked out as he continued, "A ship has been sunk, farms destroyed."

"Magic?" Raim asked looking around the gathering. "Another renegade mage?"

"A good guess," Legana grunted.

"Hardly a guess," Raim suggested as he motioned to the others in the room, "considering who's here."

"True," Legana growled before saying, "It appears a mage of some talent is targeting the king and Tesania here."

"One of Trannyth's followers?" Giddy asked frowning as she considered the general's words.

"I think not," Naisa assured her. "All of his mages were rounded up and dealt with."

"Who then?"

"We have reason to believe that Lord Dalgliesh has hired a mage from Tiadath."

"Tiadath," Giddy asked quickly. "Like in the story the old monk told us?"

"Exactly like that," Naisa replied. "At least the power they seem to wield would suggest that is so."

"But that mage was unstoppable," Giddy said, frowning. "What makes you think Raim and I can stop them?"

"We're not asking you to," Legana said as he retook his seat. "What we're asking you to do is to go to Aliaga and meet with my man there. From there you are to find out where Dalgliesh is holed up, what his current situation is, who he's associating with, and then report back to me."

"And if this mage is there?" Raim asked. "What do we do then?"

"Nothing. You bring the information back here."

"Then what?"

"What we need to do then depends on what you find out."

"If they are using a Tiadath mage to hurt my people," Tesania said quietly as she looked toward Giddy, "I will deal with them."

Reaching toward her, Deavon laid his hand on hers. "Let's hope it doesn't come to that," he said before turning his attention to Giddy. "You just need to find out what Dalgliesh is up to. See if there's anything strange going on and let us know. Can you do that?"

Snorting, Giddy looked at Raim, "You'd think he didn't know us," she said as she raised her goblet and drank deeply.

"It's important," Giddy, Deavon said quietly. "I know what you two can do. But we need to know you understand what's required?"

"Go to Aliaga, meet up with this man you mentioned," she said motioning to General Legana. "Find Dalgliesh and report back here with what we find," she continued, shrugging.

Legana stood shaking his head as he regarded the soldier. "I'm well aware of what you two did in the past," he said. "But I suggest you take this seriously."

"Please, Giddy," Tesania said sadly. "My people are being hurt . . . because of me."

Scowling at Giddy, Legana went on, "Report to Captain Eades of the King's Ship Swan at dawn. He'll be expecting you."

"Do we have any clues as to where Dalgliesh may be?" Giddy asked seriously. "Aliaga's a big place."

Retaking his seat, Legana said, "You can appreciate that this has all come about suddenly." As Giddy nodded, he went on. "We have little knowledge of where Dalgliesh currently resides. What we do know is that he had contacts and business associates there and is well connected." Opening a drawer in his desk, he took out a piece of parchment before scribbling a name with a quill and passing it to Raim.

"Rhys," Raim read before looking back to the General. "Aliagan intelligence?"

"Better," Legana grinned. "He's a thief."

"A thief?" Naisa asked quickly. "Is that wise?"

Legana considered her as he leant toward the wine bottle, offering Giddy a refill, which she refused. "Trust me," he said as he set the bottle down again. "He knows more about what's happening in Aliaga than the Aliagan intelligence do."

"I'm sure," Naisa conceded. "But is it wise to involve someone whom we have no control over? He may be working for Dalgliesh for all we know?"

"I know him well enough," Legana assured her.

"But, still . . . a thief?"

"I have used his . . . err . . . talents, many times," Legana assured her. "He has many contacts and knows things that Aliaga's king's people can only guess at. Trust me when I tell you, he's our man."

"You have dealings inside Aliaga?" General Ardel asked eyebrow rising in surprise. "What could you possibly be doing in Aliaga? Does the king know about this?"

Scowling, Legana dismissed him with a wave. "That is not for now."

"Our king may not think so."

"There are more pressing matters at hand," insisted Legana.

"Perhaps, we should be grateful . . ." Naisa said, ". . . that the general here," she added waving toward Legana, "has these contacts that we can now use."

"Well said," Legana replied, grinning at his army counterpart.

"Even if this, Rhys, does know where to find Dalgliesh," Giddy interrupted thoughtfully, as if they hadn't spoken. "How will we know if he has a mage working for him, let alone if that mage is the one casting the spells at Tesania and her people? We can't just walk up and ask."

"I think you will know," Naisa replied. "Tiadath Mages would look outlandish in Aliaga; their clothes would surely be much different to what you would normally expect to see."

"If they're not disguised," Giddy mumbled, still lost in thought. "I guess we need to find Dalgliesh and take it from there."

"That would be all it appears we can do," Naisa agreed.

"At this stage we just need to know where Dalgliesh is," Legana said. "It would be pure luck for you to actually see this mage." Considering the two soldiers thoughtfully, he shook his head and added, "Find Dalgliesh and report back to me. From there we can formulate a plan."

Tesania could take no more. "It will take too long," she said as she rose, leaning on the table. "The mage won't sit back and wait for you to traipse all over Aliaga looking for Lord Dalgliesh," she said angrily, a frown rippling her brow. Turning her attention to Giddy, she said, "We need to stop this mage quickly, before he does more damage."

"You're assuming it's a he," Naisa said softly.

"He, she, what does it matter?" Tesania snapped at the Arch Mage. "Either way, they need to be stopped." Turning back to Giddy, she said, "I'm coming with you."

"That wouldn't be wise," Ardel said. "That Dalgliesh has hired one of the Tiadath Mages is only supposition at this point," he continued while raising his eyebrow at General Legana. "For that matter, we don't even know that Dalgliesh is involved at all."

"But, if he has hired this mage," Tesania said pointedly stabbing her finger into the desk. "We can end it quickly."

"If the Mage is even there," Naisa interrupted. "They could be casting these spells from anywhere. For all we know they could even be in Eldanal."

"I doubt it. They would stand out," Raim said.

"Not necessarily. We have no idea what these Tiadaths look like. Are they similar to us?" Naisa asked hypothetically. "If so, they could easily blend in."

"Agreed," Legana said thoughtfully as he looked to Tesania. "We need hard intelligence. It's best that these two," he continued while gesturing to the two soldiers," go alone. The less people there are the more they can blend in."

Tesania considered what he said for a moment, her eyes drifting to the two soldiers. She had full confidence in what they could do, and that they would go about their task efficiently. But to just sit on her hands while more of her people might be hurt appalled her. Sadly though, she conceded that rushing into Aliaga would probably achieve little. Eventually, she said, "Just do it quickly. We need to stop them."

Giddy rose, nodding to General Ardel and the others before turning to Legana. "If that's all," she said. "I'd like to get back to my room and start packing."

"I think that's wise," Legana agreed. "There's nothing more we can tell you. I've sent word to Rhys. He'll meet you at the docks when the ship arrives in Estel."

Nodding as she started for the door, Raim in tow, Giddy stopped by Tesania laying her hand on her shoulder. "Don't worry, Tes," she reassured her.

"My people are being hurt, Giddy," Tesania whispered. "How can I not?"

Smiling wanly, Giddy promised, "We'll be back as quickly as we can."

6 - Plans of revenge

Lady Caitriona sat in a plush leather armchair in her father, Lord Dalgliesh's, office, its overstuffed arms dwarfing her slight frame as she considered the oddly dressed mage on the opposite side of the room. "And you can still cast your spells from Tiadath?"

Nodding from beneath his deep, purple cowl, the mage replied laconically, "I have the maps you have drawn. It is a simple matter of casting a spell of seeing to pinpoint the area and then send the mist in. I do not need to be close by."

"Don't let up on her," Caitriona insisted sitting forward in her chair. "She has no right to any of it! It's ours!"

"She will suffer."

"I don't just want her to suffer!" Caitriona almost screamed. "I want her to feel as we did. . . . Know what it's like to have everything taken away from you. . . . Feel the laughing eyes of people you once called friends. . . . Hear their whispers as they gossip behind your back!" Calming herself, she sat back, smoothing her dress before looking up to the mage's eyes. "No, Sergh. I don't just want you to make Tesania suffer. I want you to destroy her! Destroy everything she has, everyone she loves! I want her to feel as I felt when everything was taken from me!"

The mage's smile was only briefly visible to Caitriona from within his darkened cowl as he stood and started for the door. "She will suffer, as will the king."

"For how long?"

"For as long as your father continues to pay my fee," he replied shrugging.

"Oh, he will pay," Caitriona assured him as he reached for the door and turned the handle. "I'll make sure of it."

The mage's voice drifted back to her as his robes slipped past the doorjamb. "I shall return here at the summer's solstice to collect further fees."

Sinking back into her chair, Caitriona felt deflated. She had enjoyed watching as the mage cast his spells and even though she couldn't see the result, she reveled in the knowledge that Tesania was suffering. Now she would just have to imagine the devastation her mercenary mage would cause.

From the day they learned their family was banished from Eldanal, all their assets and possessions confiscated, she had plotted her revenge. That their banishment was because she had convinced her father to have one of his ships attack the King's Ship Triumph in an attempt to kill Tesania never entered her mind. All she could see was that this village girl, this pretender, had stolen the heart of Deavon, the man she so desired, and worse, the humiliation she had suffered at the king's ball when Tesania so blatantly showed Deavon was hers to take.

Then, she had wanted the girl dead, but now . . . now that all their assets had been handed over to Tesania as a reward for her role in the eradication of the evil mage Trannyth, she wanted her to suffer, to watch helplessly as all her assets were slowly destroyed, her people perishing one by one as everything she loved withered and died.

Her father had proved a hurdle to her plans in the beginning, wishing to forget what had happened and move on. After all, they had many assets in Aliaga and he was quickly rising up the ranks of the nobility. But she would have none of it, pouting and throwing tantrums until he tired of her antics and did as she wished. Using his new contacts in Aliaga where he learned of this man, Sergh, a mage for hire. He had no idea where he came from, didn't really care. As long as he kept his daughter happy he was willing to pay. It did however, he admitted privately, satisfy him greatly that the king, who had treated him so badly, was being made to pay. Confident that they could not trace anything back to him or do anything about it if they did, he let his daughter decide on the mage's targets and let her have her way.

7 - On a mission

Gulls floated lazily on the breeze above the King's Ship Swan as it glided slowly toward the Estel docks, their cries piercing the early morning tranquility of the still to awaken city.

Sailors scrambled over the Swan's rigging, stowing the sails in preparation for docking while others cleared the starboard rail and took station with ropes in hand, ready to cast to their counterparts on shore.

She had little headway on her by now, the water slipping by her bulbous bow almost undisturbed as it burbled down the planks of her sides.

Giddy stood with Raim, watching as Aliaga grew closer. "Land," she sighed.

"It's only been three days," Raim laughed at his friend.

"Two days too many," Giddy said, shivering. "Give me solid land any day."

"You're about to get your wish," Raim replied nodding toward a sailor as he launched his rope into the air letting it sail toward the dock before tying it off to a cleat while another sailor opened the rails and tied off a gangway that was pushed up from the shore.

Reaching down and picking up her pack, Giddy slung it onto her shoulder and started for the gangway, saying, "Can't be soon enough if you ask me."

Snatching up his own pack, Raim hurried after her, catching up to her as she stepped onto the grey, sun-worn timbers of the docks, the smells of the harbor rising to meet him. Not the sweet salty smell of the open sea, but the smell of a working port, sweating men and rotting garbage mingling with the distinct smell of a sewer. Raising his hand to his nose as his face screwed in distaste, he said, "It stinks."

"No worse than you," Giddy quipped, grinning at him.

Rolling his eyes, Raim asked, "How're we going to find this Rhys?"

"No idea," Giddy replied seriously as she started along the dock. "Legana sent him a message, so I assume he'll find us."

The docks were somewhat empty at this early hour, only what appeared to be dock workers and a few stray travelers who had obviously arrived early for their journey to some unknown port moved about. Giddy walked quickly; keen to get away from the overpowering smell of the docks. The voyage from Wyvern Harbor had been uneventful, even the weather had been merciful with relatively flat seas and accommodating winds. '*Still*,' Giddy thought as she pulled at the unfamiliar civilian clothing she wore, '*I'm glad to be off the damn thing.*'

Legana had been vague about the man they were to meet. She had no idea what he looked like, what he might be wearing. The only thing she had was his name. "There's no use wandering around," she said to Raim as they came to a worn wooden bench at the end of the docks. Slipping her pack off, she sank down. "Let's let him come to us."

"No arguments here," Raim agreed as he too sank down.

Settling in to wait, Giddy watched the now growing throng of people heading for the docks. Ladies with bonnets pulled tightly around their braided hair walked arm in arm with their husbands while their children looked up to the great masts of the docked ships, excitement in their eyes as they watched sailors move around the dizzying heights. Among the well to do also walked the normal people of Aliaga, the workers, the servants and the staff. Peddlers had also begun to arrive, setting their carts up not far from where Giddy and Raim sat, the smell of freshly baked bread assaulting their senses as they watched. "Hungry?" Giddy asked. Rising as Raim nodded, she started toward a cart laden with pastries. "You take Eldanal coins?" she asked the vendor as she approached. "Two of the crispels," she said pointing to a pile of shiny, round pastries.

"Two coins," the man said as he scooped up two of the sticky, honey coated treats and wrapped them in a large leaf before handing them over, his other hand held out for the coins.

"Perhaps you could spare a coin and purchase one for me," a voice came from behind her.

Turning, Giddy considered the man for a moment. He stood about five foot tall, coal black hair long and drifting over his face in the breeze. Other than that he was unremarkable. His clothes, while not rags, were bland and drab while his demeanor showed no emotion. Normally, in the markets near her home in Rilmir, she would have dismissed the man without a thought, but today, for a reason she couldn't fathom, she decided to oblige. Turning to the vendor once more, she said, "One more," as she reached for her money pouch, freezing when her hand grasped nothing.

Spinning, she glared at the little man, but he wasn't there. Looking quickly to Raim she spun away from the docks to where he pointed. The man was running, his hair flying back behind as he fled. "He took my money pouch," Giddy called urgently as she threw the Crispels to the startled vendor and sprinted after him. "Bring the packs."

Dodging through the pedestrians, Giddy watched as the black haired man dashed down a side alleyway. She felt vulnerable as she reached that same alley, her sword being wrapped in material and slung to her pack. But she couldn't just let the man steal her pouch, not without at least trying to get it back. Glancing back to Raim, who struggled to catch her while carrying both packs, she drew a deep breath and started into the semi darkness fully aware that it could be a trap.

Little more than six feet wide, the alley grew gloomier as she ran, darkness closing in on her with every step as she went deeper. She had lost sight of the man, but was determined to continue. Dodging a pile of rubbish blocking half the alley, she pulled up short as a sharp whistle split the air. Turning, she searched the rubbish but found nothing.

"Up here," the man's shrill voice called.

Glancing up, Giddy saw the man, the grin on his face beaming back at her from his perch on a window sill some ten feet off the ground.

"Lost something?" he asked happily while bouncing her money pouch in his hand.

"Throw it down," Giddy ordered as she stepped closer, surveying the walls of the buildings on each side for a way up.

"Or?"

"Or," Giddy said patiently dismissing a rope dangling near him as her eyes fell on the series of ledges that would have allowed him to climb so swiftly. "I'll come up and get it."

"Come," the man said nonchalantly, laughing as he dangled the pouch by its string, swaying it back and forth.

"I'll come too," Raim said, his breath coming hard as he stared up at the little man.

Shrugging, the man said as he swiveled his head around, "If you wish. But you won't catch me either."

"We'll see," Raim growled as he dropped the pack and leapt for the lowest ledge, Giddy not far behind.

The little man's laughter echoed through the alley, his long, black hair falling across his face. Shoving it aside he watched the two soldiers as they clumsily climbed from one ledge to the next. "You'll have to do better than that," he said happily as he leapt forward grasped the rope and swung to the far wall tottering for a second before catching his balance. Turning carefully he passed the rope to his other hand and grinned across at his pursuers.

Frowning, Giddy started back down. "When I catch you—" she shouted angrily.

"You won't."

"We'll see," Giddy grunted as she jumped to the cobbled stones on the alley before looking up to see a way up to the man.

"I tell you what," the little man said as Giddy turned to him. "Meet me in the King's Head Tavern at dusk."

"Why," Giddy asked suspiciously.

"So I can give you new clothes."

"What's wrong with our clothes," Giddy asked looking down at herself as Raim thudded down beside her.

Grinning, the man tossed her money pouch down. As Giddy reached out and caught it, he let go of the rope and leapt nimbly to the next ledge before turning to the window and sliding it easily open. "People will know you're from Eldanal in an instant," he said over his shoulder before climbing through and reappearing an instant later as he called down, "If you want to find Dalgliesh, you'll need to blend in."

Shoving her pouch into her trousers as he slid the window down and disappeared once more, Giddy looked sheepishly at Raim. "I guess we found our man."

8 - Friends reunited

Kailyn moved from side to side in time with the swaying carriage as its wheels ground through the gravel road leading to Tesania's stately home, the steady thud of the horse's hooves muted by the thick layer of tiny stones.

The final exams at the Mages School in Carella City had been arduous, every moment for the last year dedicated to study and practice. *'Still, it's been worth it,'* she thought as the driver yelled 'whoa' and pulled the horse to a halt while a page stepped forward and reached for the carriage door. Accepting his hand as she alighted, Kailyn smiled demurely and thanked him. Drawing a deep breath as she looked up at the grand architecture on Tesania's home she calmed herself. Distance and her studies had kept them apart for far too long and she longed to see her friend once more.

It had been four years since she had run away from her employer, Lady Ayana, and stowed away on the King's Ship Triumph determined to accompany Tesania on her grand adventure. She had grown since then; now, at eighteen, she was no longer the small girl that collected wood for the company and managed to cast simple fire spells. Now . . . she was a woman and a fully fledged mage, having graduated - with honors.

It seemed odd to her as she stood waiting for the page to lead her inside, her burgundy robes fluttering in the breeze. She hadn't visited her parents at their farm outside

Wyvern City. '*No* . . .' she mused, '. . .*Tesania and Deavon were the first people I wanted to see.*' Only just having arrived in port on the previous night's high tide, she had spent a restless night in the apartment that the king had granted her for her role in the defeat of Trannyth, excitement keeping her from sleep as she waited for the sun to rise.

Familiar to the page, he didn't ask her name as he said, "This way, if you please," and led the way to the front doors before swinging them open. "I shall inform Lady Tesania of your arrival."

Kailyn's gut clenched. She hadn't informed anyone of the date she was arriving, wanting to surprise them. Now, she worried that she should have sent word of her visit beforehand. Fiddling with her hands nervously, she admonished herself as she lowered them to her side, wishing she had brought her staff; at least her hands would feel at home on its twisting, polished wood.

Thankfully, she did not have to wait long as Tesania's excited voice floated to her, "She's here? Now?" Smiling as she heard her friend's voice, Kailyn started forward as Tesania burst from the reading room doors and rushed toward her. "Kailyn!" she said smiling broadly as she held her arms out and drew her into an embrace. "Why didn't you tell us you were coming? We would have met you at the docks."

"I wanted to surprise you," Kailyn informed her as she drew back and held Tesania at arm's length, grinning. "You look wonderful," she said.

"I don't feel it," Tesania admitted, sadness slipping over her face for an instant.

"Oh?"

"Don't worry about it," Tesania said, her smile returning as quickly as it had disappeared. "When did you get in?"

"Last night. On the Mermaid."

Regarding her suspiciously, Tesania said, "You came on one of my ships and no one informed me."

Laughing, Kailyn assured her, "Do they tell you every passenger's name?"

"I guess not," Tesania said laughing along. "Come to the reading room," she eventually said. "I'll have some cider brought for you and you can tell me all about your exams."

Rolling her eyes, Kailyn sighed, "Do I have to?"

Laughing delightedly at her friend's discomfort, Tesania conceded, "Maybe not the exams. But I want to hear everything else."

9 - Questions indeed

The King's Head Tavern hummed with life. Raucous voices rang out as waitresses did their best to keep up with the demand for more ale. It wasn't a scene unfamiliar to Giddy and Raim as they wandered in the front door. Pausing for a moment, Giddy scanned the room, her eyes finally coming to rest on the man they assumed to be Rhys.

Looking to Raim, she motioned toward the man with her chin and started toward him as he stood, beckoning them over. Still wary of him, and not sure he was Legana's man, she whispered to Raim, having to raise her voice higher than she liked to be heard over the din of voices, "Let's see what he has to say before we commit to anything."

Nodding in greeting as they reached his table, Giddy pulled a chair out, the legs scraping noisily across the stained, flagstone floor while Raim caught the attention of a passing waitress and ordered a round of ales. The little man sat grinning at them, his eyes drifting occasionally from Giddy to Raim and then back again as they waited for their ales. Scowling, Giddy eventually asked, "How did you know we were looking for Dalgliesh?"

The grin slipped off the man's face as he sat quickly forward, his greasy hair falling over his face as his eyes flicked around the crowded room. "It would be wise not to use names here."

"This place was your choosing," Giddy reminded him, irritation building in her voice.

"It was," the little man agreed as he sat back in his chair, pushing his hair back with his thumb as the waitress returned with their ales. "Thank you, Lydie," he said smiling up at her as she placed his mug down.

"You're welcome, Rhys," the waitress replied as she smiled back shyly.

"How much?" Raim interrupted as he dug out his pouch. "I only have Eldanal coins, if that'll do?"

"Put them away," Rhys instructed, scowling at the soldier before looking back to the waitress. "Tell Osst I'll fix it up later," he said, winking.

"Anything else I can get you?"

"Just the ales will be fine."

Flashing a smile around the table, Lydie said brightly, "Just wave when you want something else." With that she was gone, her shy smile now aimed at a rather large man three tables away, her voice drifting back, "What can I get for you, Rayos?"

Rhys watched her for a moment before turning his attention back to Giddy. Leaning forward, he said quietly, "Your man sent me a dispatch. For now, let's just leave it at that."

"So . . . ?" Giddy half asked, a little confused as she looked to Raim, frowning, ". . . we just sit here and drink ale?"

Shrugging, Raim replied, "Sounds good to me."

Giddy grinned and said, "You'll never change."

"I don't see you arguing too hard!"

Serious again, Giddy looked back to the little thief. "We need to move quickly. People are suffering."

Sipping his ale, Rhys considered her before lowering his mug and replying. "I'm aware of that."

"So . . ." Giddy tried again, ". . . you want us to just sit here?"

Frowning, Rhys slowly perused the people seated around them, careful not to be obvious. Leaning forward once more, he motioned the two soldiers in closer before whispering, "I have reserved a room in The Vine Inn, across the road, in the name of Arche. On the bed you'll find clothes better suited to our . . . shall we say . . . situation."

"So we're staying in Estel tonight?" Raim asked.

Shaking his head lightly, the thief looked about once more. Satisfied no one was listening, he said, "Your room's at the back of the Inn. At midnight, I want you to slip out the window. You'll find a ladder against the balcony railing."

"You'll be there?"

"I will," he replied. "I'll have horses waiting in the alley for both of you."

"Where'll we be going," Giddy asked, her suspicion rising once more.

"That's best left for tomorrow when we're well clear of prying ears," he replied as he looked around the room once more to emphasize his point. "Till then, stay here; enjoy some ale; have a meal. The roast boar's quite something."

As Giddy nodded and raised her ale to drink, Rhys sat back in his chair before lifting his tankard and draining it in one gulp. Standing, he dug into a pocket before reaching across the table and shaking Raim's hand. "I must be going," he said loudly. "It's good to see you two again."

Raim closed his hand as the thief withdrew his before looking suspiciously at what he had deposited. In his palm sat a number of Aliagan coins of different denominations. Smiling up at the man, he said, "Thank you."

"Think nothing of it," Rhys replied, winking. "Perhaps I'll see you tomorrow."

"Perhaps you will," Giddy replied as the little man dodged his way to the front door, leaving them alone. Turning to Raim, eyebrow raised as she glanced down at her empty mug, she asked, "Haven't you ordered another round yet?"

***

Midnight seemed an eternity away as Giddy paced the small room Rhys had reserved for them at The Vine Inn. She felt they had already been in the stuffy little room for hours on end, yet it had only been a short while. Having ordered a few more ales in the King's Head Tavern and talked amongst themselves about their new acquaintance and what he may have in store for them, they had eventually ordered two plates of the roast boar, sitting quietly and taking in the other patrons as they ate.

The tavern had seemed like any of the many others Giddy had visited over the years. The ale was good and plentiful, the meal satisfying and filling. It was a place she decided, under different circumstances, that she could enjoy. But, wanting to be alert for their coming journey and aware that finding Dalgliesh quickly was paramount to the success of her mission, she had suggested they leave shortly after eating and led the way across the cobbled stone street to the little whitewashed inn where she now paced.

Smiling down at Raim on the small, single bed as he began to snore softly, she leant down and pulled the thick, woolen blanket over him before walking to the balcony window and staring out. The darkness of the back alley their room overlooked was almost complete, only the wane light of a single flickering lamp fighting against its total domination. Nothing stirred in the alley, making the erratic shadows cast by the lamp seem almost eerie. Leaning against the floral paper on the wall, she yawned loudly. She knew she should have tried to sleep, if only for an hour. But the situation they were in bothered her. Used to sword in hand combat, rather than clandestine spying and sneaking about, she felt out of her comfort zone. Rhys worried her greatly. That Legana recommended and vouched for him did little to allay her concerns. *'After all,' Legana had his hands in many things that appeared beyond where he should be operating,'* she mused as rain began to patter against the window pane. Reaching forward, she traced the rivulets of water as they chased each other down the glass. Squinting to see the now obscured alley, she frowned and turned away before walking to the bed and sinking down on the end, careful not to disturb her friend. "If it wasn't to help Tesania," she mumbled to herself, "I would have told him to come himself."

"Huh?" Raim asked his voice clouded with sleep as he pushed himself up onto an elbow, blinking at her as his eyes adjusted to the candlelight.

"Nothing," Giddy replied. "Sorry I woke you."

Rubbing at his eyes, Raim then glanced at the window. "Rain?"

"Started a few minutes ago."

"That'll be fun to ride in."

Grinning, Giddy stood and ripped the blanket off him, throwing it into the corner on the far side of the room. "A big brave soldier like you scared of a little rain?"

"It's not the rain," Raim quipped. "It's the way the rain will make you smell."

Shaking her head, feigning hurt, Giddy reached down and grasped Raim's hand before pulling him into a sitting position. "Well, that's nice," she said sarcastically. "After all the nice things I've told people about you."

"I'm sure you have," Raim shot back, a grin creasing his face as he reached for his boots. "I mean, what else could you tell them?" he asked winking at her. "The truth is the truth."

Giddy's laughter rang through the tiny room. "Truth?" she managed to say.

"You know it is," Raim assured her as he pulled his second boot on and stood. "They don't come much nicer than me."

Calming herself, Giddy considered him for a moment before reaching out and touching his hand gently. "I know it," she said seriously before turning away and returning to the window, sliding it easily open.

"Hey," Raim protested as a gust of cold wind rushed into the room.

Ignoring him, Giddy said, "He'll be here soon. Let's head down."

10 - Party plans

Tesania listened intently as Kailyn spoke of her time at the Mages School. It had been many months since she had seen her friend. She had missed her and her infectious smile, she admitted, as she laughed at a story about one of the other students accidently setting a teacher's robes alight. Kailyn had truly blossomed into a self assured, beautiful young woman. Pride rushed through Tesania as she watched her talk causing her skin to tingle with goose bumps. They had been through a lot together, both having to leave their childhoods behind when they took on the task of defeating Trannyth and his beasts. She considered Kailyn her family now, like a sister, and would do anything for her. Eventually, as Kailyn finished her story and leant forward to pick up her cider, Tesania asked hopefully, "Have you been assigned to Wyvern City?"

Nodding, a grin spreading across her face, Kailyn replied happily, "I have. I'm to report to Archmage Peanne next week."

"They assigned you to Naisa?"

"I've no idea," Kailyn replied as she set her cup down and adjusted herself in her seat.

"She'll be so happy to see you."

"Me too," Kailyn agreed, her eyes lighting. "I haven't seen her since she came to Carella a few months ago."

"She's done very well for herself," Tesania said as she picked up a tiny bell and summoned a servant, the tinkling sound resounding through the room. "Walk with me," she suggested while rising and holding her hands out to help Kailyn stand. "The gardens are wonderful at this time of year." Arm in arm, the two friends made their way along the hallway and entered the gardens through a side door.

Together, they walked along the manicured lines of flowerbeds, stopping occasionally to smell the delicate flowers before seating themselves on a marble bench under a grand oak that spread its arms out in all directions, offering shade from the mid-morning sun. "Do your parents know you're home?" Tesania asked.

"Not yet," Kailyn replied, shrugging. "I wanted to see you and Deavon first."

Smiling, Tesania reached over and touched her friend's hand. "Deavon will be so pleased to see you."

"Where is he?"

"Doing ranger things," Tesania said, laughing as she shrugged. "He went to Rilmir. He'll be back in a few days."

"And Giddy?" Kailyn asked. "Raim?"

Frowning for a moment before catching herself, Tesania replied, "They're on a mission."

"Mission?" Kailyn asked eyebrow raised. "Where?"

"Never mind," Tesania replied, brushing the question aside. "I'll explain later." Standing, she took her friend's hand and drew her up before leading her back to the house.

"Where're we going?" Kailyn protested. "I like it out here."

"There are so many people that will want to see you. Your parents, Aldan, Lady Ayana . . . you know who I mean," she said happily as she pulled Kailyn toward the door once more. "Come on. We have a party to plan."

11 - Lord Dalgliesh's Estate

The rhythmic thud of horses' hooves on the muddy, puddle filled ground beat a dull chorus into the misty rain enshrouding the three riders. The sun had risen somewhere behind the curtain of rain, the early dawn's light fighting to penetrate the hazy drizzle. Rhys had arrived in the back alley behind the inn at midnight, just as he had promised, three horses plodding along behind him, heads hung low, their reins in his hand as he walked toward the two soldiers. Giddy and Raim had greeted him from where they had taken cover in a small doorway, waving him over, aware that any noise might bring unwanted attention.

Leading the horses to the edge of the city before mounting, they had then ridden through the moonless darkness mostly in silence, each lost in their own thoughts as the rain tapped incessantly on their hooded heads, water running in rivulets before splashing onto the pommels of their saddles. The going had been slow in the wet, slippery conditions, but Estel was already far behind them. Rhys hadn't given any indication where they were headed, instead, just leading the way.

Giddy bought up the rear, keeping her horse a few feet from Raim's mare. She had been in the saddle for six hours straight now and needed to dismount and stretch her legs; give her aching rump a break. Spurring her horse forward, she guided it past her friend and came up to the side of

Rhys' black stallion. "We'll need to stop soon," she called, her voice high to overcome the patter of the rain. "We need a break."

Nodding, Rhys pointed ahead. "Roadhouse. Not far."

Giddy returned his nod and fell back to Raim. "How're you doing?"

"I'll live."

"I'm sure," Giddy said, laughing. "We'll be at a roadhouse soon."

"Good," Raim replied as he adjusted his position on the saddle, grimacing as his sore rump ground across the saddle.

Giddy grinned at him. "I wish this rain would stop."

Looking up to the low clouds, Raim grunted before saying, "Doubt it."

"Me too," Giddy agreed as she thoughtfully regarded the clouds. "I'd say it's set in for the day." As Raim screwed his nose up at her suggestion, Giddy fell quiet once more, concentrating on guiding her horse through the least treacherous puddles on the muddy ground. It seemed an eternity before Raim tapped her arm and pointed ahead. "Looks like our roadhouse."

"Hope they have breakfast on," Giddy said, grinning at the little soldier before spurring her horse on a little faster. "Race you."

"I'm not racing in this," Raim called after her.

"Fine," Giddy sighed as she guided her horse into a position in front of him and dropped back to his plodding pace. "What happened to the daring young man I once knew?" she called back.

"Maybe . . ." Raim replied, ". . . he's just a little wiser now."

"Wiser?" Giddy guffawed as she turned in her saddle and laughed at him. "I'd never accuse you of that."

"Pot calling the frying pan black," Raim suggested as he nodded past her. "It'll be nice to be warm again."

Giddy turned forward once more. The roadhouse sat half obscured by the misty rain in the distance, like a ghost rising up to meet them. The windows flickered with the promising light of a warm fire and, Giddy hoped, warm mead. It was early for drinking mead; but the wet clothes clinging to her back caused her to crave the warm brew.

A short time later, Rhys led them to the barn at the back of the roadhouse and swung himself down from his saddle before pushing open the big, wooden door. Their horses nickered as they smelt the hay inside while the riders were simply pleased to be out of the demoralizing drizzle. Dismounting, Giddy and Raim joined Rhys in unsaddling their mounts, wiping them down and making sure they were settled into the barn before making the dash to the roadhouse's back door.

***

Warmth radiated into Giddy's hand from the large earthenware mug wrapped in her fingers. She still wore her wet clothes, although she had taken the time to wring what water she could from them at the back porch. It didn't make sense for them to change as they would be back on their horses before long and there was no use getting another set soaked through as well. So they had chosen a small wooden table at the side of the main room, close to the crackling fire but far enough from other travelers that they could talk without fear of anyone eavesdropping on their conversation. After ordering warm mead, which the barman already had over the fire, they sat waiting for their breakfast to arrive.

"We picked a fine night to travel," Raim remarked as he lay back in his chair and extended his legs, stretching.

Drawing his fingers through his hair, Rhys winked at him and said, "Better than you think."

Giddy laughed at his words before saying seriously, "Spies?"

Nodding, the thief drank from his mug before continuing, "There are eyes everywhere."

"Dalgliesh?" Raim asked dubiously. "Would he have spies in place just to watch who leaves the city?" Raising his mug and taking a sip, he asked through the wisps of steam, "Would he even care?"

Rhys considered him for a few moments. Eventually, he asked, "Have you ever met him? Dalgliesh, I mean."

"No."

"But you know of him?"

"I know he was a high level lord in the Eldanal Court."

The little thief shrugged and turned to watch the fire before saying quietly, "You don't get to be a high ranking lord without a little skullduggery. Dalgliesh has started his rise up the Aliagan hierarchy. He will already have connections in place."

"The city guards?"

"Guards, among others," Rhys agreed as he turned back to Raim. "Anyone who can provide him with information that might give him the upper hand in his dealings in Aliaga would be a valuable asset for him to have."

"What others?" Raim asked, confused.

Rhys turned back to the fire. "Soldiers, generals, squires who work for other lords," he said. "You have to understand," he went on. "What Dalgliesh has that you and I don't, is money. Street urchins, drunkards, the people I mentioned before . . ." pausing he leaned back to let a waitress serve their plates onto the table. Nodding thanks to her as she left, he turned to Raim and added, ". . . place enough coins in front of them and they'll do whatever you want."

"And you?" Giddy asked as she watched the thief suspiciously. "Do you work for Dalgliesh?"

"Sometimes," Rhys replied shrugging as if it meant nothing. "Not for him directly, mind," he assured them. "But, I'm not above accepting a few coins for a little information here and there."

Looking quickly toward Raim, who frowned back at her in concern, Giddy asked directly, "Are you working for him now?"

Smiling, the little thief picked up a fork and stabbed a fat fillet of anchovy before stuffing it in his mouth. Considering her as he chewed, he eventually grinned and replied, "Today, I work for Legana," he assured her before stabbing another fillet and raising it to his mouth, pausing for an instant to say, "Eat . . . before it gets cold."

Picking up a fork, Giddy ate her breakfast slowly while she studied Rhys. He was not confusing to her; she had met many like him over the years. He was a thief, plain and simple, willing to sink to any lengths for money. Not a mercenary in the traditional sense of a soldier selling their sword hand to the highest bidder; but a man who would steal on commission, sniff out information or simply report what he had seen. The consequences of that rarely bothered his type. If someone lost a prized family heirloom or even their life, he would not see past the few coins scattered in his open palm or at any stage feel that it was his burden. It didn't bother her as it might some people. After all, if it was not this little man in front of her doing the dirty work of the, so called, gentlemen it would be someone else. Deciding, as she placed her fork down on her now empty plate, that he was the best option they had to help them on their mission, she motioned to the waitress to bring more mead and asked, "Do you know where Dalgliesh is?"

Pushing his plate aside, Rhys ran his tongue along his teeth as he nodded. "He has an estate not far from here."

"You've been there?"

"No," Rhys said, shaking his head. "But it didn't take too many questions or . . . ah . . . coins to find out where he lived."

"I guess not," Giddy replied. "What else did you find out?"

Shrugging, the thief looked to the approaching waitress, allowing her to deposit their meads on the table before saying, "Not a lot. He lives with his wife and daughter."

"Anyone else?"

"The usual for a lord," Rhys grunted. "Cooks, servants, butlers, drivers, garden—"

"I get the picture," Giddy interrupted as she picked up her mead and once again wrapped her fingers around its warmth, the sweet smelling steam tantalizing her taste buds after the slightly salty fish. Looking at Rhys over the rim, she asked, "How many guards?"

Shrugging once more, Rhys took a deep swig from his mug before wiping his mouth with the back of his hand and saying, "Only one way to find out.

***

Lord Dalgliesh's home sat in a low valley beneath the spot where Giddy and the others now crouched. They had ridden throughout the dreary morning and had arrived at an outcrop of rocks overlooking the sprawling estate at around noon, although it was hard to tell the time with the overcast sky. Giddy surveyed the buildings as best she could through the continual drizzle. A large mansion stood amongst smaller out-buildings that she assumed to be quarters for the guards and household staff. Paths snaked their way between the buildings while what appeared to be ornate gardens bordered neatly trimmed lawns. A wall, some six foot tall, ran around the extremity of the estate, while two large, planked gates sat ominously closed. There wasn't much sign of life, only a few guards outside the gates stomping their repetitive rounds through the rain. "Not much going on."

"Not in weather like this," Raim replied as he blinked up to the sky. "Can't say I blame them."

"Must be drinking warm mead and sitting by the fire," Rhys said, laughing.

"Sounds good to me," Giddy replied half heartedly as she studied the layout of the grounds. "He doesn't have many guards," she pointed out eventually. "You could be over that wall in a few seconds," she said gesturing to the back of the compound. "A thief would have a wonderful time in there."

"Not really," Rhys replied, shaking his head as he pointed to a building at the near corner of the wall. "That's a guard house," he told her, "and the others over there and there," he advised while pointing to the other corners of the compound. "There would be guards on duty at all times."

"I suppose," Giddy conceded. "But someone skilled like you could easily avoid them."

Feigning embarrassment, Rhys said, "I could indeed. But Dalgliesh knows I wouldn't try."

Looking at the little thief dubiously, Giddy did not think for a second he would not try it if the reward was great enough.

"I wouldn't," he assured her when he saw the doubt in her eyes.

"Why not?"

"He has too much money . . . too much power," Rhys replied simply as he adjusted his position on the slippery rocks. "If you don't want to get bit; don't play in the serpent's burrow."

"You speak of him like he's some kind of god," Giddy accused. "He's only been here for four years. How powerful can he be?"

Rhys sniffed at her suggestion as he wiped his hand across his forehead, flinging water from his hair. "He may have lived in Eldanal before he was banished," he assured her. "But he's had his tentacles in Aliaga for decades."

"Trading?"

"Trading," the thief agreed, nodding thoughtfully. "Among other things. You have to realize that he has few scruples and will do anything to get ahead. A bribe here to a high ranking official; a deed done there for a lord. It doesn't take long to worm your way in. If . . . you can afford it."

"And the Aliagan Lords sit back and let him work his way in?" Raim asked doubtfully. "Why wouldn't they stop him wherever they could?"

Rhys turned to the soldier and grinned while rubbing two fingers together. "Money, my friend. Money."

'I'm sure this isn't what our king had in mind when he banished him," Raim said fiercely as he gestured to the buildings below. "It's like he wasn't punished at all."

"He lost his holdings within Eldanal," Rhys replied scowling. "All those years of positioning and manipulation gone in an instant. A man with his ego and pride would have suffered greatly."

"Still," Giddy interrupted, "he landed on his feet."

"That he did," Rhys agreed.

Standing and walking a few feet away, Giddy watched one of the guards near the front gate as he trudged through a puddle. "We need to know if he's employed this mage that's doing the damage at home," she said before turning to the little man. "Powerful or not. We need to go in."

"No," Rhys replied simply as he too stood and walked to Giddy's side. "You won't learn anything."

"I'm not learning anything standing here either," Giddy snapped at him. "I need to know if this Tiadath Mage is there."

"What if he isn't?"

Giddy glanced at him and then back to the guard. Shrugging, she said, "I've no idea."

"Going in and peeping through a window won't help us," Rhys assured her. "We need hard information. The only way we can get that is from their lips."

Giddy looked back at the thief quickly, concern furrowing her brow. "You want to kidnap Dalgliesh?"

Rolling his eyes at her, Rhys shook his head and replied, "Not kidnap. No. . . . We use Dalgliesh's own weapon against him," he informed her, a smug grin spreading across his face as he dug out his money pouch and bounced it in his hand.

"I doubt that will sway him," Raim scoffed from behind.

"Not Dalgliesh," Rhys replied, his voice exasperated as he raised his hand and pointed toward the gates. "But those guards would see everyone who comes and goes from the compound."

"So they would," Giddy agreed, laughing as she caught on.

"Wait here," Rhys said as he started down the rocks, jumping from one to another, careful not to slip. "A few coins," he called back, his voice not much more than a whisper, "and they'll sing like birds."

Giddy watched him go, waiting till he'd reached the bottom and started toward one of the guards, hand raised in greeting. Turning to Raim, she shrugged and said, "It's as good a plan as any."

12 - Parties and friends

The late afternoon sun speared streams of light into Lady Tesania's room, reflecting brightly off the polished silver brush she pulled through her hair. It had been a week now since Kailyn had arrived unexpectedly on her doorstep, a fully fledged mage. She was so proud of her friend, remembering the young, excitable maid she had first met in Lady Ayana's house all those years ago. She had certainly grown up, no longer a girl, now a blossoming young woman who Tesania was sure would be the talk of the young men throughout the coming night. *'I'll need to have a word with her about that,'* she thought to herself as she placed the brush aside and peered into the mirror. She could have called one of her staff to brush it for her, but she preferred to ready herself, rather than having a maid fuss over her hair and makeup and was pleased with the results. Her dark hair hung straight, *'just as mother always did it,'* she mused, smiling at the memory. After four years of living amongst the fancy curls, twists and braids that many of the women in Wyvern City wore, she had not taken to the style, thinking that it would not suit her.

Satisfied at her reflection, she stood and walked to the bed, calling for a maid to help her into her deep, royal blue, ball gown. The young girl who answered her summons began chattering before she had even reached for the strings on the back of Tesania's dress and begun to pull them tight. Smiling, Tesania indulged the happy girl, allowing her prattle on, enjoying her infectious personality. The girl reminded her, in a lot of ways, of Kailyn on the first day they had met. The difference here though, was the girl didn't have a domineering head maid standing over her, criticizing everything she did. Tesania would not allow that in her household, insisting all her staff be treated with respect and, in the case of the younger ones, patience. As the last string was pulled into place and tied off, Tesania said, "Thank you, Katie," before dismissing the girl and returning to the mirror. Smoothing the gown, she turned from side to side, the skirts of the dress swishing as she moved. Smiling, she reached for the head piece she had purchased in Rilmir with Deavon. It seemed so long ago to her now as she ran her fingers over the autumn colored leaves. Drawing a deep breath as the memories drifted away, she raised her hands and placed it on her head, the silver chain chasing through the softly woven wool and glittering in the light, the strings of beaten metal leaves hanging on either side of her head. Picking up the matching necklace and fastening it into place, she considered herself. Pleased, she started for the door.

***

The ballroom of Tesania's home was a modest size compared to that of the Royal Palace, but it still buzzed with the murmur of a hundred or more people. Standing at the top of the stairway, her hand resting lightly on the carved mahogany balustrade, Tesania glanced around the room. The pomp and ceremony of the people of Wyvern City still amazed her, even to this day. The gowns the ladies wore alone were magnificent, colors varying from pure, frost whites through greens, reds, blues and violets. It was a sight to behold as they wove their way through the crowd or stood with their men folk, talking softly, laughing along at some joke between demure sips of their drinks.

A lot of these people she now called friends, some close, some mere acquaintances. Some of them though were people she had little time for, but the politics of living in the royal city and the position she now held in that society demanded she extend them invitations despite her feelings. It wasn't that she despised them or even disliked them for that matter. It was more that they lived lives of vanity . . . lives of flaunting what they had in front of others, of always putting their desire for position in the Royal Court above common decency. These traits, she could not abide. Maybe it was because of her simple upbringing in the small village of Aryd where people treated each other as equals and respected their views. Perhaps it was that she herself felt no desire to blindly trample over another with little regard to the consequences of the need to grab more of the power and money Wyvern City offered to those willing to go to those extremes.

Kailyn stood in the centre of the room talking to her parents, a glass in her white gloved hand. Tesania smiled at the scene, grateful that they had managed to make the trip after her hurried invitation was sent. Beside them, she saw Naisa, laughing lightly as she talked to Aldan, the big ranger who had accompanied her to the wastelands and Trannyth's keep. But the person she was looking for wasn't there. Frowning, she scanned the room, passing over Lady Ayana, surrounded by her entourage of suitors, and came to the base of the stairs where Deavon stood, his eyes fixed on her, boyish grin on his face. Slowly he stepped to the first tread and then the next, his eyes never leaving hers as he drew closer.

13 - Dark magic

Oppressive heat sucked sweat through the coarse material of the mage, Sergh's robes, staining them with darkness as he stood, hands raised, in front of a large altar. Fashioned from volcanic stone, the altar stood black and ominous in the centre of the cavernous chamber under Tiadath's, Loden Mountains. Formed centuries ago during volcanic eruptions, the cave remained continually hot throughout the year, the mountain alive, magma pulsing in its veins. Rivulets of water seeped through the granite rocks above, dribbling onto the floor where they turned almost instantly to steam, adding to the eeriness of the cavern.

This was where Sergh called upon his dark magic, where he felt the power of each intoned word build to a crescendo. The flickering flames of a dozen or so sconces did their best to hold back the darkness in the cavern while his apprentices stood in the corners, plain wooden staffs in hand, faces wet and clammy as they intently watched him cast a spell, listening to every nuance of his voice, every quaver as it echoed among the stalactites above.

Focusing on a piece of parchment sitting on the altar, he traced the lines with his eyes allowing his mind to float above the ocean, the white caps of the tossing waves some hundred feet below, the mainland of Eldanal off to his left. It was easy enough for him to follow the detailed map that Caitriona had drawn for him as he let his thoughts drift above the coastline to the mouth of Wyvern Harbor before turning sharply and heading inland.

He thought the Dalgliesh girl petty with her moaning for revenge. Her father should step up and take command. After all, they had plenty of money and had landed well in Aliaga. *'Still,'* he surmised, *'as long as they are willing to hand their gold over to me; I will continue to do their bidding.'*

Admonishing himself as his mind's vision faded, Sergh stiffened his grip on his staff and drove onward, slipping over the King's Palace before coming to a large mansion on the edge of the city, his final destination.

Horses stood lazily before their carriages outside the mansion, their drivers milling about as other men, obviously pages, escorted the carriage's exquisitely dressed former occupants into the house. "A party," Sergh muttered under his breath, grinning sadistically he called upon his mist the stalactites above him trembling as his magic burst forth.

14 - Devastation

Lively music emanated from a stage at the far end of the ballroom, the orchestra's music growing to a crescendo as Tesania twirled, Deavon's fingers supporting her as she danced. It was a robust tune and she breathed hard as Deavon caught her, drawing her in closer before skipping down the room, his hand tight on her waist, supporting her as he dipped her toward the floor as the musicians ended their melody and began another. Pulling away as Deavon began to dance once more, Tesania pleaded, "Can we stop and get a drink?"

Disappointment flitted over Deavon's face for an instant before slipping away and being replaced by his usual smile. Nodding, he took her hand and led her off the dance floor, stopping beside Naisa and Aldan who stood watching the other dancers. "I'll be back in a second," he advised her as he headed toward a table laden with bowls of punch and other assorted beverages.

"Hot work?" Naisa asked lightly as Tesania wiped at her sweaty brow.

"It is," Tesania replied. "But it's so much fun."

Inclining her head in agreement, Naisa arched an eyebrow at the big ranger next to her. "Perhaps a gentleman might ask me to dance?"

Rolling his eyes to Tesania, Aldan bowed and crooked his arm toward the Arch Mage before asking, "Would milady grant me the honor of accompanying me to the dance floor?"

Placing her arm on his elbow, Naisa said, "It would be my pleasure," smiling at Tesania as the ranger led her away to the dance floor.

Tesania watched them disappear into the crowd before turning back to the table as Deavon returned, handing her a drink. "It's a wonderful party," he congratulated her as he motioned around the big room.

Tesania beamed as she turned and took in the guests. She didn't host many parties, preferring to have smaller gatherings of her friends for a meal and drinks by the fire. But for Kailyn's graduation she had thought she should put on a show. Deavon swallowed his drink in only a few gulps before looking pointedly at hers and then to the dance floor. Laughing, she said, "Be patient. I'll be finished—"

"Lady Tesania!" a page called as he fought his way through the crowd, worry creasing his face. "Lady Tesania. You must come quickly."

Tesania's eyes flicked quickly from the page to Deavon. As he shrugged, his face blank, she turned her attention back to the page. "What is it?" she asked quickly, her mind racing. "Is someone hurt?"

"Out . . . outside," the page stammered, his face ashen as he looked back to the hallway he had come from, his hand raising, shaking finger pointing. "You must come quickly."

Not at all sure what was wrong, Tesania felt the urgency as the page's frightened eyes drifted back to her. Turning to Deavon, she said, "Please ask Naisa and Aldan to meet us at the front entry." As he nodded and started for the dance floor, Tesania strode toward the hallway, the page falling in step several paces behind.

Frowning as a myriad of thoughts shot through her head, Tesania hurried along the main hallway of her home toward the two wide open oak doors. Light flickered from outside, reflecting eerily off the marble flagstones on the floor as a tortured, high pitched scream rent the air. Breaking into a run, Tesania reached the doorway in a few seconds, sliding to a halt as a man whipped past her, his flailing arms narrowly missing her head as he was flicked viciously sideways, the sickening crack of his spine shattering stabbing through the cool night air. Horrified, Tesania stood transfixed as the man's now limp body floated seemingly of its own accord, one foot in the air while his other hung grotesquely off to the side, his coat hanging down over his head, twitching arms dangling straight down below. "What is happening," she whispered raising her hand to her mouth. Piercing screams ripped through the night to her right, not a human's scream, but a sharp, ear rupturing wail. Tearing her eyes from the floating man as he disappeared above the house, Tesania groaned as she watched two horses, still harnessed to a glimmering white carriage, drifting slowly into the air, their legs kicking wildly, eyes wide with terror as they threw their heads from side to side, straining to break the bonds of their bridles. Yet another scream echoed through the still air from somewhere in the darkness, drawing Tesania's attention as she stood helplessly, heart thumping, not beginning to understand what was happening. Jumping as the first man she had watched being lifted into the air thudded onto the ground in front of her, his body twisted and broken, eyes staring lifelessly at her, Tesania stumbled backward, reeling, bile rising in her throat as she clutched at her mouth. Wide eyed, she glanced from one frightening scene to the next, struggling to take it all in as movement caught her eye.

It wasn't much of a movement, but enough to draw Tesania's eye. Watching in fascination as a tendril of mist floated down from the gutter line of the house, tracing along the fascia before slithering across the eave and feeling its way down the wall, directly above her. Enchanted by the drifting, swirling motion of the mist, she stood fascinated as it curled onto the marble floor and crept toward her feet.

Something tapped at her mind, warning her, demanding she move away. "Mist," she mumbled. "At this time of year?" Suddenly it dawned on her. "Mist," she called out, stepping quickly away. "We're being attacked." Skipping sideways, she leapt over the finger of mist as it lurched at her, its mesmerizing slowness no longer evident as it snatched at her shoe. Rushing to the door, she called to the page that crouched at the entry, trembling, drool running down his chin. "Get out of here," she yelled. "Run!"

As the page stared after her, incomprehension playing across his eyes, Tesania lifted her skirts and ran down the hallway, toward the ballroom where Deavon and the others were now coming from. "Mist," she called out urgently to them as she half turned back to the doorway, stumbling in her run and thudding into Deavon's arms. "Mist . . . Killing people . . . The horses . . . ."

Deavon helped her stand as Naisa strode past her, stopping a few feet ahead. Turning, she asked Aldan to quietly ask the other mages at the party to attend her at the front door before asking Tesania. "Are you sure it was mist?"

"It came after me," Tesania replied, her voice rising as her anger rose. "I know what I saw."

Nodding, Naisa said, as if she hadn't noticed the anger in Tesania's voice, "I have no idea how we might stop this thing."

"Surely you have a spell," Tesania insisted.

"Perhaps," Naisa mumbled, her eyes fixed on the end of the hallway. "We can only try."

"Try?" Tesania gasped while disentangling herself from Deavon's arms. "It's killing people!" she said angrily as she started toward the ballroom.

"Tes," Devon called after her, worry in his voice. "Where are you going?"

Turning back to them, Tesania looked from one to the other, clenching her fists as she controlled herself. "I'm getting my sword. Someone has to stop it."

"Your sword won't work against mist," Naisa assured her, her brow furrowing as she shook her head lightly. "It's mist . . . . Just air."

"Magic air," Tesania said as she spun and began to run to the stairs on the far side of the ballroom, dodging through party guests, not bothering to excuse herself as she jostled past them.

She knew Naisa was probably right, that her sword would simply pass through the mist like it wasn't there. But people were dying, horses and carriages being ripped apart. She couldn't just stand by while Naisa 'tried' to do something.

Flinging the door to her bedroom open, she crashed into the room and made her way to the closet sitting against the far wall. Pausing for an instant, she drew labored breaths before reaching forward and pulling the door of the cupboard open. A satisfied smile slipped onto her face as she reached in and closed her hand around the familiar shape of her ancestor's sword, the shagreen leather cool and smooth under her touch.

It had only been a few days since she had last handled the sword. The feel of it, the way it balanced perfectly in her hand, still amazed her, even after all the years since she had taken it from her slain father's room where it had molded itself to her small hand, the magic tingling along her nerves. Many evenings she would withdraw it from the cupboard and sit on her bed, polishing its ornate scabbard and blade. She had no idea why, but somehow it connected her to her mother and father, to her ancestors from long past. She assumed it had to do with her long dead ancestor who had forged the sword and imbued it with magic and his own blood. Sliding it now from its sheath, she felt the familiar pulse of power, the shiver of the grip as fire rippled and played within the mirror-like blade, twinkling in her eyes.

Spinning on her heel, she made for the door once more before rushing down the stairway. Grasping the hilt harder as she reached the ballroom floor, she ignored the gasps and screams of her guests, storming forward as they parted out of her way, the music stopping abruptly as the musicians stood and peered curiously at their hostess. The sword trembled harder in her hand, fire flickering in a growing crescendo as her heels clattered onto the marbled floor of the hallway and she strode toward the front, oaken doors.

Chest rising and falling rapidly, she broke into a run as another scream echoed off the walls around her. She could see through the doorway that Naisa stood, arms raised, obviously casting a spell, while other mages, Kailyn included, huddled around her, prodding the wisps of mist away as they crept toward the arch mages fluttering robes.

Devastation spread beyond the mages. Carriages lay on their sides, wheels torn away, their still harnessed horses struggling to rise as their frightened cries tore through the night. Men ran in all directions mist drifting after them, often jagging sideways to snare any unwary prey. Bodies of drivers and pages alike littered the pebbled drive, some still and lifeless, others struggling to stand, groaning in pain.

Reaching the door, Tesania slowed, glancing around. Deavon stood some ten feet away. He had no weapon and merely dodged the mist as best he could. "Do something," she called to the mages. "You must stop this!"

"I can't," Naisa's distressed voice cried. "We don't have our staffs."

Cursing under her breath, she berated herself for arranging a party where the city's mages would attend without their staffs in times when they might be attacked by these awful mists. *What was I thinking?* Another scream rent the air, drawing her out of her thoughts. Desperately, she looked about. Whilst the mages couldn't banish the mist without their staffs, they were managing to hold it at bay with the spells they could call forth. Deavon, on the other hand was defenseless and being driven backward. She realized it wouldn't be long before the mist had him backed against the house and so started toward him, sword raised, its internal fire flickering, casting shadows along the walls.

"Move," Tesania called to him as he looked up at her. "Get behind me!"

"No," Deavon replied adamantly, shaking his head as he flicked his eyes back to the mist. "I must draw it away from Naisa."

"It's going to trap you," Tesania almost screamed, worry for the ranger constricting her throat.

"I'll be ok," Deavon assured her, a weak grin flashing across his face, quickly replaced by concern as a tendril dashed at surprising speed at his foot, wrapping itself around his ankle, coiling like a snake around its hapless prey before plucking him into the air his head cracking against the stone verandah.

"No!" Tesania screamed as the ranger's body flew past her, the momentum spraying blood from a gaping wound on his head, covering her, filling her mouth with the iron taste. Spluttering, she spun. "Deavon!" she wailed as his body was ripped sideways and smashed against the wall, the sickening thud reverberating through her mind. Not caring if the mist would snatch her up as well, she moved forward. All she knew was that Deavon, more than ever before, needed her, and needed her now. Lunging forward, she stepped directly into the swirling mist on the ground by the ranger, feeling its clingy fingers immediately grasp at her calves, encircling, squeezing. Ignoring it, she thrust the sword at the mist, feeling nothing as the blade slipped through the wisps which offered no resistance as it swirled into a maelstrom and drew away from the frenzied vibrating of the sword. Swinging sideways, she again felt nothing as the sword sliced through empty air, the mist having fled before it. Stepping closer to Deavon, she swiped at the remaining tendrils playing around his ankles, the mist darted back, sitting up, almost as though it was regarding her, before it seemingly turned and sped away. Tears ran down her face as she knelt beside Deavon's inert body. Reaching out, she brushed his hair from his face, certain of what she would find. His face was pasty white with rivulets of already drying blood running down from his nose a bruise splashing across his forehead from where he had cannoned into the wall. Closing her eyes, she ran her fingers down the stubble on his cheek. "Why," she whispered. "Why didn't you stay inside where you were safe?" Drawing a deep breath, she gripped her sword and began to stand, removing her hand from his face as she looked away, brushing it across his lips. Freezing, her head whipped back as the faint feel of his breath caressed her fingers. "Deavon," she said hopefully, dropping to her knees and reaching for his face once more. "Deavon. Can you hear me?" When the ranger didn't respond she looked about, worried. There was no one who could help him.

Everyone else was engaged with battling the mist. Realizing he would have to fend for himself while she tried to help, Tesania leant forward and kissed him gently on his forehead before leaving him laying on his back. "I'll be back for you," she promised as she rose and spun toward the mist.

"Get back inside," she screamed at a group of lords and ladies creeping out of the front door. "You can't do anything here." Rushing toward Kailyn and the other mages, she called for them to stand still as she jabbed the sword at the mist, hope clawing at her as it once again withdrew before her assault. "Drive it all together," she yelled at them. When the mages looked at her, dumbfounded, she pointed toward an upturned carriage. "Use your magic! Herd it together," she added as she ran off to the left, jabbing her sword at the mist she passed. "Get it all to the carriage there," she called back over her shoulder. "It's our only chance."

Sliding to a halt at the left corner of her house, Tesania turned and began walking deliberately toward the carriage, stepping sideways, dodging and lunging, retracing her steps and moving forward once more. The mist moved begrudgingly before her, retreating as she thrust forward, darting to try and pass her when it thought she wasn't paying attention and then falling back when she cut it off once more.

The mages had started to do as she had commanded. Spreading out, they had formed a circle around the mist and now pushed it into the centre of an ever decreasing circle. "Naisa," Tesania called her voice cracking. "You need to block the top somehow," she instructed the Arch Mage as she pointed high in the air. "A spell . . . to stop it escaping."

Nodding, Naisa raised her arms and began to intone a spell. Her voice was low and imperceptible but the mist started to roil and roll, growing more and more agitated as it was squeezed inside its entrapment.

Tesania knew instinctively that they would have only one chance at what she intended to do. Walking forward, slashing, she waited until the mist was contained in an area no more than a few feet wide, its once wispy density now compressed to where it was a pulsing, gyrating mass which lurched at its captors in vain attempts to escape. Drawing a deep breath, she knew the time was nearly here. Raising her sword she set herself to burst forward but stopped suddenly as a face slowly materialized within the mist. It wasn't much of a face, just the semblance of one, eyes sunken into the mist, lips and chin. But it was aware of its surroundings, knew she was there. Slowly, the eyes turned toward her, seemingly studying her, moving from side to side in an almost hypnotic sway before a faint, almost imperceptible whisper emanated from its lips, "Who are you?"

"Who am I . . . ?" Tesania almost screamed, hands trembling. "You come to my house . . . Kill my people!"

"Collateral damage," the voice whispered. "They matter not."

"Matter not," Tesania spluttered anger tearing through her as the words tore at her mind. "I will not stand by," she wailed, "while you do this to them."

"You have no choice," the voice laughed.

Skipping forward, Tesania replied, "But I do," as she drove her sword into the face, feeling with great satisfaction that the blade didn't slip through as before but found something solid, something for the blade to bite. The mist froze for a split second as the blade came to rest, the swirls and eddies seeming to stand still in time before a growling scream grew from its centre forcing Tesania and the mages to their knees as the scream grew in intensity forcing them to thrust their hands over their ears, the mist boiling in upon itself before exploding in a shower of water that rained down upon them.

Lowering her arms, Tesania peered up into the falling droplets, letting them splash onto her face. Their coolness calmed her ragged nerves as she let them soak her hair and run down her bodice. Drawing a deep breath, she looked across to Kailyn who grinned at her. Smiling briefly, Tesania suddenly remembered Deavon bleeding on the verandah. Clambering to her feet, she rushed to where he lay, calling, "Naisa, come quickly."

***

Jerking away from his altar, Sergh stumbled as the force of his spell being destroyed by the girl drove him backward, the only thing saving him from falling being one of his apprentices who moved quickly to catch him.

"What is wrong?" the apprentice asked, worry in his voice as he frowned at his disheveled master.

"A woman . . . ." Sergh muttered as he looked around wildly.

"What woman?"

"There was a woman . . . ." Sergh began before catching himself and shoving the apprentice's hands away. Adjusting his robes, he walked toward his altar, reliving what had just transpired. Uncomprehending, he mumbled, "How?"

15 - Soldiers' return

Waves crashed against the rocky headland guarding the entrance to Wyvern Harbor while gulls drifted out from the shore and cried sharply above the men scrambling over the rigging of the King's Ship Swan as she glided sedately into her home port. Giddy stood anxiously leaning on the rail where it would open to allow her to disembark. It had been a rough crossing; waves smashing monotonously against the bluff bow of the sturdy little ship most of the way from Estel Harbor, having only let up a few hours earlier as she ran along the eastern coast of Eldanal.

"Not long now," Raim said from behind, the thud of his pack hitting the scrubbed decking following a few seconds after.

"No," Giddy muttered absentmindedly as she watched a small fishing boat slip along the side of the Swan.

"I'll be glad to be off this ship."

Grinning, Giddy turned to her friend. "It's been a rough one," she agreed. "Give me a horse any day."

"Agreed," Raim said as he grasped the side rail and leaned out, the breeze ruffling his hair. "Where to first?" he asked.

"General Ardel's office I suppose," Giddy replied, shrugging as she leant against the rail once more.

"Legana will want to see us."

"No doubt," Giddy replied shrugging. "But Ardel first." As Raim nodded in silent agreement, Giddy fell quiet and watched the sailors work as they slipped up to their berth and tied off. Slinging her pack onto her shoulder, she walked down the wooden gangplank, compensating for its bounce and stepped ashore before starting toward Ardel's offices.

16 - A meeting

Tesania walked slowly along the grand hallway of King Eldine's Palace, the beat of her heels on the flagstone floor echoing lightly off the high walls. Deavon walked beside her, his face stoic under the dark bruise tracing across his forehead. Tesania had pleaded with him to stay at her home, to rest and recuperate after his ordeal with the mist on the previous evening. To her dismay, he had refused, insisting that he accompany her to the hastily arranged meeting with the king and his advisors. She knew better than to argue with him and so walked sedately to allow his battered body to keep up as they drew closer to the entrance to the king's stateroom.

"Lady Tesania," a page greeted dipping his head for a moment before turning his attention to Deavon, a frown playing across his brow as his eyes took in the rangers face. "I trust all is well?" he asked nervously as his eyes flicked back to Tesania.

"Well enough," Deavon muttered irritably. "We're here to see the king."

"He is expecting you," the page replied as he once more scanned the rangers face before stepping aside and ushering them through the door to the stateroom and announcing their arrival to the people already seated inside.

Squinting in the dim light of the room after the brightness of the hallway, Tesania led Deavon forward as she nodded to the gathering. "Your Majesty," she acknowledged the king. "Naisa," she said happily smiling at her friend seated on the right side of the king before scanning past the empty seat that General Ardel would usual fill. "General," she said nodding to General Legana as she pulled a chair out for Deavon, despite his protests.

"I'm not an invalid, Tes," he grunted as he sat, groaning as his abused body objected to the movement.

Shaking her head gently at him, Tesania whispered, "You're hurt. You should be at home resting."

"Leave it, Tes," Deavon said frowning up at her. "My place is here."

Frowning back at him, Tesania took a seat next to him. She knew it was pointless arguing; besides, he was already here. It worried her though to see him in such pain. Shaking her head once more in resignation, she turned to the king who studied Deavon from beneath his furrowed brow. "A nasty business last night," he said slowly. "I trust you are alright."

Nodding, Deavon replied, "I'll survive."

"Glad to hear it," the king replied as he turned to Tesania. "And you."

"I'm fine," Tesania replied, frowning as she added, "But many people were murdered last night, dozens hurt, horses crippled, many having to be put down."

"I have read the reports."

"Then you know it was this mist? That this mage is now attacking us directly? You saw it Naisa," she said turning her attention to the arch mage. "The face in the mist? It has to be a mage controlling it."

"I concede that it was a mist," the king continued without waiting for Naisa's answer as he brought his hands in front of his chin fingers pressing together in a steeple until they began to turn white, "But we still have no proof 'who' is behind it."

Tesania considered his words. He was right of course. They had no idea where to start looking for this mage until they heard back from Giddy and Raim, let alone how to stop him. "We have to do something," she almost whispered as images of the previous night's carnage played through her head. "I can't let more people die."

The king looked at her sadly. "They are my people too," he said.

"Perhaps . . ." Naisa interrupted, ". . . We should wait until General Ardel joins us before we continue."

"You are quite right," the king agreed. "He'll be here soon enough."

"I would have thought he'd be here on time," General Legana said pointedly. "He knows the importance of this meeting."

"Indeed," the king replied. "I believe the two soldiers have returned from Aliaga. He is debriefing them."

Legana scowled. "Shouldn't that be done here?" he asked.

The king looked at him evenly before replying, "They are his people. It is expected."

"Still," Legana said as he fiddled with his shirt buttons, "They should have come to me."

"As I said: They are his people."

Legana looked away, obviously deciding that pushing the matter further would be useless. Instead he said to Tesania, "I've read the preliminary reports on last night's attack. You did well."

"We were lucky," Tesania said quietly whilst looking down at the table. "Without Naisa here," she added motioning to the arch mage, "there's no telling how much damage would have been done."

"Me," Naisa said in surprise. "I didn't contribute much."

"You held it at bay."

"For a while," Naisa conceded. "But that mist was more than I could handle."

"You didn't have your staff."

"Even so," Naisa argued. "I doubt I could have banished it. It would have wreaked havoc on all of your guests if you hadn't stopped it."

Looking down at the table again, Tesania muttered, "It wasn't me. It was the sword."

"Which you wielded," Naisa assured her. "And it was you that came up with the idea of corralling the mist."

"True," Tesania capitulated. "But still, it was the sword's magic, not mine."

"Magic that is yours to wield," Naisa said. "Don't sell yourself short."

"I—" Tesania began before the page entered the room, interrupting her by announcing the arrival of General Ardel, Giddy and Raim.

"Giddy, Raim!" Tesania exclaimed as she swiveled in her chair. "Did you find him . . . ? The mage . . . ? Where is he?"

"Not exactly, Tes," Giddy replied as she moved to a chair and dragged it out. "I'll explain what we found in a minute." Sitting, she paused as Deavon's face caught her attention. "What happened to you?" she asked quickly concern creasing her own face as she looked around the others seated at the table. "What's going on?"

"We were attacked," Tesania said. "By the mist: At my house last night."

"It attacked here?" Raim asked in surprise. "In Wyvern city?"

"It tried," Deavon replied. "Tes stopped it."

"But not before it murdered a dozen men, killed horses, destroyed carriages." Tesania said, regret in her voice. "I should have stopped it sooner."

"You did what you could," Naisa assured her. "You couldn't have saved them all."

"No," Tesania muttered. "But I could have saved some of them if I'd acted more quickly."

"Don't lay the blame for this at your own feet," Giddy said as she stood and walked to Tesania. "It's Dalgliesh you should blame."

"So it is him," Tesania uttered as she swung around to Deavon. "I knew it."

"You saw them?" Deavon asked as he looked up to Giddy. "Saw the mage with Dalgliesh?"

"Not exactly," Giddy said as she walked slowly along the room.

"Perhaps you might tell us of your mission," the king suggested as his eyes followed Giddy.

Turning, Giddy leaned on the back of Raim's chair as she began. Glossing over their travel and their meeting with the thief in Estel she told them of how they had come to the gates of Dalgliesh's Estate and how Rhys had climbed down the slippery rock face to talk to and bribe the guards for information.

"So you didn't see Dalgliesh at all?" Legana asked, scowling.

"Didn't need to," Giddy said, shrugging.

"Or the mage?"

Giddy shook her head. "As I was saying: Rhys bribed a couple of the guards at the front gate."

"And they told him about the mage?"

"They did."

"Can we trust this information?" the king asked. "They might say anything for a few coins."

"I think we can," Giddy replied as she pulled the chair in under herself and retook her seat. "Apparently there has been a strange looking mage at the estate."

"Strange?"

"His clothes, hair, mannerisms. The guards were pretty clear he wasn't from Aliaga."

"Tiadath?" Tesania asked sitting forward. "It must be."

Shrugging, Giddy said, "They didn't know where he was from. Just that he showed up one day, a month or so ago, and stayed for a week."

"He's not there now?" Deavon asked.

"Not according to the guards."

"Then how will we find him?" Tesania asked looking from Naisa to Deavon for an answer. When he looked back blankly she turned back to Giddy. "They have no idea where he's from?"

"None," Giddy replied apologetically hands spread.

"So . . . How do we stop him then?"

"Dalgliesh," Legana replied. "We need to capture Dalgliesh and make him stop the mage."

"And how do you suggest we do that?" General Ardel asked. "Remember, Aliaga is not an Eldanal State. We must be careful not to overstep our authority."

"Agreed," the king said, concern playing over his face. "We need to tread carefully. The last thing we need is a war with Aliaga."

"We can't just sit here and let our people die either," Tesania gasped. "Whether the Aliagan king likes it or not, We have to go . . . . We have to stop Lord Dalgliesh."

"We can't just send an army in," Ardel said, his voice rising. "There are protocols for this type of thing."

"My people are dying!"

"I understand that, Lady Tesania," Ardel said, his voice softening. "But we can't just land an army on their shores and not expect retaliation."

"Giddy and Raim went there."

"That was different, Tes," Giddy assured her. "We were just two; we blended in."

"So, just the three of us go."

"No, Tes," Deavon said quickly as he sat forward, gasping as his body protested.

"Why not?"

"Three isn't enough," Giddy interrupted shaking her head. "Raim will tell you. That place is like a fortress: Walls, mercenary guards. We can't just walk in and arrest him."

"Agreed," the little soldier next to her said. "We need more than three."

"We'll have my sword," Tesania assured them.

"I forbid it," the king said loudly, before addressing Tesania in a quieter voice, "I understand your people are hurting. Mine are too. But if we breach the sanctity of the Aliagan borders with our forces we will start a war and even more people will suffer."

Blinking, Tesania looked around the table. Most looked back at, some simply looked down. "I won't let him sit safe in Aliaga while my people suffer . . . I won't."

"Agreed," the king said, nodding. "Lord Dalgliesh must be brought to account and his mage stopped."

"Then we go in?" Tesania asked hopefully.

"Not with an army," Legana interrupted.

"Then us?" Tesania asked as she looked quickly to the two soldiers and Naisa. "We can get Aldan. With you three that will be five of us."

"Six," Deavon said. "You're not leaving me behind."

Spinning on him, Tesania said pointedly, "You're hurt. You can't go."

"Try and stop me."

"Six is still not enough," Giddy sighed. "You haven't seen the estate."

"This is all irrelevant," Raim cut in. "Dalgliesh has risen in the ranks on the Aliagan nobility. Even if we do manage to infiltrate his estate and capture him, the Aliagan King will demand justice. Again . . . we are at war."

"A good point," the king agreed. "We must tread carefully. I will not knowingly instigate a war."

"It seems the only way around this is through their king," Legana said as he stood and began pacing. "Tell him what is happening. Tell him that we have clear evidence Dalgliesh is behind these attacks."

"Possibly," the king replied as he considered what his general had said. "It would make sense for him to help us in this time of need; and I'm sure he doesn't wish war either."

"Right," Legana said. "You could send him a dispatch informing him of what Dalgliesh is up to and that we are sending our people to arrest him."

"No," the king said, shaking his head as he sat forward leaning his elbows on the table. "We don't know how secure that will be. Dispatches are read by many levels of aides and lords before they get to the king. Lord Dalgliesh may be informed we are coming."

Legana thought over his words before eventually saying, "Then a dispatch informing him that Deavon here, and the others, are coming to talk to him about an urgent matter."

"That would be wiser," the king agreed as he turned his attention to Tesania. "Then you can talk to him privately; let him know the situation."

"Then it's agreed," Legana said excitement in his voice as the time for planning was now afoot. "It's a given that Tesania will go: But who else?"

"Me!" Giddy said, sitting forward.

"And me," Raim added.

"Me as well," Naisa said, beaming at Tesania.

"No," the king said adamantly. "You are the Arch Mage now."

"But . . . ." Tesania began to argue.

"Her role is here. I will not enter into argument."

Disappointment filled Naisa's voice as she said, "Sorry Tes. He's right; I should stay here."

"I understand," Tesania half whispered.

"You will need a mage though," Naisa said as she looked at her hands in thought.

Tesania watched her as she deliberated, wondering if she might know who she would choose when a thought came to her. "Kailyn," she said. "She's graduated. She can come."

"Kailyn's a little young."

"We know what she can do."

"Granted, but—"

"Kailyn's who I want," Tesania interrupted. "Giddy? Raim?" she asked pleading with her eyes. "You know she can do it."

"I don't have a problem with it," Giddy said, shrugging.

"Me either," Raim said.

"Deavon?" Naisa asked.

Deavon considered the arch mage before turning to Giddy and then Tesania, his movements slow as he winced. "I think it's already been decided. But I would be happy to have her along," he said before quickly adding as he saw the look in Tesania's face. "I'm coming, Tes. It's just bruising. I'll be alright in a few days. Besides," he added as an afterthought his eyes flicking to the two soldiers, "Someone needs to keep these two in line."

"Us?" the two friends said in unison, grins flashing across their faces before Giddy turned to Raim and said, "He's talking about you, you know."

"Me?"

"Here we go again," Deavon groaned.

"See what you'v—"

"Who else?" the king interrupted scowling at the two soldiers. "Surely that isn't enough?"

"I'd like Aldan along too, if that's alright?" Deavon asked Legana.

"I'm sure we can spare him."

"Rhys might come in handy too," Giddy added. "The thief," she informed as Tesania looked at her blankly, "From Aliaga. He knows his way around."

"A thief?" Naisa asked dubiously. "Can you trust him?"

"With enough coin we can," Giddy said laughing. "But seriously," she added, sobering, "I think we can trust him."

"I'll vouch for Rhys," Legana said as his eyes flicked cautiously to his king. "I've used him many times in the past."

"Interesting," the king said. "Perhaps we should talk about this thief of yours later?"

Scowling, Legana said, "It's all legal. You could say; it's in my line of duty."

"I could," the king conceded. "But still, let us have a talk."

"As you wish," Legana said squirming in his seat as he turned to Deavon in an obvious attempt to change the subject. "Anyone else?"

Deavon looked at the two soldiers and then Tesania. He knew what they all could do and adding Kailyn and Aldan to the mix would make it a formidable team. Eventually he looked back at Legana and said, "I think that's enough. With the thief as well, we'll have seven."

"I'm sure Rhys will be able to supply more men if required," Legana assured him.

"Possibly," Deavon said. "That should be enough though. Anymore and we'll draw attention."

"Agreed," Legana replied. "So it's settled. You four, Aldan and Kailyn meet up with Rhys in Estel and see the Aliagan king. There you can acquire more men through Rhys."

"I'll have a dispatch sent to the Swan," the king informed them. "You can sail on the morning tide."

"That may not be wise," Legana said, shaking his head. "Dalgliesh is sure to have spies here in Wyvern City. They would be watching Tesania. We don't want him knowing she is on her way to Aliaga."

The king pondered on Legana's words for a moment before asking what his suggestion might be.

"Travel by horse to the southwest corner of Eldanal. There you will find a small village where you can—"

"Aryd?" Tesania said sharply. "Are you talking about Aryd?"

"That could be the name of it," Legana replied frowning. "I'm not sure. But anyway," he went on as Tesania turned to Deavon and mouthed "Aryd . . . that's my home." as Deavon nodded and reached out to take her hand.

Not noticing the exchange, Legana continued, "The Swan can meet you off the point. No one will see you there."

"But that's days riding," General Ardel protested.

"Better than being seen," Legana shot at his counterpart. "Do you want Dalgliesh to know they are coming?"

"Of course I don't. But there has to be somewhere closer."

"Where?" Legana asked, his anger rising. There's no other place a ship can safely pick up passengers along the south coast."

"Estom Harbor."

"Estom," Legana scoffed. "It will be watched just as sharply as Wyvern harbor. You don't seem to understand. They must not be seen leaving for Aliaga!"

"I understand fully."

"It seems not!"

"Gentlemen," the king interrupted angrily as he glared from one to another. Eventually he calmed and said, "General Legana has a solid point. I shall instruct the Swan's captain to meet you off this village in seven days time." Looking around the room, he paused on each of them. "Are we in agreement?"

As Ardel muttered to himself and the others nodded, the king stood. "I will arrange the dispatch to King Asden immediately as well as the instructions to the Swan." Turning his attention to Tesania, he said, "I know I don't need to tell you the urgency of this matter."

"No," Tesania agreed.

"Get to Lord Dalgliesh as fast as you can. I want him stopped."

"As do I," Tesania assured him.

"I'm trusting you all," he said as he looked at the others. "Make sure she gets there."

"We'll do our best," Giddy assured him.

King Eldine scrutinized Giddy through slit eyes before nodding and then turning to Legana. "I trust I can rely on you to work out the details."

"My Lord," Legana said as he bowed his head. "Consider it done."

"Make sure it is," the king said as he moved to the door and paused before turning back. "You have all done more than Eldanal could ever repay you for in the past. I'm afraid we must ask you to help her again." With that he turned and left the room in silence, each of the seated people looking at the door he had exited, each lost in their own thoughts.

17 - On the road

Soft shafts of sunlight punctuated the early morning darkness, reflecting off droplets of dew as they clung shivering on the edge of the gutter of the royal stables of Wyvern City. Tesania stood beside her mare, her breath condensing, pluming out into the cool spring air before dissipating away. "Cold," she said to Kailyn who stood next to her stamping her feet while wrapping her arms around herself.

"Freezing," Kailyn replied tiredly. "I wish I was still in bed."

"You haven't changed," Tesania said laughing as she remembered the times she had to get Giddy to chase the young girl out of her sleeping roll on their previous adventure.

Frowning, Kailyn said, "Well I like my sleep."

"Me too," Tesania admitted as she watched Deavon approach, his hands wrapped about the reins of his own mount as it clopped along behind him, head low. It still worried her that he was injured, although she had to admit, he did look much improved after another night's sleep. "Feeling better?" she asked.

"Much," Deavon replied. "At least I can move without so much pain," he assured her while arching his back.

"That won't last," Giddy assured him as she approached from the stables, Raim following close behind. "A day in the saddle will sort you out," she added laughing.

"I'm sure," Deavon said, grimacing at the thought.

"Rilmir today?" Raim asked.

"I think so," Deavon replied as he ran his hand down his horse's nose. "We'll need to ride hard though," he continued as he handed his reins to Raim and walked briskly toward a large man walking toward them. "Aldan," he called. "It's good to see you, my friend."

"Aldan," Kailyn said excitedly to Tesania as she too moved toward the ranger who had accompanied them years ago on their mission to Trannyth's keep.

"Kailyn," the big man responded as he bent and drew the girl into a bear hug, engulfing her.

"I'm so happy you're coming along," she said voice muffled in his shoulder.

"Me too," Aldan replied, grinning as he released her. "I heard you were assigned as our mage."

Kailyn shrugged. "It seems I was volunteered."

"She would have insisted on coming anyway," Tesania assured him as she too came into the man's embrace. Deavon's good friend had become like a brother to her in the past few years.

"I'm sure she would have," Aldan said as he grinned at the now embarrassed young mage before looking past her to the two soldiers. "They didn't tell me you two were coming along," he said in mock exasperation. "I might have declined if I'd known that."

'It's not too late,' Giddy assured him as she led the horses over to them and reached her free hand out to shake Aldan's before nodding to his other. "How's the hand?"

Aldan looked briefly down at his maimed left hand dismissing the three missing fingers as he waved it away.

"I'm used to it now," he assured them, grinning. "Can still shoot a bow as well as any man."

"Good to hear," Raim said as he smiled up at the ranger and slapped him on the shoulder.

Drawing a deep breath, Aldan looked about the stables. "It'll be good to be on the road again," he said as he looked toward Deavon. "Where to?"

"Rilmir," Deavon replied as he reached out and took the reins of his horse from Raim. "Everyone ready?" he asked as he reached for the pommel on his saddle and dragged himself up before quickly pulling on the horse's reins as it skittered forward. "Whoa."

Tesania turned to her own mount as Deavon regained control and pulled herself into the saddle. She thanked herself for having the sense to wear britches as she adjusted herself and settled in.

"Let's go," Deavon said when the party was all mounted and led the way to the city's west gate.

Tesania paused as the others moved away and looked back toward where her house would be. It worried her to leave on such short notice with repairs needed on the manor and the harvest season getting underway. But she knew she had no choice, the mage attacking her people had to be stopped. Besides, she had left instructions with her managers. They would be quite able to handle her affairs whilst she was away. "Hopefully," she muttered to herself as she turned her horse and started after the others, "we'll get Lord Dalgliesh quickly and be back in only a few weeks."

***

Rilmir was a city Tesania had visited many times since she had passed through with Deavon on her way to see the king those many years ago. She did what she could for the young street children, offering them food and clothes, but, as Deavon had remarked at the time, it wasn't much use. Mostly her gifts were quickly taken by the children's parents and sold, the money wasted on ale or gambling. The thoughts saddened her as they approached the city gates. To this day she still had her people searching for the little girl who had offered her doll to her as they entered the city. She had promised then to help her, save her. But it was useless; no one knew where the girl was or even knew her name.

Deavon guided his horse toward her. The bruise on his face had finally begun to fade but still traced a dark line across his forehead. "Thinking about the girl?" he asked softly as he saw the sadness in her face.

"I promised to save her," Tesania whispered.

"It's not your fault."

"I know. It's just that she was so dirty . . . so poor."

"You've done what you could," Deavon assured her as he reined his horse in and dismounted before reaching up, offering Tesania his hand. "Maybe, one day, you will find her."

"Maybe," Tesania said without much conviction as Deavon took her reins and led the horses toward Giddy and Raim.

"Can you two take care of these?" he asked. "Tes and I will head toward the inn and organize our accommodation." As Giddy and the others moved off toward the Rilmir stables, he guided Tesania toward the Ranger's Arrow Inn.

"Will they allow the others in?" Tesania asked worriedly. "They're not rangers."

"They will," Deavon replied as he reached out and opened the inn door. "I'll see to that."

The group ate heartily that night while sharing a few ales; some more than others. Their conversation floated from reminiscing about the past and their battle against Trannyth to what they might expect on their current mission before finally coming around to what they were all up to now.

Giddy began, explaining how she and Raim spent most of their days training other soldiers. "It's quite boring," she assured them while yawning.

"I'm sure," Deavon said laughing as he began to explain his role at the ranger's headquarters where he sifted through reports and prepared briefs for the king before saying, "Aldan?"

"Bow techniques instructor," he announced as he grinned at Giddy. "You want to know about boring!"

"It seems the king handed us eternal boredom rather than rewards," Raim said. "I for one miss the old days of travel and adventure."

"I can see that," Giddy teased as she pinched at the soldier's stomach. "Getting a bit podgy there."

"Me!?"

"You know it," Giddy grinned at him before turning her attention to Kailyn.

Kailyn took her turn, enthusing about her time at the Mage's Guild in Carella. How wonderful the teachers were. How she had passed and was now attached to Naisa at Wyvern City.

"At least someone's having fun," Giddy gibed as she winked at the young woman. Kailyn held a soft spot in all their hearts, having been only a fourteen year old girl when they last travelled together. She was almost a daughter to most of them and all of them would do anything for her.

"It is," Kailyn enthused.

"The eagerness of youth," Raim sighed.

"Well it is," Kailyn said defensively as she looked down at the table, placing her fork aside.

"He's teasing you," Aldan assured the girl. "You should know them by now."

"I suppose," Kailyn said as she looked up slyly at the two soldiers. "I guess when I'm old like them; I'll be podgy and lethargic too."

"Hey!" Giddy protested. "He's podgy. I'm not."

Raim leaned back and poked at his flat stomach shaking his head as he looked to Tesania. "How are things going with you?"

"Things were fine," she replied. "Before these attacks started happening."

Everyone at the table knew Tesania's dedication to treating her staff with dignity and how much it hurt her that they were being targeted. Silence followed for a few minutes before Giddy said, "We'll get him Tes. I promise."

Tesania looked at the soldier and smiled half heartedly. "We have to, Giddy. There's no other choice."

***

Once more, the following morning, the party pulled themselves into their saddles at dawn, the chill morning air biting at their exposed faces, turning them pink as they began the ride to the township of Lyiera.

Stopping that night at the same roadhouse by the ferry crossing they had stayed in on their journey to Wyvern City years before, they once again enjoyed one of Annie's roast joints before retiring to their soft beds.

Tesania wished she could spend more time with the old woman and enjoy her company but she knew better and that they needed to move on, and so she led her horse to the wooden ferry and coaxed it on board before hanging onto a rail and staring down river, lost in her own thoughts as she drew closer to the little village she once called home.

"Tes," Deavon said gently, jarring her out of her thoughts as he stood on the far bank with the others, waiting for her to disembark. "Sorry," she mumbled as she hastily led her horse off the old wood of the ferry, thanking Jarit as she alighted. Smiling wanly at Deavon in apology, she mounted her horse and started forward, the others falling in not far behind, no one saying much as they faced the prospect of yet another day in the saddle.

Tesania began craving the evening campsites as they rode toward Lyiera. She found the horses caused them all to be lost in their own thoughts with barely any conversation passing between them during the day, the monotonous thud of the horse's hooves lulling them into a daze. But in the late afternoon, the little group came alive with conversation as they set camp, gathering firewood, water, and herbs. Most days Aldan did his best to teach Kailyn the bow, with her usually giving up and hunting with her staff, the crackle of her spells filling the air. The few hours after their meal were the ones Tesania enjoyed the most as Giddy and Raim teased each other and anyone else they thought was fair game while the fire snapped and cracked, it's warmth offering a safe haven where her worries seemed to wash away until the cool morning mist brought them crashing back in again.

Crossing the hills where she, Deavon and Giddy had battled the beasts years before brought a chill to Tesania as she gripped her reins tight and guided her horse up the slopes, alighting regularly to lead it over rocky ground or around a particularly large obstacle. It was drawing on dark when they reached the small clearing where Tesania had first met Giddy and thought she was the most obnoxious woman she had ever met. "Funny," she whispered to herself as she glanced at the soldier who had dismounted and poked her toe at the grey ashes of the campfire, used by so many travelers, before pronouncing it dead. "How wrong I was."

"We'll need it; light it again," Deavon said as he slipped from his saddle and began to loosen the cinch strap as his horse lowered its head and nipped at the few tufts of grass available on the worn area.

"Can't we go on to Lyiera?" Tesania asked frowning as she looked at the hard ground. "I'd like to sleep in a warm bed tonight, if we can."

"It's getting dark."

"But it isn't far. A few hours on horseback."

Deavon smiled up at her before turning to the others, an unspoken question on his lips. As he scanned their faces he turned back to Tesania without saying a word to them. "I guess we go on," he said, pulling the cinch strap tight again to the grunting protest of his horse.

Reaching over, Tesania touched his leg after he had remounted and fallen in beside her. "Thank you," she said quietly. "Another night sleeping on the ground would be more than I could bear."

"I agree," he said, laughing. "No need to convince me."

A sudden thought came to Tesania as she swayed along to the movement of her horse. Turning her head toward Deavon, she asked, "Will the inns let us in this late."

"I suspect they will," he replied, grinning as he waved his hand toward the others. "What innkeeper would turn away this many customers."

"I suppose you're right," Tesania relied sheepishly before brightening. "Maybe we can stay at the Boar's Head?"

"Possibly," Deavon replied. "If they have enough rooms."

Tesania fell quite as they moved on, wondering if Bessy, the maid who had made her feel so welcome years earlier, still worked at the Boar's Head.

18 - Sad homecoming

Dust billowed from the rutted main street of Lyiera, whirling in eddies in the cool morning breeze. Tesania absentmindedly stroked the flank of her horse as she peered down the street, its skin twitching under her touch. It seemed like only yesterday that she had first walked into the small township with Deavon, a young, naive village girl intent on revenge. How little she had known about the realm then. How could she have, after her protected upbringing. But now she was returning as an adult, wiser in the ways of the world, comfortable in her own skin. And yet, she wasn't. With Aryd village within a day's ride, she felt she was still a child who had been away on an adventure and was now returning to help prepare the evening meal on the crackling hearth, while her mother hummed a lullaby. Smiling briefly at the memory, she dragged herself out of her thoughts and reached for the pommel of her saddle and pulled herself up.

"Ready?" Deavon asked smiling at her gently, obviously aware of the memories that this day would bring.

"I think so," Tesania said her voice barely a whisper as Giddy and Raim nudged their mounts forward and led the way, Kailyn falling in beside Tesania as Deavon took up a place on her other flank.

"We'll be with you," Kailyn said quietly as she reached over and touched Tesania's hand.

"I know," Tesania answered smiling briefly as she glanced at her friend. Still, the knowledge that her friends, people she now considered family; would be there did little to allay the thoughts running through her head as they plodded out of the township and started toward the woods separating Lyiera from Aryd.

Shaking her head in an attempt to drive the thoughts away, she returned to the previous evening. It had been wonderful to stay at the Boar's Head once more. The same chubby innkeeper had greeted them as they entered; a broad grin on his face. Tesania wasn't at all sure if it was in recognition of her and Deavon or if he was calculating the rates he could charge for the group filing in behind them. "You all wish to take rooms?' he had asked eagerly, eyes alight.

Tesania wandered into the main room of the inn as Deavon made the arrangements. It hadn't changed much over the years; the same crackling fire warmed the room from one corner while travelers sat at the various wood slab tables talking quietly among themselves. The smells drifting from the kitchen reminding her of the stew she had been served on their last visit, causing her stomach to growl in anticipation as she looked about taking in the familiar room, smiling as Bessy strode from the kitchen, plates balanced on her arm. She glanced at Tesania as she passed, smiling back and nodding in greeting before navigating her way through the tables. Warm and feeling at home, Tesania sighed and sat at a table, happily watching the flames lick at the wood in the hearth until the innkeeper motioned for her to follow up the worn old stairs on the far side of the inn.

The soft looking bed filling half of the room had enticed her, calling to her, daring her to lie down and forget the worries of the world. She had, however, resisted and quickly washed at a bowl and pitcher on a nightstand in the corner, before heading downstairs.

Bessy had waved and called them to a table she was wiping down, smiling at Tesania and insisting that she did indeed remember her. She stayed and talked for some minutes, chatting and laughing before taking their orders and heading for the bar. It brightened Tesania to see someone familiar, not that she had known Bessy for long, but she was a fond memory for Tesania from a time where fond memories were rare. Giddy had no such reservations, quickly falling into her teasing and raucousness, singing along with the bard strumming his lute as the ales flowed. Tesania had eventually suggested to Kailyn that they should retire for the night before thanking Bessy and heading upstairs leaving Giddy and the others to sing loudly into the night.

***

Deavon watched Tesania as they rode toward the woods outside of Lyiera village the following morning. Obviously guessing her thoughts from the look on her face, he said, "She's lovely."

"Hm?" Tesania asked frowning as she came out of her thoughts.

"Bessy?"

"Oh . . . Yes," Tesania agreed as she looked about surprised to see the trees of the woods nearby. "She is," she added softly smiling at him. "I was lost in thought."

"So I saw," he replied.

Tesania looked up at the trees as they entered. Their branches reached out, entwining with each other, the green of their new leaves blocking out the sun, drawing in the darkness and Tesania's mood with it.

These were the woods that had stood as a wall to her small village for most of her life. Not a wall that kept them locked in, but rather a wall that offered security, that acted as a buffer to the outside world. But now, she didn't remember it as friendly, now it was the barrier that she had had to break through, the barrier that once broken had disconnected her from her home forever. Staring down at the reins in her hand, she lost track of time once more as memories she had squashed for many years came flooding back in.

The others remained quiet as they travelled. Each lost in their own thoughts as they felt the blackness of Tesania's mood. Giddy eventually broke the silence, calling a halt a few hours later at a small brook and suggesting they rest for a while and eat something. Tesania dismounted without saying a word. Deavon watched her closely as she walked to a fallen branch and sat, still lost in her own thoughts. Frowning, he whispered to Aldan, "We shouldn't have come this way."

"It's alright," Tesania said, voice small. "I wanted to come," she assured Deavon as he berated himself for letting her hear.

"I just don't like seeing you like this."

Smiling wanly up at him, Tesania said, "It's something I've wanted to do. But . . ." she paused looking away into the trees before saying, ". . . but at the same time, I didn't want to."

"That's understandable," Giddy comforted her as she sat beside her placing an arm around her shoulders. "We understand."

"Thank you, Giddy," Tesania sighed, her eyes searching the soldiers. "I'm glad you're with me."

"I wouldn't be anywhere else," Giddy assured her as she stood, her hand lingering on Tesania's shoulder before she moved toward Raim who knelt at the brook refilling his water skin.

Tesania watched her go. She wanted to feel happy about coming back. After all, it was her childhood home. But, it was also a place of loss, a place of pain, a place where her childhood had been torn away from her forever. In an effort to break her mood, she stood and walked to her mount that lazily tore at the soft weeds lining the brook. Reaching under, she loosened its cinch strap, muttering, "Is that better," to the horse's appreciative eye. Smiling, she walked to Kailyn and sat beside her, shouldering her playfully. "Used to riding yet?" she inquired.

"No," Kailyn replied, groaning as she rubbed at her thighs. "I don't think I'll ever get used to it."

"It's better than walking."

"I guess," Kailyn conceded.

Accepting a small slice of cheese from Aldan, Tesania fell quiet again as she watched the water flowing past. She wasn't at all sure she could have come back without the people around her or that she could have faced the demons by herself. Reluctantly, as Deavon pulled her horses cinch strap tight and suggested they move on, she rose.

Try as she might, Tesania could not prevent the images of the past crashing back into her mind. Memories of beasts, swords raised, villagers screaming, her mother and father lying slain in the street tormented her as she gripped the reins tighter and tighter. It seemed the closer they got to the village of Aryd, the stronger they became. "Maybe I shouldn't go," she said to Deavon as he came to her side in a wide part of the path, her voice almost inaudible over the thud of the horses' hooves on the soft ground.

Deavon looked at her, his eyes concerned. Eventually he frowned. "You don't have to . . . . We can go around if you want? Straight to the ship?"

They rode on in silence, Tesania arguing with herself silently before the trees drew in and Deavon had to fall behind, his hand lingering on his arm as he said, "It's up to you, Tes. Either way, I'll be there with you."

She knew they would all be with her, that none of them would let her face the task by herself. But, this wasn't something they could protect her from. This was the past rampaging through her head, dragging up memories and feelings she had long ago suppressed. Finally, as they grew closer to Aryd, she dismissed the idea of going straight to the ship. This was something she needed to do, a past she needed to confront, a chapter she had to close. Steeling herself as the edge of the forest showed in the distance, the late afternoon sun casting dappled light into the trees, she urged her horse on a little faster breaking through the last branches a few minutes later.

The village stood at the far side of a grassed clearing, whitewashed buildings glittering in the sunshine. Frowning, Tesania looked quickly at Deavon. She had expected the village to be deserted, a ghost town. But dark smoke rose from the crude brick chimney at the back of the blacksmith's building, the smell of charcoal and heated metals reaching out, playing with Tesania's senses as the familiar scents and monotonous ring of the smithy's hammer brought pleasant memories flooding in. "Father," she cried, eyes wide as she grinned at Deavon who shook his head sadly. "It must be him! Who else could it be?" she said as she spurred her mount and raced to her father's workshop.

"Tes!" Deavon called frantically. "Tesania! Stop!" When she ignored his plea and spurred her horse on faster he groaned and spurred his own horse, slapping the reins against its neck in his desperation to stop her while the others looked at each other in confusion. "Tes!" Deavon called again as he drove his horse on. "It can't be him: Stop!"

Tesania heard Deavon's voice, even partially registering that he was frantic. But it didn't matter. Her father was in his smithy. *'Why would Deavon want her to stop?'* Determined, she drove on, the grass under her horse's hooves flying back as it raced over the soft ground. Something spoke to her as she rode, screamed at her that this was wrong, that it couldn't be her father. But she ignored it, her desire to see him overcoming her reason.

Deavon willed his mount on faster, he was catching her slowly, his stallion faster than her mare. But it seemed in slow motion and she was drawing closer to the dirt street of the village. Knowing that finding someone else hammering at father's anvil would devastate her if she wasn't prepared, he whipped the horse with the reins drawing every last ounce of its speed. "Tesania . . . Please . . . Tesania . . . . I need to talk to you."

Deavon's words floated to Tesania, they were almost indecipherable under the sounds of her horse's mad dash toward the village. She heard his words, they meant little to her, but the urgency, the pleading in his voice drew her attention. Allowing her horse to slow, she kept it trotting toward the smithy, the furrowed street now billowing dust under its hooves.

"Tes," Deavon called again as he saw her slow. Determined to stop her, he drove on, coming at her at pace before pulling the reins sharply, his horse snorting as it slipped on the loose ground. "Whoa," he called as it regained balance. Reaching out he snatched at Tesania's bridle. "Tes, stop."

Looking at him in confusion tinged with a little anger, Tesania asked sharply, "Why?"

Deavon looked at her sadly hesitating as if he didn't want to say it. Eventually he said sadly, "Think about it, Tes. It can't be your father."

Watching him in bemusement while the ring of the smithy's hammer filled the air, Tesania said, "But it must be. It's father's smithy."

Shaking his head, Deavon looked lost for the right thing to say. "Think about it, Tes," he said softly after some thought. Frowning he went on. "It's been nearly five years since you left." When Tesania looked at him blankly, he went on, "Look around . . . There are new people here . . . . They've resettled the village." As Tesania looked around surprised as she noticed the people standing watching her, some concerned some staring as if she was insane, Deavon slipped from his saddle and reached up to her lifting her easily down when she accepted his help. "There's a new smith," he told her, sadness tingeing his voice.

Tears welled in Tesania's eyes as the reality crashed in on her. Deavon drew her in, her tears now flowing freely onto his shoulder. She had been sure it was her father at the bellows of the smithy, the smells, the sounds; they had brought so many memories rushing in. It was more than she could bear to stand there now with these strangers to her village staring at her. How could she have let this happen? She knew her father was dead; she had buried him herself. Sighing deeply, she calmed herself, putting it down to the stress of returning to where her parents had been murdered. Settling, she kept her face buried in Deavon's shoulder, the strength of him comforting her as she came to terms with her mistake. "Maybe I shouldn't have come," she mumbled into his shirt as Giddy arrived and chastised the gawking crowd, suggesting as she fingered her sword, that they might have better things to do.

***

"I feel so foolish," Tesania muttered to no one in particular as she watched the flames of their campfire flicker in the early evening air. "What was I thinking?"

Kailyn shifted closer and draped her arm around her shoulder. She didn't utter a word as she drew Tesania in, but her presence reassured Tesania more than any words could have.

Giddy prodded at two fish in her pan, which they had managed to purchase off a local fisherman after Tesania had settled down. There was no inn in the small village, and so they had made camp on the edge of Aryd. The villagers had been wary at first after Tesania's maniacal arrival on their doorstep, followed by the thinly veiled threats of Giddy. But, it hadn't taken long for them to warm to the strangers when their coins began to be spread through the village as they bought foodstuffs and at Giddy's insistence, some locally brewed ale.

It felt surreal to Tesania as she sat on the edge of what used to be her village. Now it belonged to others, strangers, people she had never seen before. Even her own house had been claimed by a family, a little boy and his younger sister playing boisterously in the front garden. She didn't feel animosity toward them; in fact, it helped her to know that new life had been born into the once shattered village. Still, it had been a shock to see, especially the young smith at her father's forge. She had stood at the doors for almost an hour, watching, breathing in the smells, listening to the monotonous sound of the hammer. It had almost been therapeutic to her tired mind and she knew her father would be pleased with the neat state the new owner was keeping the smithy in.

Eventually, she drew a deep breath, thanked the smithy and walked toward her friends knowing she didn't belong here anymore, that home and new family were now elsewhere.

"It's understandable," Aldan eventually said. "The attack on your village was very traumatic for you."

Tesania looked up at the big ranger where he stood, arms crossed in front of the fire. "It was," she said quietly. "But I should have known better."

Shrugging, Aldan said, "I probably would have done the same thing."

"Me too," Raim muttered.

"And me," Giddy added.

"Alright," Tesania said, laughing. "I get it." It felt good to laugh; it was hard not to among her friends. But she knew that in the morning she would face the task she had not wanted to do in the encroaching darkness. A task she both looked forward to, and at the same time, dreaded. Taking a deep breath as she glanced at Deavon's smiling face, she put it aside and joined in as Raim began suggesting Giddy should learn how to cook.

19 - Moving on

The gently flowing water of the Lyiera River drifted silently past the grassy bank where Tesania had laid her parents to rest alongside her little friend Liale. Once her mother's favorite picnic place where they had often sat and played during Tesania's childhood, it was now a place of somber quietness.

Tesania stood with three flowers in her hand, head bowed as she stared at the grass. There was no sign of the graves now, nature having reclaimed the mounded earth. Yet she felt them; maybe because she wished to, maybe because she had an eternal bond with the grassy patch. She did not know which was true, she did not care. All she knew was that, for the first time in nearly five years, she was near her parents again. Deavon stood nearby, Kailyn at his side while the others stood at a respectful distance behind them. Each was aware of what this patch of grass meant to Tesania, none of them wished to interfere. Emotions played through her as she stood; the pain of their deaths followed by the joy of the years she had spent with them. A smile came to her for a brief moment as she remembered little Liale and her infectious laugh. Breathing deeply, she turned to Deavon, a tear running down her cheek as she asked, "May I have a few moments alone?"

Deavon didn't answer as tears welled in his own eyes. Nodding, he turned toward the others, Kailyn following close behind.

Tesania waited for a few moments before sinking to her knees, clasping the flowers in front of her. "Hello," she whispered as she released one flower and placed it down on the grass. "I miss you, Mother. I'm sorry I haven't been back sooner," she said, her voice apologetic. "You see, I've been a little busy." Pausing, she thought it was a poor thing to tell them. Closing her eyes she let her tears well out and run freely down her cheeks before dripping onto the ground. "I should have come sooner, I know," she went on, her voice snuffled as she held back her sobs. "But I'm sure you would be proud of me Father," she said. "I did it; I avenged you all . . . . The beasts are dead." Pausing she found herself waiting for an answer, for some praise. Bowing her head as she realized it would never come; she reached forward and laid the second flower on the grass. "I think you would both be proud of me," she said as she looked up to the river and wiped the back of her hand over her tears. "You see, I've made a new life for myself . . . found some wonderful friends . . . . And father, I know you would approve of Deavon." Drawing a deep breath, she settled herself before placing the last flower and saying, "Hello little Liale . . . I miss you so much." Looking out at the river, she watched a swan glide past before saying. "You would love my house, little one. There are gardens full of flowers and," she said, sniffing, "butterflies . . . butterflies everywhere, all kinds of colors . . . ." Falling silent, she stared down at the three flowers for what felt like hours before finally saying. "I have to go now . . . ." Tears ran anew down her face as she stood and looked at the flowers once more before whispering, "I love you," and turning away, walking toward her future.

***

Deavon led the way to the coast off the tip of Aryd. Tesania brought up the rear, her head hung low. No one spoke, each knowing that she needed time to collect her emotions. It pained Tesania to once more say goodbye to her parents, but it also released some of the pain she had been holding inside, some of the guilt at having left them behind. She knew there had been nothing for her to stay for at the time, nothing she could do to bring them back. Now she had some closure; now they knew they had been avenged and that their only daughter was making a new life for herself. Nodding in confirmation as the thoughts ran through her head, Tesania looked up and nudged her horse forward, working her way past the others until she was beside Deavon. "Thank you," she said.

Deavon simply smiled at her and looked ahead again, waiting for her to continue.

Eventually, she said, "Will the ship be there?"

"I hope so," Deavon replied. "We're on time, so it should be."

"And the horses? What will we do with them?"

Deavon stroked his hand along his horse's neck saying quietly, "Don't tell them, but we'll be leaving them behind."

Frowning, Tesania asked, "Will they be alright? I mean, they're used to being fed and groomed."

Deavon laughed. "Always looking out for others," he teased.

"Well," Tesania said defensively, "they are."

"You're right," he conceded. "But, Legana sent two men on the ship to take them back to Rilmir once we sail."

"Oh . . . I didn't know," Tesania said, a little abashed.

"It's my fault," Deavon said apologetically. "I didn't tell you." Shrugging, he added, "To tell you the truth. I didn't think it important."

"I guess it isn't," Tesania said as she stood in the stirrups and peered ahead. "I can see her masts!"

***

The King's Ship Swan stood off the south west point of Eldanal, her bulbous bow rising and falling with the waves as she strained at her anchor. First Lieutenant Nylor met Tesania and the others at the side rail, leaning down through the open gunwale and clasping her hand as she leapt from the little cutter that had brought them from the shore and then clambered up the side of the rolling ship. "Thank you," she said as she reached for the support of the rail. Nodding, the Lieutenant smiled briefly before turning back to his task and reaching for Kailyn's hand as the ship rolled toward the waves, the water lapping at her feet as the coxswain of the cutter fended the bobbing boat away.

Well experienced on ships by now, having traversed the coastline of Eldanal many times on her own ships as she visited her scattered farms, Tesania felt at home, swaying with the movement as the sea breeze played with her hair, tossing it about her face. Looking up at the masts she studied them with a practiced eye, tracing the yards to the futtock staves before running down the shrouds to the holly stoned deck. "She's beautiful," she said to no one in particular smiling at Kailyn as she looked at her, brow furrowed in confusion. But before she could explain, the lieutenant said, as he helped Deavon onto the deck and began to close the gunwale, "She's a beauty alright. Out of the Estom shipyards."

Nodding, Tesania continued to study the neat coils of ropes hanging over the belaying pins. "The crew keeps her well."

"The capt'n would have it no other way," the lieutenant assured her, laughing as he motioned toward the quarterdeck. "He asked that you attend him as soon as you boarded."

Nodding at the lieutenant in thanks, Tesania turned and walked toward the rear of the ship balancing herself against the roll and pitch, hand ready to grasp the rail if needed. Apart from the waves beating at the ship's sides, the day was one Tesania would consider perfect for sea travel. The sun shone from a brilliant blue sky, not too hot as it was still only early spring, but warm and full of promise. Gulls circled the masts, squawking and screeching as they chased each other from the prime positions. Tesania smiled, she had never been near a ship where the noisy birds had not been making their presence known as they waited for scraps of food to be thrown over the side. Gripping the rail on the steps rising to the quarterdeck, she grinned back at Deavon, for the first time in many days forgetting the past and looking forward to travelling to Aliaga.

"Giddy," Captain Eades said as they approached, nodding. "Raim," he added as he acknowledged the other soldier. "It's good to have you both aboard again."

"Captain," Giddy replied as she stepped in front of the others and turned to introduce them, starting with Tesania. "I hope it won't be a rough trip this time," she said after the captain had been introduced to the party.

"I shouldn't think so," the captain said as he looked up at the cloudless sky before turning his attention back to the soldier. "A clear sky; stiff breeze. Couldn't ask for more."

"I'm sure," Giddy replied as she too looked to the blue sky.

"How long do you think?" Deavon asked. "Until we reach Estel," he added quickly.

"A day," Captain Eades informed him as he stepped past and called an order along the deck to the lieutenant as the cutter was hauled over the gunwale and swung toward its cradle. "Prepare her for sea if you will, Mister Nylor." Turning back to them, he nodded apologetically to Deavon before saying, "We should be tying up at Estel early tomorrow morning."

"Will you be staying in Estel?" Tesania asked. "We should only be there a few days."

Nodding, the captain confirmed he would be remaining in Estel harbor. His instructions were to anchor and wait for their return before ferrying them back to Wyvern city.

20 - Aliaga

The dark silhouette of Aliaga filled the horizon, rising and falling as the King's Ship Swan pitched into a light swell. Tesania stood in the semi darkness by the starboard cathead at the front of the ship. She had not slept much during the night, tossing and turning in her small bunk as the real reason for her journey reasserted itself after the emotional last few days of reliving her past. Mist had invaded her dreams the few times she did manage to fall asleep, drifting in front of her, taunting her, its sunken eyes staring down at her, mocking her. Try as she might, she had not been able to block it out and after waking for the fourth time she had given up and climbed up to the deck.

It was quiet, the silence broken only by the hiss of the ocean slipping down the ship's sides, punctuated by the odd explosion of cascading water as the bow plunged into an oncoming wave. A few sailors moved about on the deck, the night watch, she assumed. Apart from nodding to her they left her alone with her thoughts. Now, as the dawn began painting the eastern horizon in shades of yellows and reds, she watched the land of her forefather's approach; a land she had never visited since she had discovered her heritage years before.

She wondered, as the sun's early light began to pick out the details of the approaching land, if she would feel any affinity for the land that her ancestors long ago called home. She doubted it. After all, it had been centuries since her great-great-great-grandfather had fled Aliaga with the sword she now called her own. *'Still,'* she mused as the land grew nearer; by now fully illuminated by the dawn light, the mouth of a harbor which she presumed to be Estel clearly visible. *'Maybe I'll feel something when I'm actually there.'* Breathing the sweet ocean air deeply, she looked around the horizon. It seemed so peaceful out on the open sea that an idea invaded her mind; telling her that she should board one of her own ships and sail away from all her worry, leave it all behind. It tantalized her for an instant before an image of the mist destroying her home flashed in to replace it. Shaking her head she cleared her thoughts and began walking slowly toward the hatch leading down to the cabins to rouse the others.

***

The Aliagan Palace seemed much less opulent than Eldenal's to Tesania as she studied the paintings lining the otherwise bland, white walls while walking slowly down the central hallway. There were none of the frescos that adorned the hallway ceiling in the palace in Wyvern city, none of the splendor that she would associate with a king. Turning full circle as she walked so she could take it all in, she eventually frowned and looked toward Kailyn who similarly looked around before catching Tesania's eye and asking, "Are they poor?"

Laughing lightly, Tesania replied, "No Kailyn. They aren't poor."

Confusion furrowed Kailyn's brow as she looked about once more. Eventually she said, "It's very plain."

Nodding in agreement, Tesania placed her arm around her young friend. "Maybe they have better things to spend their money on," she suggested.

"I suppose," Kailyn replied, doubt filling her voice.

Tesania laughed aloud now, "Not everyone likes to show off their wealth you know."

"I know," Kailyn replied defensively. "But, it's just so dull."

"It is," Tesania agreed before releasing the girl and reaching out to shake the hand of a woman who stood before them, her eyes taking each of the party members in.

"May I help you?" the woman asked a tinge of disapproval in her voice.

Deciding to ignore her tone, Tesania replied, "We're here to see the king."

The woman's eyebrow raised as the corner of her mouth lifted in a smirk, "I doubt it," she said while looking Tesania up and down with disdain.

Looking at herself, Tesania realized that she was in the same clothes she had worn on the trip through Eldanal. Drab brown britches and a creased, sweat stained shirt; it was hardly an outfit she would choose to wear when meeting a king. "I hope you will forgive our appearance," she said evenly as she looked back up to the woman. "We have travelled far to see your king. I'm sure you understand that we couldn't carry any finery with us?" she went on to ask, head tilted, her own eyebrow raised in question.

Scoffing at her, the woman turned her attention to the others, looking them up and down with as much scorn as she had Tesania. "And why would the King of all Aliaga wish an audience with the likes of you?" she sneered.

"With the likes of—" Giddy spluttered.

"Giddy," Tesania interrupted the soldier as she held up a calming hand.

"She can't talk to us like that," Giddy insisted stepping forward.

"It's alright, Giddy," Tesania assured her before turning her attention back to the woman. "I can see that our appearance might belie who we really are."

The woman sneered at her once more as she said, "Or it could say exactly who you are."

Sighing heavily, Tesania calmed herself before saying in an even tone, "May I ask who you are?"

"You may."

"And?"

The woman now looked around, a nervousness beginning to creep into her demeanor. "I am Miriam."

"And . . . Miriam," Tesania said as she looked around the hallway. "What is your role here?"

"I . . . err . . . I greet people and direct them to where they need to be."

"Well . . . Miriam," Tesania said quietly, her voice almost inaudible as she whispered conspiratorially, "Perhaps you could do that . . . direct us I mean?" she suggested more than asked. "Despite how we appear to you, or whether you believe us or not," she went on, voice growing louder. "We have an appointment to see your king. Will you deny us that . . . ? Will you tell your king that you turned us away . . . despite his invitation?"

"I . . . I . . ." Miriam stuttered, her nerve deserting her. "I suppose you need to speak with the king's page over there," she said, pointing to a man sitting at a desk at the end of the hall.

"Thank you, Miriam," Tesania said her voice full of sweetness. "You have been most helpful."

"I . . . I—"

"Good day to you, Miriam."

"Good . . . good day to you also," Miriam muttered quietly, eyes downcast.

"You didn't need to be so harsh with her," Deavon suggested as he came to Tesania's side.

"The woman is a fool," Tesania snapped, regretting it instantly as she saw the frown fall over his face. "Maybe you're right," she conceded as she approached the table the woman had pointed to. "Maybe I was too harsh."

Looking up from his stack of parchments, the man scowled. He had a haggard look about him, like someone who had been harassed and had had enough. "Can I help you," he snapped, eyes looking the party up and down as Miriam had.

"We have an appointment with the king," Tesania sighed as she saw the look of disdain creasing his face. Resisting her desire to reprimand him, she bowed slightly, smiled and said, "The lady Tesania and her entourage to see King Asden. I believe he is expecting us."

The page's eyes drifted over Tesania once more. Screwing his nose in distaste he looked doubtfully down at his parchment before shuffling through some others on the side of his desk. "Ah, yes," he said, his demeanor toward them changing immediately when he found her name. "He is indeed expecting you. But I'm afraid you can't see him today," he said shaking his head emphatically. "Definitely not today," he added as he consulted another list. "Perhaps not even tomorrow."

"But, we have an appointment."

The page looked up at her and shook his head as he raised the parchment with her name on it. "This just tells me you're expected," he said matter-of-factly. "But, as we didn't know when you would arrive, how could we have set an appointment time for you?"

"He's right, Tes," Deavon said from her side. "We didn't even know when we'd get here."

Tesania considered him and his words for a moment before turning back to the page. "We have urgent need to speak to your king," she said.

"So does everyone else," he replied in a bored tone as he swept his arm around the room of waiting people.

"But this is a matter of life and death," Tesania assured him, voice rising as she leant forward her finger stabbing into the wood of his desk to emphasis each of her next words. "We need to see him urgently."

Frowning at her until she drew back from him, the page picked up his parchment once more and studied it. "Tomorrow; an hour after midday. That's the best I can do for you."

"But," Tesania protested. "we need to see him sooner."

The page sighed and raised his arm to take in the room but was interrupted by Tesania before he could speak. Well aware of the bureaucracy of palace life, she said, "Yes, I know, so does everyone else." Discouraged, she turned to the others and shrugged apologetically. "It seems we're here until tomorrow. What do we do now?"

"I know," Giddy offered eyes alight with mischief as she nudged Raim. "There's a tavern," she said racking her memory, "The King's . . . err—"

"King's Head," Raim informed her.

"That's it. Delicious food."

"And ale I'll wager," Deavon said teasingly.

"Well," Giddy replied feigning embarrassment, "there is that. But, there's an inn across the road too," she added as Deavon looked at her dubiously. "Besides," she said more seriously, "I'd like to talk to Rhys while we're there as well."

Deavon looked to Aldan who nodded and then to Tesania. "It's as good as any, I guess," she said, to Giddy's delight.

"I would suggest," the page called after them as they walked away, his quill waving as he pointed to their weapons, "That you don't bring those with you tomorrow."

21 - Rhys

The thud of empty mugs on wooden tables seemed to never end in the King's Head Tavern, usually followed by gruff calls for a waitress to bring more.

Giddy sat silently at a table near the large fireplace at the back of the room, the flickering light of the fire playing across her face as she stared at the door of the Tavern. Raim sat at her side, his interest in the door long ago forgotten as he poked at the fire with an iron poker he had plucked from a ring of iron attached to the stone wall. Tesania and the others had already finished their meals and retired across the road to the Vine Inn where, earlier in the day, they had made arrangements for accommodation. "Another?" Raim asked as he snatched up his mug and swallowed down the last dregs.

Giddy registered his words but didn't answer for some time. Eventually she looked away from the door and grinned at her friend. "Guess."

Smirking, Raim raised his hand and caught the attention of a passing waitress, two fingers raised as he silently ordered another round of ale. "It's getting late," he said seriously as he looked toward the door that had held Giddy's attention for the last few hours.

Shrugging, Giddy replied, "Maybe he isn't coming."

"Maybe," Raim agreed as he went back to poking at the fire. "It was a long shot anyway."

"It was. But," Giddy said as she studied her empty mug and then winked at the little soldier, "there's ale."

"Indeed," Raim exclaimed as he sat up straight in anticipation of the waitress' return. Looking around the room his eyes came to rest on a waitress on the far side of the room. "Isn't that, Lydie?"

Giddy peered across the room. "I think that was her name" she replied as she watched the waitress that had served them the first time they had come to the tavern to meet Rhys. "So?"

"So?" Raim scoffed, looking at Giddy as if she were a simpleton. When she returned his stare blankly, he sighed. "She seemed to know him quite well," he prompted, eyebrow raised to emphasis his point.

"Clever boy," Giddy said in a voice she might use to praise a dog that had fetched a stick.

"Boy?"

Laughing at Raim's aggrieved expression; Giddy rose and threaded her way through the crowd toward Lydie who scrubbed at a table that had been left vacant. "Hello there, Lydie," she said as if they were well acquainted.

Smiling briefly up at the soldier, Lydie went back to scrubbing with her rag. "I'll be done in a minute," she assured her. "There's other tables free over there though," she added while pausing and pointing along the room without looking at Giddy.

"We have a table."

"Oh. Well one of the other waitresses will be able to help you."

Stepping around the woman, Giddy sank down in a chair and placed a hand on hers, stopping her scrubbing. "I was here with my friend a few weeks ago," she said to the frowning girl who looked over her shoulder to the barkeep.

"Please," she said her voice small. "I'll be in trouble if he sees me standing about."

"I won't keep you long," Giddy assured her. "Pretend like you're taking my order."

Nervously looking back at the barkeep, the woman looked for the first time at Giddy's face before saying, "I don't remember you, sorry."

"We were with Rhys," Giddy pressed as she let the waitress' hand go. "Over there." She pointed.

Glancing to where Giddy indicated, Lydie shook her head. "I'm sorry."

"It's alright," Giddy assured her. "I suppose you serve a lot of people." As the woman nodded and glanced at the barman once more, she went on, "I need to talk to Rhys urgently." When Lydie offered nothing Giddy asked, "Can you tell me where I can find him?"

"He wouldn't like it if I told you."

"But you know?"

Lydie remained quiet, but her expression told Giddy everything she needed to know. Reaching forward, she grasped her slender arm and squeezed, not hard enough to hurt, but enough to get the woman's full attention. "I need to know," she said her voice commanding. "Tell me where I can find him."

Looking from her arm to the barman and then back again, Lydie swallowed hard and then said quickly, "He only comes here when he has a meeting with someone. Usually he's at the Cunning Cockrell, two streets over." She jutted her chin toward the front entrance to emphasis the direction before glancing once more at the barman who was now looking toward her. "That's all I can tell you." Pulling her arm free, she said, "He'll be furious. Please don't tell him I told you," she pleaded before rushing away.

"The Cunning Cockrell," Giddy said triumphantly to Raim as she returned to their table and picked up the fresh ale the other waitress had deposited while she was away.

"What's that?"

Shrugging as she drank deeply from her mug, Giddy eventually said after wiping her mouth, "Sounds like another tavern."

"Funny name."

"They usually are," Giddy said laughing before draining her ale and thumping it down onto the table. "She said it's two streets over," she informed him while rising and started for the door.

"It's getting close to midnight," Raim said as they came out into the street. "Do you think he'll be there?"

"Only one way to find out," Giddy replied as she started toward a lane on the far side of the street.

Raim hurried after her. He knew better than to argue with her when she was on a mission.

Giddy walked quickly down the lane. She hardly noticed the little soldier at her side as she thought what she might say to Rhys when they found him. She knew it wasn't critical that the thief accompany them to Dalgliesh's home. But she liked him, and besides, something nagged at her, told her that he may yet come in handy before their mission in Aliaga was over.

"Will he even come?" Raim asked as if reading her thoughts.

"How many coins do you have on you?"

"Not that many," Raim replied, laughing aloud.

Giddy laughed along before saying seriously, "I suppose we can promise him payment after we sail back to Wyvern."

"With whose money?" Raim asked suspiciously.

"Yours." Giddy said winking.

"I think we both know that isn't going to happen."

"General Legana's, maybe?" Giddy added seriously.

Raim's grin was only just visible to Giddy in the darkness as he replied, "Now that's a plan I can work with."

"I'm sure he won't mind if we spread a few of his coins about," Giddy said as if reassuring Raim.

"Oh, I'm sure he won't," Raim agreed, mirth in his voice.

Rounding the corner at the second junction in the lane, Giddy pointed ahead to a building not too far along the street. Light emanated from the windows with men and women milling about on the verge of the street, the strum of a bard's lute drifting from the open doorway. "Looks like our place," she said before crossing the street and heading toward the Cunning Cockrell's front entrance.

Even with her eyes adjusted to the darkness outside, Giddy still had to squint to see in the murky light of the tavern. Far from the clean, almost wholesome, tavern they had just come from, this place radiated gloom. Patrons sat in groups around tables, their voices mingling in a constant drone that made picking out any particular conversation almost impossible. An old fireplace sat in the far corner, its flickering light fighting a losing battle against the shadows, while smoke escaped its rusty flue and drifted in plumes along the soot stained ceilings. It wasn't a place for the gentry, or even the simple folk of Estel. This was a tavern for the lower echelon, for thieves and murderers. A tavern where they could meet and talk among men of the same ilk. It wasn't a place that Giddy would normally frequent, nor was it a place she would shy away from. She had learned over the years that the types that frequented a tavern like this kept to themselves once amongst their own and she had nothing to fear.

Raim peered through the murk. "I can't see anything in here."

Without answering, Giddy walked toward the bar. There was nowhere for her to approach as men and women lent against any exposed edge it offered. Twisting her shoulders sideways, she forced her way through as she muttered, "Excuse me," to the protests of a toothless old woman who tottered on the brink of falling, the bar the only thing holding her up. At first the barkeep ignored her as she waved her hand but eventually he sauntered toward her and jutted his chin out in question to what she wanted. "I'm looking for a man named Rhys," she said simply, voice raised to overcome the din of the crowd.

"Ain't seen him."

"But he comes here."

"What'll yer be drinken?"

"I just need to find Rhys," Giddy answered. "Does he come here?" she asked again.

Shrugging, the barman turned and walked away from her without answering. With effort, Giddy managed to control herself and squeezed away from the toothless old woman. Returning to Raim, she shook her head at his inquisitive look. "Looks like we'll have to search for ourselves."

The tables in the tavern were plentiful with patrons taking up ever available chair. Giddy and Raim found it difficult to negotiate through as the seated people rarely went out of their way to allow them passage, grunting and cursing as the soldiers physically shoved against them. Giddy did not apologize as she pushed past, except when she jostled past a large man and knocked his arm as he raised his mug to drink. Stepping back, she watched as he rose before her, angry eyes boring into her as he swept the ale off his shirt with his hands. "What yer do that fer?" he demanded indignantly.

"Sorry," Giddy said quickly swallowing hard as she motioned past him. "I was trying to get through."

Frowning, the big man turned and examined the gloomy darkness as Giddy dug into a pocket to retrieve a coin. "What fer?" he asked turning back to Giddy.

Looking back at Raim who simply shrugged, Giddy returned her attention to the man. She wasn't sure if announcing their desire to meet with Rhys to this man was wise, but decided it would be easier than pushing their way through the entire room. Rotating the coin deftly between her fingers, she held it up in front of the man's eyes before slapping it down on the table, the metal clicking sharply on the worn old wood. "For your ale," she advised him before adding, "We're looking for a man named Rhys."

"Rhys?" the man said as his fingers closed over the coin.

"Yes," Giddy said nodding as she held her hand up to about the height she reckoned the little thief to be before quickly realizing it wouldn't help and lowering it again. "I was told he might be here tonight."

The big man regarded them suspiciously while wiping the last of the ale from his shirt. Eventually he pointed a meaty hand toward the far left corner of the room and grunted, "'E's over ther." As Giddy nodded in thanks and squeezed past the next table, the man called after her, "Yer better watch where yer goin' in future."

Turning her head, Giddy smiled at him. She was relieved to be away from him; for a moment or two she had thought they were in for a fight. Considering his size, she was glad he was more amicable than he appeared. "That was close," she said back to Raim when they had moved away.

"You could have taken him," Raim replied laughing as he glanced back at the bulk of the man.

Winking, Giddy said, "You know it."

Silently cursing himself for letting her get one up on him, Raim simply smiled at her and let it be.

Careful not to repeat her mistake, Giddy led them to where the man had suggested.

Rhys sat against the far wall, his eyes following the two soldiers as they approached. "Giddy," he said suspiciously, nodding. "Raim."

"Rhys," Giddy greeted as she looked about for a seat. Finding none unoccupied, she decided to stand where she was. "I need to talk to you."

Rhys looked about. The men seated at his table were obviously acquaintances of his, but he still stood, saying as he started for the front door, "Not here."

Giddy sighed at Raim as she watched the thief weave his way through the same tables they had just negotiated. "Here we go again."

"Be more careful this time," Raim suggested, laughing at the crude gesture his friend returned.

Rhys seemed to move effortlessly through the crowd while the two soldiers took considerably longer to reach the dusty street. "This way," Rhys said as he walked toward the lane Giddy and Raim had followed earlier. As they drew out of earshot of the Cunning Cockrell's patrons, he asked as he continued to walk, "How did you find me?"

"Does it matter?"

"It does in my line of business," Rhys pointed out laughing as if it was a given that Giddy should know.

Giddy shrugged. She had no desire to rat out the young waitress. Instead, she said, "I have my sources."

"In Estel?" Rhys asked, dubiously shaking his head.

"We found you, didn't we?"

Scoffing as he looked from Giddy to Raim, Rhys conceded, "I guess you did." He remained quiet for a few paces before saying seriously, "I need to know. Who told you? Was it Lydie?"

"Lydie?" Giddy asked as if she didn't know who he was talking about, feigning ignorance.

"You know exactly who Lydie is," Rhys accused as he studied the soldier through squinted eyes. "That was a mistake, you know."

"What was?"

"Denying you knew her. It told me everything I needed to know."

"She meant no harm," Giddy defended deciding to give up her charade.

"I'll talk to her later."

"You won't hurt her," Giddy asked worried that she may have put the girl in danger.

"Hurt her," Rhys said chuckling. "I'm a thief, not a thug."

"Giddy made her tell us where you were," Raim interjected. "I wouldn't be too hard on her."

Rhys considered Raim before saying, "In my line of work, it's important that I can trust people."

Raim laughed aloud. "That's a double standard," he said eventually, "coming from a thief."

Laughing along, Rhys replied, "I suppose it is."

"We came to you for a reason," Giddy interrupted in an attempt to take the conversation away from Lydie. "We may need your help."

"Dalgliesh again?" Rhys asked his curiosity piqued.

Nodding in confirmation, Giddy said to him, "We're here with some others." As the thief looked about, she added, "They're at the Vine Inn."

"Ah," the little man replied before saying, "You're going after him then?"

"Dalgliesh?" Giddy said quietly before going on. "Yes, we're going after him and his daughter, Caitriona."

"It won't be easy," Rhys muttered, his voice far off as he seemingly calculated the risks in his head. "I told you that before . . . when we were outside his estate."

"I know what you said," Giddy assured him. "But, we have no choice."

Rhys turned toward her and watched her face before saying, "You're sure it's him?"

Weighing her reply, Giddy flicked her eyes to Raim before saying, "As sure as we can be."

"If it isn't" Rhys stated, whistling as he raised his brows suggesting the trouble it might cause.

"That's a risk we're willing to take."

"We're? Who're these others you spoke of?"

"A couple of rangers," Giddy replied. "A mage . . . us" she added while motioning to herself and Raim. "And Tesania."

"Tesania?"

"Lady Tesania," Giddy corrected herself.

"A lady?" Rhys questioned mirth in his voice. "What good will a lady be? Shouldn't she be playing dress ups?"

"Not this one," Raim assured him.

"She can hold her own," Giddy added as the little thief nodded his understanding.

"So you have six?"

"Yes."

"What do you need me for?"

Giddy shrugged; she had no real answer to his question. "To be honest, I don't know," she eventually said.

"That's as good a reason as any, I suppose." Rhys said laughing aloud.

Seriously, Giddy said, "I don't know why. Maybe it's your profession. Maybe it's your knowledge of Aliaga. I just have a gut feeling you should come with us."

"A feeling?"

"Sounds stupid, I know," Giddy admitted, her tone subdued as she looked down at the ground.

Rhys walked on silently, Giddy and Raim beside him quietly waiting for his answer. As they came to the street where the Vine Inn sat, he stopped and looked at the two soldiers. "Sometimes . . ." he said, ". . . our gut knows more than we do."

"So you'll come?"

"Depends."

Giddy chuckled before asking, "On?"

"I think you know."

Replying honestly, Giddy said, "We have nothing to give you. But," she went on quickly as he scowled, "Legana will pay you for any time you give us."

"Legana," Rhys echoed as he considered her offer. "My usual fee?" he asked eagerness creeping into his voice.

"I think Legana will agree to that."

"You think?"

"I know," Giddy corrected not wanting to lose the thief's eagerness to accompany them. "I guarantee it."

"Well . . . if you guarantee it," Rhys said laughing before adding. "Seriously though: I've dealt with Legana many times. And seeing as you two were here on his behalf last time . . . ." He fell quiet as he considered the situation before grinning and thrusting his hand out to Giddy, saying, "It's a deal. I'll meet you here in the morning."

22 - Aliaga's King

The allotted time of Tesania's meeting with the King of Aliaga came and went as the group waited in the grand hallway of the palace. They had arrived well before time expecting to be seen an hour after midday. But, they had not been called and were instead being ignored. "Ask him again," Giddy insisted as she paced the floor.

"It won't do any good," Aldan assured her. The big ranger sat with his back against the cool stone seat eyes closed as he patiently waited their turn.

"He might know when we'll be let in."

Opening one eye, Aldan regarded the soldier before patting the seat next to him. "Relax."

"I don't want to relax," Giddy grumbled. "He should have seen us by now."

Deavon took up the cause as Aldan remained quiet. "It's the same at home," he said. "People wait all day to see our king."

"I'm sure they'll call us soon," Tesania added from where she sat with Kailyn's head resting on her shoulder, the young mage's soft breathing suggesting she had fallen asleep.

"Soon," Giddy scoffed. "Why make an appointment if they're going to make us wait anyway?"

"Go and ask them," Raim suggested a mischievous grin spreading over his face as he pointed to the page they had spoken to the previous day.

Giddy stopped her pacing and looked to where her friend pointed. "I will," she said with conviction as she strode away. "Coming?"

Shrugging, Raim winked at Deavon and fell in behind her.

"When will we be going in," Giddy asked the page bluntly.

Nudging her as he stepped up beside her, Raim said to the frowning face of the page, "My apologies for my friend's rudeness."

"Rude—"

"What she means to say is; could you possibly advise us of when we may expect to see the king?"

Scowling at Giddy before turning his attention to Raim, the page replied, "Some of the previous meetings have run longer than expected."

"Ah," Raim replied as he motioned Giddy to silence. "That would explain it." As the page looked back down at his parchments, Raim cleared his throat and swept his arm around the room. "Perhaps you could tell us how many of these other people are before us."

Rolling his eyes and sighing as if the two soldiers before him were the bane of his existence, the page consulted his parchment before looking up and saying, "Lady Tesania is next."

"How long?" Giddy asked.

"How should I know," the page shot at her, anger rising.

"Thank you," Raim said in an appeasing tone as he dragged Giddy away. "Tact isn't your strong suit," he accused her, laughing as she scowled.

"I just don't like waiting when we should have already been seen," Giddy said seriously. "We've already lost a day waiting to see this king."

Nodding at his friend and understanding her frustration, Raim said nothing more on the matter, instead informing the others as they returned to them, "We're next."

"How long?" Tesania asked not really expecting a definitive answer.

Shrugging, Raim replied as he patted Giddy's shoulder, "Giddy didn't manage to find that out."

"Funny aren't you," Giddy asked him acidly.

"I try," Raim said, grinning at her.

Deavon shook his head as he looked toward Tesania. "They'll never change," he said sighing.

"Would you want us to?" Giddy asked sweetly as the page's voice drifted across the room. "Lady Tesania! The king will see you and your party now."

"That's us," Tesania said with some relief. Whilst she was well aware the king would find it difficult to keep to a schedule, she also chaffed at the knowledge that they were losing time. Unlike Giddy though, she had waited patiently for their turn. Gently nudging Kailyn who looked about sleepily, she stood and reached for her hand. "Come on," she said as she dragged the girl up, "We're going to see the king."

"Finally," Kailyn muttered rubbing her eyes and then blinking at the others. "How long was I asleep?"

"Not long," Tesania assured her. Gripping her hand, she led the way to where the page stood impatiently tapping his foot.

"There are others waiting to see the king too," he said tersely.

"Sorry," Tesania said while looking down at herself and brushing self consciously at her clothes. She wasn't happy to be presented to a king looking as she did. The thought of buying a dress earlier in the day had crossed her mind, but she had dismissed it as a waste of money and time. Besides, they would not be able to take it on their travels anyway. Instead, she had picked her best britches and shirt and asked the innkeeper where she could launder them. '*At least they're clean;*' she thought as she breathed deeply and asked the page to lead them in.

The room he ushered them into was a little more opulent than the hallway, but barely. Bare of tapestries and ornaments, it left Tesania feeling a little flat. The table running nearly the entire length of the room, however, was beautiful. Carved legs curved up to cradle the corners of the giant table where cherubs looked out at the room, their faces radiating innocence and mirth. Tesania traced the table with her eyes. Each cherub had its own personality, some chubby, some thin, but each smiled back at her, the polished grain of the wood adding to their beauty.

"It's wonderful," Kailyn whispered beside her.

"It is," Tesania agreed as she scanned the length of the table stopping when she came to three men and a woman sitting at the far end. None of them seemed to notice the intruders, each staring at a parchment in their hands. She knew immediately which of them was King Asden simply by their positions at the table. But there was something else, an air about him as his eyes scanned the parchment he held. He wasn't as old as Tesania had been expecting. She guessed he might be in his early forties with the first tinges of grey touching his black hair. Admonishing herself for having preconceived ideas about a man she had never met, she straightened her back and smoothed her shirt one more time as the page announced, "Your Majesty. I present to you the Lady Tesania of Eldanal and her party."

For a moment the king did not lift his eyes from his parchment but eventually he set it aside and looked up directly at Tesania, his forest green eyes boring into her before flicking to the others as the page backed from the room. "Please," he said his deep voice resonating in the room as he indicated to the far end of the table, "Take a seat."

The sound of dragging chairs echoed through the exposed beams of the ceiling as the six travelers arranged themselves before the King of Aliaga. Tesania sat at the end, Deavon on her left while the others lined either side. "Thank you," she muttered voice shaking, the king's stare scrutinizing her clothes jangling her nerves. Clearing her throat, she said, "I believe King Eldine sent you a dispatch."

King Asden continued to regard her as one of the men at his side shuffled through his pile of parchments, eventually handing one to the king who's eyes finally left Tesania and looked down to read. "This tells me little," he said as he looked back up, resuming his baleful stare.

Shuffling in her seat, Tesania replied, "King Eldine thought it might not be wise to put what I have to say to you in writing."

"That seems a little extreme."

"What I have to say is very sensitive," Tesania assured him, her voice quivering with her nerves. She had no idea why this man was affecting her so; after all, she had spoken to her own king many times in the past few years. Yet there was something about him, his eyes, his demeanor. She couldn't put her finger on it, but something about him made her nervous, screamed at her to beware. Subconsciously, she decided to proceed with caution.

Letting the parchment slip from his fingers onto the table, King Asden asked, "What could be so sensitive that it can't be sent by correspondence?"

"King Eldine wished to ensure secrecy," Tesania advised fidgeting with her sleeve as the king's eyes continued to bore into her.

"Secrecy," the king scoffed as he flicked a hand at the men seated next to him. "Do you suggest my people can't be trusted?"

"Not just your people," Tesania muttered.

Grinning like he had won a point on her, the king sardonically said, "Just because Eldine can't control his people doesn't mean I can't control mine."

"King Eldine," Tesania said her voice growing.

"You dare to correct me in my own court!?" King Asden exploded.

Deciding that showing any more weakness in front of this man would only serve to make their mission more difficult, Tesania sat forward jutting out her chin as she said, "I mean you no disrespect. But, my king deserves the same courtesy as you."

"Respect you say." Sneering as he looked at her attire once more, he laughed aloud. "Does your king show me respect by sending commoners to insult me in my own court?"

"We are hardly—" Giddy began, stopping as Tesania reached out and touched her arm shaking her head.

Drawing a deep breath, Tesania returned the king's stare and said flatly, "You judge us by our attire . . . by the way we look . . . ."

"Do you blame me?"

Sighing, Tesania announced, "I am Lady Tesania of the court of King Eldine." Motioning to her side she added, "This is Deavon, a general in the Eldanal Rangers as is

Alden here." With the king leaning back in his chair, a smirk playing on his lips, she went on. "Giddy and Raim are generals in the Eldanal Army whilst Kailyn is attached to the arch mage of Eldanal."

The king regarded each of them as they were introduced, his eyes lingering on Kailyn for a moment before drifting back to Tesania. Scratching his chin, he once more considered each of the travelers, his attention finally coming to rest on Deavon as he said, "You say little."

"It isn't my place."

"She speaks for you?"

"She speaks for herself," Deavon replied evenly. "And for King Eldine."

"Very well," King Asden responded while turning his attention back to Tesania and warning. "Say what you need to say. But, be quick. I don't have all day."

Glancing at Deavon, Tesania silently questioned the sanity of the conversation they were enduring. When he shrugged, she turned back to King Asden. "Your Majesty." For the first time since they had entered, a smile slipped over the king's face at her words. As he nodded for her to go on, she said, "For the past two months the Kingdom of Eldanal has been suffering attacks."

"Attacks," the king exclaimed sitting forward now. "By whom?" Turning to one of his aids, he snapped, "You knew about this?" As the man stared at him dumbfounded by the accusation, King Asden demanded, "Why wasn't I informed Eldanal was being invaded?"

"I . . . I . . ." the man stuttered as he looked at Tesania, confusion in his eyes, ". . . I am not aware of any—"

"It's not an invasion," Deavon interrupted. "The attacks are localized."

Considering him suspiciously, the king asked, "And you think I have something to do with these attacks." Adding, "I suggest you choose your words carefully, General."

"The attacks are far flung. Farms . . ." Tesania took up the telling again, ". . .ships, houses . . . my estate. . . ."

Confusion crossed the king's face as the woman at his side leant toward him and whispered something in his ear. Nodding, he asked while spreading his hands, "What does any of this have to do with me?" Looking around the table, he added as he pointed to Raim and Giddy, "You have your own army. Surely they can deal with a few mercenaries?"

"You don't understand," Tesania replied regretting her words instantly as the king's eyes slit, his demeanor returning to the animosity he had shown earlier. "Forgive me," she said quickly as she stood and began pacing behind Deavon. "I meant no offence of course." Gathering her thoughts as she swung and walked the other way she looked to the king and said, "A little over four years ago a lord in King Eldine's court was disgraced and banished from Eldanal, all his assets there confiscated." As the king remained silent his eyes following her, she went on. "It is believed that this lord is now in Aliaga."

"He's here alright," Giddy interjected. "Raim and I—"

Frowning at the soldier and motioning her to silence, Tesania continued, her voice low, "In fact, we believe that very lord is now a part of your own court."

"Lord Dalgliesh?" the king inquired.

"The very same."

Considering her for some time the king eventually demanded, "You have proof of this? You are sure it is Lord Dalgliesh?"

"We have intelligence that leads us to believe he is involved."

"Believing and knowing are two very different things."

"Agreed," Deavon interjected. "King Eldine said much the same thing."

"A wise man."

"Indeed," Deavon replied. "But, we have enough reasons to believe Dalgliesh is behind these attacks."

"You captured some of the mercenaries? Informants have come forward?"

"Not exactly," Deavon replied shaking his head.

"Then how do you know Lord Dalgliesh is behind it?" the king challenged his patience seemingly wearing thin.

"Revenge," Tesania muttered almost to herself. Realizing she had spoken aloud and that all in the room were now looking at her, she said. "Sorry."

"Revenge?" the king asked her directly.

"Revenge," Tesania whispered again. "You appear to be aware of the reason Lord Dalgliesh left Eldanal?"

Nodding, the king assured her, "I am."

"When King Eldine banished Lord Dalgliesh," she went on. "He gave all his assets to me."

"That seems extravagant."

Tesania could not deny his words; she had thought the same when the king had granted all the disgraced lord's lands and assets to her. "It was a reward," she informed him. "I . . . we," she added while looking quickly to the others. "We saved Eldanal from Trannyth."

"A nasty business," the king said confirming he knew about the evil mage that had threatened Eldanal all those years ago. "So you received all his lands and assets and you now believe he is attacking those very same assets in revenge?"

"I do."

"How?"

"How?"

"How is he attacking? You said you haven't captured any mercenaries . . . no informants . . . ? How is he attacking you?"

"With mist," Tesania almost whispered knowing what was coming.

"I'm sorry," the king asked leaning forward and cupping his ear. "Did you say mist?"

"Yes," Tesania mumbled. "He is attacking with mist."

"Mist? As in, air?"

"Yes."

King Asden shook his head as he examined her. "Mist is attacking you?" he scoffed.

Tesania steeled herself and replied, "I am aware it sounds fanciful that something as innocuous as a simple mist can do the damage we are talking about. I must admit, I too was dubious when I was first told. But it is true. I have seen it with my own eyes."

"And what does this mist have to do with Lord Dalgliesh?" he asked his voice now mocking her. "He has no more control over mist than you or I."

"You're right, of course," Tesania conceded as she racked her thoughts for what to say. Breathing in heavily, she said, "Magic controls the mist . . . guides it . . . sends it to destroy my crops, kill my people, sink my ships!"

"Mist," the king cried. "Do you hear yourself? Mist cannot destroy ships."

"Magic mist can," Tesania shot back at him her anger rising.

"Lord Dalgliesh is not a mage!"

"He has one in his employ!"

Shaking his head incredulously as Tesania tried to control herself, the king turned to Deavon. "You believe this?"

Sitting forward, Deavon returned the king's gaze. "It is a fact that mist is attacking King Eldine's assets as well as Tesania's. That isn't in question." He went on quickly as the king began to protest. "Tesania's manor was attacked while we were there. We saw it with our own eyes," he added while rubbing at his forehead in memory. "It was alive I tell you. It knew what it was doing. It had a purpose . . . ." Pausing, he looked up at Tesania. Smiling at her, he said, "Thankfully, we managed to drive it away. But," he added, "We cannot stand by while Dalgliesh uses this mage to wipe everything away."

Shaking his head, King Asden sat back and growled in a low voice, "You are casting grave accusations against a lord of my court."

"With good reason," Deavon assured him.

"Explain that to me," the king insisted. "Explain this good reason. Explain why you are accusing a respected lord of this heinous crime. How did you come to this conclusion? Did this deadly mist tell you so?" he finished as he began to laugh.

"At first it was a guess," Tesania replied grimacing as she said it.

"A guess?" the king exploded the slap of his hand slamming onto the table echoing sharply through the room. "You dare to come to me, accuse one of my lord's, with a guess?"

"It was a guess," Tesania admitted as she faced the king's anger. "At first; but, as Deavon has said, it soon became apparent that the attacks were centered on King Eldine's and my own assets and people."

"That still proves nothing. I'm sure your king has many disgruntled subjects who might perpetrate this against him."

"Agreed," Tesania conceded. "But this is more than a farmstead set on fire, more than a few crops destroyed. It is high level magic that not even the arch mage of Eldanal can conjure . . . . Magic that I'm sure even your own esteemed mages could not muster."

Considering her words, the king turned to each of his own people, each shaking their heads almost imperceptibly in return. Looking back to Tesania, he said, "You still haven't said anything that suggests Lord Dalgliesh has anything to do with the attacks."

"If I may," Deavon said as he pushed his chair back and stood. "Are you aware of the attacks on Aliaga many centuries ago?" he asked the king as he began to trace the same path Tesania had been walking.

"I am not," the king said as the woman at his side sat forward and spoke.

"You speak of the Tiadath's?"

"I do," Deavon confirmed, nodding. "You know of them?"

"I've read of them in some obscure texts," the woman replied. "You believe a Tiadath mage is involved here?"

"What do you know of this, Orissa?" King Asden asked.

Orissa adjusted herself and said, "Centuries ago, a race from across the seas invaded our land," she advised. "They moved through the kingdom quickly. Aliaga's army couldn't stop them. The kingdom collapsed and Estel was overrun."

"That's correct," Tesania said absentmindedly as she listened to the woman.

"You know of the Tiadath wars?"

Surprised by her question, Tesania looked to Deavon before answering, "I do. The monks on Unastine have records of it. The . . . ." she searched her memory.

"The Tenule Chronicles," Kailyn advised her.

"That's it."

"Interesting," Orissa said. "I wasn't aware they had records of it."

"Nor were they," Giddy said laughing.

"Can we get on with it," the king asked impatiently.

"The king of the time," Orissa began the tale again, "was locked in his own dungeons. The Tiadath's had full control of Aliaga."

"Impossible," the king scoffed.

"Sadly, it was very possible," Tesania assured him, taking up the story. "You see, the Tiadath's were led by a mage," she said. "A mage of such power and magic that no one could stop her or the army she protected with her spells."

"How is it they aren't still here?" one of the king's male aides asked, enthralled by the story. "Did the king escape the dungeon and drive them out?"

"Hardly," Giddy scoffed as Tesania shook her head at her.

"The king was powerless to do anything. None of the Aliagan mages could stand against the Tiadath mage: Aliaga's soldiers couldn't defeat their armies. It was hopeless."

"So how?"

A resistance group was formed, led by a warrior named Rodus. He summoned the mages in the group to his fire one night. They discussed the Tiadath mage and how to eliminate her. Deciding that she was far too skilled to be defeated by magic alone, they devised a way to imbue a sword with spells. Spells strong enough to cut through her defenses."

"Did they?" the aide asked blushing as his king glared at him.

"Yes," Tesania assured him. "Rodus, a skilled blacksmith, forged the sword. The mages then cast spells on the steel as the sword took shape, building the magic day by day until it was complete. A plan was devised to draw the Tiadath mage to battle. She came from the capital with her army expecting to confront a small rebel group. As the Aliagan mages engaged the Tiadath mage, sacrificing themselves, Rodus made his way to her flank and drove his sword into her side destroying her magical defenses. With the mage dead, the Tiadath army quickly fell. A few weeks later Rodus and his swelling army arrived at the gates of Estel and freed the king." Deciding not to tell the current King of Aliaga that his ancestor had banished the very man that saved him and his kingdom, Tesania fell silent.

"Where did these Tiadath's come from?" the king asked Orissa.

"I have no idea," Orissa replied shrugging apologetically. "The story I know is limited. There wasn't much written about it in our history books."

"You believe it to be truth though?"

"It's truth," Tesania assured him.

The king regarded her. "You think this is another Tiadath Mage?"

"It has to be," Tesania replied. "No one in Eldanal or Aliaga can wield that kind of magic."

"Assuming it is," King Asden asked. "How do you plan to stop them? The sword you spoke of is long gone."

"But it isn't," Tesania assured him excitedly. "You see, Rodus was my forefather. The sword was passed from generation to generation."

"And you now have the very same sword?" the king asked her dubiously.

"I do."

"She does," Giddy said. "What do you think stopped Trannyth?"

"I have no idea," the king replied, his voice muffled as he ran his hand over his face, seemingly struggling to make a decision. "What do you want with Lord Dalgliesh?"

"King Eldine wants him returned to Wyvern."

Shaking his head, the king said, "I can't let that happen. Lord Dalgliesh is now an Aliagan Lord."

"Who has crimes to answer to in Eldanal."

"I can't let you take him. You don't even have proof he is involved."

"The mage was at his compound," Raim said to the frowns of Deavon and Tesania.

"How do you know that?"

"We were there," Raim replied a little sheepishly, realizing he and Giddy had been operating in Aliaga without permission when they tracked Dalgliesh down. "A few weeks ago; Giddy and I."

"Who approved this?"

"No one," Raim replied head bowed. Looking up, he added more confidently, "We didn't know for sure he was behind the attacks. All we did was travel to his compound and ask a few questions of his guards."

"Without permission to operate within Aliaga?"

"Correct."

"I shall be protesting this to your king."

"Regardless," Tesania cut in. "What matters is Giddy and Raim confirmed that there has been a mage frequenting Lord Dalgliesh's estate. They know he isn't from Aliaga because of his outlandish clothes."

The king's gaze remained on Raim as he said, "Outlandish enough for you to believe him to be a Tiadath mage?"

"Yes."

"The same Tiadath mage who is attacking your assets?"

"I believe so."

The king thought over her words before saying, "I will confer with my aides." Relaxing his scrutiny of Raim, he turned to Orissa.

Tesania retook her seat as they spoke amongst themselves. She wished she could hear what they said but their voices did not carry. Smiling hopefully at Deavon, she rested her hands in her lap and waited.

"You will appreciate," the king said eventually, his voice causing Tesania to jump with a start, "that we cannot allow you to simply walk into Lord Dalgliesh's estate and arrest him."

"We need to stop him," Tesania pleaded. "He's hurting my people."

"I understand your concern," King Asden assured her as he grasped his chin between thumb and crooked finger, considering his words. "The Kingdom of Eldanal is our ally and I will not tolerate any of my subjects perpetrating attacks against it," he said eventually. "Bring me proof," he then insisted. "Show me that Lord Dalgliesh is definitely involved in these acts and I will have him arrested." As Tesania beamed at him, he added, "But, I will not allow you to arrest him. I will, however, allow you to question him." As Tesania's joy faded, he dictated, "No more than that. No harm is to come to Lord Dalgliesh or his family. You are not to remove him from his home or Aliaga. Do you understand?"

"Questioning him won't stop the attacks!"

"Bring me proof he is involved. Then, and only then, will I order his arrest."

"And if the mage is there?"

"Do what you want with the mage," the king dismissed with a wave of his hand.

"I suppose we can't ask for any more," Deavon said. "Thank you for understanding," he added as he bowed his head slightly. "And for allowing us to at least question Dalgliesh."

"There is one other thing," the king informed.

"That is?"

"I cannot let you travel around Aliaga unsupervised."

"We know the way," Giddy assured him.

"Still," the king stated. "I want one of my people with you to . . . shall we say . . . keep an eye on things. Make sure you keep to our agreement."

"You have our word," Deavon assured him.

"It's not negotiable," the king said. Let the page outside know where you are lodging. My man will meet you there in the morning."

"With horses?" Giddy asked hopefully.

"Horses?"

"You don't expect us to walk?"

Frowning at the soldier, the king leant toward Orissa, "Instruct the stables to have seven mounts available in the morning."

"Eight," Giddy corrected.

"Eight?" King Asden asked as he scanned the group. "The six of you and my man makes seven."

"There is one more," Giddy informed him. Aware that Rhys' name was probably well known to the king and that it might raise questions, she added quickly, "He couldn't come today," as she gripped her arms around her own stomach. "Ate something last night that didn't agree with him," she lied.

Scowling, the king said, "Very well, eight mounts will await you at the stables in the morning." With that he looked down to a parchment handed to him by Orissa and began to read. Clearly having been dismissed, Tesania said, "Thank you, Your Majesty," and led the others to the door.

23 - The road to Dalgliesh

Tesania rose early the following morning and headed for the small dining room offered by the Vine Inn. It wasn't much, just a few tables scattered around a dimly lit room with a fire crackling in the corner. Nodding to a waiter who asked if she wished to be served breakfast, she sat by the fire. She had not woken Kailyn as she dressed silently in their shared room; they had a long day in the saddle ahead of them and she decided to let the young mage slumber a little longer. Staring into the fire, she re-lived the meeting with King Asden the previous afternoon. She still was not convinced he believed what they had to say. After all, who in their right mind would believe that wet air could cause so much physical damage? She regretted his refusal to allow them to arrest Lord Dalgliesh and return him to Eldanal for trial. *'But at least,'* she consoled herself; *'he agreed to allow us to question him.'* What if the Tiadath Mage was not at the estate? What then? Lord Dalgliesh certainly would not cooperate with them, and especially not with the woman that had been granted all his lands in Eldanal. *'All we can do is try,'* she lamented as Deavon walked toward her. Smiling at him she waved toward the kitchen door, saying, "I ordered gruel already."

"You're up early," he commented while walking to the door and motioned to the waiter. "Gruel please."

"Couldn't sleep," Tesania admitted, returning her attention to the fire.

"Dalgliesh?" Deavon asked as he pulled out a chair and sat heavily opposite her.

Nodding, Tesania echoed her previous thoughts, "What if the mage isn't there? Lord Dalgliesh won't just tell us he's behind the attacks . . . will he?"

"I doubt it," Deavon replied crossing his legs and leaning back in the chair hands behind his head. "I'm sure he'll have a lot to say," he added laughing. "But it won't be what we want to hear."

Tesania laughed along. "I'm sure," she agreed before looking at the ranger seriously. "Will he even be there?"

"I've no idea," Deavon admitted. "If he isn't, we'll have to make camp and wait for him."

Scowling at the thought of the Tiadath Mage sending more mist to harm her people Tesania shook her head. "We can only hope he, or at least, the mage, is there."

"He should be," Deavon assured her. "If he was in Estel, King Asden's aides would have said so."

"I suppose," Tesania conceded as the waiter deposited their gruel onto the table, asking if they wished anything else. "Cider," Tesania replied.

"Me as well," Deavon added smiling. As the waiter moved away, he picked up his spoon and plunged it into the thick, porridge like mixture, saying, "We'll find him, Tes. Don't worry about it."

Tesania took up her own spoon and dipped it into her gruel. She knew that they were doing all they could. But it pained her that it wasn't enough. Already they had spent days travelling through Eldanal to avoid Lord Dalgliesh's spies. Then another wasted day as they waited to see the king. How many attacks had there been since she had left her home? How many more of her people were suffering while she sat by a warm fire eating gruel in a far off land?

***

Returning to her room after finishing her breakfast Tesania opened a window, the ensuing cool breeze billowing the flimsy curtains and fluttering her hair as it rushed to drive the warmth from the room. Sitting on Kailyn's bed, she gently shook the girl's shoulder until she finally blinked her eyes open, complaining that the daylight was much too bright as she rolled over and pulled her pillow over her head.

Laughing, Tesania announced, "Time to get up. Deavon and I have eaten breakfast already."

"I'd rather sleep."

"Come on," Tesania insisted as she stood and whipped the covers off the young mage. "We have a long ride today. You need to eat something."

Grumbling, Kailyn reluctantly climbed from the bed throwing her pillow at Tesania as she moved to a basin of water on the bed stand. "It's freezing," she complained looking toward the flapping curtains. "Did you have to open the window?"

"I did."

"Why?"

"Because the sun is shining and it's a beautiful day."

"It's a freezing day."

"You'll survive," Tesania assured her. "Giddy and the others have just gone down to order something. If you hurry you can eat with them," she suggested before heading for the door. "Deavon's down there too. I'm going outside to see if the king's man has arrived."

The street fronting the Vine Inn was quiet at this time of morning. A few people wandered past as Tesania peered up the street and then turned and looked the other way. She had no idea who to expect or what he would look like, just that the king said he would meet them at the Inn.

Seeing no one who showed signs of being the king's man, she rubbed at her arms in the cool morning air and decided to return to the dining room where she could at least wait in the warmth of the fire. Pivoting on one foot, she walked toward the inn door sliding to a halt as a soft voice emanated from the shadows beside the entryway. "Lady Tesania?" the voice asked as a man stepped into the sunlight.

Taken aback by his sudden appearance, Tesania stepped backward eyes following his every move. He hardly looked menacing; in fact he hardly looked anything at all. Everything about the man in front of her was plain. Short mousy brown hair outlined brown eyes that gave little away. Even his disheveled brown clothes were worn and plain. She decided as her eyes travelled down to his scuffed brown boots that he could lose himself in a crowd in an instant if he wanted to. She was also sure, as she scanned back up to his face, that she would walk right past him in a busy street and not even notice he was there. Admonishing herself for staring, she shifted her gaze and asked, "Who's asking?"

A smile stretched the man's lips as he reached out his hand, offering it to Tesania. "Baird," he announced his voice no louder than the first time he had spoken.

"Baird?"

"King Asden has asked me to accompany you to Lord Dalgliesh's estate."

Abashed that she hadn't recognized that he could only know her name if he were the king's man, she stepped forward to take his hand, saying, "I was expecting you," before asking curiously while nodding toward the shadows, "How long were you there?"

"Not too long, yet long enough," Baird answered cryptically the smile on his face spreading into a grin.

Not at all sure what he meant, Tesania muttered as she moved to the door, "Yes, well, you had better come inside and meet the others."

Giddy sat with the others near the crackling fire, her empty plate pushed aside as she leant back in her chair. "Who's your friend?" she asked Tesania when she entered the room, Baird in tow.

"Baird, King Asden's man," Tesania replied as she stepped aside and let the man through, smiling as everyone at the table reacted the same way as she had, their eyes travelling over his clothing. "Take a seat," she suggested while dragging a chair out for herself.

Baird reached out and grasped the back of a chair before pulling it out and seating himself. His eyes flicked to each of the people at the table, resting briefly on each before passing to the next. "Well met," he said as he settled into his chair and motioned to the waiter, asking for a cider.

"Welcome to our little group," Deavon said as he reached over the table and offered his hand, introducing himself and explaining that he was a ranger from Eldanal.

"Thank you," Baird replied simply as he shook the ranger's hand followed by the others as they rose and followed Deavon's lead. As the waiter placed his cider before him, Baird looked around the table once more before saying, "I was told to expect seven of you."

"Rhys isn't here yet," Giddy informed him.

"Rhys?" Baird asked his face showing no emotion as he said the word but his eyes flashed to the door for a moment. "He is upstairs still?"

"Not exactly," Giddy replied eyes flickering to the door before returning to the disheveled man. "Can I ask?" she changed the subject, "What you do?"

"What I do?"

"Why did King Asden send you to accompany us?"

Shrugging, Baird replied, "Who knows why kings do what they do."

"That doesn't answer her question," Aldan interjected.

"What question was that?"

"What do you do," Aldan growled as he repeated Giddy's question and scanned the man's clothes. "You hardly look like a man the king would trust."

"Looks can be deceiving."

"Indeed," Aldan grunted.

"I think," Tesania said quietly to Baird, "that it might serve us all well if we knew why the king selected you. After all," she added quickly, "What we intend to do could be dangerous. It would be helpful if we knew a little more about you . . . so we knew what to expect in those situations."

Baird considered her words before answering, "Your words hold truth." Adjusting himself in his chair before taking a sip of his cider and replacing the mug gently down on the table, he said, "I am attached to the king's intelligence arm."

"A spy?" Deavon asked.

"Sometimes a spy," Baird agreed.

"Is that why you dress like that?" Kailyn asked curiously pointing at his shirt.

Unconsciously raising his hand to brush at his crumpled clothes, Baird replied, "It suits me to draw little attention," he assured her a grin spreading on his lips.

"I thought so," Kailyn boasted proudly at having guessed right.

"You said you're a spy sometimes," Giddy questioned. "What else?"

"Many things," Baird replied shrugging. "Whatever the king needs."

"Specifically?"

"Does it matter?"

"Maybe it does."

"Giddy," Deavon interrupted motioning for her to stop before turning his attention to the spy. "You're here to spy on us?"

"No," Baird assured him. "One of my many roles," he went on while winking at Giddy, "is gathering information on people who . . . let's just say, the king has an interest in knowing about."

"Dalgliesh," Tesania asked.

"Dalgliesh, among others."

"So you're here to help us rather than spy on us?"

"I am here to ensure you keep to your agreement with King Asden. But," he added as he saw the disappointment on Tesania's face, "If I can help you in any way, I will."

Brightening, Tesania smiled at him, saying, "Thank you," as the door behind her thudded open allowing the cold air in the hallway to flood in.

"Close the door," Giddy demanded as she rose to meet the intruder. "Glad you could make it," she said happily while clasping the man's hand. Turning, she said, "Everyone, I'd like you to meet Rhys." Starting with Tesania she made her way around the table, introducing each of the party members before finally coming to Baird, "And this is Baird, King Asden's man."

"We know each other," Baird replied his eyes narrow as he considered the little thief. "I'm surprised you would keep his company."

Tesania looked from one man to the other. She could plainly see animosity there, in their faces, in their body language. Catching Deavon's eyes she frowned at him shaking her head lightly. The last thing they needed was two people in the party at loggerheads. Their task was going to be hard enough.

"Giddy and Raim recommended him," Deavon said to the spy. "They have worked with him before."

Baird's eyes left the thief and shifted to Giddy. "I thought you were a soldier?" he questioned.

"I am."

"Then how do you come to recommend this man?" he asked his voice growing louder for the first time since he had met them.

"We . . . err . . ." Giddy began obviously confused by the animosity coming from the spy. ". . . he guided us to Dalgliesh's estate a few weeks ago."

Spinning on Tesania, Baird demanded, "Does the king know you are keeping company with this man?" he asked as he nodded disdainfully at Rhys.

"Our king is well aware—"

"Not your king," Baird cut her off. "King Asden . . . . Does he know this man is accompanying you?"

"I don't believe so," Tesania answered her voice barely more than a whisper.

"You mislead him?"

"No," Tesania replied adamantly.

Rising, Baird walked a few paces toward the little thief. "This man is a criminal."

"Does that matter?" Giddy asked angrily as she stepped in front of the spy.

"Does it matter?" Baird spluttered. "Do you hear yourself?"

"What she means," Raim pointed out as he reached toward Giddy and laid a calming hand on her shoulder. "Is that we had need of his help in the past. Without him we couldn't have succeeded in our mission."

"Which was?" Baird demanded.

"We needed to know if Dalgliesh was involved with the mage attacking Tesania."

"And you couldn't have gone through proper channels?" Baird demanded. "King Asden would have—"

"Without proof?" Raim interrupted. "He would have dismissed us off hand."

Turning away from them, Baird walked to the fireplace and leant against the mantel as he stared into the flickering flames. "What makes you think he will help you again?" he asked to no one in particular. Turning back to Giddy, he said, "Believe me when I say, his loyalty is to the highest bidder. For a few coins he will sell you out before you know what is happening."

"I have given them my word," Rhys said, speaking for the first time.

"Your word?" Baird scoffed. "That is worth nothing," he said, laughing. "And you know it."

Scowling and turning to Giddy, Rhys said, "You didn't tell me he was coming."

"I didn't know," Giddy replied defensively. "He just arrived here this morning."

"Maybe I shouldn't come with you."

"Because of him?" Giddy asked while screwing her nose up in distaste at the spy. "He can't tell us what to do."

"But the king can," Baird growled.

"Perhaps everyone needs to calm down," Deavon suggested as he rose and stepped between the two men. "Please," he said motioning to the table. "Everyone sit down."

Reluctantly, Baird moved to his chair and sat. Giddy led Rhys to the far side of the table and pointed out an empty chair before sitting in her own and glowering at Baird.

"I don't know how much you were told about our mission," Deavon said to Baird after everyone was settled.

"All I have been told is that I am to escort you to Lord Dalgliesh's estate so you can question him on a matter of some urgency to the King of Eldanal."

Nodding, Deavon confirmed his words before asking, "Do you know Dalgliesh?"

"Not personally. But I'm well aware of who he is and his dealings."

"Then you would know he is a very private man?" Deavon asked. As the spy nodded, he went on, "Do you believe he will simply let us into his compound and answer our questions amicably?"

"I doubt that would be the case."

"So you can see we may have to use . . . err . . . unusual methods to find out what we need to know?"

Shaking his head, Baird replied, "The king has expressly forbidden anything more than questioning."

Breathing in deeply, Deavon asked, "Dalgliesh has security?"

Baird nodded in affirmation before saying, "Mercenary soldiers."

"Will they let us into the compound?"

"I would say not," Baird conceded. "But I'll approach them . . . advise them that the king wishes Lord Dalgliesh to answer a few questions."

Deavon's eyes travelled down the man as he asked, "Do they know who you are."

"No," the spy replied as he too looked down at his plain clothes. "I see your meaning," he eventually conceded as he returned his gaze to the ranger.

"Then you can also see that we may need to adopt some, shall we say, unusual methods to get to Dalgliesh?"

Baird considered him suspiciously before asking, "You mean to attack the compound . . . ?"

"Not attack," Deavon assured him. "There aren't enough of us to succeed with that anyway." Considering the spy seriously he eventually said, "Our mission is urgent and cannot be allowed to fail. Hence, your own king has approved it; albeit with some conditions."

Baird nodded his understanding and acceptance of what Deavon had said before asking, "What exactly do you want with Lord Dalgliesh?"

"I'll be happy to explain everything to you on the ride to his estate," Deavon assured him before nodding toward the thief and adding, "Giddy has assured me we can trust this man, even if you cannot."

"You may regret that."

"Possibly," Deavon conceded. "But, we'll need to adapt to the situation as it arises . . . . For that reason alone, I'd rather have him along in case we need his . . . err . . . particular talents," he stated simply.

Baird's gaze drifted to Rhys. The two men held each others' stare for what seemed to Tesania to be an eternity before the spy finally said, "I should arrest you and drag you to the dungeons."

"But you won't," the little thief replied grinning at him.

"No," Baird admitted. "Not today anyway."

As satisfied as they could be with the uneasy truce between their two newest members, the party drained the last of their ciders before rising from the table and gathering their gear while Deavon paid for their lodgings. "Ready?" he asked when he had slung his own pack over his shoulder. When no one protested, he turned to Baird and asked, "Can you lead us to the King's Stables?"

24 - Thief in the Night

Tesania slipped gladly from the saddle of her grey mare a few miles from Lord Dalgliesh's estate and threw the reins over its head before leading it to where the others were tethering their mounts. They had ridden throughout the day, stopping only occasionally to rest the horses and partake of some food while Tesania and Deavon had insisted they carry on past sunset so they could be in position near the estate in the morning. Handing her reins to Raim and then rubbing at her sore rump, Tesania caught Kailyn's attention and said, "Let's gather some firewood."

Groaning as she too rubbed at sore muscles, Kailyn reluctantly followed her into a small, moonlit copse of trees nearby. "Do you think he'll be there?" she asked while bending and picking up a fallen branch. "Dalgliesh, I mean."

"I hope so," Tesania replied.

"What if he isn't?"

"I have no idea."

"We'd better hope he's home then."

"We'll see in the morning," Tesania said as she pulled a large branch from between two trees and began to drag it back to their camp.

**

Deavon shook Tesania awake as the sun crept into the foggy morning sky. "Good morning," he said smiling down at her. "Aldan's making breakfast," he informed before moving off to check the horses.

Yawning as she sat up, Tesania blinked as a shaft of sunlight found its way through the wisps of fog and played across her face. Protecting her eyes with her hand she looked about their makeshift camp. Kailyn still slumbered in her bedroll, her disheveled hair scattered across her face. Giddy sat by the fire pit warming her hands while Raim snapped a small branch and threw it on the glowing coals sending a spiral of sparks chasing each other into the cool air. "Hey," Aldan complained pulling his pan away.

"Sorry," Raim said sheepishly.

Smiling as Raim apologized; Tesania twisted toward the other bedrolls, surprised to find them empty. Shrugging, she leaned toward the young mage and shook her gently. "Wake up." As Kailyn muttered her usual protests at being woken, Tesania threw her blankets aside and climbed to her feet, rubbing at her arms as she stepped toward the warmth of the fire and the inviting smell of breakfast.

"Good morning," Giddy said smiling up at her.

"Morning," Tesania replied while looking around the camp and then peering into the fog. "Where're the others?"

Shrugging, Giddy replied, "No idea. They were gone when I woke up."

Shrugging also as Tesania looked toward him, Raim added, "We were up before dawn and they were already gone."

Frowning, Tesania looked toward Aldan who shook his head. "I hope they're ok," she said quietly while once more studying the dissipating fog.

"They're big boys," Giddy assured her.

"I know," Tesania replied as she sank down and sat on the log next to the soldier.

"Maybe they're sorting out their differences," Raim suggested, mischief in his voice. "You know . . . duel at sunrise and all that."

"You're not helping," Giddy informed her friend tartly.

"I'm just saying—"

"I don't think they'd go that far," Deavon interrupted as he walked toward them.

"Well, they'd hardly be off on a morning stroll," Raim insisted.

"I've no idea what they're doing," Deavon replied before saying, "Eat your breakfast and then get your gear packed. I want to move out as soon as possible."

"What if they're not back by then?"

Deavon scanned the trees ahead of him as he thought. "I'm sure they'll be back by then."

"And if they're not?"

"We go without them."

"Would that be wise?"

"We can't wait," Tesania cut in.

"I know," Raim assured her. "But we should wait until they return at least," he counseled. "I want to know what they've been up to."

"From what I saw at the Vine Inn," Aldan said as he lifted a piece of cured meat from his pan and offered it to Tesania, "they hate each other. I doubt they'd be together. Not in a friendly way anyway."

"There you go," Raim quipped at Giddy. "Aldan agrees; a duel at dawn," he boasted while looking into the distance. "I wonder who won."

"They didn't duel," Giddy assured him rolling her eyes.

"How do you know?"

"Trust me."

"You don't know—"

"They wouldn't . . . would they?" Tesania asked Deavon concern edging her voice.

"I don't think so," he replied smiling at her reassuringly. "I'm sure they have their reasons for leaving camp so early.

"To warn Dalgliesh?" Aldan asked thoughtfully while wiping out his pan.

"Would they?" Tesania asked Deavon quickly as she stood and looked in the direction of Lord Dalgliesh's estate as if she could see what the spy and thief were up to.

"Rhys wouldn't," Giddy said adamantly.

"Do you know that for sure?" Aldan asked. "Baird warned us he might sell us out."

"He wouldn't," Giddy replied her surety fading as she spoke.

"I don't think that's it," Deavon said. "If it was only Rhys missing . . . then maybe. But both of them?" he asked no one in particular while shaking his head in confusion.

"Rhys snuck off and Baird followed him?" Aldan suggested.

"Then we can only hope that Baird stopped him in time," Deavon said.

"If . . ." Giddy insisted, ". . . if Rhys was going to warn Dalgliesh," she added adamantly. "We don't know that."

"Agreed," Deavon said as he once more looked around. "Their horses are still here," he said pointing to the line of horses in the lifting fog. "And their gear," he added while nodding to the blankets they had left on the ground. Frowning, he seemed to come to a decision. "Finish your breakfast," he suggested to them all. "Giddy . . . can you wake Kailyn up."

"I'm awake," Kailyn's muffled voice carried to them from under her blanket making Tesania laugh at the disappointment that slipped over Giddy's eager face.

***

Pulling herself into her saddle, Tesania took the reins in hand and guided her horse toward Deavon and then Lord Dalgliesh's estate. The two Aliagans' hadn't returned by the time they had broken camp, their mounts being led by Raim as they moved off. "Where could they be?" she asked more to herself than the ranger as she stared down at the horse's mane in thought.

"I know where one is," Deavon said motioning ahead.

Looking up quickly, Tesania saw the thief walking toward them, a grin on his face as he called out. "Weren't going to wait for me?"

"We didn't know where the two of you had gone," Tesania accused raising her voice so it would carry to the little man.

"Two of us?"

"You and Baird."

"Baird?" Rhys said spitting on the ground in distaste. "Why would he be with me?"

Turning in her saddle and looking back at the two empty saddles behind Raim, Tesania said as they grew closer to the thief, "He wasn't at the camp this morning. I thought he must have been with you."

"I was," Baird's voice drifted from the distance.

Spinning on his heel, Rhys glared into the trees, head whipping from side to side as he searched for the spy. "You were following me?" he demanded hotly.

"Of course," the spy replied matter-of-factly as he appeared ahead of them from seemingly nowhere.

"Why?"

"You slipped out of camp in the middle of the night."

"And . . . ? That gave you the right to sneak around behind me."

"The king gives me my rights."

"Bah . . ." Rhys snarled spitting once more. ". . . your king isn't here now."

"I am his humble servant," Baird replied shrugging as he skirted past the thief and approached Deavon's horse. "He headed out before dawn, toward Lord Dalgliesh," he informed while looking up at the ranger. "I thought it prudent to see what he was up to."

"Thought it prudent?" Rhys exploded, voice raised, face red.

"With your past recor—"

"Bah," Rhys snarled again. "What I've done in the past is irrelevant."

"Is it?"

"I've promised these people . . . . My loyalty's to them."

"For a fee!"

"So?" the thief exclaimed hands spread in frustration. "Whether they're paying me or not makes no difference," he insisted while looking up to Giddy and then the others one by one until his eyes came to rest on Tesania's worried face. "Whilst I'm employed by you," he informed her passionately, "my loyalty is to you."

"Until you speak to Lord Dalgliesh and he offers you more," Baird said sneering.

"Did I?"

"Did you what?"

"Did I talk to Dalgliesh?"

"Well . . ." Baird said looking down and kicking at the ground. ". . . no."

"Exactly," Rhys said glaring at the spy.

"What exactly were you doing then?" Tesania asked the question that seemed to be on everyone's lips.

"He went to the edge of the compound," Baird informed her.

Scowling at the spy, Rhys turned his face back up to Tesania. "In my business," he informed her, "We don't sleep much during the night."

"So you went to Lord Dalgliesh's estate?" Tesania asked suspiciously, accepting without comment that the hours the thief worked were not what honest people would be used to. "To what end?"

"Reconnaissance."

"In the middle of the night?"

"Makes sense," Baird said, unexpectedly backing up the thief's words.

Glowering at him, Rhys said, "The more we know about the compound guards and their habits, the better."

"You can tell us what you saw on the way," Deavon suggested to the two men standing before him. "Mount up."

Rhys stalked to Raim and snatched the reins of his horse from the soldier. Pulling himself into the saddle, he muttered at the spy who was similarly mounting his own horse, "If you want to know what I'm up to in future, ask."

"Will you tell me?" the spy asked dubiously.

"While we're on this mission," Rhys said as he spurred his horse forward. "Yes."

Tesania observed the exchange as the two men parted. Baird watched the thief ride away, the look on his face puzzling her. She couldn't tell if it was doubt over what Rhys had said or doubt over his own mistrust of the little thief. When he saw her watching though, the usual featureless expression fell over his face as he nodded and spurred his own horse forward. Frowning at Deavon who shrugged back at her, Tesania turned her mount and followed into the trees.

No one spoke as the small company rode along, each concentrating on guiding their mounts through the trees. Eventually as the trees opened out into a grass clearing she nudged her horse forward toward Deavon. "What do you think?"

"About Rhys?" he asked. As Tesania nodded, he went on, "If he'd wanted to inform Dalgliesh we were coming, he wouldn't have come back."

Tesania considered his words before saying, "Maybe, if Baird hadn't followed him . . . ."

Smiling, Deavon assured her, "But, he didn't know Baird was there."

Looking ahead to where the thief sat hunched in his saddle, Tesania eventually said, "He seems honest enough," before asking quickly, in response to Deavon's laughing face, "What?"

"You do know he's a thief?"

"Well . . . yes," Tesania admitted laughing along. "You know what I mean."

"I do," Deavon replied as his laughter settled. "Giddy seems to trust him though."

"Giddy doesn't trust too many people."

"Exactly," Deavon agreed before pointing ahead at Baird and the thief. "They're stopping." Spurring his horse, he called back, "Let's see what they're up to."

***

Rhys' finger traced the outer walls of Lord Dalgliesh's compound as he explained the security positions from the party's perch among the rocks overlooking the low valley beneath them. They had left the horses a few hundred yards behind and continued to their current position on foot, creeping from rock to rock in a crouched position until they could see the sprawling estate below them.

"And that's Dalgliesh's dwelling?" Deavon asked pointing toward a large mansion standing amongst smaller outer building.

"I'd say so," Rhys agreed. "I've never been in there," he admitted, shrugging apologetically.

"It would make sense," Aldan said. "He'd hardly live in the smaller ones," he added motioning to the smaller buildings surrounding the large house.

"Agreed," the little thief said, nodding.

Housing for the guards and household staff?" Aldan asked, more as a statement than a question.

"Looks that way."

"And that's the only way in?" Deavon asked, nodding toward the two large, planked gates at the front of the estate.

"As far as we know," Giddy replied.

"It would make sense," Baird added. "One entry means only one way in and one place for them to watch."

"Not necessarily," the thief growled at him.

Sighing, the spy said, "In normal circumstances."

"The gates look to be locked from the inside," Deavon cut them off. "It won't be easy to get in without a fight."

"Absolutely not," Baird said adamantly. "His Majesty has forbidden that."

"So we just knock?" Rhys asked sarcastically.

"Excuse me, Mr. Guard" Giddy took up the sarcasm, "Can you please let us in so we can arrest and question your master?"

"I agree," Tesania said her voice quiet as she surveyed the buildings below them. "I don't want anyone hurt. We can't just attack them."

"Thank you," Baird said, grinning in triumph at the thief.

"Not because of your king," Tesania said, anger rising suddenly at the grin on the spy's face. "I don't care what he said," she assured him, sneering. "But," she went on as she shook her head sneer slipping away, "I won't let any of these people," she gestured toward the guards stomping their rounds in front of the gates, "be hurt because of him!"

"They knew the risks when they took on their jobs," Aldan said.

"No, Aldan," Tesania said, her eyes searching his, pleading. "Why should they suffer because they work for a monster?"

"Because, they choose to work for that monster."

"No," Tesania repeated, shaking her head. "That's not enough. They aren't the ones attacking us . . . sinking my ships. I won't allow them to be hurt."

"We won't be able to just walk in, Tes," Deavon soothed her. "As Giddy said, we can't just knock."

"There are not enough of us anyway," Raim said as he surveyed the valley below. "There have to be dozens of guards down there."

"Agreed," Rhys said from where he squatted on the ground. "I've seen at least fifteen since we've been here. Add the others that are off duty, sleeping, eating. We don't have the numbers to deal with that head on."

"Not head on," Raim said a grin slipping onto his face. "We could throw Giddy over the fence . . . come at them from another direction?"

"Throw me . . ." Giddy protested, ". . . just try it."

"It makes sense," Rhys said. "Not just Giddy though."

"You are not throwing me—"

"We go in after dark," Rhys continued as he pointed toward the compound and a building at the near corner of the wall. "That's a guard house, and the others over there and there; and that larger building toward the back looks to be the barracks," he advised while pointing to the various buildings in the compound. "There'll be guards on duty at all times, mind. But there is a change of guard just before midnight. They stay on until the next change at dawn. We'll need to act in those few hours and need to be decisive."

"And how are you going to get to Lord Dalgliesh once you're in," Baird asked dubiously. "The guards will be on to you before you get far."

"Eliminate them."

"No," Tesania gasped.

"Not kill them," Rhys said to her quickly, smiling wanly. "We jump them, subdue them and tie them up."

"That won't give us much time," Aldan said dubiously. "It won't take long before they're found and the alarm raised."

"So we take them all out."

"All of them?" Giddy asked excitement in her voice as she massaged the pommel of her sword. "Sounds like a plan I can go with."

"Tie them up, Giddy," Raim sighed at her.

"I know," Giddy replied defensively.

As Raim laughed at his friend, Deavon said, "That wall's over six feet tall. How do you propose all of us get over it?"

"Not all of us," Rhys replied, eyes alight. "You and Aldan help Giddy, Raim and I climb over the wall," he said pointing. "We work our way toward the gate, taking guards out as we come to them, while you, Aldan and the others do the same from the front."

Baird shook his head dubiously. "How are you going to subdue that many men?" he asked.

"It'll be the middle of the night. Most of them will be asleep in the barracks by then," Rhys replied. "Besides, we have plenty of rope. We can cut it up along with the saddle cloths, blankets," he added, "Use them to tie and gag as we go."

"And none of them will be hurt?" Tesania asked.

"A few bumps on their heads," Rhys replied.

"It seems to be the only way," Deavon said to her gently. "We'll make sure none of them are seriously hurt where we can."

"And the domestic staff?" Baird asked. "What if a maid comes outside and sees you?"

"The same as the guards."

"You would hit a woman?"

"If she's going to raise the alarm," Rhys replied. "They'll be alright after a few days," he added in supplication as Baird shook his head in disgust.

"I think Deavon's right," Aldan said in a thoughtful voice. "We can't just knock . . . . Nor can we carry off a frontal assault with the numbers we have." He shook his head. "It seems this is the best plan to get to Dalgliesh while not permanently harming his people."

"You are not to harm Lord Dalgliesh himself though," Baird interrupted.

"Only if we have to," Giddy assured him.

"You will not," Baird said. "The king has expressly forbidden it."

"We know, Baird," Tesania said to the spy. "But we need to know who this mage is . . . . Need to stop him."

"What about the mage," Kailyn asked from behind them all, her voice soft as she wrung her hand around her staff nervously. "Have you thought about that . . . ? What if he is there? What'll we do then . . . ? He'll fight."

Tesania's hand unconsciously dropped to her sword as she listened to the girl's questions. "I hope he is," she said eventually when Kailyn fell quiet. "We can stop it here and now."

"You will attempt to kill him?" Baird asked.

"I will," Tesania answered defiantly, chin jutting forward.

"Isn't that a little hypocritical?"

"What is?"

"You don't want any of Lord Dalgliesh's people harmed," Baird accused. "Yet you will happily kill this mage; who is in fact, just an employee like the others."

"He is a murderer!" Tesania exploded. As Deavon frowned at her and nodded toward the compound. She calmed herself and in a lowered growl said, "You are correct. He is an employee . . . . But," she added to the victorious smile on Baird's face. "He isn't just guarding a gate . . . he is murdering my people . . . our king's people." Drawing a deep breath as the smile slipped off the spy's face, she said, "He has forfeited any right he has for leniency and I, for one, will show him no quarter."

"I see," Baird muttered before asking, "And Lord Dalgliesh? Will you show him no quarter?"

"I will bring no harm to your precious Lord," she said in disgust. "As you have reminded us many times, that is a matter for our king."

"My king," Baird insisted.

"This isn't getting us anywhere," Deavon interrupted laying a calming hand over Tesania's before turning to the spy. "You already have our word that Dalgliesh will not be harmed." As Baird nodded, he added, "But his mage is a different matter."

"I see," Baird conceded.

"He's very powerful," Kailyn said, swallowing hard. "I don't know that I can—"

"You won't need to," Tesania assured her friend while patting her sword and smiling. "I'll take care of him. You just watch my back . . . ok?"

"Ok," Kailyn mumbled unconvinced. "He's very powerful though," she went on eyes lifting to Tesania's, concern radiating out.

"I know," Tesania assured her as she reached out and grasped her hand. "I'll be careful."

Deavon watched them as they reassured each other before turning to Rhys, "What time?"

The thief shrugged. "They aren't expecting any trouble," he advised. "There were minimal guards on duty this morning. Shortly after midnight I'd say. That'll give us time to get in, find out what we need and be out by dawn."

Deavon considered his words as his eyes scanned the compound. "Very well," he said. "We all work on cutting down our ropes and blankets to make restraints and then get some rest." As the others agreed, he said, "Let's head back to last night's camp and wait until midnight."

25 - Infiltration

Crickets chirped in the moonlit darkness surrounding Tesania where she sat by the dying fire, the still radiating coals painting her clothes in an eerie, ever changing, orange glow. She hadn't slept much, although she had tried in vain to do so. Her mind would not settle as she lay on the hard ground, the soft sound of Kailyn's breathing in her ears. So she had risen and walked to the fire to wait for midnight, rubbing at her arms to warm them against the cool night breeze. The others had managed to find some sleep, except Raim, who sat with his back against a tree on the edge of their little clearing, his eyes and ears trained in the direction of Lord Dalgliesh's estate. She didn't speak with him, not wanting to wake the others, and not wanting to interrupt his guard. Instead, she watched the remnants of the fire and went through their plans over and over again. Shaking her head to clear it, she stood and walked to her horse. "Shh," she whispered as the mare nickered into the night. Reaching forward, she ran her palm down its nose. "You're a good girl, aren't you?" It calmed her to be near the placid animal, her own image reflecting in its eye from the wane moonlight. "We have to succeed," she said, voice almost inaudible. The mare nickered once more and nudged her before turning its attention to a clump of grass by its feet. "Thanks for listening," Tesania said as she patted the horse's flank and then returned to the fire, jumping in a start as Deavon said from the darkness, "It's almost midnight. We'd better wake the others."

***

The smooth stones of the compound walls joined each other almost perfectly, allowing little purchase and certainly no way for the small party gathered at its foot to climb. Rhys ran his hand over the stone as he whispered, "We go over here."

"Very well," Deavon replied as he looked around the group, his face barely visible in the shadowed moonlight. "You all have your ropes?" he asked while adjusting his own supply in his belt. As they all nodded silently in the dark, he went on, "Right. Giddy, Raim and Rhys go over here and work their way to the front gate, eliminating guards as they go." As they nodded, he added, "Make sure they're tied up properly; I don't want any getting loose before we've completed our mission . . . . Aldan, Baird and I go to the front gate."

"And us," Tesania said. "Kailyn and I are coming too."

Deavon nodded, "I'd like you to follow a few paces behind," he suggested. "Back us up; if needed."

As much as Tesania wanted to be a part of bringing Lord Dalgliesh down, she understood the wisdom of allowing the trained fighters to go ahead of them. "Alright," she replied, her voice betraying more nerves than she would have liked.

"You clear the inside to the gate," Deavon said to Giddy. "No more than that until you let us in . . . Understand?"

"Yes, boss," Giddy replied her teeth visible as she grinned.

"Raim?"

"I'll keep her in line," the little soldier promised.

"And the barracks?" Aldan asked. "What do we do about that?"

"Nothing," Deavon replied. "They should sleep through like any other night if we keep the noise to a minimum."

"And if they don't?"

"We'll deal with that if it arises," Deavon replied. "The important thing is to get the gate open. Once we're together we can overcome any threats that come our way." Without waiting for any further questions, he asked, "Everyone knows what to do?" When no-one replied, he said, "Alright . . . Watch each others' backs. I want everyone out safely. Do you hear me?" Motioning Aldan forward after another moment's silence, he bent by the wall and cupped his hands. "Rhys, you're first."

***

Rhys slipped down the inner side of Lord Dalgliesh's security wall and melted into the shadows of the buildings, his heart thumping in his chest as he waited for the two Eldanal soldiers to join him. It wasn't fear that caused the blood to rush through his veins rather than the excitement of the situation, the unadulterated joy he felt whenever he entered another's property without their knowledge or consent. Tonight was a little different though. Normally he worked alone and rarely did he engage any guards; preferring to slip in and out unseen. Controlling his breathing, he motioned Giddy over as her feet crunched onto the ground, followed by Raim. "The guard house," he whispered pointing.

Giddy nodded and then poked Raim in the ribs, "You're in first," she said in a hushed tone.

"Thanks," the little soldier replied.

Ignoring them, Rhys moved toward the guard house in a half crouch, Giddy and Raim falling in close behind.

***

The compound enclosure cast a shadow in the soft moonlight as Tesania followed a few steps behind Aldan, her fingers running along the stone wall as a guide. She didn't know if the shadow was a blessing as they followed Deavon toward the front gates, or a curse as she stubbed her foot on yet another protruding stone. Cursing silently, she glanced back to where Kailyn followed, only just managing to make out a small movement as the mage's robes fluttered in the breeze. Satisfied that her friend was close, she turned her attention back to where she reckoned Aldan to be, her pulse thundering in her ears, adrenaline pumping through her veins. It had been years since she had been in a situation like this, years since she had crept toward Trannyth's Keep and wielded her sword against his dark magic. But this somehow felt different; there were no beasts to stand in her way, no army of fanatical mages or a keep with walls higher than she could imagine. Here, she was creeping toward men such as she would employ herself, men that protected Lord Dalgliesh not because they owed him allegiance but because he paid them a handful of coins. Slipping her hand down to her sword, she drew it slowly from its scabbard. Immediately she was aware of its lifelessness; there was none of its usual pulsing power when she was in danger, no shivering in the grip or fire rippling within the blade. "They're not our enemies," she whispered to herself as she contemplated the meaning of the sword's dead weight. "Aldan," she whispered more urgently, quickening her step. "My sword," she said as he looked back at her. "It's dead."

"Quiet," he whispered back.

"But it proves that the guards aren't our enemies," she insisted. "Please be gentle with them."

"Gentle," Aldan whispered back mirth in his voice. "I'll be as gentle as I can be," he assured her. "Now be quiet; we're nearing the end of the wall."

Tesania knew they had already covered this earlier, but it clawed at her gut that the guards were just hired help and not to blame for the dreadful attacks being perpetrated against her own people. She also knew that they were about to battle people that would possibly fight to the last to do the job their Lord paid them to do. Shaking her head to clear it, she thudded heavily into Aldan's back as he stood motionless in front of her, followed shortly after by Kailyn following suit into her own back. "Shh" Aldan hissed back, his voice almost inaudible as he stepped back against the wall to allow Deavon through.

"Two guards," Deavon informed them quietly with two fingers raised. "Alternating route, crossing over each other. Swords and crossbows."

"What's the plan?" Aldan asked.

"We take one out as he comes to our corner."

"And the other," Tesania asked nervously. "What if he raises the alarm?"

"We take the first guard down and then wait until the other one comes to find him?"

"Sounds feasible," Aldan replied. "As long as he does come and doesn't just raise the alarm."

"They aren't expecting anything. I'm sure he'll come."

"And if he doesn't?"

"Kailyn?" Deavon asked the mage. "Can you stun him?"

"I can try," Kailyn replied. "As long as I can see him."

"Good," Deavon replied. "The next rotation, I'll take the first guard out. The rest of you be ready."

Swallowing hard as Deavon nodded at her and then the others, Tesania drew a deep breath. As Deavon turned away and the moment of action came closer, she had a sudden thought. Squinting into the darkness, she asked, "Where's Baird?"

***

The coolness of the guardhouse stones seeped through Rhys' shirt as he pressed his back hard against it. Slowly drawing his knife from its scabbard, he leant forward and peered for a fleeting second into the building's doorway before whipping back to his original position. "Closed," he said quietly to Giddy.

"Probably asleep?"

"No idea."

"Only one way to find out," Giddy suggested.

"Agreed," Rhys replied. "Ready."

"Right behind you."

Adjusting his knife in his right hand, Rhys leant toward the door once more and reached for the handle. It moved without resistance. For a moment he held it closed, nodding back to the two soldiers before driving forward and bursting through the door. Blinking as his eyes adjusted to the light of a candelabrum on a single table in the middle of the room and the flickering light of a fireplace in the far corner, he quickly made out two startled guards rising from their chairs, confused faces flashing between himself and his two companions who forced their way into the room beside him. "You take the woman," he called as he drove forward at the large male guard who had by now shaken off his confusion and reached for his sword. Stepping three paces, Rhys leapt, driving into the guard's midriff as the sword had only been half drawn from its sheath. Stumbling, the man tried desperately to keep his balance, arms flailing, but failed as he tottered back and fell his body thudding into the hungry fire sending sparks cascading into the room. Bounding forward, Rhys snatched at the guards flailing legs dragging with all his strength as the man's screams filled the guardhouse. Struggling, he managed to pull the man a little way but he was too heavy. Desperately he jerked again as the flames of the fire continued to lick at the man's clothes, the stench of burning hair and flesh permeating the small room. "Raim!" he called. "Help!"

Raim looked at Giddy who nodded for him to go. She had the other guard pinned with her knees clamped firmly down on the woman's biceps. Shoving the table aside as he dashed toward the burning guard, Raim grabbed at his shirt and pulled with all his might. Between them the two small men managed to haul the guard from the fireplace where he lay motionless on the floor, small groans escaping his swelling lips. Snatching at a cloak hanging from a hook on the wall, Rhys threw it to Raim, crying, "Douse the flames," as he fell to his knees on the far side of the man's head and began beating at the flames that had taken hold of his clothes. Finally, as the flames died away Rhys looked down at the smoldering mass of burnt, shriveled hair sticking to charred flesh, blisters forming where the flames hadn't had time to do fully their work. "That didn't go as planned," he growled, admonishing himself.

"Things happen in battle," Giddy assured him as she slipped a piece of cloth from her belt and began tying it around her captives head. "How bad is he?" she asked as the woman she sat on struggled, throwing her head from side to side. "It's going to happen," Giddy assured the woman gripping her chin tightly and holding her head steady. "Stop struggling."

***

Tesania peered into the darkness ahead of her. She had no idea where Baird had got to. The last she had seen him he had fallen in behind Kailyn but now he was missing. It worried her as she watched Deavon's silhouetted shoulders, waiting for his command. Had the king's spy done exactly what he had warned Rhys would do? Had he slipped away to warn the guards, or even worse, Lord Dalgliesh himself? She had no idea. "I guess we'll find out," she muttered to herself as Deavon's hand rose, his five digits spread. Slowly, he closed one over followed by another in a countdown. At three, she decided to worry about Baird after they had finished their mission and gripped her sword tighter. At two, she swallowed hard and looked back at Kailyn, reassured to have the young mage there. At one, she shuffled forward as Deavon sprung their trap.

Cursing silently that she couldn't see what was happening past Aldan's big frame, Tesania stepped sideways in time to see Deavon stumbling backward dragging the dead weight of the guard. "That was fast," she said when he reached their cover.

"He didn't put up a fight," Deavon informed her as he began looping a rope around the man's arms. "Let's hope the other guard is just as easy."

"Is he coming?" Tesania asked Aldan who now stood at the corner of the wall.

"I'll see," the big ranger replied before leaning out and peering toward the second guard. "I can't see—"

"Stand where you are," the guards staccato command came.

Aldan's hands came slowly up. "Relax, friend," he said easily as if he were talking to an acquaintance at a bar.

"I'm not your friend," the guard's suspicious voice replied. "Now step away from the wall. All of you."

Tesania looked quickly to Deavon who motioned for her to do what the man demanded. Not at all sure that it was a good idea to leave their cover, she did as he said and stepped to Aldan's side. Ten or so feet away stood the second guard, crossbow drawn and set wavering between Aldan and herself and then Kailyn as she stepped forward as well. "We mean you no harm," she said, cringing at her own lie.

Stepping sideways, the guard made his way around them until he could see into the murky darkness where the other guard lay unconscious. "All of you," he said as the point of his crossbow travelled to Deavon's chest. "Now."

As Deavon stood and raised his arms, the guard swiftly moved his aim to Kailyn and commanded, "Drop the staff," before motioning to Tesania's sword with the point of the arrow. "And the sword too."

Reluctantly, Tesania crouched and laid her sword on the ground as Kailyn laid her staff down nearby. "It's not vibrating," she whispered to Deavon as she straightened. "He won't hurt us."

"Your weapons," the guard said motioning to Aldan and Deavon.

Deavon nodded to Aldan before unbuckling his own sword belt. "We mean you no harm," he said echoing Tesania's words. "We just want to talk to Lord Dalgliesh," he added while holding the sword out and then dropping it.

"In the middle of the night?" the guard scoffed as he leant and looked past Deavon at his fellow guard. "Did you mean him no harm too?"

"That was unfortun—" Deavon began as he looked back at the inert body.

"Save it," the guard cut him off. "You can tell it to the capt'n."

"Yes," Deavon agreed. "To your captain."

"Move," the guard said while circling to their rear. "Toward the gate. And don't try anything. I'm not afraid to shoot."

"Yes he is," Tesania whispered. "He's bluffing."

"Do as he says," Deavon whispered back. "We don't know that for sure."

"But my sword," Tesania protested as she looked down at the lifeless blade of her forefathers' weapon.

"It's not infallible, Tes," Deavon insisted as he gripped her arm and guided her after Kailyn who had already started toward the gate.

"But," Tesania protested again. "I can't just leave it . . . . What if the Tiadath Mage—" Mid sentence she swung around as a sickening thud echoed through the night. Watching as the guard's arrow tip slowly sank toward the turf, she looked at his face. Barely visibly in the moonlit darkness were his eyes, dazed and blank as he sank to his knees and collapsed forward, head smacking into the ground. "How . . . ?"she whispered as her eyes travelled up past the scuffed brown boots behind the unconscious man to the grinning face of Baird.

"It looked like you needed some help," he said while slapping the end of a shattered branch into his hand.

"You didn't kill him?" Tesania asked worry rushing through her as she stepped forward and knelt to inspect the man, feeling for a pulse in his neck whilst avoiding the blood oozing from the gash in the back of his skull.

"He'll live," Baird assured her.

Satisfied, as she felt the blood pulsating in the man's veins, Tesania stood. "Where were you?"

"In the trees," Baird replied motioning into the darkness.

"Why didn't you stay with us?"

The spy's eyes narrowed as she asked the question. "I scouted around the far side." Shrugging, he added, "I do things my own way."

"Even though we expected you to be with us?"

Shrugging again, Baird replied as he motioned to the guard at his feet, "The way things were going . . . perhaps it was lucky that I did."

"He's right, Tes," Deavon interrupted as he walked toward them and handed Tesania her sword which he had recovered along with his own. Nodding to Aldan, he said, "Tie him up and move him around the corner with the other one." As Aldan pulled rope from his belt and knelt, Deavon looked toward the gate. "Let's hope Giddy and the others are having a better time of it than we were."

***

"Not much more I can do for him," Rhys conceded as he stood and stretched his back. "They'll have to look after him themselves once we leave."

"At least he won't be raising any alarms," Giddy replied as she shoved herself off her captive's shoulder and stood as well. "The others will be at the gate by now. We'd better head out."

With one more regretful glance at the moaning guard on the floor, Rhys nodded and started for the door. Pausing, he gently pulled it open and peered into the darkness. Satisfied that no other guards were in the vicinity, he motioned the two soldiers to follow and slipped out. "Straight to the gate," he whispered. "Watch for wandering guards."

As his companions muttered agreement, Rhys started in the direction of the main gate. Moving silently from building to building, he soon came to the open courtyard lying just inside the entry to the compound. Glancing cautiously around the corner, he muttered, "One guard sitting by the gate. Seems to be asleep."

"Tch, tch," Giddy admonished almost inaudibly. "His captain will give him a mouthful in the morning."

"I can't see any others," Rhys advised as he leant farther out from his hiding place."

"Might be walkers though," Raim suggested. "Giddy and I will watch the paths leading in while you take care of him."

"Deal," Rhys replied as he vanished around the corner.

"Try not to hurt this one," Giddy called softly after him to Raim's mirth. "I'll go right; you take the left," she said more seriously.

Rhys crept across the small clearing under the gate. The guard didn't stir as he approached, making him surer of his assumption he was asleep. Looking about quickly to ensure no other guards overlooked the area, he drew his knife and flipped it in his hand, blade facing back, blunt end protruding from his hand. Stepping lightly, he made his way to the sleeping man's side. "Sorry," he whispered as he raised his hand and cannoned it down on the side of the guard's head. Not waking, the man grunted before slumping forward and slithering to the ground.

Pulling a length of rope from his belt, the little thief quickly tied the man's hands followed by a gag across his mouth. Satisfied that the threat was nullified, he glanced over at Giddy and Raim. Both faced away from him, eyes intently looking into the darkness beyond. Stepping a few feet away, he reached out and grasped the timber gate bolt and lifted it from its cradles. Gently pulling the gate, he held his breath for a moment wondering if it would creak and announce his presence to the whole compound. To his relief it swung easily on hinges and left the cool night soundless. Squinting through the gap, he grinned and pulled the gate farther open when he saw Aldan's big frame on the other side. "Welcome," he said, voice low as he bowed and swept his arm toward the inner compound.

***

"You took your time," Aldan grunted as he walked past and moved toward Giddy.

"Yes . . . well . . . we had a little trouble."

"Trouble?" Tesania asked as she entered the compound.

"One of the guards was hurt," Rhys admitted. "It was an accident."

"How bad?" Deavon asked before Tesania could say anything.

"He fell into a fire. Burned him pretty badly."

"Where is he now?"

"Guardroom," Rhys replied motioning into the darkness.

"Can we help him?"

"I made him as comfortable as I could," Rhys replied spreading his hands. "There wasn't much I could do."

Nodding, Deavon said, "They'll have to look after him themselves."

"But he'll be in pain" Tesania protested her eyes searching Deavon's.

"We have to move on," Deavon insisted. "Dalgliesh is the priority."

"He's right," Baird said from the shadows. "The longer we're here, the more chance there is of being caught."

"He's as comfortable as I could make him," Rhys assured her. "What more can we do?"

"Kailyn," Tesania said. When the girl looked at her, she asked, "You have your potions?"

"I do."

"Then at least we can relieve some of his pain."

"Later," Deavon insisted. "Right now, we go after Dalgliesh."

Frowning as she considered his words, Tesania looked from the ranger to Kailyn and then toward Lord Dalgliesh's home. She knew they were right, that stopping the attacks on her own people took precedent over one mercenary guard. Still, it bothered her that he was lying there in pain and they were just going to simply leave him. Shaking her head to clear it, she looked to Deavon, "You're right," she whispered.

Smiling at her sympathetically, Deavon nodded before motioning the others over. Once they were gathered, he said, "We need to move fast." When the others nodded and muttered their agreement, he went on, "Right. Same teams as before. Giddy, you clear the guard house to the south. We'll take the wandering guards and clear the way to Dalgliesh's manor."After a brief pause, he asked, "Agreed?"

"Agreed," Giddy muttered as she began to move off.

"We'll meet you at the manor," he whispered after her as she disappeared into the night.

***

Lord Dalgliesh's whitewashed manor house glowed in the moonlit night. Marble pillars reached high into the air at the top of sprawling stairs, their thick girth supporting a roof protecting the carved wooden entry doors. Tesania looked up at the enormity of it. It reminded her of the entryway to her own opulent home. Considering it was once Lord Dalgliesh's family home, she thought she shouldn't be surprised by the resemblance. Drawing her thoughts back to the situation, she looked to Deavon and asked, "Do we knock?"

Shrugging, Deavon grinned at her. "It's as good a plan as any."

"Will they answer?"

"I should think so. They wouldn't be expecting uninvited guests at this time of night."

"I guess not."

"Would they expect a guard to knock though? Won't it be out of the ordinary?"

"I've no idea," Deavon admitted. "I can't see they would be expecting anything though."

"They would feel fairly secure, I should think," Baird said. "I can't see any reason for them not to answer."

"So we knock and say what?" Deavon asked.

"Do we need to say anything?" Aldan responded. "Knock and then force our way through once they unlock the door."

"That might work," Deavon said dubiously. "But I would rather be prepared if the question is asked.

"An urgent message?" Baird suggested. "Pretend to be a messenger from the king."

"Not a bad plan," Deavon replied as Giddy and the others approached through the darkness. "All clear?" he asked the soldier.

"Trussed and ready for the fire," Giddy replied grinning at Rhys' rolling eyes.

"Alright,' Deavon said, ignoring her. "You and Raim stay out here as backup. Watch for wandering guards or shift changes."

"Yes, boss."

"If we need you, we'll call," he instructed. "Otherwise, stay put."

"Got it."

"Rhys, you're with us . . . Kailyn?"

"Yes?" the young mage asked, voice nervous as she wrung her hands around her staff.

"The mage could be in there," Deavon advised her. "Are you ready for that?" When the girl nodded almost imperceptibly, he said, "You need to be ready. Understand?"

"Yes," Kailyn muttered unconvincingly.

"Good," Deavon said as he turned to the others. "We knock; tell them we have an urgent message, then storm in once the door is unlocked." Looking from one to another he waited for their nods of understanding. "There shouldn't be too many people awake at this hour. Just night staff. We silence them and then search room to room . . . Got it?" When no questions came, he went on, "This Tiadath Mage could be deadly. Everyone be on your guard. Support Kailyn as best you can."

"I'll take care of him if he's here," Tesania said softly gripping her sword harder.

"We do it as a team," Deavon insisted. "If you have an opening, take it. Otherwise, support the others." As Tesania reluctantly nodded, he said to the group, "No harm is to come to Dalgliesh or his family. Understand?"

Tesania didn't care what happened to Lord Dalgliesh. As far as she was concerned he deserved everything that came his way. But she was aware of the promise she had made to the Aliagan King and so nodded agreement. The mage, though, was another matter entirely. If she had the chance to kill him, she would take it. Breathing in a long breath as Deavon said, "Let's go," she ascended the stairs, eyes fixed firmly on the carved wooden doors.

26 - Dalgliesh's Manor

Tesania cringed as three knocks rang out into the still night air, the sharp, staccato sound echoing through the empty compound.

"Sorry," Baird said sheepishly as he looked about.

"Don't worry about it," Deavon said motioning the spy's attention back to the door as the sound of bare feet slapping on the floor inside grew louder. "They're coming."

"What is it?" a young woman's muffled voice drifted through the heavy doors.

"An urgent message," Baird called as he leant closer to the door in an obvious attempt to curb the loudness of his voice.

"At this time of night?"

"My apologies. It is an urgent message from the king." Baird said. "It is imperative that Lord Dalgliesh receives it immediately."

"My Lord is not here," the woman said.

Frowning, Baird turned to the others and shrugged.

"Ask her to let us in anyway," Deavon whispered.

"For what reason?"

"I don't know," Deavon snapped before saying more thoughtfully. "She'll be a maid. Make something up."

As Baird looked blankly at the ranger, Rhys stepped forward and spoke to the door. "Perhaps you could let my companion and I in for a few moments. It's frightfully cold out here tonight."

"I couldn't," the woman replied.

"We won't hurt you lass . . . Do you think the guards would have let us come this far if we meant you harm?"

"Well . . ." the maid said thoughtfully. ". . . I guess not. But . . . I will get in frightful trouble if I open the door for you, seeing as My Lord isn't here."

"We just ask a few minutes in by a warm fire," Rhys pressed. "Perhaps a few morsels of food before we start the cold ride back to the capital." When the woman stayed quiet for a moment, he added, "There'll be a coin in it for you if you'd be so kind as to offer us a few moments of succor."

A few moments passed as the maid seemingly weighed up the offer before the scratch of a lifting latch echoed through the door. "Only for a few momen—" the woman said as the door sung inward and her young face came into view, her voice stopping suddenly as her eyes darted from one of the group on her doorstop to the next before falling to their weapons. "What is the m—?"

"Sh," Rhys said as he pressed forward and snatched the girl's arm before spinning her around and clamping his hand over her mouth. "We mean you no harm," he said into her ear as he dragged her back into the manor. "Be quiet now . . . you hear."

Tesania stepped into the extravagantly furnished hallway as Deavon and the others moved quickly forward and peered into the doorways along the hall. "He won't hurt you," she assured the girl who starred back at her, eyes wide with terror. "We mean you no harm." As the maid's eyes darted over the party once more, the fear emanating from them not abating, Tesania moved closer and placed a calming hand on her forearm. "Be calm," she said voice almost a whisper. "We will be gone soon. You're safe."

"In here," Deavon said, motioning to a doorway.

Tesania followed as Rhys guided the girl into the room. It appeared to be Dalgliesh's drawing room with plush leather chairs surrounding a low table in the middle of the room. Nodding at a chair at the far end of the room, she followed as Rhys forced the maid over to it. "We won't hurt you," she promised the girl. "If you promise to be quiet." When the maid's eyes looked back at her with the same terror, she stepped closer. "I understand why you're afraid. Believe me, I would be too if I were in your situation." As the girl's eyes fixed on her own, Tesania went on. "We came to see Lord Dalgliesh. You said he isn't here?"

Slowly the maid shook her head before saying something that Tesania couldn't understand behind the thief's hand. "Release her," Tesania instructed.

"Tes," Deavon warned. "We don't know if there are guards. She might alert them."

Frowning at him, Tesania turned her attention back to the girl. "You won't . . . will you? Yell out I mean?"

Slowly, the maid shook her head, Rhys' hand following the motion.

"You promise?" Tesania asked. "Because if you do . . . I can't control what happens after that." She hated saying this to the scared girl in front of her, but she knew they needed to maintain their secrecy. "He's going to release your mouth now," she said while nodding at Rhys. "We only want to ask you a few questions and then we will let you be . . . . Understand?" As the maid's face became uncovered she looked about the room once more, fear still radiating from her eyes as she focused once more on Tesania.

"I understand," she said, voice trembling.

"Good girl," Tesania said unable to help herself from talking to the young maid like she was one of her own staff. "What's your name?"

"Cinna," the girl replied slowly.

Tesania nodded before saying, "Now, Cinna; you said Lord Dalgliesh isn't home?"

"N . . . no," the girl stuttered. "He went away."

"When?"

"A few weeks ago."

Tesania's head flicked around to Deavon who stood guarding the door. "Weeks," she muttered before turning back to the maid. "Where did he go?"

The blank look on the girl's face told Tesania all she needed to know. "I guess you wouldn't know," she said almost apologetically. As the maid nodded in agreement, Tesania wracked her mind before asking suddenly, "And the mage?"

"Mage?"

"The Tiadath mage?" When Cinna looked at her blankly, Tesania then said, "A strange looking man . . . dressed in mages robes. He would have looked very different from any other mage you have ever seen."

"Oh, him," the maid said. "He left many weeks ago."

"Many weeks?" Tesania gasped as Kailyn let out a sigh relief and visibly relaxed her grip on her staff.

"Yes. He stayed here for a few weeks and then left."

"And you haven't seen him since?" Rhys asked from behind the maid, causing her to jump."

"No . . . ." she said while shuffling sideways and turning so she could see him.

Scowling, Tesania asked, "Where did he come from?"

Reluctantly the girl dragged her eyes away from Rhys and looked blankly at Tesania. "I don't know," she said apologetically. "I'm just a maid."

"I know," Tesania consoled her. "You've been very good." Stepping backward, she sank down into a plush chair, her fingers running along the arm as she considered what the maid had said. Eventually, she looked toward Deavon. "What now?" she asked voice small as she realized their chances of finding and stopping the mage had taken a serious blow. "How can we stop him now?" she asked weakly. "There's no one here who can tell us where he comes from."

"Lady Caitrio—" the maid began before gasping and stopping herself, hand coming quickly to her mouth.

"Caitriona's here?" Tesania asked hope rising once more. "Is she?" she demanded. "Is Caitriona here?"

"Yes . . . ." the maid replied voice trailing off.

"Upstairs," Tesania said to Deavon unable to control her voice. "She'll be asleep." Deavon frowned at her. "She might know something!" Tesania insisted.

"She may know nothing either," Deavon insisted.

"Lord Dalgliesh isn't here," Tesania said adamantly. "She might be our only chance to find the mage."

Deavon grunted. "She's a spoilt brat."

"But she might know . . . we have to at least try."

"If we must," Deavon replied in a disgruntled voice.

Tesania ignored his distaste for the lady of the house and looked back at the maid. "You've been very helpful," she said to the girl. When Cinna couldn't help but smile at her, she asked, "How many guards are in the house?"

"Guards," the maid asked, confused. "There aren't any guards in the house. Only us maids and the butler."

"Thank you," Tesania said smiling as the girl admonished herself for giving up more information. "I promise you, we will not harm any of them." When the maid's frown eased with relief, she asked, "And Caitriona?"

"Upstairs, second door on the right."

"Is anybody else upstairs? Guests, family?"

"No. Only Lady Caitriona."

"Thank you," Tesania said while motioning toward the thief. "You will need to stay here with, Rhys." When the girl frowned and stepped away, Tesania added. "He won't hurt you . . . . As long as you behave. Understand."

"I understand," the maid said as she moved farther and positioned a chair between herself and the little thief.

"Rhys?" Tesania asked. "You understand?"

"I wish her no harm," he replied simply. "But perhaps we should gag her?"

"Why?" Cinna asked sharply as she spun to Tesania. "You said he wouldn't hurt me."

"And I won't," the thief promised. "And that's exactly why I suggested it."

"What do you mean?" Tesania asked.

"Think about it," the thief said as he motioned toward the maid. "The others will be bound and gagged when you bring them in?"

"I see," Tesania said as she understood his meaning. Turning to Cinna, she said in a soft voice. "He's right." When Cinna looked at her blankly, she explained, "When the other maids are brought in here, they'll be bound and gagged."

"So?"

"So . . . you won't be. You'll be standing here free to move and speak."

"So?" the girl asked again frowning in confusion.

Sighing, Rhys said, "Do you want them to think you're working with us? That you let us in and told us everything we needed to know?"

The realization of what they were saying slowly dawned over Cinna's face as the frown slowly disappeared and fear crept back into her eyes. "They wouldn't," she gasped.

"With you unbound," Rhys assured her. "They most definitely would."

"But I didn't . . . ."

"They don't know that."

"It might be best if we tie you up," Tesania interrupted. "I don't wish any trouble for you once we leave."

"I won't tie the knots tightly," Rhys assured the frightened girl as he stepped toward her and drew a length of rope from his belt. "It'll be just for show."

"It's for the best," Tesania said smiling at the girl in an attempt to calm her. "You'll be alright. I promise."

Reluctantly, Cinna allowed Rhys to slip behind her offering no resistance as he pulled her hands back. "Good girl," he muttered as he began to tie his knot.

Satisfied that the maid would co-operate, Tesania rose and walked to Deavon. "We need to capture Caitriona."

Deavon scowled at the mention of the obnoxious girl who had hunted him relentlessly in the Eldanal Royal court. He obviously had no desire to see her again. But he just as obviously knew that he must. Adopting his usual stoic face, he said, "We go room by room. I want everyone in the manor accounted for before we go after Caitriona." When they all nodded, he added, "Staff quarters first. They'll be on this floor at the back." Moving off, he called back softly, "Room by room. Stay together."

***

Rounding up the rest of the household staff proved simple. Most were dazed and still half asleep as Deavon and Aldan entered their rooms and slipped gags over their mouths. Within ten minutes they had entered every room on the ground floor and herded their captives to the drawing room where they stood despondently with the maid who had first let them in the door.

"Co-operate," Deavon said to the gathered household staff as he massaged the pommel of his sword, "And no harm will come to you. Understand?" When none of the staff challenged him, he nodded turned to the others. "Baird, Rhys, Aldan; you stay here while Tesania, Kailyn and I go and pay Her Ladyship a visit."

27 - Lady Caitriona

Tesania counted twenty two steps as she ascended toward the first floor of Lord Dalgliesh's manor. She had mixed feelings as she climbed closer to the woman who had embarrassed her on the dance floor all those years ago. She knew the girl was just like her father; Lord Dalgliesh, ambitious and cunning, and that she would stop at nothing to get what she wanted. After all, she had convinced her father to send his ship, the Lady Roslyn, to sink the vessel she and Deavon sailed upon in their quest to bring down Trannyth. She had had little to do with the Dalgliesh girl apart from that one meeting in the king's ballroom. Still, it bothered her to now be creeping toward her bedroom and she worried about what feelings the coming meeting might bring forth in Deavon. She wondered, as the big ranger stepped off the last step and began to walk along the candlelit hallway, if Caitriona would still be in love with him after all these years. Would she even remember him? Shrugging as she fell in behind him, she cast the thoughts from her mind and stood against the wall next to the first door on the right.

"Ready?" Deavon asked as he reached for the handle.

Nodding, Tesania grasped the hilt of her sword and raised the blade as Deavon shoved the door open. Surging in, they found the room empty as Cinna had said it would be.

"Right," Deavon whispered as he left the room. "We clear the rest, and then onto Caitriona's room."

"I don't think there's any danger here," Tesania whispered back as she peered at her silent, inanimate sword in the soft candle light. "My sword isn't vibrating."

"Still," Deavon said. "I'd rather be sure."

Door by door, they cleared each room along the hallway. True to the maid's word there were no other occupants on the floor. Satisfied, Deavon gathered them before the last unopened door and said in a low voice. "Kailyn, you stay in the hallway. Let us know if anyone approaches." When the mage nodded he said to Tesania, "Gently now. She's just a girl."

"Just a girl?" Tesania gasped. "She's a nasty pi—"

"You know what I mean," Deavon interrupted. "She'll be unarmed. We don't need to use force."

"She's a serpent," Tesania hissed vehemently. "Don't give her a chance to strike."

"I know, Tes," Deavon sighed, brow creasing. "Just let me do the talking."

Tesania knew Deavon could handle himself against Caitriona, but it worried her that the woman who had for so long vied to win the ranger's favor was now about to re-enter his life. Admonishing herself for letting the thoughts distract her, she shook her head and said, "Let's get it over with."

Deavon smiled down at her. She could tell he guessed her thoughts. "It'll be alright, Tes," he assured her. "I've handled her many times before."

"I know," Tesania said as she gripped her lifeless sword. "Still . . . I'll be ready."

Grinning at her this time, Deavon reached for the handle and raised his other hand, collapsing three fingers one by one as he counted down and then pushed the door open.

Darkness greeted them as they entered the room. Heavy curtains were drawn across the windows blocking even the smallest amount of moonlight from the room. "Candle," Deavon whispered back to Kailyn. When the mage returned with a small, flickering candle on a gold leaf candle holder, Deavon turned and held it high. The room came into dim view in the candles wane light. Plush chairs sat along one wall while the entire north-eastern corner was taken up by an elaborately carved dressing table, a mirror reaching toward the ceiling. In the middle of the room stood an enormous four posted bed with heavy, embroidered drapes hanging down on all sides, the soft breathing of Caitriona emanating from the depths of darkness. Stepping forward, he grasped a curtain on the side of the bed and drew it back.

Caitriona's eyes flickered open as the candlelight invaded her sleeping area. Disorientated at being woken at this time of the night, she blinked and rubbed at her eyes while mumbling, "What is it?"

"It's me, Caitriona," Deavon announced.

Head drifting up and turning to the ranger, still half asleep, Caitriona muttered, "Deavon?" as a dreamy smile crept over her lips and she reached her arms toward him. "I knew you'd come for me one day, my darling."

Stepping forward into the light, Tesania snapped, "He's not here for you!"

"You," Caitriona exclaimed her sleepiness disappearing in an instant as Tesania's sword burst into shivering life. "What are you doing here," she demanded eyes flicking from Tesania's face to the sword. "Get out! Do you hear me?" she ranted gesticulating toward the door. "How dare you come into my home and threaten me! Do you know who I am?" she challenged as she stood and stepped uneasily toward the far side of the bed.

"I do," Tesania replied. "You are a nasty little—"

"Tes," Deavon interrupted while reaching out and pushing her sword hand down.

"Well she is."

"Not now," Deavon warned. As Tesania frowned at him, he turned his attention back to Caitriona. "We need information."

"And you just barge into my room in the middle of the night?" Caitriona demanded as she pulled one of the bed curtains across her nightgown. "Where are my staff?"

"They're safe," Deavon assured her. "We have a few questions to ask you," he continued.

Caitriona sneered toward Tesania. "I have nothing to say to her," she growled before looking back at Deavon, her cold demeanor changing in an instant to warmth. "But you, my love. We can still be together. It isn't too late. Father would be thril—"

"That isn't going to happen," Tesania said guffawing.

"Why?" Caitriona demanded the sneer on her face returning. "Because of you?" she asked. "You think you're good enough for him . . . hmm . . . ? You're just a village girl!"

"Enough," Deavon roared, face flushing red. "We didn't come here to listen to your insults. Nor did I come here to carry you away." As the woman shrank away from him, he calmed himself and went on, "We are here for information about the attacks on the king's farms."

"And hers," Caitriona sneered.

"So you know about the attacks?" Tesania asked hope rising as she asked quickly, "Where can we find him?"

"Him?"

"The mage?"

"I'll tell you nothing," Caitriona blurted, stepping closer to the far side of the bed and pulling the curtain closer to herself. "Especially you!" she screamed.

"Tes," Deavon said, his face flaring with hues of orange from the fire flickering inside the blade of her sword. "Let me speak to her." As Tesania nodded hesitantly and stepped a few feet away, he said to Caitriona, "We know that your father has summoned a mage from Tiadath; and that he is paying him to attack Tesania and our king."

"Yes," Caitriona agreed, nodding while glaring at Tesania. "Father summoned him," she went on. "But it was me who organized his attacks."

"Why!?" Tesania exclaimed. "What did my people do to you!?"

"Your people . . . ?" Caitriona exploded anger crashing over her face. ". . . your people . . . ? Everything you own was my Father's . . . was mine!" Calming as Tesania stared at her; she said flatly, "You stole everything I had." Turning to Deavon, eyes saddening, she reached for him and added, "Everything I ever wanted."

"I was never yours," Deavon said emptily as he drew away from her like he would from a venomous snake. "That was all in your own mind."

"It wasn't," Caitriona said tiny voice pleading. "You loved me . . . you wanted me . . . . Until . . . until this dirty farm girl came and took you . . . took everything away!"

Tesania watched the woman as she sank to her knees, tears welling in her eyes as she stared incredulously into Deavon's eyes. She felt no remorse for her, no pity. All she felt was animosity and disbelief that the woman could be so deluded. "I took nothing," she said slowly. "The king removed your father's holdings. Not I."

"The king!" Caitriona cried, her distraught voice echoing from the vaulted ceiling. "The king is a fool . . . . He banished my father . . . banished me . . . ! For you . . . ! He sent his loyal subjects into exile for a filthy, disgusting, farm girl."

"Not because of me . . . . Because of your father's actions."

"Actions?" Caitriona shrieked. "For trying to protect the very kingdom he was banished from."

"He wasn't protecting the kingdom at all," Tesania said sadly shaking her head. "He was trying to murder me."

"I wish he'd succeeded," Caitriona hissed.

Shaking her head once more, Tesania looked up at Deavon. "This is getting us nowhere."

Nodding, Deavon looked back to Caitriona. "How long will this mage keep attacking?"

"Until the money father gave him runs out."

"How long?"

"Months," Caitriona replied, an insane grin spreading across her face. "Months; you hear me? Months of pain for your farm girl here. Months of dying and destruction." Cackling insanely, Caitriona then exclaimed, "And then we'll pay him to do more!"

Tesania watched the woman in horror. She obviously bordered on insanity. "You can't," she eventually said in almost a whisper. "Innocent people are dying."

"Let them die. What are they to me?"

"Does that matter?" Tesania asked incredulously. "They're innocent people."

"So!?"

"Tes," Deavon interrupted, holding his hand up to her before turning his attention to Caitriona. "Where is your father?"

"Eldanal."

Frowning in confusion, Deavon asked, "Eldanal? How can he be in Eldanal? He's been banished."

Caitriona laughed aloud. "My father does what he wishes . . . where he wishes. And there's nothing you or your king can do about it."

Obviously deciding that he wouldn't get a straight answer, Deavon asked, "When will he be back?"

Shrugging, Caitriona replied, shoulders slumping despondently, "Weeks . . . months. I don't know. He's doing business. That's all he cares about."

"We can't wait that long," Tesania said to Deavon, worry straining her voice. "We need to stop the attacks now."

"You won't stop Sergh," Caitriona said cackling again, eyes alight. "He'll continue until you're all destroyed."

"Sergh?" Tesania asked quickly. "Is that his name?" When Caitriona realized her mistake, she fell quiet. "That's it, isn't it? A Tiadath mage named Sergh." Looking up at Deavon, Tesania felt excitement at finally having new information. "We know who he is now, at least," she said, frowning as the enormity of actually finding him dawned on her. Looking back at Caitriona, she asked, "How do you contact him?"

"I'm not telling you anything more," the woman announced adamantly, lips pouting like a spoilt child.

"Is it enough?" Tesania asked Deavon.

Scanning the young woman on the bed in front of him, Deavon eventually said, "We know the mage is in a land called Tiadath, and we know his name."

"But is it enough?"

"I think it's all we'll get," he conceded, shrugging. "But at least it's more than we had."

Nodding as a sudden thought came to her, she suggested, while cringing at her own words, "Take her with us?"

"To what end?"

"Make her show us where he lives."

"How would I know where he lives?" Caitriona scoffed laughing hysterically.

"You hired him."

"Father hired him," Caitriona corrected.

Frowning, Tesania considered the woman's words. Eventually, she asked, "You have no idea where he comes from? Where Tiadath is?"

"I wouldn't tell you if I did," Caitriona cried as she scrambled to the top of the bed, her wild, tousled hair adding to Tesania's thoughts that she might be quite mad.

"People are dying!" Tesania exclaimed. "Because of you!"

"They deserve it!"

"Deserve it . . ." Tesania repeated in exasperation. ". . . deserve it . . . . How can you even begin to say—?"

"It's no use, Tes," Deavon interrupted, reaching out and touching her arm. "I believe that she doesn't know where the mage comes from. Besides," he added while shaking his head despondently, "she wouldn't help us; even if she could."

"True," Tesania agreed. She knew by the look in Caitriona's eyes that she would never tell them exactly where this Sergh was or how to find him. Frowning as she shook her head at the sad woman on the bed, she asked, "What next?"

"We find Tiadath and then Sergh."

"Unastine?"

"I think so," Deavon replied thoughtfully as Baird's head appeared at the door. "The monks should have something that mentions it."

"Time to move out," the spy warned. "We need to be well clear by dawn."

"We'll be down in a minute," Deavon replied, waving Baird away before turning back to Caitriona. "What you have done is evil, Caitriona. Evil beyond words." As the young woman looked up at him, eyes wide like a doe caught in front of his bow, lips trembling as she stared at her heart's desire, a desire she could never fulfill, he went on. "You can't have everything you want in life simply because your father has money. You can't just walk over other people regardless of their feelings or desires."

"But—"

"You cannot . . . can never have the quality of this woman you call a farm girl," he went on adamantly while nodding toward Tesania. As Caitriona whimpered up at him he turned and started for the door saying over his shoulder, "And you will never have me."

"No!" Caitriona cried after him, reaching out, hands grasping air. "Deavon . . . . Stay with me . . . . Deavon . . . . Don't leave me again!" As the big ranger went through the door, she leapt from the bed and ran after him. "I will wait for you," she called into the hallway. "I will wait here for you and someday we shall reunite our love!"

Pushing past her into the hallway, Tesania laughed and said, "Don't hold your breath."

"You dirty—"

Stepping closer, Tesania moved to within inches of the other woman's face. "We will stop this mage of yours," she snarled. "And then," she added while raising her sword blade to the girl's ear, "I'll be back for you."

Stumbling backward into her room, eyes wide, Caitriona cried, "You wouldn't!"

"Wouldn't I?" Tesania muttered as she slammed the door shut, motioned to Kailyn to follow, and hurried after Deavon.

Deavon strode down the stairs two at a time causing Tesania and Kailyn to have to rush to catch him at the drawing room. Pausing to catch her breath, Tesania perused the room. Cinna sat on the floor with three other young maids, her legs crossed, while the older maids and the butler sat bound in the various chairs in the room.

Rhys leant against the far wall tapping a dagger into his palm. "Anything?" he asked curiously pushing forward and walking toward the doorway.

"A few bits of information," Tesania replied. "We can cover it later." When Rhys nodded his understanding she motioned toward the front door of the manor.

Understanding her meaning, Rhys turned to the staff. "As promised, you are unharmed," he said. When the butler spoke in a muffled voice, Rhys informed him, "I can't understand you, sir." Walking to Cinna, he then said, "Next time, do as you're asked . . . . You could have got yourself and all of these good people killed," he said while sweeping the room with the dagger's point. As the maid whimpered and pulled back, he added while winking at her, "I like your pluck young lady, but there's a time for it, and today wasn't it." Turning to the others, he said, "That goes for all of you. No bravery, no heroes. We haven't harmed anybody here today. Let's keep it that way." With that he walked past Tesania and the others and headed for the front door.

Tesania looked at Deavon and then Kailyn, shrugged and followed. Catching the little thief on the front steps, she said, as Giddy and the others walked toward them, "Nicely done."

Rhys grinned at her. "I thought so," he said. "Couldn't have her being blamed for letting us in so easy."

"It was a little easy," Tesania said laughing. "Hopefully it'll stay that way."

"It will," Baird said from behind her. "If we move now we'll be well clear by dawn."

"Everyone here?" Deavon asked as he looked around counting. "Right, let's head to the gate. Keep your eyes out for stray guards."

"But the other guard," Tesania said quickly, eyes searching his. "We need to help him."

"Other guard?"

"I think she means the one I managed to singe," Rhys suggested.

"Kailyn can help him," Tesania insisted as Deavon looked at her dubiously. "It's the least we can do."

"We need to move, Tes," he said looking toward the gates.

"I'm aware of that," Tesania replied adamantly. "But it's our fault he's hurt. I won't leave without at least trying to help him."

Deavon frowned at the gate once more and then at Rhys. "Where is he?" he asked obviously deciding that trying to convince Tesania to leave the injured guard unattended would take longer than actually helping him.

"Guard house," Rhys replied pointing into the darkness.

"Lead on," Deavon growled. "Let's make it quick."

Motioning for Kailyn to follow Tesania pursued Rhys between two buildings. "You have your potions?" she asked.

"Yes," the mage replied. "I don't know what I can do for him though."

"Just ease his pain," Tesania suggested. "It's the least we can do."

"I have fermented lungis berries," Kailyn informed her. "That'll have to do."

Tesania smiled at her friend. "That'll do nicely," she said as Rhys stopped at a door and turned to them.

"In here," he said. "There are two of them. The woman is bound."

"Go," Tesania said as she moved her hand to the hilt of her sword, ready in case the woman had managed to escape her bonds. She need not have worried though, as the female guard lay tied and gagged where Giddy had left her. When she heard them enter the room she began shouting expletives, most unrecognizable through her gag. Tesania ignored her and looked toward the burned guard who simply lay there, skin contorting in spasms followed by low moans.

Kailyn knelt by the man, grimacing at the gruesome sight of his charred skin. Rummaging in her bag, she smiled down at him. "I have something," she said pulling forth a small vial of clear liquid. "It will help with your pain. At least until the healers wake in the morning." When the man paid no heed to her words as if he hadn't heard her, she looked to Tesania.

"Go ahead," Tesania urged.

"We need to go," Baird said from the doorway voice agitated.

"I know!" Tesania grunted back at him before returning her attention to Kailyn. "Just a few drops in his mouth."

Kailyn swallowed, unstopped the vial and then moved her hand toward the frightful mess that was the man's face. Carefully, she tapped the vial until three drops had spilt from the end and landed on the guard's swollen tongue. "There," she said, "That should make you feel better."

"Come on," Tesania said to her, reaching for her arm and pulling her up. "That's all we can do. Let's go."

With one last look at the poor man on the floor, Kailyn stood, swaying on her feet.

"Are you alright?" Tesania asked her, concerned as she reached out to support the mage.

Breathing in heavily, Kailyn closed her eyes before muttering, "Yes, I think so. It's just that he's so badly hurt."

"I know," Tesania said soothingly as she glanced down at the mass of burns, regretting it instantly. "You did what you could," she assured the young mage while taking the vial from her hand and re-stopping it before placing it into her bag and then guiding her toward the doorway. "They'll care for him in the morning."

"I know," Kailyn whispered.

"Is she alright?" Deavon asked as they stepped into the night.

"She'll be alright in a few minutes," Tesania said. "It's fairly gruesome in there." Looking at Kailyn who had by now regained some control, she said, "I'll look after her. Let's just get out of here."

Deavon needed no more coaxing than that. Leading the way, he moved to the front gate, pausing to check that the guards were still tied and that no others had arrived. Satisfied, he waved to the others to follow and slipped into the expanse of the Aliagan countryside.

28 - A change of plans

Steam rose from the neck of Tesania's mare in the morning sunlight. She had ridden the horse hard in the last of the darkness, pressing on through dawn as the party put as much distance as they could between themselves and Dalgliesh's guards. She had no idea where they were now, except that the sun rising to her right told her they were heading predominately north. Deavon had called a halt periodically throughout their dash, conferring with Rhys and Baird, changing directions, following roads and then barely visibly tracks to confuse any pursuers. Weary and saddle sore, she eventually called out, "Can we stop soon. I need to get out of this saddle."

"Me too," Kailyn said glumly from behind her.

Rhys turned in his saddle while pointing ahead. "There's a roadhouse ahead. Less than an hour."

"An hour?" Kailyn grumbled.

Laughing, Rhys said, "We can stop here and you can gather firewood and help us set up camp. Or . . ." he said as the young mage groaned and frowned at him, ". . . we ride for another hour and have a hearty breakfast delivered to our table as we sit before a crackling fire and sip warm cider?"

"Warm cider," Giddy voted winking at Kailyn.

Scowling, but obviously not going to argue, the mage nodded and nudged her horse forward.

Tesania agreed on both accounts. She longed to step down from the horse and rest her aching thighs and rump. But the thought of a warm cider in a comfortable chair beckoned her on more strongly. Smiling knowingly at Kailyn as she rode past, Tesania spurred her own horse into motion, falling into the rhythmical sway of the mare's stride as her mind drifted away.

They had been away from their homes for what felt like weeks now. She assumed there had been more attacks since their departure and worried that she was traipsing around Aliaga looking forward to a hot meal when innocent people may be suffering in her name. She knew there was nothing more she could do, that she could proceed no faster. Yet, it had been a gut wrenching blow to not find Lord Dalgliesh, or indeed his hired assassin at the compound. She had hoped to end it then and there. But that had not been the case and now she and the others would need to find another way to put an end to the mage and his dark magic. The enormity of the task they faced sickened her. Not only did they need to find a far off land that seemed to exist only in the past, but they then needed to scour that land and find one single man; a man that she must find at all costs, a man that she must destroy. Lost in her thoughts, she relived Caitriona's vile words over and over. How could the woman be so deluded as to think everything that had happened to her was Tesania's fault; how sick in her own mind must she be?

"Tes," Deavon said gently from beside her, causing her to start. "The roadhouse," he informed her pointing ahead to a mud brick structure a few hundred yards along the road.

"Sorry," Tesania mumbled. "I was lost in thought."

"I saw," Deavon assured her, laughing lightly as he reached over and touched the back of her hand for a moment before adding, "We'll find him."

Smiling briefly at him, Tesania then shook herself to bring herself fully back into the present.

"A warm cider will do you a world of good."

"And some food."

"That too," Deavon agreed as their horses plodded closer to the roadhouse. Looking toward the sky as a gust of wind plucked at his hair, he said, "Storm coming in by the look."

Tesania looked up glumly. "At least we'll be at the roadhouse," she said, shrugging.

"Barn's at the back," Deavon pointed out as he patted his horse's neck. "You'll be grateful of a rest as well I imagine?" he asked the stallion before nodding to Tesania and spurring his mount forward to organize the others.

***

Fried meat wobbled on the end of Deavon's fork as he pointed out for the second time since reaching the roadhouse that they had no idea where the land of Tiadath was. "The monks are our best hope," he said before stuffing the spicy morsel into his mouth.

"I'm not saying they aren't," Baird said between mouthfuls. "But there are other ways."

"Such as?"

"This Tiadath Mage—"

"Sergh."

"Right; Sergh. He travels to Aliaga somehow?"

"Ship," Deavon stated rather than asked.

"Or he flies?" Baird said.

"Impossible," Kailyn interjected. "No one has magic like that."

"Do you know that for certain?" Baird asked the mage. "After all, you didn't think anyone could sink a ship out at sea; until he did."

"Good point," Deavon said as Kailyn looked down at her cider with no answer to the spy's question.

"He can't fly," Tesania said adamantly.

"What makes you so sure?"

"The Tenule chronicles," Tesania replied. "Remember?" she asked Kailyn. "When Rodus forged the sword, the Tiadath mage followed her army on foot."

"Right," Kailyn agreed remembering as she screwed her nose at the spy. "I told you so."

"So you did," the spy agreed winking at the girl. "But that still doesn't discount that he might be able to fly."

"Does it matter?" Aldan asked from the end of the table. "Even if he does fly, we can't."

"Well said," Giddy agreed, cider in hand. "We'll need to sail there . . . . Wherever there is."

"And we're back to the same problem," Deavon sighed as he pushed his empty plate aside and took up his own cider. "That's why the monks are our best hope."

"Let's assume," Baird said nodding to Kailyn, "that he can't fly."

"He can't," Kailyn muttered.

"Then he would have to come by ship."

"That doesn't help."

"It may," the spy said as he rolled his mug between his hands thinking. "Ships have captains and crew, correct?" he asked the girl.

"I guess."

"And crews talk."

"Captains don't though."

"For the right price, they will," Rhys assured her, winking.

"What if he came on a Tiadath ship?" Aldan asked.

"I can promise you that no ship enters Estel Harbor without being identified," the spy assured the big ranger. "If a ship from an unknown country arrived, my people would know about it."

"Even I would know about it," Rhys added as he sat forward and peered down the table at Baird. "Estiel?" he asked.

Baird considered his words as he took a sip from his mug and swirled it in his mouth before swallowing. "Possibly," he answered eventually.

"Why Estiel?" Giddy asked as rain began to patter onto the roadhouse's roof. "Why's that any different to Estom."

"Oh, it's very different," Rhys said laughing aloud. "Very, very, different," he assured her.

"In what way?"

"Where do I begin . . . ?" the thief asked.

"A bit seedy?" Raim asked.

"A lot seedy," Rhys informed him. "It's not a place for the gentry. Let's put it that way."

"And you think you can find the ship the Tiadath mage came on?" Kailyn asked.

"Probably not," the little thief conceded. "That would be a long shot, at best."

"But," Baird said thoughtfully. "The ships and their captains you'll find there don't ply the usual . . . shall we say . . . trade routes."

"Pirates?" Raim asked.

"I doubt it," Baird replied evenly. "Piracy isn't a problem in these waters."

"Smugglers?"

"You're getting warmer," Baird replied.

"Smuggling is just the tip of it," Rhys said laughing again. "We don't have time to list the things Estiel plays host to."

"I don't think I want to know," Kailyn said in disgust. "Why doesn't your king take care of it?" she then asked Baird curiously.

"That's a difficult question," the spy answered slowly. "Let's just say, there will always be a place like Estiel. If it's shut down, it will just pop up somewhere else. Better to keep some things where they can at least be seen."

"And for when the Lords and Ladies want some dirty work done," Rhys interjected grinning at the spy.

"Yes . . . well. Sometimes things are better left unsaid."

Motioning them all to silence as a waitress approached, Deavon ordered another round of ciders and then said as she left with an overloaded tray of empty plates, "It's a long shot, at best."

"Possibly," Baird conceded. "But it's a chance at least. Those ships go to many places that the king's ships do not. Perhaps one of them may have the information we require."

"Do we have time for it?" Tesania asked concerned. "It'll take days, maybe even weeks. What if there's no one there who can tell us where Tiadath is?"

"Or won't tell us, even if they do know?" Raim added.

"They'll tell us," Rhys assured them as he jangled his coin pouch in his jacket pocket. "If they know, that is."

"Exactly," Tesania said. "If they know." Turning to Deavon, she said, "We can't waste weeks hoping they 'may' know something."

"The monks mightn't know anything either," Aldan suggested. "That's a long shot too."

Tesania sat in confusion for what seemed an eternity as the others stared at her. Eventually, she said, "It seems either way is a long shot."

"Do both," Aldan suggested.

"We don't have time."

"Split up," the ranger said. "Some go to Unastine and the monks, the others to Estiel."

Tesania beamed at Aldan. "Sometimes," she said to his quickly reddening face, "You're a genius."

"Only sometimes?" the ranger asked head bowed, feigning embarrassment.

"Rarely," Giddy assured him.

"Enough from you," the ranger growled before looking to Deavon. "What do you think?"

Nodding slowly, Deavon said, "It makes sense. Two irons in the fire at once." Still nodding, he asked Tesania, "Tes?"

"I can't see why not," she replied slowly. "We don't need all of us to go to the monks. Giddy and Raim could ride down to Estiel and ask questions there while we sail to Unastine."

"And me," Rhys said.

"I don't think General Legana will be too happy about continuing to pay your exorbitant fees," Giddy said scowling.

The little thief grinned at her. "It's on the house," he said.

Considering him suspiciously, Giddy said with eyebrow raised, "I wouldn't have thought you'd do anything on the house."

"I'm curious is all," Rhys said a little excited. "It's not every day you find a new country that may be open for my kind of, err, business."

Baird laughed aloud. "Always on the make."

"Not always," the thief assured him. "But I'm a businessman."

"It has nothing to do with you wanting to help us does it?" Raim asked more teasing than serious.

Blushing furiously, Rhys replied, "Actually . . . ." before fading off.

"Who knew," Baird said laughing uproariously. "Friendship before money. Who would've thought it?" As the thief scowled at him, he turned to Giddy. "May I accompany you also?"

Shrugging, Giddy replied, "The more the merrier."

"So it's decided," Deavon said as the rain outside grew heavier. "Giddy, Raim, Rhys and Baird head down to Estiel and ask around about any strange ships or mages." When the four new travelling companions nodded, he then said, "That leaves Tes, Kailyn, Aldan and I to travel to Unastine to see the monks."

29 - Shipping out

Water plumed into the air above the bow of the small fishing boat Tesania huddled in before plummeting down and crashing over her, rivulets cascading down the back of her neck. Dragging the wet hair from her eyes for what seemed like the hundredth time, she groaned as the little boat climbed yet another wave, balancing for a moment, before tipping over the top and rushing to bury its nose in the salty water of Estel harbor once again. Ducking as another wall of water crashed down on her, she turned back to Deavon. "Maybe this wasn't the best idea!"

Clinging onto a wooden seat in the middle of the open hulled boat, knees awash where he knelt on the rough, weather worn planks, Deavon shouted back, "Perhaps not."

"We should have waited until it was calmer."

"The storm could be in for days," Deavon protested. "And no one else would venture out."

Daring to peer over the bow as the tiny boat crested another wave, Tesania identified the King's Ship Swan anchored outside the harbor mouth where it had sat awaiting their return. "She's just off the port bow," she called back to the others while gripping the gunwales as the fishing boat plummeted down the far side of the wave.

They had reached Estel late in the afternoon having split with Giddy and the others at the roadhouse. The ride to the king's stables, where they returned their horses, was cold and miserable with the downpour alternating between light drizzle and driving rain. At first, they had considered returning to the Vine Inn and waiting the storm out where they could be dry and warm. But Deavon had pointed out that they could be stuck for days if the storm didn't pass quickly. Wet through and exhausted, Tesania had agreed to allow him to find a captain who would be willing to brave the agitated sea and take them out to where the Swan lay at anchor.

Cringing when the ranger pointed to the little fishing boat bobbing in the tumultuous swell like a cork, Tesania had eventually, with much trepidation and reluctance, agreed to step aboard. It was a decision she wished, as Kailyn's ashen face disappeared over the side rail once more, the sounds of her retching carrying over the crash of the waves, she hadn't made.

30 - Estos City

Peering ahead, Giddy could just make out the bedraggled tail of Rhys' horse ahead of her in the driving rain. It had a been a miserable journey since parting with Tesania and the others, the rain only ceasing for the odd short period before crashing down once more. Adjusting herself in the saddle, she looked back and was just able to see Raim's mount struggling through the mud behind her. Satisfied that he was still following, she turned her attention back to the sodden ground in front of her. There wasn't a lot she could do; it was hard enough just to see the ground properly in the gloomy light. And so she let the horse pick its own way along the narrow road, only interfering when it wandered too far toward the treacherous verge.

Estos City lay somewhere ahead of them in the rain. Baird had suggested they make their way to the city and hole up for the night before setting off in the morning for the day long ride to Estiel. They were hoping they would get there soon as a lightning bolt crackled through the air nearby followed almost instantly by a booming thunder clap which sent her horse skittering on the wet road. "Whoa," she called urgently pulling at the reins. Nudging the nervous animal forward a little faster, Giddy caught Rhys and fell in beside him. "How much farther?" she shouted over the wind.

"Nearly there," the thief yelled back, water streaming off his face as he turned to her. "Warm fire," he said loudly. "And ale!"

Grinning at the thief, Giddy reined her horse in and waited for Raim. "Not long," she called. "Rhys wondered if you'd want ale," she shouted. "I told him you'd prefer a warm cider."

Regarding her suspiciously for a moment, Raim eventually smiled, teeth barely visible in the horrid weather. "Right now," he called back. "I'd settle for anything."

31 - Unastine

The King's Ship Swan's sails fluttered in the light wind over Unastine's small harbor, the sharp, staccato sound of the flapping canvas rushing along the deck to where Tesania watched the crew scramble along the foot-ropes of the yards. It always amazed her how easy they made it seem considering the height and the thinness of the rope they almost ran along.

"We'll be at anchor soon," Captain Eades informed her from his position by the ship's wheel. "Mister Nylor," he called to the first lieutenant standing by the rail. "I'll have the cutter away as soon as you can."

"Aye, sir," the lieutenant replied as he hurried forward calling commands to the men.

"He's a good man," Deavon said.

"He'll do," the captain replied almost absentmindedly as his attention switched from the sails to the water slipping by below.

"I wonder if Tean's here?" Kailyn said as she stood on tip toes and peered toward the imposing stone monastery on the shore.

"I'd say so," Aldan said, looking toward the shore as if he might pick their old friend out among the dozens of similarly dressed monks. Grinning as he realized the impossibility of the task, he said, "I guess we'll have to wait to find out."

Draping her arm around the young mage and urging her forward, Tesania said, "He might be. He spends most of his time here."

Rolling her eyes, Kailyn said, "I know. You'd think he'd stay at the apartment the king gave him."

"You'd think," Tesania agreed as the splash of the dropping anchor carried along the breeze. "He sees things differently to us though."

"I guess so," Kailyn replied nodding despite the frown of incomprehension that played across her brow.

Laughing, Tesania nudged the mage aside as the cutter swung past them and began to disappear over the side. "Get your bag," she urged. "Maybe you can ask Tean about it if we see him. I'm sure he would be happy to explain his devotion to The Lord," she added laughing harder at the look of dismay on her friend's face.

"That's all we need," Aldan groaned from behind them.

"He's not that bad," Deavon said slapping his colleague on the shoulder.

"Err . . ." Aldan began before saying, ". . . we are talking about the same, Tean . . . aren't we?"

"I guess not," Deavon muttered as his attention moved to the first lieutenant who had opened the side rail and now motioned them forward. "We hope to be back aboard tomorrow," he informed the man.

"Very well," Lieutenant Nylor replied as he held his hand out to Tesania and helped her over the side. "We'll be replenishing our supplies this afternoon and will be ready to sail when you're ready to re-board."

Nodding, Deavon stepped to the rail. "I'll send word as soon as I can."

Tesania waited for him in the small boat. Thankfully, she thought as the cutter bobbed up and down on the slight swell, it wasn't going to be like the arduous journey they had endured just a few days ago. Shifting on her seat as he sat down beside her, she looked toward the wharf. A single monk stood facing them, head cowled, hands hidden inside his robe sleeves. "Our greeting party," she suggested, nodding ahead as Deavon looked at her questioningly.

"It seems so," he said after following her gaze and peering ahead.

"Not much of a welcome," Aldan complained.

"You want an orchestra?" Deavon asked, laughing.

"I guess not," Aldan replied sheepishly as the sailors pulled at their oars sending the cutter skimming toward the wharf. "They do know we're coming though?" he then asked.

"They should," Deavon replied. "The king sent a dispatch asking them to find any information they may have on Tiadath."

"I wonder what they've found," Tesania almost whispered as the cutter bumped against the barnacle covered wharf.

"Only one way to find out," Deavon said as he stood and held his hand out to help her.

Clambering onto the firm wharf, Tesania swayed for a moment, her body still used to the constant movement of the sea. As Deavon leapt up next to her and turned to help Kailyn, she nodded to the monk. "Tean?" she asked hopefully.

"Greetings," a deep voice answered from within the darkness of the monk's cowl dashing Tesania's hopes it might be their friend. "The Abbot has requested I convey you to him directly."

"Very well," Tesania replied before asking. "Is Tean here?"

"Brother Tean is in the library," the monk replied simply.

"Oh," Tesania said sighing in disappointment. "I'd hoped he'd meet us."

"Brother Tean has devoted himself to the king's request," the monk advised her. "He has dedicated himself to finding the answer."

"Has he found anything?" Tesania asked, brightening.

Extracting his hands from his robe sleeves before spreading them apologetically, the monk said, "I know not," before then sweeping one arm toward the stone monastery and saying, "Please accompany me." With that he turned and started toward the impressive building before them, the large arched windows with stained glass depicting angels and gods reflecting the sunshine into their eyes.

Leading them through the grand arch and into a hallway that seemed to go on forever as it angled down into the earth, the monk moved on in silence. Having been down these dark halls previously, Tesania didn't worry as the light faded; soon only the evenly spaced candles mounted in the walls showing the way.

"I forgot how cold it got down here," Kailyn said quietly as she drew her cloak around herself.

"It is the perfect place to store our texts," the monk explained as he stopped before an elaborately carved door and pushed it open. Standing aside, he motioned them through. As last time, the room was well lit, the rows of shelving seeming to hold even more of the musty old scrolls and parchments than Tesania remembered while the ancient tables scattered throughout the room overflowed with stacks of parchments where monks sat studying and transcribing.

At the far end of the room was a podium, upon which sat a huge stone table, also overflowing with parchment. Between stacks sat an old, hunched man; his pure white hair a mere ring around the back of his head, crown bald.

Recognizing the abbot immediately, Tesania headed toward him, shoes scuffing on the smooth, worn stone floor.

Rising as they approached, the abbot made his way around the table a smile spreading across his face, eyes alight as he shuffled toward them. "My dear girl," he said. "It is good to see you again."

"You remember us?" Tesania asked, beaming at the old man.

"Remember you . . ." the abbot said before chuckling, "You are quite famous," he assured her. "Why, I have personally spent many months writing the records of your deeds against Trannyth for our collection," he said while pointing a crooked, arthritis filled finger toward a pile of parchment before then motioning to a monk seated on the far side of the room. "And, of course, Tean never lets us forget either."

"Tean," Tesania said her voice rising in excitement as she turned to the monk the abbot had pointed to. When he remained with his back to them, head bowed as he read a parchment, Tesania's excitement waned.

"Tean," the old abbot called. "Tean!" he called louder, falling into a bout of dry coughing as the monk looked up and turned toward them.

"Tesania," he said and stood before coming toward them, his eyes taking them all in. Reaching out, he clasped her hand, nodding before grasping Deavon's hand then Kailyn's and finally Aldan's nodding to each in turn before looking past them, disappointment etching his face. "Giddy?" he asked. "Raim . . . ? Naisa?"

"Giddy and Raim are on a mission," Tesania told him. "Naisa is the Arch-mage now . . . she couldn't come."

"Quite," Tean said. "I trust you are well?"

"I am," Tesania assured him. "But my people are suffering," she added deciding to be direct. The last thing she wanted was to spend hours reminiscing even though she had missed her former companion.

Nodding, Tean said, "So I have heard. A nasty business."

"Have you found anything?" Tesania asked as she peered past him to the desk he had been seated at.

"Many of us have been searching the texts," the abbot interrupted.

"And?"

"In a moment," the abbot said as he looked wearily back at his chair. "If I might?" he said as he started toward the seat, Tean quickly falling in beside him to offer support. Sighing as his weight came off his feet, he smiled up at Tesania. "My old bones," he said apologetically.

"It's alright," Tesania said smiling back at him as she picked up a pitcher of water from his desk and motioned toward his mug.

"Please," the abbot said. As Tesania poured the water, he said, "We have had some success."

"You know where Tiadath is?" Tesania asked excitedly, spilling the water as she turned to Deavon.

"Not exactly," the abbot replied.

"Oh," Tesania said in disappointment. "When you said you'd had some success . . . ."

"And we have," Tean said. "We have found texts that mention Tiadath."

"So you know where it is?" Deavon asked.

Tesania watched the monk dreading that she might already know his answer.

"Not exactly," Tean replied, his eyes sad as he looked at Tesania. "But we have found mentions of a far off land called Tiadath."

"Mentions?"

"The Tenule chronicles," the abbot said. "But you know of them of course," he added waving her protest away. "Other parchments tell of trade with a people said to be Tiadaths."

"And that's it?"

"It proves Tiadath exists," Tean said.

"We know Tiadath exists," Tesania said anger rising as she looked from Tean to the abbot. "That was never in doubt."

"Tes," Deavon cautioned.

Drawing a deep breath, Tesania leant against the abbot's table her eyes searching his. "Please tell me there is something more."

"Well," the abbot replied before clearing his throat and taking a sip of water while Tesania waited impatiently. "We have at least two accounts of where this land of Tiadath lies."

"You have?" Tesania asked her excitement rising once more. "Where?"

"South-east."

"South-east," Tesania repeated before waiting for more, her attention shifting from the abbot to Tean and then back again. When neither offered any more, she asked, "Just south-east?" as if by that simple question they would now add more.

Spreading his hands, Tean said, "That's the best we have, Tesania. If we had more . . . we would tell you."

"I know," Tesania said her voice soft with disappointment. Drawing a deep breath, she then said, "I'm sorry I spoke to you as I did." She then said to the abbot, "It's just that people are suffering . . . ."

"It's quite understandable," the abbot dismissed. "Perhaps, if we had more time . . . ?"

"No," Tesania said sadly. "That's something we don't have." Looking at the others, she frowned and said, "South-east? Is that enough?"

"Probably not," Deavon replied shaking his head.

"It's a big expanse of water out there," Aldan added. "A few degrees off and we could miss it entirely."

"And sail around for months," Deavon added.

Scowling, Tesania turned back to the Abbot. "There's nothing else?" she implored. "Nothing that might suggest exactly which direction to go?"

The abbot shook his head. "That is all we have," he apologized. "Would that I could tell you more."

Smiling at him, Tesania then turned to Deavon. "Let's hope Giddy and the others have more luck."

"There's probably more chance," Aldan said.

"Agreed," Deavon said as he rested his hand on Tesania's shoulder. "And don't forget they have Rhys and Baird."

"I am sorry we could not do more for you," the abbot interrupted. "Perhaps we could offer you a meal and lodgings for the night?"

Shaking her head, Tesania thanked him but insisted they return to the Swan immediately, saying, "I'd like to get to Estiel as soon as we can."

32 - Estiel

The snort of Giddy's horse echoed through the late afternoon air above the coastal town of Estiel. "Easy," Giddy said as she rubbed her hand down the horse's neck, its hide flicking nervously under her touch. "Doesn't look like much," she said to the others who sat astride their own horses nearby.

"It isn't," Rhys assured her before suggesting with a wink, "Keep your coins close."

"Let them try," Giddy replied laughing as she unconsciously felt for her money pouch.

"I seem to remember it was easy enough to take," Rhys teased a grin spreading across his face.

Frowning at the little thief, Giddy growled, "I owe you for that one. Thanks for reminding me."

"Hey," Rhys protested. "You made it so easy . . . What was I supposed to do?"

"Err . . . Keep your hands off!"

"But that wouldn't have been any fun!"

"It was fun," Raim interjected laughing at Giddy. "Your face wa—"

"Enough from you," Giddy snarled at her friend while once more feeling for her pouch before nudging her horse forward as she looked to the sky. "Let's get in before it gets dark."

The rain had held off for a good part of the afternoon, but it was still wet, drops of moisture shimmering as they fell from the surrounding foliage and splattered onto the slippery cobblestoned road. They had made good time after leaving their lodgings in Estos City. At first miserable as the incessant rain continued to beat down, it had grown into a pleasurable ride once they could throw their oilskins off and feel the bright sun on their faces. Now, as they approached their goal, Giddy studied the town in front of them. Ships of varying sizes sat at anchor in the small harbor, others were tied up to the docks, their many masts reaching into the darkening sky like a forest of trees. The harbor itself was filthy with flotsam gathering in oily clumps everywhere, the smell drifting up the road and beginning to assault her senses. The dwellings were no better, there were no mansions here, no manicured gardens or brightly painted window frames. Instead, the buildings were dilapidated, the whitewash that had once been haphazardly slapped onto the walls, faded over many decades, the exposed mud and wood rotting and collapsing in the sun. "A lovely place," she muttered to no one in particular as they entered through gate posts that were more decomposing stumps than posts.

"The Dirty Flask would be our best bet," Rhys said pointing to an alley on the left.

"Dirty Flask? What's that?" Giddy asked suspiciously. "Or do I not want to know?"

"It's an Inn," Rhys said laughing at her.

Cringing, Giddy looked to Raim, the disgust she felt echoed on his twisted face. "Isn't there somewhere cleaner," she eventually asked the thief.

"It's clean," he assured her, laughing again at her obvious doubt. "It's just a name."

"I suppose," Giddy conceded admonishing herself. She laughed inwardly as the little man led the way into the alley. Where was the young, adventurous soldier that didn't care what the name of the establishment was but rather cared what they served inside? "I must be getting old," she muttered to herself glaring at Raim when he chuckled and agreed.

"You'll need to settle down soon," he teased. "Maybe some babies . . . ?"

"You'd like that, wouldn't you," Giddy shot back at him.

"Actually," Raim replied seriously, "I would."

"You think I'm goi . . . ." Giddy began voice drifting away as she realized what he had said. Regarding him through slit eyes, she asked suspiciously, "What did you say?

"You heard me," Raim replied a little sheepishly as Rhys called back that the stable was at the back.

"You want babies?" Giddy pressed.

"Maybe," Raim said grinning at her. "Let's get the horses settled," he suggested changing the subject. "And then some ales."

"I won't be able to drink ales if I'm with child," she pressed again.

"Then let's drink plenty now," Raim said evasively, winking as he led his horse into the stable.

Watching him go, Giddy ran her hand over her flat, toned stomach and for the first time in her life considered what it might feel like to bear a child. "Bah," she muttered to herself and led her own horse in after him.

***

Rhys drained his mug of ale and placed it down on the worn wooden table in the Dirty Flask Inn. "We won't get any information here," he said as he looked about the room.

"True enough," Baird agreed. "The taverns by the docks are where we'll find the people we're after."

Pushing her mug aside, Giddy stood. "Let's head there then."

"Let me do the talking," Rhys suggested as they spilled out the front door of the Inn and started for the dock area. "I know these sorts of people better than you."

"You're welcome to them," Giddy said as she stepped aside to let a party of drunken sailors past, screwing her nose up at the reek that followed them.

"You are getting old," Raim said laughing.

Apart from snarling at him, Giddy let him get away with the comment as they made their way through the seedy back streets of Estiel. Rhys led the way without wavering as they came to cross roads or had to choose a direction at an intersection. He was quite familiar with the town, she decided, maybe more-so than he let on. Still, she conceded, it was to their advantage. Happy to let him lead, she took in the sights. It was no worse than a back street of any town or city she had been in, except that the buildings were in a sad state of disrepair. Apart from that though, it was much the same, drunks milling about, singing and yelling, stumbling and cursing with the odd puddle of sick wafting unpleasant odors into the air.

"This one will do," Rhys said as he came to a halt in front of a tavern that exuded the sounds and smells of a well used establishment. "Let's find a table," he suggested as he forced his way between a group of burly sailors who stood across the doorway, ignoring their belligerent protests as he muttered, "Perhaps, if you didn't stand in the doorway!"

Giddy chose not to comment as she shoved past the men who obviously had no intention of moving aside. Once past them the room opened a little. She doubted they would find a table that was free in the overcrowded tavern and instead tapped Rhys on the shoulder and motioned to a space by the far wall where they could at least stand together. Nodding, the thief moved that way as Raim called out that he would order a round of ales and headed for the barkeep.

"Are we in the right place?" Giddy asked, voice raised enough to carry over the din. "I mean . . . these look like sailors to me . . . . Don't we want the captains?"

Baird nodded in agreement as Rhys perused the room stopping occasionally to study a sailor that took his interest. Eventually, as Raim arrived with four ales, he said, "You're right." Reaching for a mug, he said, "After this one, we'll move on."

"The Whale?" Baird suggested. "We should find some there."

"The Whale?" Rhys said considering the spy with a raised eyebrow. "You know more about this place than you've been letting on."

"All in the job," Baird assured him as he lifted his ale and drank deeply before wiping his mouth and saying to the two soldiers in explanation, "The Whale's a bit quieter than here. We'll find more captains there I should think."

"You're right," Rhys conceded. "I should have thought of it myself."

"A bit up market for you," Baird suggested.

Rhys looked in amusement at the spy and winked before draining his ale and saying, "Perhaps it is. Let's find out."

Hurriedly downing her ale as Rhys strode away, Giddy handed the empty mug to Raim, smirking as he frowned at her and rushed after the little thief catching him as he forced his way past the same group of sailors blocking the door. "We haven't got time to go to every tavern in town," she called after him. "Are you sure about The Whale?"

Rhys paused and turned back to her, shrugging as Raim caught up with them. "As sure as I can be," he said.

"That's comforting," Giddy growled as she fell in beside him.

"I think Baird's right," the thief said. "The Whale is as good a place as any to start."

"Then why did you start there?" Giddy asked motioning back to the tavern they had just vacated.

"A lapse in judgment," Rhys replied shrugging again. "But The Whale's not too far," he assured her pointing ahead. "Just around the corner."

Just around the corner turned into three corners before the outline of a bedraggled whale hanging above the front door of a tavern came into view. "The Whale," Rhys announced with a flourish as if it were his pride and joy.

"Lead on," Giddy suggested as she looked at the tavern. Unlike the previous one, this one was much quieter with only the subtle murmur of voices whispering from the door as they approached. "This is better," she whispered to Raim as they entered. Whilst crowded, the tavern still had a few spare tables that they could choose from. As they moved toward the back of the room, Giddy looked around. The men in this tavern were more austere than the ones they had previously had to fight their way through. These men had an air of position about them, an air of authority.

"Ale?" Raim asked.

"Cider," Giddy replied.

"Cider?"

"You heard."

"A cider it is," Raim said in some shock. "Rhys? Baird?"

As he left to get their drinks, Giddy leaned forward jutting her chin toward the room as she asked, "Which one?"

"No idea," Rhys replied as he scanned the room. "I don't know any of them."

"Me either," Baird responded to Giddy's questioning look.

"That's a big help," Giddy said sighing in exasperation.

"It was a long shot that we would know any of the captains currently in port," Rhys defended. "But that doesn't stop us asking them."

"True enough," Baird agreed. "It's only a matter of asking the right questions."

"To the right person," Rhys added.

"And which one is that?" Giddy asked as Raim returned.

"I have no idea," the little thief replied winking at her.

Rolling her eyes, Giddy reached for her cider and stood. "Perhaps we should split up." The others agreed, Rhys deciding to accompany her while Raim and Baird teamed up and headed for a lone drinker on the far side of the room. "Him?" she suggested gesturing to another lone drinker.

"As good as any," Rhys agreed as he started toward the man. "Evenen'," he said merrily as he approached him. "Mind if we sit?"

The man glanced up at him, steel grey eyes flicking quickly between the thief and Giddy before returning to the mug cradled in his hands. "Plenty of other seats in 'ere," he said, voice like rolling gravel.

"Aye," Rhys agreed falling into a sailor's brogue. "But this 'ere one bores me," he said jutting a thumb at Giddy. "I long fer some intelligent conversation."

The man looked up at Giddy once more, his eyes travelling over her face and then down to her toes. "She'd do fer me," he said gruffly.

"Thank you," Giddy said glaring in triumph at the thief.

"Yer wouldn't be saying that after a day or two," Rhys assured the man as he pulled a chair out, to his unwilling host's disgust, and sat. "What yer drinken'?" he asked pointing to the man's all but empty mug. "Ale?"

"Aye, ale," the man conceded.

Looking up to Giddy, Rhys slapped her on the rump and commanded, "Two ales luv. And 'urry it up too."

With a look of daggers, Giddy decided to play along and left to speak to the barkeeper as Rhys leaned across the table and offered his hand. "Rhys . . ." he said. "And yer'd be?"

Giddy didn't hear the man's reply as she left, assuming he had volunteered his name at all. It was probably for the best, she supposed, that Rhys be left to do what he did best. Glancing around the room, she saw that Raim and Baird had deposited themselves at the table with their mark and were attempting to engage him in conversation. It appeared, by the scowl on the man's face and the frown on Raim's, that they weren't having much luck. "Two ales," she informed the barkeep. "And a cider." Turning, she watched as Rhys spoke to the man they had approached. It seemed all one way traffic with the little thief doing all the talking while the man stared down at his hands. Shaking her head and wondering if they were going about this the right way, she turned back to pay the barkeep and then carried the mugs back to the table.

"'Bout time," Rhys growled at her as he reached up and took the two mugs of ale from her, passing one to the man. "Capt'n Berring here was saying he just got in ter port terday."

"Oh," Giddy said as she pulled a chair out and sank down, interest peeked.

"I only told yer to shut yer up," Captain Berring growled.

"Right, yer did," Rhys said frowning at Giddy as the captain continued to look down at his hands. "What ship did yer say yer were from?"

"I didn't."

"Right," Rhys said again. "Bus'ness been good?" he asked.

"Bus'ness is what bus'ness is. Now if yer'd be kind enough to leave a man alone with 'is drink."

"Look," Rhys said dropping all pretences. "We are in need of information. Information that only someone like you can supply."

"Like me?" Berring asked laughing as he looked up at the thief. "What can I tell yer that any of ther others in 'ere can't?"

Leaning forward and looking about the room before turning his attention back to the captain, Rhys whispered conspiratorially, "We want you to take us to Tiadath?"

"Tiadath?" the man grunted. "What's that?"

"Where's that," Rhys corrected continuing to look at the captain intently as he pulled forth his coin pouch, dropping it on table with a thud. "And that's what I want you to tell us."

"Tiadath," Captain Berring repeated the word licking his lips as his eyes fixated on the pouch of money sitting tantalizingly on the table. "I might know of such a place," he said. "Depends."

"On what?" Rhys asked as he picked his pouch up and bounced it in his hand smiling knowingly at the man whose mesmerized eyes followed the path of the pouch up and down. "How much?" he asked.

"We don't even know that he's been to Tiadath," Giddy protested as she leant forward and caught the pouch in mid air.

"Oh, I've been there, lass," the man said attention now on her hand, his own hand twitching as it moved toward hers.

"Prove it."

"Ther' ain't no way ter prove it," the captain grunted his face changing in an instant to a sneer as he changed focus from the pouch to Giddy's face.

"I can handle this," Rhys said snatching his pouch away from Giddy as he frowned at her and shook his head suggesting silently that she should stay out of the negotiations.

"Fine," Giddy said sitting back heavily in her chair. "It's your money."

Frowning at her once more, Rhys slowly turned his attention to the captain. "Perhaps the lass is right—"

"Lass," Giddy scoffed. "Do I look lik—"

"How do we know you can guide us to Tiadath . . . Apart from your word?"

"Me word is me bond."

"I don't doubt it," Rhys replied as he began to bounce the pouch again. "Tell us . . . when did you last embark on a journey to Tiadath."

"Few months back."

"A few months," Rhys repeated flashing Giddy a triumphant grin. "Ferrying someone?"

Berring looked from Rhys to Giddy and then back again. "Aye . . . it were a passenger. Paid me 'andsome like too."

"He's guessing," Giddy said scowling at the little thief. "You all but told him that was the answer we're looking for."

Ignoring her, Rhys asked, "Who was this passenger?"

"That'd be private," the captain protested his eyes once more on the pouch.

"Oh, I'm sure a few coins could make it un-private," Rhys suggested as he stopped bouncing the pouch and slipped the drawstring open. "Perhaps two . . . three maybe."

"You're wasting your money!"

"'E ain't," Captain Berring growled at the soldier as his hand snaked forward. "Three might do it," he conceded as he returned his attention to Rhys. "Just fer the passenger, mind. Nothen more," he added quickly.

"Indeed," Rhys nodded as he fished out three coins and threw them onto the table, the clatter of the metal on wood ending abruptly as the captain's hand snatched them up.

Studying them for a moment, Berring looked about the room and then leant forward. "It ain't normal fer me ter talk 'bout me passengers and all."

"I'm sure it isn't," Rhys said nodding his understanding before flicking his finger at the man's closed fist. "But I'm sure that makes it worth your while."

Considering his words, Berring stared at his closed fist before looking up to Rhys and then Giddy, obviously lost for what to say.

"He doesn't know anything," Giddy said as she frowned at Rhys. "A waste of money."

"It ain't," Captain Berring insisted as he looked from her to the thief and back again over and over, his mind obviously working as hard as it could.

"Well?" Giddy demanded leaning forward and glaring into his eyes. "Who was it!?"

"It wer' a . . . a . . . man."

"A man," Giddy repeated loudly guffawing. "There you have it," she said to Rhys as she swung her arm to take in the captain. "It was a man . . . What more proof do we need? Give him your pouch and we can sail on the morning tide!"

Desperately, the captain looked from the now laughing Giddy to Rhys. "It were a man . . . that be fer sure," he said as his gaze fell to the pouch once more. "Not just any man though . . . he were special."

"Special?" Rhys asked waving Giddy to silence. "In what way?"

Once more Berring floundered to find an answer. Eventually he offered, "He were a mage."

"A mage?" Rhys repeated quickly as he darted Giddy a knowing glance.

"Yer," the captain replied his confidence lifting. "He 'ad a staff and all."

"It must be him," Rhys said to Giddy.

"He doesn't know the first thing about Tiadath."

"How would he know about the mage then?"

"He guessed," Giddy almost screamed before adding in a quieter voice, "I can't believe you're falling for this. Especially you."

"I don't know," Rhys replied as he considered her words. "Maybe you're right."

"She ain't right," Captain Berring assured him quickly. "'Ere . . ." he said as he stubbed his fingers into a bowl of salt and threw a pinch across the table. ". . . I'll draw yer a map." As Rhys leaned forward, he added, "For ther whole pouch, mind. Not one coin less."

Caught up once more, Rhys considered his pouch before saying, "Done . . . . But remember this my friend. If you lie to me, I'll be back to recover all of my investment."

"Yer won't be wasten' yer money with me," the captain assured him, a new found confidence in his voice as he began to draw on the table. "We be here," he explained as he made a dot in the salt. "If yer 'ead down," he went on drawing a line with his finger, "under Aliaga and then strike out south-west from ther eastern headland of Estan Harbor. Keep true to south-west for twenty days and yer'll come to the land of Tiader."

"Tiadath," Giddy corrected.

"Yer, Tiadath," Berring quickly agreed. "Ther be a harbor on the north east tip."

"Convenient," Giddy scoffed.

"Giddy," Rhys said before asking the captain. "Twenty days?"

"Yer, twenty, depending on ther winds. Just keep sailing till yer hit ther land."

Standing, Rhys thanked the captain tossing him the bag of coins as he said, "In forty days I'll be back. I'll see you then shall I?"

Pulling nervously at his collar, Captain Berring muttered, "I'll be at sea."

"That's a surprise," Giddy said standing and following the little thief and shaking her head. Eventually, as they joined Raim and Baird at their table which was now empty of the man they had approached, she said, "That was a waste of your money."

"Three coins isn't a big loss."

"Three," Giddy protested. "You gave him the whole pouch."

"Did I?" the thief said, grinning as he dug into his pocket and produced a pouch that was obviously full of coins.

"But I saw you give it to him," Giddy began as she looked back at the man who was tugging eagerly at the draw strings of the pouch in his hands. "You—"

"We'd better make ourselves scarce," Rhys suggested winking as he tried unsuccessfully to withhold his mischievous grin.

A cool breeze met them as they stepped from the tavern. Giddy breathed in the air, regretting it immediately as the town's stench filled her senses and she began to cough.

"Any luck with you?" Rhys asked Raim.

"He didn't know anything," Raim replied. "Or wasn't willing to talk about it. Either way; we came up with nothing," he added spreading his hands.

"I think that might be a problem that we'll keep running into," Rhys said thoughtfully. "We're going about this the wrong way."

"No luck for you either then?" Raim asked.

"We got quite a bit of information," Rhys advised him winking at Giddy. "But I have no desire to sail twenty days to the south west on that man's word."

"You don't believe him?" Baird asked as a cry of anguish rang from the tavern.

"Not one word," Rhys replied as he grinned at Giddy and began to run.

33 - Sergh

Sergh sat at his desk staring from the window of his home in the small township of Adena. It had been weeks now since his attack on Tesania's stately home, weeks since his spell had been so violently torn apart. The woman now infested his psyche, inhabited his dreams. "Who is she?" he whispered for what seemed the thousandth time to his assistant standing by the door.

"Does it matter?" the assistant asked tentatively, hand sliding nervously over his plain, unadorned apprentices' staff.

Rubbing at the pain in his temples, Sergh sighed before answering, "She wields power I have never seen . . . power I cannot fathom."

"She was lucky," the assistant ventured.

"No!" Sergh spat angrily, slapping his hand down on the desk, regretting it immediately as the pain in his head exploded. Closing his eyes, he began to gently massage his temples again. "She's dangerous," he eventually muttered.

"To you?" the assistant scoffed.

"Even to me," Sergh said quietly.

"No one has power like yours."

"You didn't feel it," Sergh said calmly as he squeezed his eyes harder to block out the pain that had resided in his head since the woman had banished his spell. "I still do."

"The Arch Mage of Eldanal perhaps?"

Shaking his head lightly, Sergh said, "No. This was magic I have never felt before; magic their Arch Mage couldn't begin to have." Rising, he walked to the window, squinting as the late afternoon sunshine bit at his eyes. "I can't explain it . . . but it was different."

"You're going to cease the attacks?" the assistant asked.

Sergh didn't reply for some time. Eventually, he said, "No . . . I made a commitment . . . ."

"Those fools won't know you have stopped," the assistant said. "The lord and his spoilt brat . . . What does it matter?"

"It matters to me," Sergh replied rubbing once more at his head. "Besides, their gold is as good as any others . . . If we want more of it, we must follow through."

"And the woman?"

Staring out the window as he considered the question, Sergh finally replied, "I'll concentrate on the farms and ships. She can't be everywhere."

"What if . . . ."

"If?"

"What if she comes here?"

Considering his words for a few moments, Sergh eventually replied quietly, "I can't see it. She wouldn't know who I am, let alone how to find me?"

"The lord . . . ? His brat?"

"No," Sergh said thoughtfully. "They know my name. That is all."

"And that you're from Tiadath."

"That won't help her," Sergh replied. "Even if they do find their way to Tiadath, they'll never find us here."

"You're probably right . . . . But if she does?"

Turning, Sergh looked at the apprentice the pain drumming in his head rising to a crescendo as he considered what he had said. Frowning, he dismissed the apprentice with a wave before returning to the window. Reaching out, he plucked his staff off the desk, running his hand over the familiar knotted wood as he muttered to himself, "She can't possibly find me."

34 - Captains and Thieves

Giddy lifted a slice of honey soaked bread, tearing a corner off with her teeth as she watched Raim dive into a plate of anchovies. "Don't come near me today," she said as he stuffed a plump fish into his mouth.

"No problem there," Raim replied, grinning as Rhys and Baird approached and dragged out their chairs, the thief catching a waitress' attention as he sat.

"I'll have the fish," he advised. "And a mead."

"Same for me," Baird added.

"Don't go near Giddy then," Raim suggested as he stabbed another anchovy.

"What . . . ?"

Shaking his head and grinning once more, Raim mumbled, "Nothing," around his fish and picked up his mead.

"I hope," Giddy said to the new arrivals, "that we have a better plan for today."

"Agreed," Baird replied. "Last night was a waste of time."

"It was definitely flawed," Rhys agreed. "Randomly asking captains if they know where Tiadath is won't work."

"Assuming he was a captain," Giddy scoffed as she remembered the man they had spoken to the night before.

"My point," Rhys said.

"So . . . ?" Giddy asked leaving it hanging in the air.

"Wait and see what Tesania and the others have uncovered?" Raim suggested.

"I'll leave it to you," Giddy said mirth in her voice, "to tell her we sat here drinking ale for a few days because we couldn't come up with a plan."

"Well . . . err . . . ."

"Exactly," Giddy said before turning her attention to the thief. "Contacts?" she asked. "Surely you know someone here?" she added before looking to Baird with the same question.

"We might have an operative here," Baird replied spreading his hands. "But I have no idea who they might be. Estiel has never been a priority for me. You?" he then asked Rhys.

Scowling, Rhys moved back and allowed the waitress to deposit his plate. As she left, he said, "One."

"Do I know him?" the spy asked.

"I'd imagine so," Rhys replied scowling again as he said, "Lafric."

"Lafric?" Baird spluttered into his mug, chocking on his mead.

"Yes," Rhys replied. "Lafric."

"You trust Lafric?" Baird asked incredulously.

"Not particularly," Rhys replied flatly as he stabbed sourly at his plate.

"Lafric?" Giddy asked looking from Rhys to Baird.

"A stand up citizen by the sounds of it," Raim said, laughing as he too looked at the Aliagans.

"Far from it," Rhys growled.

"Lowest of the low," Baird added.

"Sounds like he can't be trusted," Giddy said frowning. "Anybody else?"

Rhys shook his head. "Not here."

"What's so wrong with him?" Raim asked.

"What isn't?" Baird replied as Rhys began to talk.

"Believe it or not," he said, "There is honor amongst thieves."

"Let's pretend we believe that," Baird scoffed.

Rhys shrugged. "Either way," he said. "But there is . . . most of the time."

"But not with this Lafric?" Giddy asked.

"No," Rhys replied simply. "He would sell his proverbial grandmother to make a profit."

"Can we trust him then?"

"Probably not."

"Then we can't use him."

"What's there to lose though?" Raim asked. "He's at least worth a try."

"True enough," Rhys replied.

"You'll have to do it without me," Baird said. "He knows me."

"Good point," Rhys agreed. "He'll clam up and go to ground if he sees one of the king's men. Better I go alone."

"Is that wise?" Giddy asked. "Wouldn't we be better off together."

"No," Rhys disagreed. "He knows me, whereas, he doesn't know you."

"I see your point." Giddy nodded before asking in concern, "Will you be alright?"

Rhys laughed out loud as he pushed his empty plate aside and stood. "It's not like it's my first time. I'll see you in a few hours."

Giddy watched him go. He knew these parts and these people better than she ever would. But waiting and doing nothing while others did the work she should be doing bothered her greatly.

"Ale?" Raim asked breaking her from her reverie.

Smiling at the little man, she replied, "Why not?"

***

Hours passed as the midday sun hit its zenith and began to sink inexorably toward the darkness of night. Giddy sat in the common room of The Dirty Flask Inn with Raim and Baird, whiling the time away as Baird told them the little he knew of the town and the seedy underworld it was home to. As she wondered for the hundredth time when Rhys would return, he appeared at the door and made his way to their table, dragging a chair noisily over the worn wooden floor. "Any luck?" Giddy asked.

Nodding, Rhys motioned a waitress for ale. "He knows a captain."

Giddy sniffed. "Another one."

"Different," Rhys assured her. "At least we have someone else's knowledge of him this time."

"I suppose," Giddy conceded. "Cost much?"

"We did a deal," Rhys said evasively.

"I'm sure," Baird grunted.

"Do you need any coins?" Giddy asked reaching for her pouch. "Not that I have much."

Waving her away, Rhys replied, "You wouldn't begin to have enough."

"But you did?" Baird asked smiling knowingly.

"Not gold; no," Rhys conceded. "Let's just say; there are other commodities in the back streets of this town."

"I'm sure you're not losing out," Baird remarked.

"Possibly not," Rhys replied, shrugging. "Deals are done every day. Some pay off, some don't."

"Let me have a stab at it," Baird said. "A partnership with Lafric to relieve Tiadath of its gold."

Rhys scowled at the spy and dismissed him with a wave. "I'm not about to discuss it with you."

Shrugging, Baird assured him, "What you do in Tiadath is no business of mine."

"Exactly," the thief growled. "Let's leave it at that."

Giddy watched the exchange and decided to stay out of it. Eventually, she asked, "Where's this captain?"

"I'm meeting him at sundown."

"I'm coming."

"Suit yourself," Rhys said before scowling at Baird. "But not you."

Baird shrugged. "Suits me fine."

***

Lafric was a large man, not only in height but in girth, his soft, sagging body hanging over the edges of his chair in the Crossed Daggers Tavern. "Ale?" he asked Rhys as Giddy pulled a chair out and sat. At the little thief's nod he turned his attention to Giddy. Nodding, she moved her attention to the other man sitting on the far side of the table. "Giddy," she said when the man's eyes met hers and rose to reach across and grasp his hand. "This is Raim and Rhys," she added motioning to her companions.

"Captain Rygal," the man replied as he took her hand in his firm grasp and shook.

"And you'd be Lafric," she said releasing her hand and moving toward the big man who took her hand but declined to answer. Sitting again, Giddy decided to get straight to the point and said to the captain, "You've been to Tiadath?"

Nodding slowly, his eyes fixed on Giddy's, Rygal eventually replied, "Aye; a few times."

"Trade?"

A smile played at the edge of the captain's lips for a moment before slipping away. "Let's say trade," he replied voice even.

"Fair enough," Giddy said.

"I wouldn't have brought him here if he hadn't been to Tiadath," Lafric snarled.

"Fair enough," Giddy said once more glancing at Lafric before turning her attention back to Rygal. "Can you tell us where it is?"

"I can take you," Captain Rygal replied. "The three of you . . . . For a fee."

"That won't be necessary," Giddy said. "We have our own transport. Just give us directions and we'll handle it from there." As Rygal shook his head, she asked, "You won't give them to us?" Turning to Lafric, she then asked, "Why'd you bring him here if he won't tell us?"

"I didn't say I wouldn't tell you," Rygal said.

"You shook your head."

Rygal nodded. "What's your ship?"

"The Swan," Giddy replied.

"Out of Eldanal?" he asked.

"Correct."

"You can't just sail an Eldanal ship into their waters and tie up at the Tierra docks."

"Tierra?" Raim asked. "Is that a city?"

"One of them," Rygal replied.

"And your ship?" Giddy enquired, cutting Raim's next question off. "It's an Aliagan ship I presume?"

"Indeed," Rygal replied, adding before Giddy could ask, "But they know me . . . know my ship."

"They didn't always," Giddy said frowning in frustration. "Yet you obviously sailed there."

"Does it matter?" Lafric growled. "Who is this woman?" he then asked Rhys. "And why is the good captain here," he added motioning to Rygal, "being harassed by her?"

"I'm hardly har—"

"Giddy is the leader of this mission," Rhys said. "Well, at least this part."

"Mission?" Lafric asked shoving himself forward in his chair with some effort. "What mission?" he asked suspiciously, breath ragged from the effort of moving. "You're not going to cross me now, are you . . . ?" he asked ominously, eyes slit, chest rising and falling like a bellows as he stared down at Rhys.

Darting a quick look at Giddy and Raim, Rhys replied, "Our deal has nothing to do with this. It's a completely different matter."

Lafric's attention moved from Rhys to Giddy and then onto Raim before he eventually said, "You had better not try . . . ."

"We have a deal," Rhys said waving the matter aside.

"Why do you want to sail to Tiadath?" the captain eventually asked Giddy as the others fell quiet.

"Does it matter?"

Shrugging, Captain Rygal replied, "It could. Anything you do might reflect badly upon me."

"Then don't come," Giddy said. "They'll never know you told us anything. Just draw a map and we'll be on our way."

"It won't work," Rygal said. "As I said; you can't just sail into Tierra."

"Let us worry about that," Rhys interrupted. "We appreciate your advice," he added as the captain scowled at him. "Truly, we do. But we can handle it ourselves. Just draw us a map."

Shrugging once more, Rygal produced a parchment from inside his coat. "It won't do you any good," he said as he spread it on the table and repeated once more, "They will not let you sail into Tierra harbor."

"Then we won't," Giddy said as she peered down at the scrawling on the parchment. "South-southeast," she said glancing at Rhys who smiled back at her aware that she was making a point about the direction the previous captain had given them. "Would have been a long sail for nothing."

"What would?" Rygal asked.

"Nothing," Giddy said, dismissing it. "And Tiadath is how many days away?"

"Depends on many things," Rygal replied. "If you're lucky, you'll do it in as little as ninety eight days. If you're unlucky . . . ." He shrugged.

"Ninety eight days?" Giddy repeated trying unsuccessfully to hide her surprise.

Rygal laughed out loud. "What did you expect?" he asked. "If it were only a few days sail, everyone would know how to get there."

"I guess you're right," Giddy replied, abashed. Reaching out, she picked up the map and folded it away, slipping it inside a pocket as she rose. "A pleasure meeting you," she said nodding to Lafric and then the captain.

"Pleasure," Rygal replied as he stood and offered his hand to her. As she shook it, he said seriously, "I meant it. Do not try and sail into Tierra Harbor. It will not go well for you if you do."

"Thanks for the advice," Giddy said as she nodded goodbye and turned to leave, walking to the door and stepping into the cool evening air. "That went well," she said as Raim and Rhys joined her.

"You trust them?" Raim asked.

"I think so," Giddy replied. "Rygal seemed genuine enough."

"He wouldn't cross Lafric," Rhys assured them. "The map's as bona fid as any we'll ever see."

"You're sure?"

"I'll bet Rygal's life on it."

"He'd kill him?" Raim asked eyebrow raised.

"Probably," Rhys replied matter-of-factly before explaining, "Lafric runs the, shall we say, less than legal side of Estiel."

"Ah, an example," Raim said, nodding in understanding.

"Exactly." Rhys shrugged as if it were a natural thing. "Rygal knows that all too well."

"Rygal seemed honest enough," Giddy said.

Rhys scoffed. "If he's involved with Lafric," he assured her. "Honesty isn't one of his strong suits."

"So we can't trust him?"

"As I said," Rhys said while peering back into the tavern. "He wouldn't risk crossing Lafric."

"And . . . do we trust Lafric?" Giddy asked.

"He's a criminal," Rhys conceded. "But I have an arrangement with him . . . ." he trailed off.

"It'll have to do then," Giddy said as Rhys started back into the tavern suggesting she and Raim return to the Dirty Flask and turn in.

"You think it's enough?" Raim asked as they walked back to their lodgings.

Shrugging as she thought through her answer, Giddy eventually replied, "It'll have to be. We don't have anything else."

"Hopefully, Tesania and the others have had more luck."

"Let's hope," Giddy replied.

"Where are we meeting them?" Raim asked, frowning as he seemingly wracked his mind.

"No idea," Giddy replied, also frowning. "The docks, I suppose."

"Makes sense."

"We'll need to spend time down there . . . so we can see when the Swan arrives."

"There's an Inn down there, isn't there?"

"I imagine there's a few," Giddy replied grinning. "Tomorrow, we'll find out."

35 - Reunited

Tesania grasped Deavon's hand tightly as he leant over the Swan's rail and helped her walk down the swaying gangplank and onto the Estiel docks. Giddy waited at the foot of the gangplank offering her hand to assist as Deavon let go. "Welcome," she said beaming as she nodded toward the filthy town. "It's not much," she went on, "But it's home."

"Home," Tesania muttered before regarding the soldier seriously. "Even you wouldn't live here . . . would you?"

"I wouldn't," Giddy admitted as she motioned to the little man beside her. "But Raim here would fit in like a pig in mud."

"Would I just?" Raim asked shaking his head before turning his attention to Tesania as Deavon stepped from the gangplank onto the dock. "Anything?" he asked.

"Not much," Tesania replied disappointedly before asking more brightly, "You?"

"Perhaps we should wait until we're all together," Deavon suggested as he drew aside and let Kailyn, followed by Aldan, step from the gangplank.

"On the ship," Raim said. "There's nothing worth coming ashore for," he informed them grimly.

"I'm beginning to see that," Tesania replied screwing up her nose in distaste.

"Wait here," Giddy said as she gripped Raim's sleeve and drew him away. "We'll get Rhys and Baird from The Dirty Flask."

"Dirty Flask?" Tesania asked.

"The Inn we're staying at," Raim informed her. "A lovely little place."

"Sounds like it," Aldan said laughing.

"We'll be back soon," Raim called back as he and Giddy slipped into the throng of sailors ambling along the docks.

Tesania swept the dirty harbor with her eyes deciding that the soldiers were more than likely correct about Estiel. Turning, she held her hand out to Deavon for support and started up the gangplank again. At the top she waited for the others and then started for their cabins, saying to Lieutenant Nylor as she passed, "Giddy and Raim will be back soon, along with two others." As he nodded his head in understanding, she added, "Could you please ask them to join us in our wardroom."

"Certainly, Ma'am"

Smiling at him briefly, Tesania made for the hatch that led to their quarters. She couldn't help but like the young man. Tanned and toned, he was always quick with an affable smile and seemed to naturally hold the respect of the men. She wondered, as she made her way to the wardroom and settled herself into a seat, if he might not be someone she could use in her own fleet.

"Care to share?" Kailyn asked.

"Sorry?"

"You were miles away," the young mage said smiling gently. "Care to share?"

"Not really," Tesania replied. "I was just thinking how nice the lieutenant is."

"Oh," Kailyn cooed. "He is nice."

"Not in that way," Tesania said quickly as she glanced guiltily toward Deavon. He appeared deep in conversation with Aldan, so she said to Kailyn, "I was just thinking he might make a fine captain of one of my ships one day."

"I know," Kailyn teased.

"I was!"

"He's a little young," Deavon said his eyes now on her.

Blushing, Tesania muttered, "I said, one day."

"He's a fine seaman," Deavon said.

"That's what I mean."

"In the future perhaps," Deavon said as he went back to speaking with Aldan.

"He's more than just a fine seaman," Kailyn whispered.

"Kailyn!" Tesania admonished the girl.

"Well, he is," she said blushing redder than Tesania had.

"Shh . . . ." Tesania said shaking her head at the girl as she grinned at her. As Kailyn looked down at her hands, blush not subsiding, Tesania turned her attention to Deavon as he talked to Aldan. She enjoyed watching him as he spoke to his friend. They were always so relaxed talking about anything from the state of the Rangers of Eldanal to the size of the fish they might have caught. It gladdened her that he had such a good friend that he could let his guard down with. Others could find him a little serious at times, but she saw the glint in his eye, the slight crinkle in the corner of his mouth as he stifled a grin. It was a part of who he was, the stoic Ranger General, but she knew him for who he really was. A gentle, loving man who would do anything to keep her and his friends out of harm's way. Their relationship had developed over the past four years to a stage where they were mostly inseparable aside from her work and his duties with the Rangers. She ached with loneliness when he was away, longing for him to return. Watching him now she felt compelled to whisper, "I love you," so quietly that even Kailyn, who sat right next to her, didn't hear. She supposed one day they might marry, actually, she admitted with a small laugh, she hoped for that with all her heart. But for now, she was happy to just be with him and sat watching him talk until he looked at her, the dimple appearing in his cheek as he smiled causing her heart to skip a beat.

***

"Captain Eades," Tesania acknowledged the captain as he entered their cramped wardroom and took a seat at the end of the table. "Lieutenant Nylor," she greeted nodding to the young man who took a seat at the captain's side.

"Are we all here?" Captain Eades asked eventually.

"I believe so. Giddy and the others arrived a few minutes ago."

"Very well," he said before clearing his throat and peering at each of his passengers in turn, his eyes eventually coming to rest on Tesania. "I trust you have some new information?"

Nodding slowly, Tesania glanced at Giddy before returning her gaze to the captain. "As you already know," she began now glancing at Deavon. "We didn't find much information with the monks." As the captain nodded, she went on, "They did however suggest that Tiadath is southeast."

"As you informed me in Unastine harbor," Captain Eades growled. "And as I said then; that simply isn't good enough."

"I am aware of that," Tesania answered shortly. "But thanks to Giddy; we now have more to go on."

"So I presumed," the captain replied, smiling at her apologetically. "Otherwise I wouldn't have the men provisioning the ship."

"Thank you for your trust," Tesania muttered looking down at her hands.

"Not at all," Captain Eades said dismissively while looking around the table once more. "And what is this new information?" he asked, eyes coming to rest on Giddy. "I trust it's solid?"

"Solid enough," Giddy replied, shrugging.

"From some sodden captain collapsed in the corner of a tavern?" the captain asked a glint of mirth in his eyes. "Perhaps a sailor who claims to have a maiden in every Tiadath port?"

"Neither," Giddy replied seriously while slipping her hand into her pocket and producing the map Captain Rygal had provided and tossing it on the table toward Captain Eades. "A map," she informed him as he leant forward and picked up the folded parchment.

"Indeed," Captain Eades muttered as he unfolded it. "From whom?"

"A reliable source."

"Reliable?" the captain grunted his eyes running over the scrawled writing. "In Estiel?"

"As reliable as we'll ever see here," Rhys said.

"And it's all we have," Raim added.

"Quite," Captain Eades said as he continued to peruse the parchment. "Who gave you this map?"

"A captain," Giddy informed. "Captain Rygal, I believe his name was."

"Never heard of him," Eades said as he continued to study the map. "Whoever he is," he said flicking the corner of the parchment with his finger, the sharp snap causing Kailyn to flinch. "He knows his stuff."

"Well, he is a captain," Rhys sighed.

"Says he?"

"We have strong enough reason to believe he is," Giddy said. "He was vouched for."

"By?"

"Does it matter?"

Captain Eades' eyes met Giddy's, all semblance of mirth now gone. "You are asking me to set my ship on a course by this," he said while waving the parchment at the soldier, "Of course it matters."

"To be fair," Rhys interrupted, "Giddy had the same trepidations as you."

"And?"

"And," the little thief said squirming under the captain's gaze which was now firmly fixed on him. "I can assure you that the map," he said pointing, "Is as real as any we'll ever see."

A few moments of silence followed as Captain Eades continued to study the thief dubiously before finally turning his attention to Tesania and waving the map toward her, asking, "You trust this?"

"I have little choice," she replied evenly.

Nodding slowly, the captain laid the map on the table and straightened it out with the side of his hand before stabbing his finger onto it. "We are here."

Leaning forward, Tesania peered over the captain's hand, his finger sat on blank parchment below the scrawled name of Estiel. She followed it as he traced down the parchment explaining the long days of sailing they faced if the map was to scale.

"Ninety eight days," Giddy informed him. "With favorable winds."

"Ninety eight days?" Tesania gasped as she turned to Deavon, eyes searching his as she said, "It's too long. We need to stop him sooner."

As Deavon shrugged, face blank as he obviously had no answer for her, the captain interrupted, "At least three and a half months . . . or more," he muttered to himself as he ran his finger to the north-west tip of the land mass drawn at the lower end of the parchment.

"But—" Tesania began to protest.

"I can't get you there any sooner," the captain said gruffly. "Assuming this map is correct."

"He's right, Tes," Deavon said.

"I understand," Tesania said before muttering, "And in the mean time his attacks will continue."

"We can only do what we can do," Aldan said consolingly to Tesania. "The Swan can only sail so fast."

"I know," Tesania conceded morosely.

Captain Eades' weathered face softened as he looked at her and said, "I am aware of the situation, and I will do my best to land you as soon as I possibly can." As Tesania smiled briefly at him, he returned his attention to the map and tapped his finger on the north-west coast of Tiadath. "Tierra City. I suppose you can start your search there."

"No," Giddy said adamantly.

"I'm sorry?" the captain asked Giddy, a frown playing over his brow.

"We can't go to Tierra," Giddy said as she sat forward. "We can't land at any of their towns or cities as a matter-of-fact."

Frown growing deeper, Captain Eades asked, "And why not?"

"They'll be hostile."

"The Tiadaths."

"So I'm told."

"And the Swan?"

"It would probably be wise not to be seen."

"They would sink us?" the captain asked his frown changing to a worried crease.

"Or capture us," Giddy replied, shrugging. "Take the ship."

"What about us?" Kailyn asked quickly.

"Slavery . . . ?" Giddy said shrugging once more. "I've no idea."

"They wouldn't make us slaves . . ." Kailyn half whispered to Tesania, eyes wide. ". . . would they?"

"I don't know," Tesania admitted before turning to Giddy. "This Captain Rygal of yours said as much?"

"Not the slavery," Giddy admitted. "But he was adamant that we shouldn't approach any of the cities."

"We don't know that's necessarily true," Aldan said.

"We're back to the same question then," Giddy said shaking her head as she spread her hands. "Do we trust Rygal or not?" When no one answered her, most staring down at their own hands, she added while nodding at the parchment, "If we're going to trust his map, I think it prudent to trust everything else he had to say."

Nodding slowly, the captain stared down at the map for some time before saying, "You're right. And I will not send this ship, or its crew, knowingly into danger."

"How do we get ashore then?" Kailyn asked, eyes flicking from Tesania to Deavon and then to Giddy as she swallowed deeply. "I can't swim very well."

"We won't be swimming," Tesania assured her.

"It's a possibility," Captain Eades said half to himself. "We could stand offshore—"

"I can't," Kailyn gasped.

"The cutter, sir," Lieutenant Nylor said as he shuffled forward in his seat and looked down at the map. Reaching out, he pointed off the north-west coat of Tiadath. "We could sail past the point here," he said tracing a line with the tip of his forefinger. "Out to sea," he added before starting his finger toward the coast. "At night, we sail in close and lower the cutter," he said smiling at Kailyn. "Then you wouldn't have to swim."

"Thank you," Kailyn said, returning his smile shyly.

Winking at the girl before turning his attention back to the captain, Nylor said, "I will take them in myself . . . with the cutter crew."

"You'd do that for us?" Kailyn asked.

"To save you from getting wet," Nylor replied grinning. "Anything."

"Such a gentleman," Giddy shot at him before turning her attention to Deavon and saying, "Sounds reasonable."

Deavon considered it but before he could reply Tesania said, "That doesn't help us."

"It gets us ashore," Aldan said.

"On the coast; maybe in the middle of nowhere . . . What then . . . ? How can we possibly find this Sergh from there?"

"We'll have to work it out when we get there, Tes," Deavon said reaching for her hand and cupping it. "I think Giddy's right," he then said. "We can't simply sail into one of their ports."

"I can see that," Tesania said. "But to land in the middle of nowhere."

"Can't we sail in close during the day?" Kailyn asked. "Then we can see where there's a town or something? Land there?"

"No," Lieutenant Nylor replied. "We can't be seen at all."

"They wouldn't know we're not from Tiadath," Kailyn said in confusion.

"From shore they may not," Nylor said gently. "But any ship, or indeed sailor who might be on shore, would know we were not a Tiadath vessel immediately."

"Mister Nylor has the right of it," the captain said. "I will not take the Swan in sight of land during daylight."

Tesania drew her hand away from Deavon's and asked, "And if we land in the middle of nowhere?"

"Then we work our way along the coast until we find a town or city," Deavon replied.

"Do we have time?"

"Not really," Deavon conceded. "But I can't see that we have any other choice."

"We'll find somewhere," Baird assured her, speaking for the first time in the meeting. "There's usually a road running along the coast in any country," he informed her. "Fishing villages, small townships."

"Will they know where he is?"

"Probably not," Baird admitted. "But they'll know where the bigger cities are."

"It's a problem we were always going to face, Tes," Deavon said gently. "Even if we land right in the middle of their main city, we would still have the exact same problem we face now."

"Exactly," Baird agreed. "We are assuming that everyone in Tiadath knows who this Sergh is. But, in reality, he may be as unknown to them as we are."

The enormity of Baird's words crashed in on Tesania. Shaking her head, she muttered, "Will we ever find him?"

"First," Baird replied, "We must get safely ashore. From there we can formulate a plan."

Shaking her head, Tesania said, "I don't like it."

"We don't have much choice. Besides," he added as he slapped Rhys on his shoulder, "Between us; we can find anyone."

"I hope you're right," Tesania said quietly as she smiled up at Deavon's reassuring face.

"We'll find him, Tes," he said.

"But first, we need to get you there," Captain Eades said as he rose and excused himself, Lieutenant Nylor following behind, pausing to help Kailyn stand before hurrying after his captain.

"Thank you, Lieutenant Nylor," Kailyn called after him.

Pausing, the Lieutenant turned back and winked at the young mage, "Call me Lee," he said, winking again before turning and disappearing along the companionway.

"Lee," Kailyn whispered, sinking back in her seat.

Deavon nudged Tesania, a look of concern on his face as he mouthed, "Watch her."

Giddy sighed, obviously oblivious to the worried look on Tesania's face as she leaned back in her chair, hands behind her head and said, "Ninety odd long days . . . with you lot."

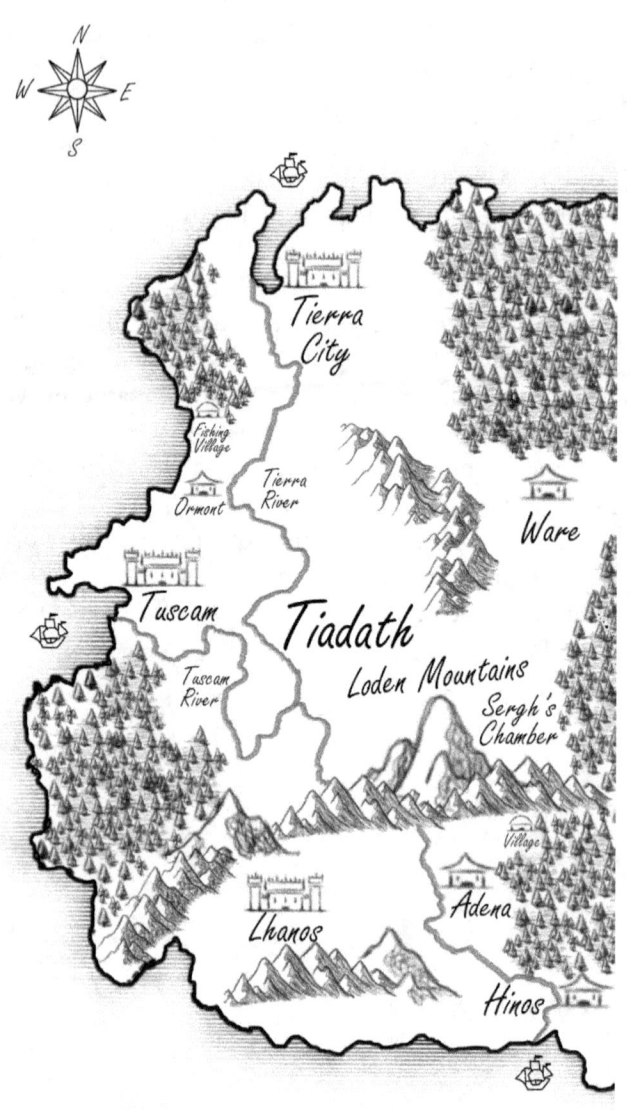

Tierra City

Fishing Village

Ormont

Tierra River

Ware

Tuscam

Tiadath

Tuscam River

Loden Mountains

Sergh's Chamber

Village

Lhanos

Adena

Hinos

36 - North-westerly

The Swan ran under three quarter sail before a freshening north-easterly breeze, her burbling wake glittering in the late afternoon sunshine. Tesania leant against the stern taffrail, eyes following the white trail, toward Eldanal; toward home. Sighing deeply, she pushed herself upright and turned, smiling briefly at Deavon before suggesting they should retire to their wardroom.

They had sailed from the filthy port of Estiel more than three months earlier after loading provisions for a nine month return journey, the captain insisting that over supply was much preferable to running low in the middle of an unknown ocean. No one had disagreed, each acutely aware of the fact that they were sailing into uncharted waters that could very quickly become hostile. And so, Tesania had waited patiently as Lieutenant Nylor supervised the nets of kegs and boxes that swung and swayed as they were hauled up onto the deck.

The journey had been almost relaxing once they had settled into the daily routine of ship life. Knowing that for now there was nothing else she could do, Tesania had fallen into the habit of walking the decks with Deavon and the others in between talking with the captain or reading the many books he kept stowed in his cabin. But as the days drew on and the Swan's full sails pushed them closer to Tiadath, she began to feel restless, eager to get on with the task ahead. With practiced ease she negotiated the deck of the ship as it rolled under her, eventually coming to the side rail where Kailyn watched Lieutenant Nylor demonstrate tying a knot, his hands deftly flicking the hemp rope over itself and through the loop he had created. "We're heading down," she informed the girl who barely glanced from the lieutenant's hand for more than an instant.

"Alright," she said.

"Are you coming?"

"Not just y—"

"Sail ho," a cry came from high in the rigging.

"Where away?" Nylor called, immediately throwing the rope aside.

"Off the port bow. Hull down."

Swinging to the rail, Nylor peered across the blue water before rushing toward the wheel as the lookout's voice rang down once more, "Bearing north-east, into the wind. Running away from us."

Tesania followed the lieutenant to the ship's wheel as the captain stepped onto the deck. "Ship off the port bow," he reported. "On a north-easterly course, tacking away."

"Very well," the captain replied before calling up to the masthead, "How much sail does she have?"

"Royals aren't set," the lookout called down, "She's doesn't appear . . . wait, she's coming about."

"They've seen us," Tesania gasped.

"Not necessarily," Captain Eades growled as he peered into the distance. Tesania followed his gaze but could only see water as he barked a command, "I'll have full sail, if you will, Mister Nylor." As the lieutenant began to bellow orders at the men, he said, "Coxswain. Steer sou-sou-west."

"Aye, sir," the coxswain replied the wheel already spinning through his seasoned hands.

"They're coming after us?" Kailyn asked Lieutenant Nylor. When he didn't answer, she asked again, "Lee!? Are they coming after us?"

"Possibly," Nylor replied smiling briefly at her before returning his attention to the sails. "You men there," he called, "Get those sails up."

"They may just be changing tack," the captain informed her. "We shall soon see," he added calmly.

"What if they are coming after us?"

"I shall deal with that when the time comes," the captain replied, irritation rising in his voice as he frowned briefly at the girl.

"Come away," Tesania said pulling at Kailyn's sleeve as she recognized that the ship's officers needed to concentrate on their jobs. "Let's go by the rail and see if we can see her," she suggested.

As Kailyn reluctantly followed, the captain called up to the lookout, "Masthead! report."

"She hasn't set more sail," the lookout called down. "Looks to be beating into the wind on a north-westerly heading."

"She's not coming around?"

"Nay, sir. She's running straight. Looks like she's on her port tack."

"Keep me informed," the captain called before turning and talking quietly to Lieutenant Nylor.

"See," Tesania said to Kailyn as Deavon came and stood beside them. "They didn't see us."

"I hope so," Kailyn replied.

"They would have come around immediately if they had," Deavon assured her as the captain strode toward them. "A close call," Deavon said.

"Very," the captain agreed.

"We must be getting close then?" Tesania said hopefully.

"I should think so," Eades agreed. "We've been at it for over ninety days. And," he added, "for him to have no lookouts set can only mean he feels safe in his home waters."

"They must have been sailing out from Tierra," Tesania ventured.

"Possibly," the captain agreed again, nodding. "We have no way of knowing where they came from though, or where they are going."

"I suppose," Tesania replied.

"Still," Deavon said. "We must be getting close."

Captain Eades considered it for a moment as Lieutenant Nylor approached and stood beside him before saying, "We need to head east tonight under limited sail. See if we can't find this land of Tiadath."

"We'll be landing tonight?" Kailyn asked her voice edged with sudden concern.

"If the winds hold," Eades replied.

"And we actually find Tiadath," Deavon said ominously.

"Indeed," the captain grunted before saying, "As I said, east under limited sail until we sight land."

"In the darkness?" Kailyn asked, her concern falling into confusion.

"There will more than likely be lights on shore, fires, candles in windows," Nylor assured her smiling as she blushed.

"And if there isn't?" Tesania asked. "If it's an uninhabited coastline?"

"That's why we go in under limited sail while taking soundings as we proceed," Eades replied. "The last thing I want is to run the old girl up on a reef."

"We'll see it either way," Lieutenant Nylor assured her as he looked to the cloudless sky. "With a near full moon the shore breaks will be visible for miles."

"Quite," the captain said.

"And if we do find Tiadath?" Tesania asked. "Can you get us in close enough to land?"

Shaking his head, Eades replied, "Nay . . . I won't take her in any closer than two miles."

"Two miles?" Kailyn gasped.

"Inshore reefs," Lieutenant Nylor explained. "From there, I'll be taking you in with the cutter," Nylor reminded her.

"Oh," Kailyn muttered.

"It draws a low draught so we will be able to land without much difficulty."

Nodding his agreement, the captain said, "And once we have safely deposited you ashore, we will stand out to sea."

"How will you know when we're ready to be picked up again?" Tesania asked worriedly, realizing that there were details they had not begun to plan. "We have no idea where this mage is; let alone how long it'll take to find him."

Eades nodded thoughtfully as he stared over the starboard rail. Eventually he turned his attention back to Tesania and said, "I will bring the ship in on the seventh night from today and then every night from there on."

"But how will you know we're there?" Tesania pressed. "Or that we're ready to be picked up?"

"A signal," Nylor suggested shrugging as he looked about the faces of the group. "A fire?"

"Too dangerous," Eades dismissed. "Anyone could light a fire for any reason. We might send the cutter crew into danger."

"And any fire might be investigated by those on shore if it's seen," Deavon added.

"My staff," Kailyn offered brightly. As the others looked to her expectantly, she explained. "I can call forth its light but direct it only out to sea."

"Clever," Nylor said.

"It's not hard," Kailyn said blushing as she looked down at her feet.

"But still, clever," Nylor insisted.

"It is settled then," Eades said ignoring the banter between the two as he turned and stepped away. "Have the cutter ready to slip when we sight land, Mister Nylor."

"Aye, sir."

Tesania watched the captain walk away. "We're nearly there," she whispered to herself before smiling up at Deavon, the excitement coursing through her tempered only by the trepidation and fear that had begun to claw its way through her gut.

37 - Dark Shores

Dull Moonlight reflected from the swirling eddies left like footprints in the waves by the cutter's six oars as she glided across the small swell off the western coast of Tiadath. Captain Eades had brought the Swan about as the afternoon wore on and steered directly east. It was a gamble, as they had no idea if they had sailed far enough south to be parallel with land they searched for, but as the ship moved slowly onward into the growing cover of darkness they were rewarded by a cry from above. "Land ho!"

It wasn't much of a sighting, just a shadow stretching along the horizon. But it was enough to drive them on as the excitement of finally doing something other than whiling away the days aboard ship began to churn in the travelers stomachs.

Now six of the Swan's sailors pulled at their oars as Lieutenant Nylor stood at the stern of the cutter, hand guiding its tiller as his eyes flicked from the gentle roll of the waves to his target onshore. It wasn't much of a target, just a few lights emanating from what appeared to be windows along the shore. It didn't look to be a city or even a town; possibly a small village or farmstead. Either way, it was Tiadath, and so they had clambered down the ship's side and stepped into the cutter before pushing away from their only attachment to home, setting themselves inexorably on the path to finally confront the Tiadath Mage.

"The northern point," Aldan called back from his position in the bow of the boat. "Looks calm enough to pull up to."

"Aye," Nylor replied as he stretched up and looked to the yellow, moonlit reflection of a small sandy beach that the ranger pointed to. "I'll set you ashore there."

"It's far enough away from the buildings to keep us unseen."

"We'll need to pull the boat up on shore," the lieutenant said lowering his voice now as they came closer to the beach. "We don't want the ladies feet getting wet."

"Don't worry about us," Tesania growled at him, eyes intently scanning the unknown land. "Just get us ashore."

"We'll have to beach it anyway," Nylor explained as he shifted the tiller and started the boat in on the back of a small wave. "Supplies to unload," he explained as the sand ground against the keel, the sound rasping through the wooden cutter. "Over the side," he ordered the two sailors at the front. "Get that anchor set."

As the two leading sailors disappeared, the splash of their entry into the shallow water seeming to be loud enough to alert all of the people ashore, the other four followed them and began to pull at the cutter as she rose on the incoming waves, shifting it farther up the beach with each swell. "That'll do her," Nylor ordered as he tied the tiller off and started forward, reaching his hand out to Kailyn to help her rise as the waves shifted the boat from side to side. "M'Lady," he said.

"Thank you," Kailyn said as she rose and stumbled to the bow where Nylor gripped her waist, lifting her like he would a doll as he handed her down to one of the sailors who roughly deposited her on the sand and reached up to grasp Tesania as she sat on the side rail and threw her legs over.

"I'm fine," she assured the sailor as she pushed forward off the rail landing on her feet before turning and reaching up for her pack which Deavon handed down as Lieutenant Nylor thudded down on the beach next to her and turned to retrieve Kailyn's pack. "We'll need to find cover," she said as Deavon jumped down beside her, stumbling forward as he lost balance.

"Makes sense," Aldan agreed as he prepared to alight from the boat, waiting for a swell to pass. "We can hole up until dawn and see exactly where we've landed."

"The trees up on the ridge there will do us," Raim said as he pointed at the shadows of what seemed to be a forest that crept down to the edge of a village.

"It's as good as anywhere," Tesania agreed after quickly scanning the shore between themselves and the illuminated windows along the beach. To their left was a near vertical cliff face that stood some twenty feet away while to their right was beach and waves for as far as she could see in the dim light. She couldn't see any other choice than to make for the trees beside the little village.

"I'll help you," Lieutenant Nylor said as he picked up Kailyn's pack and began to walk toward the trees.

"Shouldn't you be getting back to the ship?" Tesania asked, her frown invisible to the others in the darkness. "The captain will want to be away from land as quickly as he can."

"It's early," Nylor assured her. "We have hours of darkness to stand away. Besides," he added, the white teeth of his smile visible even in the darkness, "This pack is heavy."

"Heavy?" Tesania grunted. "It's no heavier than everyone else's."

"Still," Nylor insisted. "I'll carry it to the trees for her."

"And tomorrow?" Giddy asked mirth in her voice. "Who'll carry it then . . . ? Not me!" she added adamantly.

"I can carry it myself," Kailyn insisted reaching out and snatching the pack away from the sailor.

"I was only—" the Lieutenant began to protest.

"I know," Kailyn interrupted while pulling the pack onto her shoulders. "Giddy's right though. It's my pack, and I'll carry it."

"As you wish," Nylor conceded before adding softly, "I'll walk you up to the trees though." As Kailyn began to protest, he said quickly, "It's not far. I just want to know you're safe . . . . That all of you are safe," he added defensively before addressing the cutter's crew and instructing them to wait for his return.

The journey to the trees started out quickly, the traveler's footsteps sure on the still wet ground, but as the sand became dryer, they began to struggle as their feet sank ankle deep. Fighting for each step, Tesania found her foot stuck every time she planted it into the soft ground. Not glued, like it might be in mud, but all the same it was an effort to pull her heels free. What worried her more, however, as they grew closer to a row of fishing nets strung out to dry beneath the lighted windows of the houses, was the sharp squeak that emanated from the dry sand each time she stepped forward. "We'll need—" she began falling quiet as light sprang from an opening door.

"Burton?" a woman's voice called into the night. "You're back early? Is every—" the woman's voice cut in mid sentence as she reached inside the door and produced a lantern holding it high in the air as she squinted toward them, "Who are you?" she asked voice low and suspicious, but before Tesania could answer, she cried, "Thieves!"

"We're not—" Tesania began.

"It's no use," Deavon interrupted, placing his hand in the small of her back and pushing urgently as the doors to the houses along the shoreline began to burst open, men appearing quicker than Tesania would have thought possible. Not needing any more prompting, she began to run, the sand clawing at her feet making it feel like she was running on the spot. Shouts echoed through the darkness as the villagers gave chase, their cries shattering the still night air. Glancing back, Tesania could make out at least a dozen men on their trail, thankfully struggling in the loose sand as much as she was. Breath ragged, legs burning, she turned her attention back to the trees in front of her. Raim led the way, his small, athletic frame visible against a strip of moonlit sand as he struggled up a slope toward the forest they had seen from their landing spot. There wasn't much sand now, just the strip they ran along between two jagged piles of rocks protruding down from a dark ridgeline, funneling them toward the trees that stood like a wall of blackness above them.

"Keep moving," Deavon said from behind her, his breath as ragged as her own.

Fearing she wouldn't be able to keep up the effort for much longer, Tesania drew on her reserves and pushed on, step after agonizing step as her calves protested each thudding footstep she took forward. Reaching the top of the rise, it was too much, her legs, after months of idleness at sea, could take it no more. Exhausted, she looked back expecting to see their pursuers gaining ground. Instead, she stopped, Deavon careening into her back almost knocking her to the ground as he desperately reached out and supported her. "Move," he managed to say voice labored insistent hands pushing her toward the darkness of the trees.

"They aren't coming," she managed to say between deep, drawn breaths, throat burning.

"What?" Deavon said as he turned and stared down toward the villagers.

"They've stopped," Tesania said pointing at the huddle of men standing at the base of the rise gesticulating toward them, their voices drifting up the slope with threats of what would happen to Tesania and the others if they dared come back down. "We mean you no harm," she managed to call down to them, having somewhat recovered her breath.

"Mean us no harm?" a man's scornful voice asked. "Sneaking around in the middle of the night?"

"We weren't sneaking at all," Tesania protested.

"Stealing the nets, I'll wager," the man said ignoring her words. "We won't have it, you hear."

"We have no interest in your nets," Tesania assured him as Kailyn and the others gathered around her.

"Why aren't they following us?" Kailyn asked peering down the slope.

"They're fishermen," Aldan replied, adding as the girl's face turned to him in confusion, "They don't have weapons."

"Oh," Kailyn said as she looked back at the men.

"And," he added, "They have no way of knowing if we do."

"Then why were you sneaking about?" the fisherman demanded.

"We were just . . . ."

"We were just . . . !" the man mocked before adding, "Just stealing our nets."

"It's no use," Aldan said from beside her.

"The road in is over yonder," the man suggested, his waving arm visible in the moonlight. "You didn't come in that way or we would have heard you."

"You're quite right. We didn't come in that way," Tesania assured him.

"Tes," Deavon said quietly, warning her she was giving too much away.

"Where did you come from then?" the man asked as he turned and looked back at the sea.

Acutely aware of the cutter and its crew, Tesania looked toward the headland but could see no sign of them against the whitewash of the waves. Frowning as she wondered where they might be, she could only think of one thing to say and blurted out, "Tierra City."

"Tierra," the man echoed. "And what would city folk be doing sniffing around our nets in the dead of night?" he asked before adamantly adding, "Stealing them!?"

"We were not—"

"We have ways of dealing with thieves," the man continued.

"We are not—"

"You say you are from Tierra City?"

"Yes."

"Why are you here then?"

"We are travelling."

"To?"

Tesania turned to Deavon. She had no way of answering the question. The only place they knew in the whole of Tiadath was Tierra City. When he shook his head with no helpful suggestions, she frowned, wracking her brain. Eventually, she called down the slope, "South."

"South!" the man scoffed. "South you say. Well that explains everything," he added as his colleagues laughed and murmured beside him. Eventually, he asked, "South . . . to where? Ormont?"

"Yes," Tesania said a little too quickly as she grasped onto the name he offered. "To Ormont . . . to visit my family."

"To visit your family," the man said. As Tesania thought she might be convincing the man that they meant no harm, he accused, "And yet you sneak into our village under the cover of night."

"We weren't sneaking."

"Sneak past our homes . . . make your way to the nets!"

"We have no interest in your nets."

"Come down here!"

"Why?"

"So we can show you how we deal with thieves."

Sighing in exasperation, Tesania replied her voice terse, "We are not thieves."

"It's no use, Tes," Deavon said, touching her arm lightly before calling down the slope. "She speaks the truth." As the man began to speak he cut him off. "But I can see you will not believe this. So we will take leave of you now."

"Take your leave," the man called up. "But know this; we are on to you. You hear me? Come near the nets again and we will not be so forgiving."

Without another word to the man, Deavon turned and motioned toward the trees. "Let's move on before they change their mind."

Glancing down the slope, Tesania shook her head, acutely aware that the men still staring up at her could have been a valuable source of information had things transpired a different way.

"What about Lee?" Kailyn's voice came from beside her, causing her to start.

"Lee?" she asked, confused.

"He'll have to return to the Swan?"

"She's right," Lieutenant Nylor said from behind them. "I'll need to be back aboard soon so the captain can get us well clear of the coast before dawn."

Once again scanning the seemingly empty headland where they had landed such a short time ago, Tesania shook her head and said gently, "I'm afraid they've left you behind."

"Left him?" Kailyn asked confusion in her voice. "But they're waiting for him."

"It appears not," Tesania said as she motioned toward the empty headland. "They've gone," she said as she looked sadly at the lieutenant's face.

"I guess they would have," he said slowly, swallowing hard as the reality of it set in.

"They'll come back," Kailyn assured him. "They won't leave you here."

"I'm afraid they will," Nylor said, voice tinged with sadness as he stared out to sea.

"But they can't," Kailyn said adamantly. "You're their first lieutenant."

"They did what they must," Nylor replied matter-of-factly. "What I would have expected them to do once we were compromised."

"Leave you!?"

"For the ship's safety? Yes . . . . And for ours," he added turning to her. "They did the right thing," he said a smile growing across his face, "Besides; now I can protect you."

Scowling, Kailyn muttered, "I don't need protecting." Spinning, she strode heavily into the trees, Lieutenant Lee Nylor, first officer of the King's Ship Swan, mumbling apologies close behind.

Shrugging, Tesania glanced back to the sea once more, back to where the Swan and her only link to home lay.

Breathing in deeply before slowly exhaling, she turned and followed the others into the trees.

38 - Prying eyes

Yawning, disheveled hair sporting a myriad of dried leaves, Tesania sat up in her bedroll in the little clearing they had found during the night. It wasn't much of a camp as they had barely been able to see in the darkness amongst the dense trees, even with the light emanating from Kailyn's staff. No one had argued when Deavon suggested it was as good a place as any and had sunk down onto the leaf littered ground. Their meal hadn't been much, just a few morsels of dried bread and cheese washed down by a little water. But it sufficed as each of them sat in their own silence seemingly contemplating the enormity of being in an unknown land where every person they might meet would more than likely want to harm them rather than offer any help. Feeling weary, Tesania had suggested to Kailyn that they turn in as Raim offered to take first watch.

A fire now crackled in the middle of the clearing where Giddy stood poking at a pan that hissed and sizzled and spat back at her. Aldan and Deavon stood nearby discussing she could only imagine what. Throwing her blanket aside, she stood, stretching her arms to the sky as she yawned once more. "Morning, sleepy head," Giddy called. "Breakfast?"

"Please," Tesania mumbled as she picked her way over to the soldier, avoiding the sharp twigs and sticks amongst the leaf litter.

"Sleep well?"

"Well enough," Tesania replied as she picked the leaves from her hair smiling as Deavon approached. "Good morning."

"It is indeed," Deavon said while peering through the canopy of the trees to the bright blue sky. "A good day for travelling."

"To where?" Rhys asked from the far side of the clearing where he sat cleaning his knife, a small piece of material sliding up and down the blade as he considered them, eyebrow raised.

Looking to Deavon and then Aldan and finally Giddy, Tesania conceded she had no real idea, suggesting finally, "Ormont."

"Ormont, you say," Rhys said amusement in his voice as he glanced about the clearing. "And where is that?"

"South," Tesania ventured. Knowing what was coming, she quickly added. "I know . . . it's vague."

"Vague it is," Rhys replied as he slipped the piece of material into his pocket. "But it's a start, and better than anything else we have."

"True," Tesania agreed as Giddy shoved a plate at her. "Thank you," she muttered before looking back to the little thief. "It's more than likely on the coast."

"I would think so," Aldan said as he moved to her side, also accepting a plate from Giddy.

"And what will you do when you get to Ormont?" Lieutenant Nylor asked, looking around the group.

"We," Kailyn said sleepily from her bedroll as she pulled herself into a sitting position. "You are coming with us, Lee . . . . Remember?"

Frowning at Kailyn for a moment before gazing toward the west where his ship would be, Nylor shook his head sadly before taking a deep breath and turning to Tesania, asking, "And what will '*we*' do when '*we*' get to Ormont?"

"We," Tesania replied, smiling at the Lieutenant consolingly before going on, "will find out when we get there."

"Ormont will be a start," Baird interrupted from where he sat by the fire. "Whether it's a city or just a town, we don't know. But there we will find out more than we know now."

"Agreed," Aldan said. "But first," he added while thumbing the collar of his shirt, "we need to get rid of these clothes."

"Our clothes?" Kailyn enquired as she stood and walked toward the fire.

"To fit in," Rhys informed her. "Dressed as we are, we'll never disappear amongst the masses," he added.

Confusion contorted Kailyn's face as she said, "But the men last night didn't seem to notice our clothes."

"It was dark, you ninny," Tesania said laughing as realization dawned on Kailyn's face.

"We could visit the fishermen again," Rhys suggested eyes alight as he spoke.

"No," Deavon said flatly.

"But they're close," Rhys defended. "Probably out fishing."

Shaking his head, Deavon once more said, "No," before explaining, "They've seen us once. That's enough."

"What does it matter?"

"Deavon's right," Baird said to the thief. "The less we are seen, the less people will remember us. I should think you of all people would know this."

Scowling at the spy, Rhys spat and flipped the knife in his hand before pointing it at Baird. "Don't tell me what I should know."

"It was just an observation," Baird assured the thief, spreading his hands conciliatorily.

"He's right though," Tesania said to Rhys.

As Rhys spat once more in disgust, Aldan said, "We move inland. There has to be a road nearby."

"Agreed," Deavon said, nodding. "Let's find the road and then head south."

"And our clothes?" Tesania asked.

Shrugging, Deavon replied, "We'll need to play it as it comes. Farmsteads, villages . . . ." he trailed off.

"South it is then," Giddy said as she began kicking dirt over the fire.

39 - The Tiadath Mage

A bead of sweat sat on Sergh's forehead, glistening in the flickering torchlight before breaking and running down the side of his face in a rivulet. Wiping it away, the Tiadath mage looked toward his assistant on the far side of the volcanic cave in the Loden Mountains. "Who are we visiting today?" he asked mater-of-factly as if he were asking what was for supper.

"A small farm owned by their king," the assistant replied while pointing his finger at a map in his hand. "Just outside Rilmir."

Rubbing at his temple, Sergh asked, "Grain?"

"Livestock. Pigs and chickens it seems."

"Pigs and chickens," Sergh muttered shaking his head. He was beginning to tire of the task he had taken on for the Dalglieshs. But he knew he must carry on for the time being, must do as the fools wished. Still, it irked him that his decades of work toward his goal, his thousands of hours of research and study were being used for what? "For what?" he whispered aloud, mirroring his thoughts. "To serve some lord and his brat!"

"I'm sorry?" his assistant said. "What was tha—?"

Waving his question aside, Sergh stepped to his altar and attempted to clear his mind. For now he would do the Lord's bidding to get his gold; gold that would fund his army, gold that would see him rise to be emperor of the entire world. '*Then,*' he thought sadistically, a sneer playing across his face, '*Dalgliesh . . . his daughter . . . all the pompous fools . . . will grovel at my feet.*'

40 - Clandestined journey

Tesania raised herself onto her elbows on the small hill she lay upon and pulled at the rough cloth of her new dress. It was hardly the ideal attire she would have chosen to steal, but it was all that the little farmstead had had. She still felt guilty for having stolen it, along with clothes for the others, from the farmers as they worked out in the fields. But they had come across no other habitations on their journey south and she had little choice other than to allow Rhys to pick the inadequate lock of the home and rummage through the meager belongings. There wasn't much in the rough hewn, wooden cupboard, just a few dresses and folded trousers and shirts. She wondered for the hundredth time what the poor woman must have thought when she came back from the fields, exhausted and filthy, to find her best clothes gone. Looking toward the little thief now, she shuddered and shook her head, wondering how he could do what he did for a living, leaving his victims empty handed and bereft while he profited from their hard work. The only consolation she had as she pulled at the coarse material once more, was that at least the farm woman was similar in size to herself, whereas Kailyn's dress floated on her like a ship's sail flapping in the breeze. Shaking her head once more at the thief, she let it slip from her mind and turned her attention to the township in front of them. "Ormont?" she asked of no one in particular.

"I doubt it," Deavon replied from where he lay on the small grassy hillock beside her. "It's a little small."

"Agreed," Aldan said. "I got the impression from the fisherman that it was a place more substantial than this."

"All he said was Ormont," Raim interrupted. "It could be this place."

"Only one way to find out," Giddy said, rising to her feet and adjusting her oversized shirt. "Who's coming?"

"I will," Tesania replied, standing and moving to the soldier's side.

"And I," Deavon said as he also stood.

"Three's enough," Raim said as he rolled onto his back, crossing his legs and closing his eyes before mumbling, "I'll wait here."

Laughing out loud, Giddy said, "Fine by me. More ale for us."

"Ale?" Raim asked, his interest in the little town suddenly renewed as he shifted and peered over the hillock once more. "You think they have a tavern?"

"You'll never know," Giddy teased. "Now go to sleep."

Rising, Raim brushed himself off. "I think you might need more than three," he suggested while smiling lopsidedly at Tesania and then Deavon. "I mean, will Giddy be enough to protect you?"

"Protect us?" Tesania asked in mock surprise. "Protect us from what?"

"Err—"

"I think Deavon might be able to protect Giddy," Tesania went on. "Assuming Giddy ever needed protection."

"Not Giddy," Raim insisted seizing onto an idea. "You. I'll protect you."

"But I'll protect her," Giddy insisted. "We don't need you along."

"But . . . I . . . ." Raim sought for the right words, eyes darting from the distant town and back to Tesania.

"Just let him go," Aldan sighed. Motioning to Kailyn and the rest of the party still sitting on the ground, he added, "We'll never hear the end of it if you leave him here."

"I suppose he could come along and stand guard outside the tavern door," Giddy conceded. "Make sure we don't get any unexpected visitors."

"Outside . . . ." Raim said glumly before obviously realizing that Giddy was teasing and grinning.

Shaking his head at the two soldiers, Deavon spoke to Aldan, "We'll be back in an hour or two. Make sure you stay out of sight."

"Will do," Aldan replied as his four companions began to walk away.

"Enjoy your ale," Rhys called nonchalantly after them from where he sat. "We'll visit you in the lockup afterwards."

"Lockup?" Tesania asked as she stopped and turned.

"Lockup in exchange for your ale."

Still perplexed, Tesania looked around the others.

"Money," Baird said. "He's referring to your lack of Tiadath coin. Which," he added, scowling at the thief, "He could have simply said."

"I'll say it as I wish," Rhys growled.

"Obviously," the spy replied screwing his nose in distaste as he looked Rhys up and down. "But you might have come straight to the point."

Scowling at the spy, Rhys turned his attention to Tesania distaste replaced by a wry smile as he said. "You won't have Tiadath coin to pay for Giddy's ale."

"He's right," Tesania said as she looked at Deavon in concern.

"We should have searched the farmstead," Rhys went on. "They would have had a stash of coin somewhere."

"Don't you think we took enough from them?" Baird asked. "They'll struggle to recover from what we did take."

Shrugging, Rhys replied, "Then they need a better lock."

"Would it have kept you out?"

Rhys gave a mocking laugh and replied simply, "No."

"Baird's right," Deavon interrupted, "We took enough from those poor folk."

"Agreed," Tesania said as she unconsciously felt at the collar of her shirt. "We couldn't have taken their money too."

"Then you won't be drinking ale any time soon," Rhys said in fake sympathy as he winked at the two soldiers.

Looking from Rhys to Raim who simply shrugged back at her, Giddy turned to Deavon and searched his eyes as she said, "We must have something we can exchange . . . ?"

"No," Deavon said adamantly as he began to pace back and forth thinking for a moment before saying, "We can't risk compromising ourselves."

"But—"

"No buts, Giddy," Deavon said waving her to silence as he began to pace in thought. "No ales then," he eventually said. "We ask questions and leave."

"That'll raise its own suspicions," Giddy said seriously, having obviously forgone the desire for ale. "Four strangers walking into an inn and asking questions while ordering nothing. No," she said, shaking her head. "It won't work."

"I'll go," Rhys offered as he pushed himself up and gained his feet, slapping at the dirt on the knees of his pants.

"You have no money either." Aldan suggested. "It won't solve anything."

"He won't need money," Baird assured them.

Ignoring the Aliagan spy, Rhys said, "Trust me."

***

Rhys paused under a weathered wooden sign that swung in the light breeze, its rusted iron hooks groaning softly in protest at each movement back and forth. "Ormont," he muttered to himself as he read the faded writing and then shifted his attention to the dusty main street in front of him. A few dozen people wandered about the street in the afternoon sunshine, men and women about their daily business of trading and purchasing goods while a few children ran raucously behind a hoop they rolled along a furrow in the well worn and compacted ground. Ignoring the children, his practiced eye roamed over the adults. It always amazed him how easy folk made it for people of his ilk to do their work. Grinning wryly to himself, he watched a man with the string of his purse hanging from his pocket, not only announcing the whereabouts of his valuables but openly inviting its theft. Deciding the man was a little large and well built, the little thief turned his attention to a woman inspecting vegetables outside a store, her purse held loosely in her hand allowing the mouth to gap open, an easy target for someone with his skills. Deciding that the street was too open for his work, Rhys began to walk forward, making his way to the buildings on the left hand side of the street where he could keep to the shadows. "Ma'am," he said, nodding as he approached a woman looking at the vegetables, smiling as she snatched at her purse and drew it to her side. "Would you be able to tell me where the tavern might be?" he asked.

Regarding him suspiciously as her eyes ran over his ill fitting clothes, the woman motioned along the road toward a cross street. "Down to the right; a few doors."

"Thank you, ma'am" Rhys said smiling thankfully at her as he bowed slightly. "I'm a bit parched, you see," he added as he gripped his own throat between thumb and forefinger.

"I'm sure," the woman said as she edged away.

"Is everything alright," a man's voice asked from behind Rhys.

Turning, the little thief took the man in. judging from the apron adorning his body, he guessed him to be the shopkeeper. "I was just asking where the tavern was."

Scowling, the shopkeeper also looked down at Rhys' ill fitting clothes before pointing to where the woman had pointed previously, "Down the road. Now be on your way."

"There isn't any need to be rude," Rhys protested. "I was just asking."

"I'll thank you to be on your way," the shopkeeper said as he once more looked down at the thief's clothes. "Or I'll call the sheriff."

Raising both hands disarmingly, Rhys groaned, "No need to be calling the sheriff. I was just asking an honest question."

"Did you get those clothes honestly?" the shopkeeper asked and then growled without waiting for an answer, "On your way."

Not wanting to push the situation any further, Rhys began to back away, hands still in the air. "I'll be going," he said. Slowly, he turned and made his way along the street, glancing back as he reached the corner. The shopkeeper seemed to have forgotten him already as he helped the woman pick out a bunch of turnips. "This place would be easy pickings," he whispered to himself thinking of how he would be able to get his associates down to Tiadath and then back again. It would be easy enough, he surmised.

After all, Lafric would be able to supply the contacts to plenty of captains like Rygal. But would it be worth it, he wondered as he walked toward a sign that read, The Black Goblet Tavern. The weeks of sailing, sitting on their idle hands, while they could be plying their trade in the cities they knew so well. Probably not, he surmised as he stepped onto the worn stone threshold of the tavern and moved cautiously inside.

Musty darkness greeted Rhys as he squinted his eyes, trying to adjust to the dimly lit room. There didn't appear to be any windows in the tavern, at least none that allowed any light in to chase away the darkness. Instead, candles flickered on a few dozen or so crowded tables, acrid smoke rising lazily from their tips to pool and swirl amongst the blackened roof beams. It wasn't unlike many of the taverns Rhys had visited in his life. In fact, it was exactly the type of atmosphere he preferred. Too much light hindered him when he was working or allowed others to see what he was doing when he was in his downtime.

Looking about the room as his vision adjusted, Rhys found what he was after and walked to a table on the western wall. "Mind if I join you?" he asked to the seemingly drunk man sitting by himself, near empty mug clasped between his hands.

Taking Rhys in through bleary eyes, the man slurred, "Suit yerself," motioning to the chair opposite him.

"Thank you,' Rhys said while pulling the chair back and sitting down. "Rhys," he said reaching a hand out.

"Rhys," the man repeated as he stared at the thief's hand. "Funny name."

"Indeed," Rhys replied without missing a beat as he drew his hand back. "My father travelled a lot," he explained. "Never told me where he picked the name up from I'm afraid." As the man looked away disinterestedly,

Rhys asked, "Can I ask your name." Grinning disarmingly, he added, "Wouldn't want to drink with a stranger."

"Brianus," the man mumbled before swilling the last of his ale down, swaying in his chair as he lost balance for a moment.

"Steady there," Rhys said as he quickly rose and stepped around the table grabbing at the man even though he had already found his balance.

"I'm right," the man insisted, weakly shoving Rhys' hands away.

"Alright then," Rhys said as he returned to his seat. "I thought you were about to fall."

"Yer think I'm drunk," the man accused. "I can hold me ale as well as any man."

"I'm sure you can," Rhys said, winking as he pulled a plain leather purse from under the table and sprinkled out a few Tiadath coins onto the table. "Care for another," he asked. "My treat," he added, winking once more.

Staring at the purse in the thief's hand for a moment, the man struggled to focus as he swayed in his chair, shaking his head sharply, he looked back up and squinted at Rhys, "Generous of yer," he said slowly.

"Not at all," Rhys said as he caught the eye of a passing waitress and ordered two ales before saying to the man, "So, Brianus; are you from around these parts?"

Belching loudly, Brianus adjusted himself in his chair, the movement seeming to take an inordinate amount of effort and time. As he scratched at his crotch, he replied, "I were born here."

Smiling up at the waitress as she arrived and deposited two jugs of ale on the table, Rhys paid her a few coins and turned his attention back to the local man. "Drink up," he insisted pushing a mug toward Brianus' hand as he took a small sip of his own ale. Watching the man over the rim of his mug, he decided to get straight to the point before Brianus collapsed. "I'm looking for a mage," Rhys said simply.

"A mage?" Brianus muttered in confusion. "In Ormont?"

"Specifically a mage called Sergh. You know him?"

"How would I know him," Brianus asked laughing aloud, whole body shaking before he lost his balance once more and suddenly grabbed at the table to support himself.

Shrugging, Rhys said nonchalantly, "I heard he spends a lot of time in Ormont. With the other mages."

Shaking his head and peering at Rhys as though he thought he might be a simpleton, Brianus slurred, "Ther ain't no mages in Ormont."

"Oh," Rhys said trying to keep the disappointment from his voice. Gazing down at his mug for a few moments he began to spin it between his fingers as he thought, eventually looking back up at the man, he asked, "None at all?"

"Nah," Brianus growled. "I just said ther weren't none here."

"So you did," Rhys said disarmingly, smiling as he added, "Forgive me."

"Maybe a few Sha- charlatans," the man offered stumbling over the words.

"I was assured there were real mages here," Rhys said this time allowing the disappointment to show through in his tone. "I must have heard wrong. What a waste of time," he added shaking his head sadly. "Mother will be so angry with me."

"Yer mother needs a mage?" Brianus asked before taking another swill of his ale.

"Yes," Rhys replied. "She won't be very happy with me, I'm afraid. What, with the crops dying."

"Dyen?"

"Cursed," Rhys said sadly. "Looks like we'll lose the whole crop." Pausing, he then looked the man straight in the eye. "I shouldn't bother you with my problems, friend." As the man began to reply, Rhys asked, ale, my friend?"

The drunken man seemed deep in thought as he nodded yes, eventually he offered, "Maybe ther Mages' Guild?"

"Mages' Guild?" the thief asked as he motioned for ale for Brianus.

"Tuscam. Ther be a whole mess of them mages ther," Brianus replied as the waitress approached and placed his new ale on the table by his arm.

"Tuscam," Rhys echoed. "You know where it is?"

Swigging more ale, the man scowled at Rhys before leaning forward, reeking breath washing over the little thief as he growled angrily, "Course I do. Yer think I'm dumb or sumfen?"

Cringing away, Rhys replied easily, "Not at all. I sat here because you looked like the most intelligent person in the room."

Brianus considered his words dubiously, before sitting back and taking another swig of ale. "Maybe not ther smartest, but I'm not ther dumbest," he eventually said, the words slurring worse than before.

"As I said," Rhys said grinning, "I sat here for a reason." When the man didn't reply, Rhys said, "Forgive my ignorance, but where is Tuscam . . . ? From here, I mean?"

"Sssouth," Brianus slurred "Three days from 'ere if yer on foot."

"I have a horse," Rhys lied.

Draining his mug, Brianus slapped it down on the table and said, "Day or two then,"

"Another?" Rhys asked gesturing at the empty ale mug jingling his new coin bag in front of the man's face.

Blinking as he tried to focus on the bag, Brianus said, "Yer generous fer a stranger."

"Let's say I came across some easy money," Rhys replied, smiling delightedly at his own joke. "Ale?" he asked whilst motioning to the waitress once more.

"One more," "Brianus agreed swaying in his chair as he blinked at the waitress when she arrived with a fresh mug of amber ale.

"Thank you," Rhys said to the woman, handing her a coin as he picked his own ale up and drained it. Standing, he said to Brianus, "It's been a pleasure drinking with you."

Staring up at him for a moment, Brianus squinted once more as if trying to decide if he knew the man in front of him.

"Enjoy your ale," Rhys said as he threw the coin bag up and snatched it out of the air feeling alive as he laughed aloud at the drunk man who had no idea his own purse was being displayed in front of him. "Maybe next time, you can shout the ales," he suggested winking once more as he turned and headed for the tavern door.

41 - Gathering information

"Tuscam," Rhys said happily as he returned to the others waiting outside of Ormont and tossed the purse of coins to Deavon.

"Where's that?" Kailyn asked.

"Farther south. A couple of days."

Prizing the purse open and peering inside, Deavon asked, "What's in Tuscam?"

"My friend," Rhys said laughing as he motioned to the purse in the ranger's hand, "said there's a Mage's Guild there."

Pulling the purse strings shut, Deavon threw it to Aldan as he said, "Well done" to Rhys slapping him lightly on the back before turning to the others. "Tuscam it is."

"We could stay the night in Ormont," Giddy suggested as she eyed the purse in Aldan's hand. "Get an early start in the morning."

"I wouldn't advise it," Rhys said winking at her.

"Why not?"

"First rule of his business," Baird answered for him. "Don't be anywhere near your mark when they discover they've been robbed."

"Exactly," Rhys reluctantly agreed while scowling at the spy. "The farther we're away by the morning, the better."

***

Tesania sighed in relief as she slipped her feet into the cool water of a brook burbling through the little copse of trees where she and the others had stopped to survey the walls of the coastal city of Tuscam. Barely visible now through the swaying foliage, the walls stood high and proud with bastions protruding every few dozen yards.

"Impressive," Aldan said from where he crouched peering through the trees.

"Very," Deavon replied as he too scanned the walls, his eyes stopping on the gates while he studied the movements of the people entering and leaving the city. "I don't see any guards," he eventually said.

"I'm sure someone would be watching," Aldan said as he motioned toward the arrow loops that adorned the heavy outer stone of the bastion nearest the gate.

"It's just another city," Rhys said nonchalantly from where he sat by the brook. "Unless they were at war, they wouldn't have guards, would they?"

"I guess not," Deavon conceded.

"War or not," Baird interrupted, "they would have people watching the gates."

"For?" Lee asked in interest.

"Anything that catches their interest," Baird replied easily.

"Such as?"

"Kings, counselors, anyone in power has a vested interest in knowing who, and indeed what, is coming into their cities."

"Such as?"

"Many things," Baird said evasively.

"That doesn't help much," Kailyn said coming to the young lieutenant's aid.

"They watch," Rhys said laughing at Baird, "but they don't always see."

"We see more than you may think," Baird said slyly and he considered the thief.

Scoffing, Rhys replied, "You see what we let you see."

"On the contrary," Baird assured the little thief, "We see, but often do not act."

"This is getting us nowhere," Tesania interjected, frowning at Rhys and then Baird before asking, "Do you think we would attract the watchers attention?"

"I would say so," Baird replied, ignoring the look on Rhys face.

"Why?" Tesania asked as she looked down and pulled at her shirt. "Our clothes?"

"No," Baird replied.

"Our number?" Kailyn asked.

"Clever girl," he said to Kailyn's delight. Looking about at the others, he explained, "The people assigned to watch would think nothing of the regular faces that come at go through the gate; except," he added while glancing slyly at Rhys, "people of interest."

"If they saw me," Rhys growled.

"When they saw you," Baird assured him before turning back to the others. "A stranger however," he said, "Would be noticed and noted but usually dismissed unless something in particular tweaked the watcher's suspicions."

"Like?" Aldan asked.

"Demeanor," Baird suggested, "what they carry with them, weapons and such."

"So they would be suspicious of everyone?" Tesania asked.

"Not necessarily," Baird replied. "But a party of nine," he said motioning to the gathered group, "would most definitely draw their attention."

"What could they do?" Aldan asked. "I don't know Tiadath very well, but I'm sure travelling in a big group wouldn't be against the law."

"Who knows," Baird said shrugging his shoulders. "As you say, we have no idea what their laws are."

"So, they might arrest us."

"I doubt it," Baird dismissed. "But they would more than likely watch us."

"A tail?" Deavon asked.

"I would think so. At the very least."

"That would cramp us. We need to be able to move around freely" Aldan said.

"Exactly," Baird replied.

"So we go in twos," Lee suggested. "Then they wouldn't suspect anything.

"We could meet at the town square," Rhys said as he stood and peered toward the city gate. "And then decide what to do from there."

"Not all of us," Deavon said as he too stood. "We would still draw too much attention if we arrived together at an inn."

"True enough," "Baird agreed. "The innkeeper may very well report such a gathering to the authorities."

"No innkeeper I know," Rhys interjected. "They hate the law as much as we do."

"Do they?" Baird asked simply a knowing smile spreading over his face.

Considering him for a moment, Rhys squinted at the spy as if trying to read him and then shook his head. "I don't believe that for one moment."

"Perhaps," Baird replied his smile growing, "that's a good thing." As the thief scowled at him, he turned to Deavon and said, "I suggest that, like at Ormont, the majority withdraw into the woods and make camp while only a couple enter the city and scout around."

"Looks like no ale for you again," Raim said, digging Giddy in the ribs and grinning at her.

"Or for you," Giddy replied, remaining stony faced as Raim's grin slipped away.

"I'll go," Rhys volunteered, ignoring the two soldiers' banter as he looked about the group. When no one objected, he asked, "Who's coming with me?"

"I'll come," Baird replied standing and walking to the thief's side.

Scowling, Rhys said, "Plainly, someone else would be better suited."

"Better suited?" Baird asked eyebrow raised as a smile flitted playfully across his lips at the little thief's obvious discomfort. "Who is more suited to the task than I?"

Snorting, Rhys stepped away from the Aliagan spy. "Surely you want to come instead," he asked Deavon, almost pleading as he sneered back at Baird.

"He's right," Deavon said as he tossed the purse of Tiadath coins to the spy. "He's the best man for the job."

"Bah," Rhys spat. "I'll go in by myself."

"I think you should take Baird," Tesania said, rising and walking to the thief. "Like he says, his background makes him best suited."

"It's not like we're spying," Rhys protested. "All we're doing is finding the Mage's Guild and asking a few questions. Any of you could do it."

"If anyone can do it," Baird said cheerfully as he began walking through the trees toward the city, "Then you won't mind me tagging along. Coming?"

"Coming!?" Rhys spluttered at the spy's back before glaring around at the others. "Any of you could have volunteered, any of you!"

"But he did," Giddy replied, grinning at the thief. "You'd better hurry and catch him."

Looking around, Rhys watched the spy for a moment before looking back at Giddy and sighing. "I'll be back as soon as I can." Turning, he hurried after Baird.

***

Baird waited for Rhys to catch him at the edge of the trees. Although he would never admit it, he actually liked the little thief. But he was aware that their different positions in life would preclude them from ever truly being friends. Still, he mused as Rhys reached his side, whilst the thief would never turn on his own, he was now a contact on the inside of the Aliagan underworld: a contact well worth grooming. "Best we head through the trees to the road," he said motioning to the dusty road in the distance. "If they see us coming in across the field it may raise suspicions.

"Agreed," Rhys said as he started forward.

Baird fell in beside him remaining silent until they reached the road and fell in behind a turnip laden wagon, its bullocks straining at their yokes while the farmer swore and cursed at their slowness. "I suppose we could have had worse positions in life," he said to Rhys.

"Indeed," Rhys replied adding nothing more to the conversation as he brushed away the hordes of gnats that seemed to be following the wagon.

Suggesting they slow their gait, Baird allowed the farmer to get some distance ahead of them relieving them of the swarms and the rather unpleasant odor of the farmer and his bullocks. It suited him to stay behind, allowing their approach to the city gates to be easy and unassuming. Eventually, as they got to within a few hundred yards of the gates, he looked down at Rhys and asked, "Does it look promising?"

"What?" Rhys asked looking up at the spy and then at the walls.

"Tiadath?"

"Oh," Rhys said looking down at the road in thought.

Assuming he wasn't going to get an answer, Baird said, "It's a long way from home."

"Yes, it is," Rhys said before surprising the spy and adding, "I thought it might be a bit more, shall we say, primitive here."

"Un-organized you mean?" When Rhys simply nodded, he asked, "You came across a gang in Ormont?"

"No," Rhys replied shaking his head.

"What makes you think it's organized then?"

"That," Rhys replied looking up at the walls now looming over them. "You don't have a city like that without having crews working it."

"True enough," Baird replied as he also looked up at the forbidding walls. "You could make a deal with them," he suggested wondering as he did why he was talking in such a manner.

"No," Rhys said. "Why would they want to cut in an unknown from another land?"

"I guess they wouldn't."

"I wouldn't . . . if they came to Aliaga, that is."

Smiling wryly, Baird thought of the uproar if another syndicate arrived in Estel and tried to muscle in on the action. Shuddering as the implications hit home, he said, "It would start a gang war."

"Exactly," Rhys said, voice low as he nodded in agreement. "I think I'll stay with what I know;" he stated. "With the people I know."

Chortling to himself, Baird said, "I'll be sure to tell the king you will be staying on as his loyal subject."

"You do that," Rhys said grinning up at the spy.

"I'm sure he'll be delighted," Baird quipped.

"I'm sure," Rhys replied laughing along as they walked through the open gates of Tuscam.

Immediately, the road opened into a sprawling quadrangle as they entered the city. Horses, bullocks and carts littered the area, laden with goods and livestock, their owners busily negotiating and yelling at one another as the slow moving bullocks blocked others' ways. Baird couldn't have asked for a better scene, the chaos allowing for himself and Rhys to slip in and quickly disappear amongst the throng. Tapping Rhys on the arm as they slipped between over laden wagons, Baird motioned toward the eastern wall and began weaving his way through, eyes searching the crowd and surrounding walls as they went. "Brown tunic, against the wall to our left," he muttered to the little thief while looking the other way.

"I'd say so," Rhys replied without looking at the man leaning against the wall. "Doesn't seem too interested in us."

"No," Baird replied, risking a glance at the man whom he had identified as a city agent. Thankfully, Rhys was right, the man had seemingly dismissed them as a threat and had his attention firmly fixed on a group of disheveled farmhands that had just come through the gate, their raucous cries rising above the din of the already packed quadrangle. Reaching the wall, he forgot the man and turned right, walking swiftly toward what seemed to be a street running between the houses at the far end of the quadrangle.

Having no idea where the Mage's Guild would be, Baird surmised that the best place to start asking would be the drinking houses where peoples' tongues tended to be looser after a few ales. "We need to get to the inner parts of the city and find a tavern or inn."

Nodding in agreement as he stepped aside to allow two women to pass, Rhys approached a well dressed gentleman who hobbled toward them, the crack of his silver tipped cane hitting the cobbled street echoing off the walls around them. "Excuse me," he said. "Would you be kind enough to point us in the direction of the nearest tavern?" When the man looked him up and down with a scowl playing over his face, Rhys added, "We're here on business you see and it's been a long, dry trip. We'd like to refresh is all."

"What's your business here," the man asked his scowl turning to interest.

Nudging the little thief to be careful, Baird decided to be as truthful as he could be and replied instead, "We have business at the Mage's Guild."

"The Mage's Guild," the man repeated eyebrow raised as he once more looked the two men up and down. "You don't look like mages."

"Well, no," Baird said pulling down on his shirt unconsciously. "We aren't mages. But we have business with them."

"Business?"

Baird's instant thought was to say they were tailors hoping to secure a contract with the guild, but as the man's eyes still lingered on his poor quality farmers' clothing, he scrambled to say, "We're farmers"

"Farmers you say," the man said suspiciously screwing his nose and looking down at their attire again before asking, "What business would farmers have with the Mage's Guild."

Baird racked his brain as Rhys shuffled nervously beside him, motioning they should move on. Struggling for an answer as the man became agitated his face changing from distaste to distrust Baird suddenly remembered Kailyn tending to the burnt man at Dalgliesh's estate. "Herbs," he said. "We grow herbs and berries for their potions and spells."

"Herbs and berries you say," the man said his demeanor changing back to interest.

"Lungis berries, specifically," Baird said, the lie now coming easily as he gained confidence in it. "Although we do grow quite a variety for them."

"Lungis berries," the man said nodding his head, obviously believing the spy's story. "Can't say I've heard of them."

"They ferment them. Tastes quite vile,' Rhys stepped in having obviously also remembered Kailyn's ministrations to the burnt man. "But their pain numbing qualities are quite extraordinary."

"Perhaps I have had them," the man said rubbing at his thigh. Raising his cane, he said, "Had a nasty fall last year. Broke my leg."

"You had Lungis berries then?"

Shrugging, the man grinned at them and said, "I have no idea. But whatever the healer gave me for the pain was repulsive."

"But it worked?" Baird asked. "With the pain, I mean?"

"Yes indeed," the man said

"That would have been our Lungis berries then," Rhys said feigning pride. "It's nice to meet someone who's benefited from our hard work in the fields."

"Anyway," Baird interrupted thrusting his hand out to shake the man's hand before he could answer. "You were saying the nearest tavern was . . . ?"

"Yes," the man said, a little confused at the sudden turn in the conversation. Turning, he raised his cane once more and pointed along the road ahead of them. "The nearest tavern would be The Seven Stars. A hundred yards or so that way," he informed them.

"Straight ahead?" Rhys asked looking into the distance as he tried to see past the people walking along the street.

"Yes, you can't miss it," the man said as Baird and Rhys thanked him and started off. "But I wouldn't go there," he added bringing them to a sudden halt.

"You wouldn't?" Baird asked turning back.

"Not if you're bound for the Mage's Guild afterward."

"Where should we head then?"

"The Crown's down that way," the man said motioning to a street on their right. "Three blocks."

"Why's The Crown better than The Seven Stars? A tavern's a tavern, isn't it?"

"Yes; but The Crown is almost directly across the street from the Mage's Guild. It might save you some time after you . . ." once again the man looked down at their clothes, ". . . freshen up."

"Again," Baird said as he reached forward and shook the man's hand once more, "we owe you our thanks."

"Not at all," the man replied. "Just keep growing those berries," he added, winking as he turned and began to hobble away.

"The Crown it is," Baird said grinning at Rhys. "Your treat I believe."

Scanning the people of Tuscam as they walked to The Crown, Baird decided they were much like the people in any other city he had been to. Whilst their clothes were a little different in cut than he was used to, the materials were much the same. Given that, and that they spoke essentially the same language as the people of Aliaga and Eldanal, he surmised there must have been trade in the distant past, probably centuries ago. Or perhaps Tiadath's population was made up of people who had fled Aliaga in the past to avoid persecution or indeed starvation in a long forgotten famine. Shrugging to himself, he decided he would probably never know. Reaching a crest in the street the harbor below the city came into view, blue water dotted with ships and boats, their masts reaching for the sky. "Substantial," he said to Rhys as he too surveyed the harbor.

"Bigger than Estiel," Rhys agreed.

"Definitely," Baird replied as they reached The Crown Tavern. Stone bench seats ran along the length of the front of the tavern with a few other people enjoying their drinks in the sunshine their voices drifting along the slight breeze. Baird considered sitting in the sun also, but years of habit drew him to the far corner where the shade of a swaying oak tree created a darkened pocket. Sitting, he nodded to Rhys when he asked if he would like an ale.

As the man had suggested, the Mage's Guild sat almost directly across from the tavern, its impressive, wide stairs sweeping up from the street to an imposing stone doorway. Allowing his eyes to travel over the carved stonework of the two story building, he could only marvel at its grandeur. Scanning further, he paused for a moment on the gardens; enclosing the front of the building were manicured lawns with patches of bright flowers and shrubs punctuating the greenness, butterflies and other insects flitting between. Farther back, along the eastern side of the guild was a low stone wall dividing the front of the gardens from the areas at the rear. He could plainly see courtyards where hooded mages sat conversing on stone seats while others sat in what seemed to be classes or lectures, their teacher's hands weaving intricate patterns. Farther back still appeared to be the more mundane part of the guild's daily activities; living quarters and outhouses lined the far wall while seemingly wet robes and other clothes hung over ropes strung between grand old oak trees. Breaking off his inspection as the thief arrived back, he reached for his ale, muttering, "Thank you."

"Impressive," Rhys said as he sat beside the spy running his eyes over the building across the street.

"Indeed," Baird replied taking a sip from his mug. "They obviously take their magic seriously."

"I'd say so," Rhys replied as he too sipped at his ale, still studying the building. "Probably why this Sergh can cast spells that our mages could only dream of producing."

Nodding in agreement, Baird continued drinking while watching the comings and goings of the guild. Hooded figures came and went at irregular intervals, their hands always gripping staffs. Draining the last of his ale, he said in a disappointed tone as a group of three mages stepped from the guild's front door, "We won't get any information."

"Why not?" Rhys asked, frowning as he too watched the mages.

Baird watched the thief as he struggled to understand, smiling as he saw it dawning over his face. "Exactly," he said.

"I see your point," Rhys said, eyes following the three mages as they walked down the stairs toward them. "We could say we're mages," he suggested half heartedly.

"It wouldn't work," Baird replied shaking his head as he placed his empty mug down onto the bench before looking Rhys up and down. "We hardly look the part."

Nodding slowly, Rhys considered their situation before suggesting, "We could always ply one of them with ale."

Shaking his head, Baird replied, "I don't think so. It would be a long shot to find one that even knows Sergh, let alone where he can be found."

"True enough," Rhys conceded. Scuffing his foot along the ground, he sat in thought as he scanned the street and the building in front of them. Suddenly he grinned and looked at Baird before nodding toward the ropes strung between the grand old oaks at the back of the guild's courtyards.

Raising an eyebrow as he got the gist of the thief's meaning, Baird considered the proposal before saying, "We will need more than robes."

"Like?"

"Staffs," Baird suggested, nodding toward the mages as they walked away from them along the street. "They seem to never be without them."

"Steal them."

"No," Baird replied sadly. "They may leave their robes out to dry," he said motioning to the oak trees. "But they would never leave their staffs where they could easily be taken."

"That's never stopped me before."

Laughing lightly, Baird replied, "I'm sure. But, it could raise the alarm. The last thing we need is to be caught. Besides," he added, "There are other obstacles."

"Such as?"

"Knowledge," Baird said, winking at the thief. "What if they start talking in terms we don't even understand."

"I see your point," Rhys said looking sullenly down at the ground.

"So," Baird said as he stood and stretched his back. "We need mages' robes—"

"Easy enough," Rhys replied.

"And staffs, not to mention knowledge . . . ." Baird trailed off.

Rising, Rhys said, "I have an idea." Starting for the low stone wall leading to the old oak trees he said over his shoulder, "I'll be right back."

42 - Ingress

"Me!?" Kailyn exclaimed flinching as a deep burgundy-red robe flew at her from Rhys' hands. Snatching it from the air, she drew it down to her lap where she sat beside Tesania. Caressing the material between her fingers, she looked up to the little thief and then the spy. Frowning as she realized they were serious, she shook her head and looked aghast at the others gathered around the crackling fire. "Why me?"

"You're a mage, aren't you?" Rhys asked eyeing her staff leaning against a tree behind her.

"Well . . . yes . . . ." Kailyn stammered.

"Then you're the obvious choice," he insisted while dropping his pack and laying a second robe he carried on top of it.

Shaking her head once more in disbelief, Kailyn looked to Tesania, eyes widening as she said, "But I don't know their spells . . . or their symbols. What if they're different from the spells we use in Eldanal?" Looking back to Rhys, she quickly looked down at the robe and whispered, "I can't."

"You have to," Rhys said bluntly. "We . . ." he went on motioning to himself and Baird, ". . . know even less than you do."

"I just said I don't know their ways," Kailyn defended.

"You won't need to," Tesania said gently as she reached over and laid her hand on Kailyn's arm.

"Exactly," Rhys said. "All you need to do is look the part."

"Then you do it," Kailyn said sharply as she looked up and pointed at the second robe.

Following the line of finger, Rhys sighed and shrugged before turning and starting toward the staff leaning against the tree. Reaching out, he said, "I'll need to borrow—"

"No," Kailyn exclaimed, jolting upright as she snatched for her staff.

"I would think that you've come across enough mages," Aldan said moving his large frame between Kailyn and the thief, "to know better."

Holding his hand up in placation, Rhys stepped back. "I meant no offence," he said. "I was merely making a point."

"So you see now why it must be you?" Baird asked softly while stepping to her side. "Everyone we saw coming and going from the guild," he said whilst looking at her earnestly, "was a mage . . . with a staff."

"But what will I say?" Kailyn asked as she looked once more at Tesania for support.

"We'll cover that," Baird said drawing her attention again.

Swallowing, Kailyn shook her head. "What if I forget something?"

"You won't," Baird assured her.

"How can you be so sure," Kailyn asked doubtfully.

"Because I'll be there with you."

Brightening for a moment, Kailyn smiled at him before slipping back into her doubts. "But you don't have a staff."

"No," Baird agreed.

"He won't need one," Tesania said catching on to the spy's plan.

"But Rhys just said—"

"Ninny," Tesania interrupted grinning at her friend. "Did you have a mage's staff before you graduated?"

"No," Kailyn said in confusion.

"But you had a staff?"

"An apprentice's staff, yes," Kailyn agreed catching on. Looking at Baird, she said, "Apprentices staffs are plain. They don't have an imbued gem."

"Precisely," Baird said grinning at her. Motioning to the robe on Rhys' pack, he said, "I'll come with you, as your apprentice."

"Isn't she a little young to have an apprentice," Giddy scoffed while looking the spy up and down. Especially one your age."

"She has a point," Deavon said. "You are a little old to be an apprentice."

"As are you," Baird pointed out, eyebrow raised.

"Tesania's the only one young enough," Aldan suggested before Deavon could answer the spy.

"Me?" Tesania asked in surprise. "I'm older than Kailyn. too."

"True," Aldan replied. "But you are the closest. There's only a few years between you."

"Four," Kailyn said softly, more to herself than anybody else.

"Four," Aldan repeated. "That's close enough? Isn't it?"

"A late starter," Raim suggested before adding mischievously while winking at Tesania, "A slow learner."

"We know who the slow learner here is," Giddy scoffed at her friend as she reached out and clapped him lightly on his shoulder.

"I learn well enough," Raim defended.

"It could work," Tesania interrupted them as she looked at Deavon. "If Kailyn weren't my master, but rather an assistant to my master."

"It still leaves the age difference?" Rhys said.

"I started late," Tesania suggested, shrugging at the little thief as she thought. "I just started this year even . . . . That way I can play naive when it comes to the ways."

"It could work," Rhys conceded.

Growing into the task, Tesania added as she pointed at Kailyn, "You've finished your apprenticeship and have been asked to run an errand for our master. An errand to find, Sergh."

"And you're along for support?" Kailyn asked also starting to take the task seriously now that her friend would be coming along.

"That," Tesania agreed, "As well as support and company."

"It may just work," Deavon said as he considered it.

"Won't they ask who your master is?" Lieutenant Nylor asked from where he sat by the fire, concern on his face as he looked up at Kailyn.

"They couldn't possibly know the name of every mage," Kailyn replied frowning uncertainly.

"I doubt it," Giddy agreed. "There are plenty of generals in the army; I wouldn't know most of them by sight let alone their names."

"Giddy's right," Baird said. "There were dozens of mages entering and leaving the guild in the short time we were there. They couldn't know every mage in Tiadath by name."

"Then will they even know who Sergh is?" Lee asked.

"That's something we will need to find out," Baird replied.

"Either way, we don't have a choice, Lee," Kailyn said, having obviously accepted her role. "If they don't know where he is we will probably never find him."

"It's settled then," Deavon said. Turning to Tesania, he said, "You'll need something that will pass as a staff," before moving into the trees with Aldan close behind.

***

Tesania adjusted her robe nervously on the bench seat outside The Crown whilst she watched the front door of the Mage's Guild across the street, her fingers running anxiously over the knotted branch that Deavon had returned from the trees with. It wasn't much of a staff, just a gnarled old length he had found in the copse of trees, but once stripped of its bark and rubbed with some oil taken from their cooking supplies it looked as if it might be something presented to a novice just starting out on their journey of magic.

"I'll wait for you here," Baird said as he cupped Kailyn's shoulder to reassure her. "You'll be fine."

"I suppose," Kailyn said her tone unconvincing. "I have no idea what to say, though."

"I'm sure they have mages coming and going all day asking questions," the spy suggested. "Just try to be natural and play it by ear."

"Play it by ear," Kailyn muttered unconvinced.

"We'll be alright," Tesania assured her as she stood and smoothed her robes. "Let's just get on with it."

"You'll do fine," Baird called after them as they headed towards the wide stairs leading to the guild door.

"What shall I say?" Kailyn asked as they climbed the stairs and stood before the doorway, stepping aside to let a young mage past.

Reaching out, Tesania adjusted her friends robes for her, smoothing the shoulders and brushing a small piece of lint from the collar. "Ask exactly what we want to know," she suggested. "Don't try to create some elaborate story. Stay with what you know and keep it simple."

"Simple," Kailyn repeated drawing a deep, quick breath as she glanced at the door.

"Simple," Tesania said again smiling at her friend, trying not to project the fact that she felt just as nervous about what they were going to do. "Ready?"

Eyes flicking to the door once more, Kailyn drew one more deep breath smiled at Tesania and with a swish of her robes strode into Tiadath Mage's Guild. Gone instantly was the uncertain girl as the two walked into the cavernous foyer of the guild. Instead was a purposeful young mage intent on doing her masters bidding, a young mage suddenly exuding the confidence she had earned through years at the Carella Mage's Guild in Eldanal, years that had seen her emerge as a fully fledged mage. "Well met," she said to a young, seemingly apprentice mage.

"Well met," he replied voice bored as he looked past them with little interest.

"You might pay me the courtesy of paying attention when I talk to you." Kailyn snapped.

Surprised at Kailyn's clipped tone, Tesania quickly played along as the young man looked from Kailyn to herself. Smiling sympathetically, she rolled her eyes toward Kailyn, suggesting she felt for her fellow novice and knew his lot.

A hint of a smile appeared briefly on his lips before he looked back to Kailyn and asked sullenly, "How may I assist you?"

"Much better," Kailyn said aloofly as she glanced about the room. "My master," Kailyn said emphasizing the words "wishes some information about a fellow mage. Where might my assistant and I go," she said motioning to Tesania, "to enquire about such things?"

Drawing himself up to his full height, "the young man announced, "You need an appointment."

"An appointment?" Kailyn asked. "Do you know who my master is," she demanded, her confidence in her role seeming to grow as she went on.

"N . . . No."

"What is your name?" Kailyn asked looking him up and down disdain in her voice. "My master will be most interested in knowing who stood in her way."

"I'm not standin—"

"Then tell me whom we should speak with?"

Unsure of himself now, the young man's eyes flashed from Kailyn to the hallways at the back of the room and back again, finally settling on Tesania. "Please," she pleaded frowning at Kailyn nervously, "I will be punished," she mouthed to him before looking sadly away.

Obviously in a quandary, torn between his duty and helping a fellow, seemingly downtrodden apprentice, the young man stared at Tesania for what felt like an age before stumbling over his words as he said, "Mast . . . Master Cemal."

"And where would this Master Cemal be?" Kailyn asked while once more looking pointedly around the room. "Do you think I can read minds?" she then snapped looking back at the man in annoyance. "Well . . . ? I don't have all day."

"I'll take you to him, shall I?" the young man muttered looking nervously from his feet to Kailyn and back again.

"I think that would be prudent," Kailyn said. When the young man simply stood there, she added, "Perhaps now would be as good a time as any!"

As the young man scuttled away toward the back of the room Tesania fell in beside Kailyn and whispered in an accusing voice, "You're enjoying this . . . . Aren't you?"

"A little," Kailyn replied quietly, slipping Tesania a quick smile before falling back into her roll and looking sternly ahead as the man lead them into a hallway and past three doors before stopping and knocking tentatively on the frame.

"Pardon my interruption," he said flinching as if he expected a lightning bolt to sizzle from the doorway and engulf him.

"What is it?" a gruff voice came from the room followed by the distinct shuffle of parchments. "I don't have any other appointments today."

"These. . ." the apprentice began looking apprehensively at Kailyn before glancing at Tesania and smiling briefly, courage seemingly bolstered as he continued, ". . .people are here on the bidding of their master to enquire the whereabouts of a err. . . mage."

"You know the procedure," Cemal growled. "Tell them to speak to my assistant and make an appointment for next week sometime."

"That won't do," Tesania whispered, her tone urgent as she shook her head at the young man and looked fearfully at Kailyn. "Please," she whispered almost inaudibly doing her best to plead with him with her eyes.

Fear mirrored in the young man's face as he swallowed hard and looked from Tesania to Kailyn's stern face. Coughing apologetically, he said to the mage inside the room, "Forgive me, but they have travelled a long way."

"So has everyone else."

"Please," Tesania mouthed again as the young man looked at her in a loss for what to do.

"I. . . I—"

"Stand aside," Kailyn said, pushing past the young man and entering the doorway, Tesania hurrying behind. "Well met," Kailyn said curtly to the mage sitting behind his desk, parchment piled high on each side in small trays that seemed dwarfed by the piles. "You may go," she said, turning to the young man and waving him away. As relief flooded over his face and he turned and hurried away, Kailyn sat down at the opposite side of the table without waiting to be asked and motioned for Tesania to take a second empty chair. Smiling disarmingly at the mage, she said in a cheerful voice, "Thank you so much for seeing us on such short notice."

Rising, the mage said angrily, "I did not agree to speak with you." Finger lifting toward the door, he continued, "Now, if you would kindly lea—"

"My master will be very pleased that you chose to speak with us so quickly." Kailyn went on unperturbed. "I'm sure you will be rewarded handsomely."

Finger still pointing at the door, Cemal's voice changed from anger to intrigue, "Rewarded?"

Tesania watched the conversation, amazed and silently proud of the way Kailyn had stepped so outside herself and forgotten her nerves. She looked every part the confident spokesperson of a powerful mage. The mention of a reward was a master stroke, she could see by the glint in Cemal's eye and the change in his demeanor. Deciding Kailyn didn't need her help, she sat back to enjoy the show.

"Indeed," Kailyn replied. "Naisa can be very generous to those who help her."

'Naisa,' Tesania almost snorted but managed to hold herself together.

"Naisa," Cemal repeated obviously wracking his mind. Doubt crept into his voice as he said, "I can't say I have heard of her."

"I'm sure there are many mages in Tiadath you haven't come across," Kailyn dismissed lightly.

Cemal considered her words for a moment, glancing at Tesania and then back to the young mage in front of him before running his eyes along her staff to the gem inlaid at the tip.

"Need I demonstrate my skill?" Kailyn asked her voice icy as she flashed the gem for an instant.

"No," Cemal replied, his attention coming back to Kailyn's face. "I did not question your knowledge of the ways."

"Your actions suggest otherwise," Kailyn said looking up at the top of the staff, her voice returning to normal.

Peering at Kailyn through slit eyes, Cemal asked, "What can this . . . Naisa, possible offer me."

"Gold," Kailyn said simply.

Seemingly unimpressed, Cemal assured her as he motioned to the piles of parchment, "Offers of gold are not something I am in shortage of."

"My master," Kailyn said without missing a beat, "has also authorized me to offer you a debenture."

Sitting forward, Cemal's face lit up with more interest. "A debenture," he repeated. "Tell me, what good would your master's debenture be to me?"

"I'm sure . . ." Kailyn said slowly as she for the first time struggled for the right thing to say, ". . . that . . . a debt . . ." she went on before seizing on an idea, ". . . with a mage of her standing would place you in a position of power when negotiating with her in the future."

"Her standing?" Cemal asked. "As I said, I have not heard of her."

"Not here," Kailyn said quickly. "But in the north, where she lives, she is building her contacts and power base at a remarkable rate."

"You speak very highly of her," Cemal said as he clasped his hands together and put his forefingers to his chin.

"She is my teacher," Kailyn said simply nodding to herself. Before adding, "As well as my master."

Lowering his hands and nodding slowly, Cemal sat back and once more studied Kailyn and then Tesania. Eventually he asked, "You will put this debenture in writing?"

"Of course," Kailyn assured him.

"And you guarantee she will abide by this debenture?"

"My word is her bond."

Once more, Cemal studied the pair in front of him for some time, his attention switching between them as he studied their faces. For some moments his eyes rested on Tesania's staff causing her to hold her breath until he turned his attention away. Eventually, he leant to a drawer and produced a blank parchment. Pushing it toward Kailyn he motioned to a quill and ink on his desk, suggesting he accepted the debenture as he asked, "What is it that your master has sent you to ask?"

Picking up the quill, Kailyn dipped it in the ink and began to scrawl a commitment that she knew she, or Naisa would never have to fulfill. "She wishes to know the whereabouts of a mage by the name of Sergh," Kailyn said simply, not looking up as she continued to write.

"Sergh?" Cemal asked in surprise.

"Yes, Sergh," Kailyn repeated as she signed the bottom of the debenture with bold cursive hand writing.

"Reaching across, Cemal picked up the parchment and read it before looking to Kailyn and saying, "Caitriona. An interesting name."

"Thank you," Kailyn replied demurely before asking, "Now, can you tell us where we can find Sergh?"

Cemal waved the parchment in the air a few times to dry the ink before carefully folding it slipping it into the same drawer he had taken the blank page from. "Anyone could tell you that," he said grinning triumphantly. "Why, even that imbecile," he said gesturing at the door, "that brought you to me without an appointment could have told you Sergh abides in Adena."

"Adena," Kailyn echoed before looking at Tesania a little confused. "Forgive me," she said as she looked back at the mage. "I haven't travelled much," she explained. "Could you tell me where Adena is?"

Cemal considered her dubiously before asking, "You don't know where Adena is? What kind of a Teacher is this Master of yours?"

"She taught me magic, not geography," Kailyn fired back defensively before asking abruptly. "Is it near here?"

Looking down at the closed drawer as if he wondered if the debenture would be worth much now that the girl's lack of knowledge about Tiadath became apparent, Cemal replied, "South east. Maybe your Master might give you a few geography lessons in future."

Dismissing his jibe, Kailyn asked, "How many days walk is it from here?"

"Walk," Cemal said guffawing. "Don't tell me you haven't heard of the Loden mountains?"

"Of course I have," Kailyn lied hotly before steadying herself and asking, "So it is on the far side of the mountains?"

Shaking his head, Cemal muttered to himself, "What are they teaching young mages these days." Reaching to the drawer, he produced another parchment. Dipping the quill, he began to draw a crude map showing the position of Tuscam, where they now were, the mountains and the township of Adena, adding a few other city and town names as he went.

Watching him intently as he drew a solid line of mountains across the width of Tiadath, Kailyn asked, "Is there a road through the mountains?"

Looking up as he finished the map, Cemal shook his head and muttered, "I hope I do meet your master one day. I will be having words to her about your education." Looking to Tesania, he said, "I hope she is doing a more thorough job with you."

"Is there no road?" Kailyn asked again. "Through the mountains?"

"No," Cemal replied his anger rising. "You have to sail around the south west point," he said, indicating by stabbing his finger onto his map. "Anybody who knows anything about Tiadath knows you need to sail to Hinos to get to Adena."

"I didn't," Kailyn said simply, smiling at him as his anger rose. Reaching out, she plucked the map from his fingers and rose. "Thank you for your time," she said quite honestly as she made for the door.

Smiling briefly at the angry mage, Tesania hurried after Kailyn, whispering as she caught her, "You did so well."

"I know," Kailyn whispered back, eyes wide, body shaking with adrenalin. "I think I upset him though," she added, laughing as she reached back and tried to rub between her shoulder blades. "I could feel his eyes burning into my back."

Walking from the hallway and into the front foyer, Tesania quickened her step, eager to be out of the place. Nodding to the young apprentice who had shown them to Cemal's office, Tesania flashed him a smile and mouthed, "Thank you," before pushing Kailyn out the front door.

43 - Ship for hire

"A ship," Deavon said as he listened to Kailyn recount what the mage in the guild had said.

"Cemal said it was the only way," Tesania said as she pointed at the map the mage had drawn which now sat on a stone in the middle of the huddled travelers. "The Loden Mountains run all the way across Tiadath."

"Impassable?" Aldan asked.

"According to Cermal; yes," Tesania replied. "He said the only way to get to Adena was by sailing to Hinos," she recalled pointing at the name on the lower right of the map.

"Sail on a Tiadath ship," Lee said whimsically.

"Settle down," Giddy said to the lieutenant. "It's just another ship."

"Another ship," Lee gasped, shaking his head in disbelief. "Every ship's different," he assured her.

"Every ship?" Giddy asked. "Most of them look the same."

"Even so," Lee said, eyes alight. "They all ride differently, hold to the wind differently. No two ships are ever the same, not even the same design built by the same shipwrights."

"If you say so," Giddy replied looking at the young sailor as if he were inebriated.

"How long have you had your sword?" Lee asked, pointing at Giddy's scabbard.

"Years," Giddy replied her hand moving unconsciously to the hilt.

"Swap it with Aldan," Lee suggested.

"Swap it?" Giddy asked stepping back.

"Yes," Lee went on enthusiastically. "Exchange swords."

"What . . . for a minute or two?"

"No; forever. Give him your sword and you take his."

"No!"

"Why not?"

"Because it's mine," Giddy said defensively, hand rubbing the pommel.

"And you know its feel . . . its weight . . . its balance?"

"He's got you there," Raim said to Giddy, laughing at her discomfort.

"You see?" Lee said. "A ship is like your sword. Each one of them has its own characteristics."

"I see your point," Giddy conceded. "Just tone it back a little," she suggested. "We don't need you wandering about a Tiadath ship like a besotted puppy, drawing attention to us."

"He's just excited to see a new type of ship," Kailyn came to his defense. "I can see why."

'So can I," Giddy surrendered before turning to Deavon and asking seriously, "You think there will be any for hire?"

"There's only one way to find out," Deavon replied shrugging. "Tomorrow morning we go into the city a few at a time and meet at the docks."

"The Crown Tavern is near enough to the docks," Baird suggested. "We could all meet there."

"Agreed," Deavon said, to Giddy's delight. "But for now, let's move farther back into the trees and make camp."

***

Tesania sipped at her cider before placing it down on the bench beside her. So far there were only five of them at the tavern. Rhys had come in with Giddy and Raim, all three of them sitting at a table in the sunshine, on their second ales, while Tesania had accompanied Deavon in, enjoying the walk as they had time to talk privately, something they rarely got to do of late. Kailyn and Lee were due in next followed by Aldan and Baird.

"He suits them," Deavon said motioning to Rhys.

Tesania watched the three for a few moments, smiling as she said, "Giddy seems to like him."

"A rare thing," Deavon said laughing.

"It can be," Tesania agreed, also laughing. "They certainly all like to drink ale," she added as Giddy motioned for another round from a passing waitress.

"That they do," Deavon agreed. "It's been months for them though," he said sympathetically. "So I guess we can allow them another before we stop them."

"Good luck with that," Tesania said as Kailyn came into view. "Over here," Tesania called, waving to her friend. As the young mage and Lee approached, she offered them a cider, Lee deciding he would prefer an ale. Catching the waitress' eye as she deposited Giddy and the others' drinks on their table, she ordered, adding two ciders for Baird and Aldan assuming they wouldn't want ale.

"You might be right about Baird," Deavon said laughing as he raised his ale and sipped. "Aldan . . . cider?"

"He'll survive," Tesania assured him grinning.

"I guess he'll have to," Deavon agreed.

Falling silent as she sipped her drink, Tesania's gaze fell on the forest of masts at the bottom of the hill. There were dozens of ships at anchor in the harbor while just as many were tied up along the docks. There appeared to be many types, square riggers and caravels were among the few she could name. She supposed Lee might know more of them but decided not to ask. Instead, she turned her attention to the spy and the big ranger as they walked toward her. Smiling, she handed them their drinks. Aldan looked at his and sniffed, disappointment flooding over his face before he caught himself and said "Thank you."

Laughing, Tesania said, "You can have an ale, if you wish."

"I can?"

"Of course," Tesania said as she reached out and took his cider. "Order an ale."

"Thank you," Aldan said, this time meaning it. "Baird?" he asked, nodding at the spy's mug as he started off in search of the waitress.

"Cider's fine," Baird assured him before turning to Tesania and thanking her. "We're all here then," he said, looking around at the others.

"Some in worse shape than others," Deavon said as Raim called for another round. "Last one," he called to the soldier's disappointed look. "We'll hopefully be sailing today. The last thing we need is the captain turning us away for drunkenness." When the soldier nodded his understanding, Deavon said to Baird, "I think we'll only need a few of us to search for passage."

"I should think so," Baird agreed. "It's not far down to the docks anyway."

"I'll come," Tesania offered.

"And me too," Lee added finding it hard to control his eagerness.

"And you too," Deavon said laughing. "Just try and curb your enthusiasm."

"I'll try," Lee assured him.

"Good man," Deavon said. "Kailyn?" he then asked.

"Hmm?" Kailyn enquired over the rim of her mug.

"Would you like to come down to the docks with us?"

"Yes please," Kailyn replied, brightening as she lowered the mug and beamed at Lee. "Maybe I can keep you under control," she said.

"Maybe," the lieutenant replied sheepishly.

"Drink up," Deavon said as he stood and drained his mug. "The sooner we get this lot . . ." he said motioning to Giddy's table, ". . . onto a ship, the better."

***

A cacophonous screech of seagulls engulfed the dock area as Tesania walked past a fishing boat unloading its daily catch. It felt good to be by the sea again, the breeze ruffling her hair carrying the salty smells of the ocean along with the not so pleasant odors of the men hauling crates of fish from the bobbing boat. "Plenty to choose from," she said as she looked out into the harbor and took in the many different types of ships.

"Truly," Lee replied his attention dashing from one ship to another barely pausing long enough to take them in.

Shaking his head at the lieutenant, Deavon motioned toward a group of sailors approaching them. "Excuse me," he said. "We're looking for passage to Hinos. You don't happen to know any ships heading that way that might be able to board us?"

"Can't 'elp yer," one of the sailors replied, turning and raising his arm to point down the dock. "I'd be askin' at the Lazy Wench down yonder if I were you."

"Thank you," Deavon said as the sailors moved past.

"Sounds like the tavern might be a good starting point," Tesania suggested as they began to walk again.

"I'd say so," Deavon replied.

"Where all good captains spend their time when in port," Lee said, laughing.

"It seems to be," Tesania agreed.

"Makes it easy to find them," Kailyn said happily.

"Most definitely," Tesania said, smiling at her friend as they came to the Lazy Wench. Looking up at the heavily weathered sign, she could make out the faded old image of a rather large woman draped over a barrel. "Who names these taverns?" she asked seriously.

"Men," Kailyn replied, shooting Lee a sideways glance.

"Not me," he defended. "If I owned a tavern I'd name it The Swan."

"After your ship?" Tesania enquired, growing to like the young man more and more as he nodded affirmatively.

"Shall we?" Deavon asked as he pulled the door open and ushered the others inside.

The usual dark, musty scene of a tavern greeted them as they entered. Squinting as her eyes adjusted, Tesania motioned toward the barkeep who stood behind his bar talking to a sailor. Nodding, Deavon led the way.

"What'll it be?" the barkeeper asked, excusing himself from the sailor.

"Nothing today," Deavon informed the disappointed man. "We're just looking for passage to Hinos. Some sailors suggested there might be a captain here that could help us?"

Jutting his chin toward a table with three men sitting at it, the barkeeper said, "Captain Bolow over there'd be your man."

"Thank you," Deavon said as he turned and moved toward the table. "Captain Bolow?" he asked.

"That would be me," one of the men replied standing and nodding to Tesania and Kailyn before sitting again. "How can I help you?"

"We're looking for passage to Hinos."

Nodding, the captain asked, "Just the four of you?"

"Nine, actually."

"Nine," the captain repeated, still nodding. "I can manage that."

"Where will we meet you?" Deavon asked.

"Not so fast," the captain said holding his hand out. "You've got your passes?" he asked.

"Passes?"

"Travel passes," Captain Bolow said as if Deavon should know what he was talking about.

"I'm afraid we don't," Deavon said honestly, not knowing what else to say. When the captain's eyes floated over the group suspiciously, Deavon hurriedly said, "We're from inland. We don't travel by ship much."

Seemingly accepting the explanation, Captain Bolow said, "I can't take you I'm afraid. Not until you get your passes."

"We're in a hurry to get to Hinos," Deavon said. "Can we pay you a little extra and forget the passes?"

Shaking his head, the captain said, "Not worth it. If I was caught with you on board and no passes I'd lose my ship."

Obviously deciding that they were not going to get any further with the captain, Deavon asked, "Forgive my ignorance. But where do we get these passes?"

"Harbor master's office at the end of the docks."

"We'll go and get them now," Deavon said as he started off.

"I'm sailing in a few hours," Captain Bolow informed him. "On the ebb tide."

"I'm sure we'll be back in time."

Uproarious laughter erupted between the three men at the table. Settling himself, the captain said, "Maybe . . . if you're lucky . . . you'll get your passes in six or seven days."

"Six or seven days," Tesania repeated. "We can't wait that long."

"You don't have a choice," the captain informed her. "They'll want to check your identity. Confirm where you've travelled from."

Looking at Deavon in concern, Tesania turned back to the captain. "Is there some other way to Hinos?"

"Only by ship from here."

"We can't wait another week," Tesania said limply. "We need to get to Hinos as quickly as possible."

"May I ask why?"

Suddenly aware of the position they were in as the three men at the table stared up at her expectantly, Tesania shook her head and said, "I feel we have wasted enough of your time. It seems we will have to wait until our passes are issued."

"That might be wise," Captain Bolow said nodding. "I should be back by then. Perhaps I can offer you passage then?"

"We'll keep an eye out for you," Deavon said as he touched Tesania's elbow and started her toward the door. "Thank you for your time."

"Not at all," the captain replied smiling up at them. "I hope to see you in a week's time."

"That didn't go as planned," Tesania said, blinking in the sunshine outside the tavern.

"Not at all," Deavon said as he looked down the dock to where Captain Bolow had suggested the Harbor Master's office might be.

"There have to be other captains," Tesania suggested as she followed his gaze. "We can't wait a week."

"They'll all say the same thing," Lee assured her. "The honest ones at least."

Turning, Tesania looked at the young Lieutenant. "You might just have something there," she said, smiling delightedly at him.

"Me?" Lee asked in surprise.

"The honest ones won't," Tesania echoed.

"But, the dishonest ones," Lee said catching on.

"Where would we even find a dishonest one?" Kailyn asked.

Turning back to the tavern, Deavon said, "Not in there."

Shaking her head as she looked along the docks before turning and looking the other way, Tesania said, "We won't be able to afford their fee anyway."

"You're right," Deavon said. "Smugglers and their ilk don't risk their ships for a few coins."

"Giddy has probably drunk most of the ones we have anyway," Kailyn suggested.

"Quite possibly," Tesania agreed, laughing aloud as she pictured a pile of empty mugs in front of Giddy and the others.

"She better not have," Deavon said seriously.

"I doubt it," Tesania said soberly the smile slipping off of her face as she returned to the dilemma. "So we have no choice?" she said, more as a statement than a question. "We'll have to apply for passes."

"With?" Deavon asked. "We have no identification. No proof to say we are who we say we are."

"Then we're stuck here," Kailyn said sadly before seemingly catching onto an idea. "Maybe Rhys can steal more money? Even some identification certificates?" she suggested brightly.

"Or," Lee said as he stared out into the harbor. "We borrow that caravel out there and sail tonight."

"Lee," Kailyn gasped.

"You just suggested Rhys steal money and documents," Lee defended. "What's the difference?"

"He has a point," Deavon said as he studied the fore and aft rigged ship rolling on the swell in the middle of the harbor.

"There doesn't seem to be many crew on her," Lee said as he turned his attention back to the ship. "A caretaker crew maybe."

"Possibly," Deavon said.

"If she's in harbor for a long stay, the crew would mainly be ashore," Lee explained to Kailyn his eyes alight as he studied the ship's masts. "We could climb on board and take her over; slip her mooring and be out to sea before they can raise an alarm."

"Won't they send other ships to chase us?" Kailyn asked worry in her tone.

"Probably," Lee replied shrugging. "But she looks fast. By the time they raise an alarm and organize a chase we'll be well away."

"You can sail her?" Deavon asked seriously as he too studied her masts. "The rest of us aren't sailors."

"I can teach you all," Lee assured him. "She's lateen rigged; just the two fore and aft sails to worry about."

Tesania also studied the ship. Compared to the spider's web of rigging on the huge square rigger moored beside her, the Caravel looked like a training ship. Looking up at Deavon, she said, "Do we have a better alternative?"

"Probably not," he conceded.

"And you can definitely sail her?" Tesania asked Lee.

"With my hands tied behind my back," Lee assured her.

Laughing at the enthusiastic look on his face, Tesania spoke to Deavon once more, "Can we do it tonight?"

"I can't see why not," he replied. "Lee?"

Looking up at the clear sky, Lee replied, "It's as good a night as any."

"It's settled then," Tesania said happy to have found a solution to their problem as she slipped her arm through Kailyn's and guided her toward The Crown Tavern. "Let's head back to the others."

***

Dull moonlight played on the swells and ripples of Tuscam Harbor lending its wane light to Tesania as she stepped down from the wharf into a small row boat. Stumbling as the boat rolled on a small wave, she managed to clutch the gunwale and steady herself as Aldan reached out and grasped her arm. "I'm alright," she assured the ranger as she turned and sat on a thin thwart seat running across the bow of the boat. Space was limited in the little wooden, clinker built boat, offering barely enough room for Kailyn to squeeze onto the thwart beside her while Aldan and Deavon sat on the centre thwart, shoulders tight against each other.

"Ready?" Baird asked from the wharf.

"Ready," Deavon replied.

Untying the boat's rope from a bollard on the wharf, Baird handed it down to Kailyn before reaching down and accepting Deavon's help as he climbed into the back of the boat.

"They could have found something bigger," Aldan growled as he fitted his oar into the rowlock and waited for Deavon to push them away from the wharf.

"There wasn't much choice," Deavon replied as he too fitted his oar and nodded to Aldan to start pulling out into the harbor toward Giddy and the others who sat waiting for them in a marginally smaller and tightly packed boat. "As long as it gets us out there," he said as they drew closer to the other boat. "You know what to do?" he asked Giddy and her companions.

"Steal the ship," Giddy replied from the near darkness.

Ignoring her, Deavon said, "We'll come in on her port side. You head around to starboard." When Raim acknowledged, he went on, "In the mean time, try to keep as quiet as you can."

"Will do," Giddy replied as Raim and herself began to pull at their oars and moved off.

Tesania watched them as they melted into the darkness while Deavon and Aldan began to row toward the other side of the ship. It worried her that they might have to use force to take the ship. The last thing they needed was an injury to slow them down when they landed at Hinos. *'Or,'* she thought with a shudder, *'a death.'* Casting the images from her mind, she peered ahead at the silhouette of the caravel as it loomed closer, its masts seeming to grow twice as tall against the starlit night as Aldan pulled his oar from the rowlock and gently laid it along the side of the boat as they glided up to the ship's side.

"Silently," Deavon whispered also removing his oar. As Baird tied the little boat off, Deavon said. "Aldan and I first." Looking at Tesania, his eyes barely visible in the shadowed darkness, he added, "Follow us in a few moments, but be careful."

Nodding, Tesania watched Aldan and then Deavon grasp the rungs of the ship's ladder and scramble up the side before she turned to Kailyn and motioned her to keep close. While Baird held the rocking boat against the side of ship she reached out and snatched at the ladder. Drawing a breath, she waited for the swell to push the boat upward before thrusting forward, managing to secure a foothold as she clung desperately to the ropes. Cautiously, she climbed, one rung at a time until Deavon reached out to help her onto the deck before moving to assist Kailyn. "Thank you," Tesania muttered as she peered around the deck. A single lantern swung from the main mast, casting an eerie light over the seemingly crewless deck. Giddy and Raim stood on the far side of the ship helping Rhys board as Lee climbed easily up the masts rigging and vaulted onto the deck, enthusiasm flushing his face as he took in the scene. "She's a beauty," she heard him say, to which Giddy quickly suggested he be quiet.

"Where are the crew?" Kailyn whispered beside her, looking along the deck both ways.

"I've no idea," Tesania replied shrugging. "Asleep probably."

"No Guards?" Baird asked as he stepped on board.

"No need," Aldan assured him, voice quiet. "They're in a friendly port."

Baird scoffed. "There's no such thing as a truly friendly port."

"They obviously think there is," Aldan insisted.

"Granted," Baird conceded. "The lantern though . . ." he said pointing to the swaying light, ". . . suggests they might at least partially agree with me."

"Periodic watch," Lee suggested as he walked toward them, easily negotiating the rocking movement of the deck. "Or a lazy watchman."

"Either way," Deavon said, voice low as Giddy and the others approached. "We need to move fast." Looking at Lee, he asked, "How many can we expect?"

"There would be twenty or so crew," Lee replied.

"Twenty!" Kailyn exclaimed, worry flashing across her face as she looked to Tesania. "Twent—"

"Most of them will be ashore," Lee interrupted his tone reassuring. "There'll only be a small watch crew aboard. Two or three maybe."

Studying the flat deck running to the bow of the ship, Deavon turned to the stern where the quarterdeck rose above them. Motioning to the door in the middle, he asked the lieutenant, "Crew quarters?"

"More than likely," Lee replied as he turned and scanned the hatches on the main deck. "The front holds would be for cargo."

Nodding, Deavon instructed as he pointed to the stairs leading up to the quarterdeck, "Rhys, you and Lee clear the upper deck. Make sure we don't miss anyone." When the thief nodded, Deavon went on, "Giddy, you and Raim go into the crew quarters first. Take the first cabin on your right."

"Will do," Giddy replied slipping her sword from its scabbard.

"Don't hurt them," Tesania said quickly.

"As long as they do as they're told," Giddy assured her.

"Tesania's right," Deavon said. "We can't afford to hurt anyone. Stealing the ship is bad enough, but . . . ." he said leaving it hanging in the air.

"Right," Giddy said. "No killing."

Shaking his head, Deavon said, "If you come across anybody, just subdue them. Aldan and Baird will follow you in and take the first cabin to the left while you clear yours and so on. Understand?"

"Got it."

"And the rest of us?" Tesania asked as she too drew her sword noticing immediately that it was lifeless in her hand.

"You and I will check the second cabin on the right; assuming there is one. We'll have to play it by ear," Deavon said. "Try to be as quiet as possible," he added. "We don't want to alert them until we reach their actual cabins."

"And me?" Kailyn asked.

"Stay on deck," Deavon said. "If you see any boats approaching let Lee know immediately."

Seemingly happy with that, Kailyn nodded and turned to look toward the distant wharf.

"Everyone knows what to do?" Deavon asked, the rasp of his sword being drawn ringing out into the night. When all of them nodded, he said, "Right, let's go."

As Rhys and Lee headed for the stairs, Giddy led the way to the cabin door. "Ready?" she asked voice edged with excitement.

"Go," Deavon said.

Tesania watched nervously as Giddy opened the door and slipped inside, Raim close behind. Deavon reached out and caught the door before it could shut and motioned to Aldan to enter, followed by the spy. Looking to Tesania, he said sternly, "Follow me and be careful."

Tesania didn't answer, instead she raised her sword and wrung at the hilt with her hand. She wanted to tell Deavon exactly the same thing, wanted to tell him to stay safe. But she knew he would be highly aware of the situation and wouldn't do anything rash. As he stepped inside, she followed making sure to close the door softly behind her. "Clear," she heard Giddy whisper as she emerged from a door on the right and started down the lamp lit companionway, Rhys close behind. Happy to let the soldiers forge ahead of her, Tesania stayed close to Deavon as he peered into the left room and asked Aldan if they had found anyone. When the ranger replied no, he came out of the room and started toward his next doorway, soon emerging and shaking his head. This went on as Giddy and Raim reported no joy at each of the right side cabins with Aldan and Baird echoing their findings. "Could they all be in the Captain's cabin?" Tesania wondered aloud.

"It looks that way," Deavon replied as he nodded to Giddy to take up position.

"Partaking of the captain's wine while he's ashore, I'd suggest," Aldan said.

"Possibly," Deavon replied voice low. "Let's find out, shall we?" he added as he motioned Giddy forward.

From Tesania's position she couldn't see much as Giddy threw the door open and stormed into the cabin at the end of the companionway. Standing on tiptoe she tried to peer around Deavon but was blocked by Aldan's big frame as he pushed in behind the two soldiers, Giddy's voice drifting back to her. "I wouldn't if I was you," she said voice demanding as she added, "Against the wall . . . both of you."

"What's happening?" Tesania asked Deavon as she once more peered past his shoulder but could only see the lamp lit doorway and no movement beyond. Placing her hand in the small of Deavon's back, she steered him forward and finally entered the cabin. Two glasses and a number of empty bottles sat on a basic wood table in the middle of the cabin, along with some kind of dice game whilst two men, obviously sailors by their garb and the tattoos decorating their arms, stood against the far side of the cabin.

"What's ther meanen' of this?" one demanded his eyes flicking around the group confronting him. "We ain't got no cargo worth stealen' . . . Ther 'olds are empty they is."

"We're not here to steal your cargo," Giddy assured him.

Confusion ran across the man's face as he looked to his fellow captive. When the man looked blankly back at him, he turned back to Giddy. "We ain't got no valuables neither," he announced as he seemingly came to the conclusion they were a band of thieves after the ship's treasure. "We're just coastal cargo runners," he added, voice fading away as he glanced down at the array of weapons facing him. "Yer won't be finding nothen' valuable ere," he repeated.

'We don't want your valuables," Deavon said as he lifted the point of his sword to his scabbard and guided it home.

"Ain't nothen' else 'ere for yer," the man said in confusion.

"Except the ship itself," Giddy said a grin flashing onto her face as her words sank in and the man's face went pale.

"Ther sh-ship," he stuttered. "Yer can't be taken' ther ship."

"Why not?" Giddy asked as she waved her sword at his stomach. "It seems you have little say in it."

"Ther capt'n," the man began fear playing in his eyes as he looked from Giddy's sword to his shipmate. Swallowing hard, he turned back to Giddy and then to Deavon. "He'll 'ave us," he stated. "We was on watch," he said, swallowing again before stating boldly, "Yer can't take 'er. We won't allow it."

"Maybe you should have kept better watch then," Giddy suggested as she motioned to the glasses and dice on the table. "Instead of drinking your captain's best wine."

"It were'nt 'is best win—"

"It doesn't matter," Deavon interrupted him. "We're taking this ship. End of conversation." As the man looked at him, mouth agape, the fear he obviously felt almost palpable as he looked desperately around the room. "No harm will come to you," Deavon assured them.

"When ther cap'n—"

"Tie them up," Deavon instructed Aldan and Baird. "Make sure they're secure and load them into the port boat.

Then bring the other boat aboard." As Aldan nodded and began looking around for rope, Deavon walked with Tesania back onto the deck. "That went well," he said smiling down at her.

"Thankfully," Tesania replied before asking, "Will they be alright in the boat?"

Nodding, Deavon stepped onto the ladder leading to the upper deck. "They'll drift through the night, but they'll soon be found once the sun comes up."

Satisfied, Tesania followed him up the ladder as Deavon announced to First Lieutenant Lee Nylor of the King's Ship Swan that he was now in full control of his first command.

44 - Adena

Giddy gripped the main mast's shrouds, steadying herself as the caravel they had 'borrowed' a few nights earlier rolled over the top of a swell and hastened down the far side. It had been an uneventful journey thus far with no sign of chase being given by the previous owner, or indeed the authorities. Perhaps they had been lucky and the searchers had guessed the wrong way and sailed north along the coast in pursuit. Maybe they were hot on the little ships tail and only just over the horizon. She didn't know the answer and so dismissed it from her mind, instead casting her gaze to the Tiadath coastline as it slipped by. It hadn't changed much in the hours she had been watching, forests of trees marching down from the distant mountains to dip their roots in the salty brine of the sea. But it suited her to be alone, to sift through her troubled thoughts.

"Mind if I join you?" Raim's voice came from behind her.

Turning, Giddy considered her friend as he swayed with the ship's movement before smiling and nodding. "I'm not sure I'll be much company though."

Smiling back dismissively as Giddy turned back to the rail, Raim stepped forward leaning against the weathered rail of the ship and stared out at the coast in silence.

Aware of his presence nearby, Giddy remained quiet for some time before frowning and turning her head toward her long time friend. "Did you mean it?" she asked.

"Mean it?" Raim replied, confusion playing on his face as he looked back at her. "Mean what?"

"The thing you said back in Estiel?"

The confusion on the little soldier's face increased as he seemed to cast his mind back to when they had been in the port city in Aliaga. Eventually he looked at her apologetically and shook his head.

Considering him earnestly for a moment, Giddy felt hollow inside. The feelings she felt were foreign to her. The thoughts had been clouding her head for days, as though she was seeing the world through someone else's eyes. "Don't worry about it," she finally said, turning back to stare across the waves, admonishing herself for speaking out so foolishly. Feeling Raim's eyes on her, she raised her arms and placed them on the rail, hands covering her face.

"What is it?" Raim asked, the worry evident in his voice.

"Nothing," Giddy replied. "It was silly of me to bring it up . . . . Forget it."

"I won't forget it," he said as his hand gently grasped hers and drew it away before lifting again to her chin, fingers lightly guiding her to look at him. "I'm sorry if I don't remember what I said in Estiel," he said his mind still obviously racing as he tried to recall. "But obviously . . . ." Trailing off as his confusion slipped away and a broad smile slipped just as quickly onto his face. "Babies?" he asked simply.

"Babies," Giddy whispered as she looked away, feeling ashamed at having such thoughts.

Drawing her face back once more, Raim looked directly into her eyes, his own eyes alight. "Giddy," he said, voice nearly a whisper. "I would like nothing more in this world than to have a family with you."

"You would?" Giddy asked, her tone changing from elation to disbelief as she spoke.

"Do you think I haven't thought about it?" he asked her. "That I haven't agonized over asking you?"

"Asking me?" Giddy inquired, suspicion replacing the disbelief. "Asking me what . . . ? To help you find some tavern wench to raise your brats?"

"I don't want some tavern wench," Raim dismissed the idea, anger rising for a second in his voice. "I want you," he stated as he calmed himself. "I've always wanted you . . . since the day I met you."

"You have?" As the soldier nodded, she went on suspicion rising again in her voice. "Why haven't you asked me then?"

Shrugging, Raim smiled at her weakly, "I thought you would laugh at me."

"Laugh?"

"You're not exactly a wench in need of a husband to look after you," he replied accusingly.

"You want me to be a wench?"

Laughing, Raim replied simply, "No, Giddy. I want you to be you. I want you to always be you."

"Always?"

"Don't make this hard," Raim begged. "You heard what I said."

Giddy watched Raim closely, studying the defiant lift of his jaw as he stared her back, the glow in his eyes. "So you want to have a baby with me?" she asked her voice falling back to almost a whisper.

"Babies," Raim corrected as he stepped closer placing his arm around her shoulder. "Lots of babies."

As she turned back to the rail and looked once more to the shoreline slipping by, Giddy drew a deep breath and wondered what she was getting herself into.

***

"What's up with those two?" Deavon asked Tesania, motioning to the two soldiers leaning against the ship's rail on the far side of the ship.

"I've no idea," Tesania replied as she peered at them. "I've never seen them that close before," she added. "I wonder what's going on?"

"Maybe they've finally admitted it?" Deavon suggested.

"Admitted?"

"That they love each other."

Looking at the soldiers again, Tesania considered what Deavon had said.

"Come on," he said. "You can't say you haven't seen it."

Eventually, Tesania turned away from the pair and looked up at Deavon. "I have," she replied. "But like others, they hide it well."

***

The coastal town of Hinos was much like any other Tesania had seen. Fishing boats bobbed and played on the evening swell, having returned with their day's catch, the smell of fresh fish drifting along the breeze. Larger ships lay at anchor in the small harbor, their bundled sails tightly clinging to the yards as they swung to and fro on the tide. Wishing to avoid questions and the harbor master, they had sailed past the town and laid anchor in a secluded inlet a few miles to the east and walked in, parting as they drew closer and entering the town from varying directions in twos and threes, taking care not to draw attention.

Each had a task to fulfill, Tesania and Deavon were to purchase a small amount of cheese and dried bread along with any available herbs and spices, while Giddy and the others would also buy bread as well as cured meats for their travel inland to Adena. She felt relaxed as they walked, hand in hand, along the town's main street, stores along each side bustling with customers. She felt a calmness she hadn't felt in some time. Perhaps it was Deavon, she wondered as a group of children ran past, their cries of joy filling the air as they chased a scraggly chicken under a wagon. Unable to control it, Tesania smiled broadly and looked up at Deavon. "Do you remember when you were a child running after chickens?" she asked. "Without a care in the world."

"I do," Deavon replied as he watched the squawking chicken scurry from under the wagon and squeeze between two fence palings, disappearing from sight to the dismay of the children. "A different time."

"I miss it," Tesania said quietly as images of the village she grew up in flooded her mind.

"Innocence is fleeting," Deavon said seriously squeezing her hand. "All too soon the responsibilities of growing up pile on top of us."

"Indeed," Tesania replied, sighing as the task at hand slipped back into her mind. "We'd better move on," she said motioning to the Grocer's store. "The other's will be waiting for us."

***

A small fire crackled, spitting embers into the cool morning air, filling the travelers' camp with the musky odors of smoke as they sat quietly eating a meager breakfast. They had reached the outskirts of the town of Adena on the previous evening and had decided to make camp a mile or so away, again not wishing to arouse suspicion so close to their goal.

Tesania ate in silence, picking small morsels of fried meat from her plate and unconsciously raising them to her mouth. *'This is it,'* she thought to herself, stomach twisting in knots. "Will he be here?" she whispered to herself.

"What was that?" Kailyn asked from beside her.

Jumping as the young mage's voice startled her from her thoughts, Tesania smiled briefly at her friend before saying, "I was just wondering if Sergh will even be here."

"We'll find out soon enough," Aldan answered from the far side of the fire.

"We won't all be able to go in," Deavon interrupted as he brushed the residue of his breakfast from his plate and stood.

"But we have to," Kailyn insisted. "Isn't that why we all came?"

"True," Deavon conceded while folding his bedding. "But we can't just charge into Adena with swords raised," he informed her. "We need intelligence, where he lives, guards etc . . . and, as Tesania pointed out," he said motioning, "If he's even here."

"And if he's not?" Kailyn asked. "What then."

"We'll cross that bridge when we come to it," Deavon replied. "In the mean time, I want you and Tesania to come with me. The rest of you stay here."

"Me?" Kailyn said looking around the others and then at Lee. "Why me?" she then asked, looking back to Deavon. "Surely Giddy or Raim would be a better choice to—"

"Need I remind you we're here looking for a mage, Kailyn," Deavon interrupted.

Looking down at her robe for a moment, Kailyn muttered, "Oh. I see," as Tesania shook her and teased, "Ninny."

"Well I . . . ."

"I know," Tesania assured the girl. Rising, she held out her hand and helped Kailyn up. "Just play the part of Naisa's assistant again and you'll do just fine."

Visibly brightening, Kailyn grinned. "I hope Naisa never finds out I've been using her name."

"I'm sure she wouldn't mind," Aldan replied. "Considering the circumstances."

"I'm sure," Kailyn agreed before turning her attention back to Tesania. "You'll be my assistant again?"

"I wouldn't want to miss the show," Tesania assured her, winking as Kailyn blushed. Rising, she followed Deavon's lead and attended to her bedding before lifting her sword, wondering as she did that it remained lifeless, no vibration or excitement in the blade demanding her attention. Slipping the scabbard's belt around her waist, she slowly buckled it as she stared in the direction of Adena. Fear nibbled at her throat and knotted her stomach as mixed feelings rushed through her mind at the thought of finally confronting the mage who was doing so much harm to her people. *'Will the sword even recognize him as an enemy?'* she worried. After all, this mage had no direct quarrel with her. He simply carried out the commands of Lord Dalgliesh and his twisted daughter. Adjusting the hilt, she thought, *'I guess we shall soon find out.'*

"Ready?" Deavon asked.

"Tes shouldn't go," Aldan said from where he sat beside the fire.

Turning, Tesania looked down at the ranger, frowning, "Why not?" she asked.

Shaking his head, Aldan looked back at her as he motioned to Tesania's hip and said, "Granted, you and your sword are our trump card. But, you shouldn't engage him until we're ready . . . and definitely not while half of us are sitting out here in the trees."

Unconsciously moving her hand to the hilt, Tesania replied as she caressed it, "We're just gathering information. I won't do any more than that."

"It's too risky," Aldan told her, shaking his head again. "What if he recognizes you?"

"How could he?"

Shrugging, Aldan replied, "Your sword's magic . . . ."

"Plenty of things have magic in them," Kailyn interjected. "My staff for instance," she added holding it forward, the gem at the crown flashing for an instant.

"Sergh has not directly encountered you or your magic before," Aldan went on. "Tesania's sword; he has."

"The night of Kailyn's party?" Deavon suggested from the edge of the camp.

"Exactly," Aldan agreed, nodding.

Sniffing in dismissal, Kailyn said, "Magic has no signature."

Spreading his hands, Aldan said, "To you."

"To anyone."

"Do we truly know that?" Aldan asked as he stood and looked around at the others before turning to Tesania. "There was a face in the mist that attacked your home?"

"Yes," Tesania replied.

"So we can only assume he has seen you?"

"Could a mist see?" Giddy questioned.

"It knew what it was doing," Tesania replied, concern clouding her mind as she considered Aldan's words. "We can only assume he could see what was transpiring."

"And you and your sword drove him off . . . shattered his spell?" Aldan pressed.

"Yes."

"Your sword is unique," Aldan went on. "Naisa said herself that the magic in it is unknown to her or the other mages in Eldanal. Who knows if it leaves a signature?" Stepping to Tesania, Aldan laid a hand on her shoulder and said in an apologetic tone, "I know you want to end it, Tes, but he knows you, all-be-it vaguely, but still, he knows you." As Tesania took his words in, Aldan removed his hand and swept it over the party surrounding the little fire saying, "You have the right people here to do the job . . . you need to let them do it."

"He's right," Deavon said. "We can't risk confronting Sergh before we're ready."

Breathing in deeply, Tesania felt deflated having built herself up to confront Sergh. "You're right," she said finally as she began to unbuckle her sword belt and looked about the others. "Who will do it then?"

"Baird is trained in these things," Aldan suggested. "He should go along with Kailyn."

"Giddy and I will be able to plan any attack once we get a look at the town and where Sergh's house is located," Raim suggested, rising from his place by the fire. "Rhys could come with us," he added before saying to Deavon, "You and Aldan could go in a few minutes after we do and get a feel of the place as well."

Nodding, Deavon turned to Lee, "You can stay here with Tes, if you wish?"

"That's fine," Lee replied smiling over at Tesania before looking apologetically at Kailyn. "Be careful," he mouthed to the young mage as she turned away and started into the trees.

"She'll be alright; Baird will guide her," Tesania assured him as she watched the others push through the low hanging branches of the trees. It pained her greatly to let them walk into Adena without her. She could see the sense in Aldan's argument, but she was so close to Sergh, so close to stopping the violence he was perpetrating against her people that she wanted to grasp her sword and rush into the town screaming his name, demanding he account for his actions. Sighing deeply she accepted the need to wait and turned to the Luitenant, asking, "How did the ship handle on the voyage down?" a smile creeping across her face as the young man's eyes lit up.

45 - Mountain path

Disappointment flooded though Tesania. "Not here?" she repeated Kailyn's ominous words.

"That's what they said at his home," Kailyn said, sitting down beside Tesania.

"Where then?"

"Up there," Kailyn informed her pointing to the tip of the Loden mountains, barely visible through a gap in the foliage.

"It seems he has a chamber in a cave up in the mountains where he casts his spells," Baird informed her.

"Are you sure?" Tesania asked, frowning as she peered up at the distant mountain.

"That's what his house staff said," Kailyn replied, shrugging.

"And you believe them?"

Shrugging again, Kailyn picked up a stick and prodded at the fire, watching the sparks dance into the air as she said, "Why would they lie?"

"To protect him?" Lee ventured from where he lay on the ground on the far side of the fire.

"From what? All we told them was I was here to speak to him on behalf of my master, Naisa."

"Kailyn's right," Baird said. "They showed no sign of suspicion."

"I would assume he receives many visitors," Lee said as he rose and moved around the fire, sitting beside Kailyn and picking up his own stick to prod at the fire.

"You're probably right," Tesania conceded adjusting her position on the log she sat upon. "I suppose it would have been too easy if he had been home."

Kailyn looked at her sharply, "Easy?" she asked. "You've seen what he can do."

"You know what I mean," Tesania said, drifting into silence as Kailyn turned her attention back to the fire. It had always been the risk, she conceded. Whilst she had prayed Sergh would be at his home and they could simply walk into Adena and confront him, she also knew that he could well have been anywhere in Tiadath. Laughing to herself, she admitted, he could have even been back in Aliaga where they had just come from. Drawing a deep breath, she consoled herself with the knowledge that at least he was in Tiadath and within their reach.

It was an hour or more before Deavon and the others returned to report what they had found.

"It doesn't matter," Tesania informed them. "He isn't here anyway." Adding before Deavon could speak, "He's up in the mountains." Gesturing through the trees, she said, "Apparently he has a chamber up there where he casts his spells."

Turning, Deavon looked up at the peak of the mountain before asking, "How far up?"

"I've no idea," Tesania admitted looking toward Kailyn and then Baird, eyebrow raised in question.

"They didn't say," Baird answered. "All they said was he's in his chamber in the mountains."

"And you didn't think to ask where that chamber was?"

"We did actually," Baird replied, voice defensive. "All the staff knew was that he has a chamber in a cave up there.

Not much past a little village at the foot of the mountain." he indicated with his finger pointing to the distant peaks. "I didn't want to push them too hard and give anything away."

Nodding agreement, Deavon replied, "A good call."

"They did say he'd be back in a week or so," Kailyn ventured.

"A week or so," Tesania repeated looking up at Deavon. "It's too long."

Nodding once more, concern clouding his face as he turned and looked back up at the mountains, Deavon said, "We'll need more information." Turning back to the group, he motioned to Baird and then Rhys. "We'll need you to go into town, visit the taverns and inns, find out what you can." Looking around the others, he added, "The rest of us will stay here to avoid any unwanted attention."

Coughing, Raim suggested, "Perhaps Giddy and I could ask around one of the taverns."

Rolling his eyes, Deavon nodded affirmation before saying, "Co-ordinate yourselves with Baird and Rhys." Shaking his head as the two grinning soldiers leapt up and started for the town waving the spy and the thief to follow, Deavon called after them, "And see if you can purchase some torches." Looking up at the mountains, he muttered, "We may just need them."

***

Sweat trickled down Tesania's neck before running like a rivulet to the small of her back. Wiping at her brow, she squinted up at the blazing sun. Not a single cloud floated in the blue sky to offer them any shade on the exposed mountainside while heat emanating from the rock beneath their feet stifled the air around them, ensuring their utter discomfort. "Why would he want to come all the way up here?" Tesania asked of no one in particular jerking at her shirt a few times in an attempt to waft some of the heat away. "It's so oppressive."

"Privacy?" Deavon guessed from directly behind her on the narrow, winding path they followed up the side of the mountain.

"Or insanity?" Lee offered from a few feet below.

"He's probably drawing from the mountains energy," Kailyn said, her breath labored as she struggled up the path in front of Lee.

"Is that possible?" Tesania asked, pausing to look back at the mage. "I haven't heard of that before."

Shrugging, Kailyn took the opportunity to rest and find what little shade she could from an overhanging rock before replying, "I read a few texts that spoke of using the earth's energy to enhance spells." Fanning her face with her hand, she went on, "But it doesn't make much difference. Not enough for mages to use it much anyway."

"But you think Sergh might be?"

Shrugging once more as she accepted a water skin from Lee, Kailyn replied, "We know that the ways used in Tiadath are different to the ways we use at home." Taking a long drink from the skin, she smiled thanks at Lee and handed it back before returning her attention to Tesania. "He's casting spells from here," she said motioning up the mountain slope, "all the way to Eldanal. For all we know, he could be drawing on the mountains energy to increase the strength of his spells."

"Or the range," Deavon said.

"Possibly," Kailyn conceded.

"You said it didn't make much difference in the texts you read."

"But with a spell cast over that distance," Kailyn said, nodding as she picked up on his thoughts. "Anything would help."

"Does it matter?" Lee asked looking from Kailyn to Deavon, hand shielding his eyes from the sun. "I mean, we know he's up there. Can't we just get up there and get out of this infernal heat?"

"Lee," Kailyn said frowning at the young lieutenant.

"He's right," Deavon said. "Why Sergh performs his magic in the caves is irrelevant at this stage."

"Is it?" Tesania asked peering up the mountain. "If he is drawing on the mountain's energy, won't it make his spells stronger when we confront him there."

"It's a big 'if'," Deavon said, also looking up the mountain. "We don't know anything for certain."

"He wouldn't be up there for no reason," Tesania said, shaking her head as she thought it through. "I mean, he wouldn't come up all this way for privacy." Motioning to the trees far below, she added, "There's plenty of places he could have privacy near his home." Frowning, she looked back up the mountain path toward Giddy and the others in the distance. "No," she said shaking her head once more, "It's not for privacy. He's using the mountains energy." Looking up at Deavon, she searched his eyes, "It has to be that. What else could it be?"

Deavon looked back at her with obviously no answer. Eventually, he conceded, "You're probably right. But, as Lee says, either way, we need to go up there and find out."

"And get out of this heat," Lee added as he started up the path toward the others.

Tesania watched Deavon and Kailyn fall in behind the sailor. She stood for a moment before glancing back down the mountain path to a little village they had skirted around, its thatched roofs barely visible through the trees marching right up to the mountain's roots. Imagining sipping a cool drink in the shade of a verandah as a bead of sweat traced its way down her face, she ran the conversation through her head once more, eventually conceding they were right. Drawing a deep breath while subconsciously running her palm over the pommel of her sword, she wiped the dripping sweat from her brow once more and started after them toward the cave mouth they knew, from Baird and Rhys' mission into Adena the previous evening, was only a few miles ahead.

46 - Mage's promise

Power surged through the Tiadath Mage's body, tingling at his nerves as his mind's eye watched his mist drift over the Eldanal landscape toward a farmstead. It wasn't a large farm he surmised, just a few wooden barns beside a small dwelling that looked as if it would only house a few people at most. His targets had been growing smaller in the months since the woman and her sword had destroyed his spell at the party near Wyvern City. The headaches it had caused had all but subsided in those months, now barely a memory as he watched Eldanal float by below. Sighing deeply, he decided that this would be the last day he would work for the petty lord and his brat. From tomorrow on, he promised himself, he would not follow the Dalgliesh girl's orders. No longer would he scour her maps and do her petty work. This, he swore to himself as his mist floated to the front of the homestead and hung expectantly in the air, would be the last order he would take from her or her spineless father. 'No' he mused to himself. '*After today, I will attack the Eldanal King directly, his farms, his harbors, his cities, his palace . . . . Soon, all of Eldanal will know my power; will learn to fear my name.*'

Breaking himself from his indulgent thoughts, Sergh focused once more on his expectant mist. Drawing himself tall, he called forth the energy from the bubbling and spitting lava far below, the cave floor shaking and trembling as he unleashed his magic, driving the mist forward to smash against the homestead's door. The tiny house stood proudly for a moment under the onslaught, shivering as its timbers groaned under the weight of the spell before shattering and imploding inward.

Emotionlessly, Sergh watched the destruction, a smile lifting the corner of his mouth as his mind heard a woman scream.

47 - Treacherous footing

Dirt and rubble slithered down the side of the Loden mountains as they trembled and shook. Steadying herself inside the entrance of the cave mouth they had come to, Tesania grasped onto jagged rocks protruding from the wall as she watched the landslide pour over the front of the cave and disappear down the slopes. "An earthquake?" she asked Deavon sharply, concern filling her voice as tiny shards of dislodged rock from the ceiling rained down on them. "Should we stay in here?"

Pointing at a rock rushing past the cave entrance before clattering on the path they had just left and careening away, Deavon said, voice raised to overcome the noise, "It's better than out there."

"Is it an earthquake?" Kailyn repeated Tesania's question, eyes wide as she watched a stream of dust and debris cascade past her face.

"I don't know," Deavon said peering into the darkness of the cave as the tremors subsided. Turning his head, he looked up at the ceiling of the cave and then out of the entrance where only a trickle of sand and stone now flowed. "Whatever it was, it seems to have subsided."

"Thank goodness," Tesania replied, coughing as she waved a cloud of dust away. "Maybe we should go back outside," she suggested, coughing again as she nodded toward the daylight.

"Better to let the rubble out there settle," Aldan suggested from beside Deavon.

"He's right," Baird said his face barely visible in the gloom. "There could be loose stones above the entrance waiting to come down at any moment."

"What if the cave collapses?" Lee asked, obviously wishing he was out on the open seas as his eyes darted around the cave.

"I don't think it will," Baird replied. "Not with a small shake like that."

"Small?" Kailyn said, shaking her head in disbelief.

"It wasn't a big one," Baird assured her. "You would know if it was a big earthquake . . . believe me."

"So it was an earthquake?" Tesania asked once more.

"It seemed that way," Baird replied, shrugging his shoulders in the murky darkness.

"What else could it have been?" Raim asked from nearer the entrance, his silhouette highlighted by the daylight behind him.

No one spoke as they each dusted off their clothes and adjusted their gear. Eventually, Deavon said, "I don't think we have much choice. Sergh is in these caves, so we must push on."

"We could wait for him," Lee suggested. "He has to come out eventually."

"He does," Deavon agreed. "But when?"

"I have no idea," Lee admitted looking away from the ranger. "But he has to."

Wiping at the grit and grime sticking to her sweat covered face, Tesania said, "We can't wait."

Mistaking the meaning of her comment, Lee suggested hopefully as much as asked, "Back in Adena then? Where it isn't so hot."

Frowning at the sailor, Tesania shook her head and said, "His house staff said he would be up here for at least a week."

"A week," Kailyn groaned, wiping at her brow. "How can he bear this heat for so long."

"I've no idea," Tesania replied, turning to squint into the back of the darkened cave. "But if he's here, it means he's casting spells." Looking back at the others, she said, "We need to stop him before he can hurt any mo—"

"Spells," Kailyn gasped.

"What?" Tesania asked turning her attention to the girl.

"He's casting spells."

"We know that," Tesania said irritably. "That's why we're h—"

"No," Kailyn cut her off. "I mean; we think he's drawing from the mountain's energy, right?"

"Yes," Tesania replied, "But—"

"Don't you see?" Kailyn cut her off once more, delight in her voice as she went on. "When he draws the energy the mountain reacts . . . ." As Tesania stared at her, obviously not understanding, she sighed in exasperation and said, "His magic caused the earthquake!"

Continuing to stare at her young friend for a moment Tesania took her words in before a smile slipped onto her face and she muttered, "Clever girl." Turning to Deavon, she said, "She might be right?"

Nodding, Deavon said, "It's possible."

"It makes sense," Aldan said, his shadowed face all but blending with the gloom behind him.

"But, it could also just be an earthquake," Baird said.

As Deavon continued to nod in agreement with the spy, Tesania said, "It's him casting his spells . . . I know it."

"We can't jump to conclusions," Baird said snatching his hand out to grip the cave wall and steady himself as another tremor shook the mountain.

"Either way," Tesania said steadying herself as the tremor passed. "He's in here somewhere destroying crops, maybe sinking ships . . . ." Turning toward the back of the cave once more, she said, "I'm not waiting here while he hurts my people."

"She's right," Aldan said. "We can't wait on the side of the mountain for a week or more. It's too dangerous."

"And we can't wait in Adena either," Rhys said. "It's too long to not arouse suspicions."

"Tes is right," Giddy said. "He's hurting people. We have to stop him now."

"So it's settled," Deavon said. "We have no choice but to risk the tremors and go in." When no one responded or protested he went on, "Raim, get Kailyn to light one of the torches for you and take point. Giddy, you back him up. The rest of us will follow." As the two soldiers stepped eagerly forward, he said, "You know what to do."

As Raim's white teeth caught the light from the cave's entrance and flashed for a moment in the gloom as he smiled, Tesania drew a deep breath. They were close now, she could feel it. But still her sword remained impassive as she ran her palm over the pommel, as if it were oblivious of the danger that lay not very far beyond. As Kailyn's staff flickered and set light to the torch Raim held forward, Tesania adjusted her pack and prepared to follow, her mind recalling the caves in the Britath mountains where they had spent days crawling on their hands and knees into the darkness before falling into a chasm. Shuddering at the memory, she pushed the thoughts from her mind and stepped in beside Deavon as he followed the two soldiers deeper into the cave.

Walking through the semi darkness with only Kailyn's staff and a torch held by Aldan casting eerie light that appeared to struggle to drive the shadows away; Tesania ran her hand along the rough surface of the wall. The cave itself, which had at first offered enough room for the travelers to spread out and walk beside each other had drawn in to be more like a tunnel, forcing them to walk in a single line. Thankfully it at least had remained large enough for them to walk comfortably upright and not have to stoop or crawl, yet the oppressive heat sapped at them, soaking their clothes with sweat and testing their resolve. It had only been an hour or so since they had left the cave's entrance and started into the blackness but it felt an eternity to Tesania as excitement and fear fought each other to occupy her knotted stomach. She knew they were near, knew that the Tiadath mage might be only a few hundred feet away. Doubt infested her thoughts as she stepped carefully on the uneven floor. She had her sword, she knew, and it was made by her forefather to defeat a mage exactly like this. But . . . it couldn't do it itself. She and the others would need to expose themselves to a mage who had the power to control mist thousands of miles from where he stood; a mage that had already demonstrated he would willingly kill without remorse. Frowning, she glanced back to look at Kailyn but could only see the tip of her staff. Did she have a right to ask the young girl, just graduated from the Carella Mages School, to pit herself against a fully fledged Tiadath mage? Would Kailyn even have the power, let alone the spells to confront such a mage? Sucking in a deep breath, she conceded that there was no choice now; Kailyn wouldn't leave her and she herself had no choice but to go on. Vowing to herself to do what she could to keep her friend out of danger, she glanced over Kailyn's shoulder at Lee's dark outline. "We're all in the same situation," she sighed to herself quietly and turned back to look at Deavon's shadowed back, stopping in mid stride as her sword burst to life. Grasping the vibrating hilt, heart pounding, mouth suddenly dry, she drew the blade slowly from its scabbard. Light burst forth casting a flickering glow on the cave walls as the blade slipped free of the sheath; fire pulsed excitedly within the polished blade, hues of orange and red fighting for her attention, warning her danger was near. "Stop," she called out to Deavon before realizing he had already stopped and turned back toward her as Giddy's voice came from not far beyond.

"We found him," Giddy said skidding to a halt, the light from the sword playing over her face. Pointing back into the darkness, she said, voice labored from running, "There's a large chamber up ahead."

"Are you sure it's him?" Deavon asked.

"Who else would it be?' Tesania asked, brandishing her excited sword at him.

Nodding, Deavon chose not to answer but instead addressed Giddy again. "Did he see you?"

"No," Giddy replied her breathing coming easier as she wiped her hand over her sweaty face. "Raim's keeping an eye on them now."

"Them?" Deavon asked. "How many?"

"Five that we could see," Giddy replied. "One standing at an altar in the centre, looks like he might be our man."

"And the others?"

Shrugging, Giddy said, "Apprentices, I assume."

"I'm coming to have a look," Deavon said. Turning he sought Aldan out in the erratic light. "I want you to come along too. The rest of you," he instructed as he reached out and squeezed Tesania hand for a brief moment, "wait here."

48 - Confrontation

"Five," Deavon said to Tesania, holding his hand up in the light of Kailyn's staff, fingers and thumb spread as he confirmed Giddy's earlier count.

"And Sergh?" Tesania asked, knowing the answer already as her sword continued to vibrate excitedly in her hand.

"Looks like he's the one at the altar, as Giddy said," Deavon replied.

"Casting spells?" Tesania asked, her thoughts flashing to home where her people could be facing his foul mist.

Shaking his head, Deavon replied, "Not at the moment. He appears to be studying a map."

"Of Eldanal?" Kailyn asked.

Shrugging, Deavon replied, "I have no idea."

"He must be," Tesania said, sure that the Tiadath mage was attacking Eldanal once more. "Either way . . . ."

"Raim's keeping watch," Aldan assured Deavon as he walked in from the darkness with Giddy, sweat glistening in the light. "What's the plan?"

No one spoke for what seemed an eternity as Deavon contemplated his answer. Eventually, Rhys offered, "It isn't going to be easy."

"That's an understatement," Deavon said laughing nervously before going on. "There are five of them . . . Sergh and what appear to be four of his apprentices, judging by their plain staffs." Wiping at his face with his sleeve before pointing a finger at the side of his palm to draw, Deavon explained, "The tunnel comes out here. Sergh is near the altar in the middle." He indicated the centre of his palm and then swiped down and across before pointing to each corner of his hand. "The four apprentices are at each corner of the cavern."

"How big is it?" Baird asked. "The cave?"

"About a hundred and twenty feet or so long, I would guess," Aldan replied. "And," he added turning his attention to Deavon. "It looks like there's another tunnel on the far side."

"How do you know?"

"Just from the darkness over there."

"He could be right," Giddy said. "The light from the sconces is reflecting off all the cave walls except there."

"Maybe the cave just gets deeper there?" Deavon suggested.

"Possibly," Aldan conceded.

"It could make sense though," Tesania said. "Some caves are formed by water erosion. If so, it would have to get out somehow."

"Possibly," Deavon said, echoing Aldan. "But it's irrelevant," he went on. "They'll stand and fight."

"Agreed," Aldan said, nodding. "With power like his, he won't run."

"That's what scares me," Kailyn's voice came softly as she looked earnestly at Tesania. "He has power not even Naisa has seen."

Reaching out, Tesania placed her arm around the young mages shoulder and pulled her closer. Holding her sword up so the excited light flashing within played over Kailyn's face, she said, "That's what this is for."

"Don't get too cocky, Tes," Giddy said. "You have to get to him first."

"And that will be no easy task," Aldan added.

"Exactly," Deavon said. "We need to distract Sergh while at the same time engaging the other four."

"If they're apprentices they won't have anywhere near the power of Sergh," Baird said.

"Don't underestimate them," Kailyn interjected ominously.

"Kailyn's right," Deavon said. "We have to treat them as if they were fully fledged mages."

"And take them down quick," Giddy added. "Swords against staffs won't work in a long fight."

"Agreed," Deavon said. "The safest way is to storm the room . . . . Give them no time to react." Turning to the soldier, Deavon indicated with his hand once more. "Giddy, you and Raim take out the mage on the right." As she nodded he emphasized. "Don't hesitate. Be quick and decisive."

"Yes boss," Giddy said voice full of excitement as she grinned, teeth flashing in the light of Kailyn's staff.

Shaking his head, Deavon turned to Aldan, "You and I will take the one on the left." Turning to the spy and the thief, he instructed, "You two go for the far right one."

"We don't have enough," Aldan said. "Tesania can't be in the first wave."

"I can do it," Kailyn volunteered her voice betraying her reluctance as she looked at Tesania swallowing hard.

"No," Deavon said. "You'll need to distract Sergh so Tesania can get close to him."

"Distract him," Kailyn said eyes wide as she looked up at the ranger. "He casts spells all the way to Eldanal . . . ."

Tesania drew her into both arms, hugging her as she said, "Just cast some spells at him and get back into the tunnel." Kissing the young mage on the head, she added,

"When he turns his attention to the others, come out and cast at him again."

Drawing back, Kailyn looked at Tesania as if she was mad. Pulling away, she tugged her sweat soaked robe from her body and said, "I'll do my best," voice betraying her fear.

"You'll do fine," Tesania said sympathetically, knowing the fear and dread running through Kailyn mirrored her own. "But," she went on, trying to smile at her friend to reassure her but only managing a grimace. "Stay safe."

"Stay safe," Kailyn muttered before repeating, "He casts spells all the way to Eldanal."

"I'll stay with you, Kailyn," Lee offered brandishing his sword.

"Thank you," Kailyn whispered shaking her head in denial. "But I don't want you to be hurt."

"Me either," Lee assured her. "But, I'll be with you all the same."

"And the fourth apprentice?" Aldan asked.

"Once the other three are eliminated, we all move to the fourth," Deavon replied.

"Sounds easy," Giddy said. "Rush into a cavern full of mages . . . take three down while the dangerous one stands in the middle of the room and then rush across the room to get the fourth one . . . while the dangerous one still stands in the middle of the room."

"Got anything better?" Deavon fired at the soldier.

"No," Giddy replied turning her attention to Kailyn. "You'll need to be at your best," she said seriously, tone tempered. "It isn't going to be easy. Like the Tiadath mage Tes' sword was forged to kill, he will have defensive spells in place, so you won't be able to hurt him. Just keep him occupied until Tes can get close enough."

Smiling weakly at Giddy, Kailyn muttered something unintelligible as she wrung her hand on her staff and looked away.

"There isn't much choice," Aldan said, looking at each of them. "Tesania, if you see an opening . . . if he turns his back to you or isn't paying attention . . . take it."

As Tesania nodded in understanding, Lee suggested, "We could talk to them? Appeal to his humanity. Maybe he'll stop the attacks if he understands what he's doing."

Guffawing loudly, Tesania said, as Deavon urgently motioned her to lower her voice, "He knows exactly what his attacks are doing. He's a murderer who will happily kill you before you get half way through your appeal."

"Tes is right," Deavon said, cutting Lee off as he started to reply. "If we give them time to think and react it will cost us dearly. Surprise is the biggest weapon we have."

"And the apprentices?" Lee asked. "Are they murders that deserve to die?"

Tesania considered his words. To a degree, she admitted, he was right. They were his staff and were not directly casting the spells. Should they die because of their master's actions? Confused, she frowned and looked to Deavon for help. As he shook his head and spread his hands with little to offer, she turned back to the Lieutenant. "I appreciate what you're saying," she said as she came to a decision. "But they aren't maids that are innocent to what their master does; they aren't stable hands or cooks. They're mages . . . ." Sweeping her arm toward the dark tunnel, she went on, "Mages that willingly came to the cave with him; willingly watching him kill; standing by while he murders innocent people on the other side of the world." Shaking her head sadly, she finished, "They are no better than he is."

"Besides," Aldan said, "We can't just ask them to stand aside while we attack their master. They'll fight and fight hard. We need to neutralize them as quickly as we can."

Laying her hand on the lieutenant's arm, Kailyn said to him, "We have to, Lee. Can't you see?"

"I do," Lee replied softly before looking back to Tesania. "Forgive me," he said. "I'm a mere merchant sailor. The thought of killing is new to me."

"None of us enjoy it," Deavon assured the lieutenant, glancing quickly at Giddy as he said it. "But what must be done, must be done."

Nodding, Lee moved closer to Kailyn and said, "I understand. I'll do my best to help."

"Good man," Deavon said, smiling briefly at the sailor before addressing the rest. "I admit, it isn't the best plan. But there isn't much choice in these caves," he said, looking around at the walls. "Sergh is in here casting spells that are killing people, destroying crops and livestock. He has to be stopped and as I see it, there's only one way in . . . ." When no one disagreed, he went on, "Let's move forward quietly. I'll let you know when to put the light out." Looking down at Tesania's flickering sword, he suggested. "It might be an idea to sheath your sword until we engage." Pausing he looked at the others one by one as Tesania slipped her sword into its scabbard. "Stay sharp, watch each others' backs and we'll come out of this alright," he said. With one last look and weak smile at Tesania, he turned to the tunnel and started after Raim.

It seemed only a few minutes to Tesania before Deavon motioned to douse the lights. Sudden darkness engulfed them, pitch black, making it impossible for Tesania to see even Kailyn who stood right next to her.

"Use your hands on the wall as a guide," Deavon's voice floated out of nowhere. "Move slowly and be careful of your footfalls."

"It isn't far now," Aldan added. "You'll see the lights from the cavern soon to give you a bearing. From here on in, no talking."

"Is everyone ready?" Deavon asked. When a soft murmur of affirmation came from the darkness, he said, "You all know what to do. When I give the signal, attack." When no one answered, he said, "Let's move up to the cavern."

Carefully sliding each foot along the invisible cave floor so she wouldn't trip on a jagged piece of ground, Tesania inched forward, hand running along the coarse tunnel wall to help keep her bearings. She felt her heart thudding in her chest, seemingly rising in tempo with each step she took. Months of travel had now come down to just a few hundred feet of lightless tunnel. Soon she would be in reach of the Tiadath Mage, soon they would all be in a battle for their lives. Casting the thoughts from her head as a dull light grew in the distance, she felt for the reassuring grip of her sword, wishing she could slip it from its sheath and let its magic steel her resolve. Resisting, as Raim's silhouette became visible against the cavern's light, she walked the last few dozen paces and stopped next to Deavon. As Giddy explained the situation to Raim with hand motions Tesania couldn't begin to understand, she looked toward the cavern, surprised by the amount she could see. Raim's position was obviously far enough back in the tunnel to remain unseen by the mage and his apprentices, whilst it afforded a view of the cavern beyond. Scanning the large cavernous chamber she saw an apprentice, his robes drenched in sweat as he waited for his master to cast more spells amongst steam rising from the floor as rivulets of water touched the hot rock. Pulling at her own wet, sticky clothes, she wondered how they could stand to be in this place for days as her attention moved to a mage standing in front of a large altar, her heart jumping, mouth suddenly dry as her sword jangled insistently on her hip. Finally, they had found the man responsible for so much hurt, so much pain. Finally they were in arm's reach of the Tiadath mage.

Focusing on a piece of parchment sitting on the altar, Sergh was seemingly oblivious to the party of intruders standing no more than seventy feet away. Raising his staff he began to intone a spell.

Spinning, Tesania tugged at Deavon's sleeve and motioned urgently to the mage, mouthing, "We need to go now!"

Glancing into the cavern, Deavon nodded, drew a deep breath and motioned to the others to attack.

No longer needing to hide as Giddy and Raim rushed forward followed by Deavon and Aldan and then Baird and Rhys, Tesania drew her sword. It shivered and shook in her grip, the fire in the blade brighter than she had ever seen it before. Mesmerized for a moment she stared at the myriad of colors, the hues of reds and yellows, the flashes of oranges and greens. Shaking her head, she admonished herself as a spell fizzed off Kailyn's staff, shattering inches from Sergh as his defensive spells took the brunt of her attack. "Move!" Tesania cried, lurching forward and shoving Kailyn sideways as Sergh spun toward her, staff spitting fire as he unleashed a spell that passed perilously close to the young mage's ear before cracking against the cave wall behind them. "Get into cover," Tesania demanded, pointing toward the tunnel as Kailyn looked toward her, tears streaming down her cheeks.

"He's too powerful," she almost screamed, face white with fear. "I hit him . . . you saw it . . . it didn't even scratch him!"

"Get into the tunnel," Tesania called desperately as Sergh raised his staff once more. Realizing that this time he probably wouldn't miss, Tesania leapt forward, sword swinging up as she called to Lee, "Get her into the tunnel." Hesitating in his spell as she rushed forward, Sergh momentarily froze, not knowing who was his biggest danger, the girl who was obviously a mage or the woman rushing toward him with sword raised. Obviously deciding the latter he released a spell that sizzled at frightening speed toward her. Throwing herself forward, she landed on her shoulder and rolled, scrambling to her feet to face the mage, sword raised as he glared at her, anger and vitriol burning from his eyes as he raised his staff to cast another spell, hesitating as his eyes moved to the point of the sword blade and traced the fire along its blade to the hilt and then up to his assailant's face.

Instantly the malevolence slipped from his eyes, replaced with disbelief as he howled, "You! How?" Backing away, doubt and fear played across his face. "You can't . . . ." he fumbled for the words, grimacing as his hand shot to his temple. "I can't . . . ." Turning, he fled.

Starting after him, Tesania heard his voice carrying to his apprentices demanding they stop her at all costs. Sliding to a halt as she remembered the fourth apprentice she spun, lunging sideways, barely avoiding a bolt of fire as it ripped through the sleeve of her shirt searing her skin as it crackled past. Realizing that she would have to let the Tiadath Mage go for the time being, she dared to glance at the others. Giddy and Raim had their apprentice cornered, his staff shattered at his feet, but they were still engaged and couldn't help her, Deavon and Aldan were likewise still engaged while the two Aliagans had their apprentice down on the ground, blood oozing from multiple wounds. But, they were on the far side of the cavern and not near enough to help her. Turning her attention back to the fourth apprentice as he muttered a spell, a smile appearing on his face as he prepared to release, she decided attack was the only option. Sword raised, adrenaline pounding through her veins, she charged at him, knowing it was too far and another bolt of magic would soon be coming her way. Eyes darting either side, she knew she would need to dive away to survive as the apprentice thrust his staff forward, smile growing into a grotesque grin. Sucking in a deep breath she watched the tip of his staff and prepared to dive sideways, but nothing came; no sizzling spell, no crackling fire. Confused, she looked to the apprentices face; he stared back at her, eyes widening, grin slipping away, smoke rising lazily from a black, ghastly hole in his temple as his body slumped to the floor.

Skidding to a stop, Tesania looked around the cavern, eyes falling on Kailyn at the mouth of the tunnel, arms raised, staff trembling as tears streamed down her face. Nodding thankfully at her for a moment, Tesania spun and rushed to Deavon. She wasn't needed though when she arrived. The apprentice lay dead at the two rangers' feet. Looking quickly at Giddy, she saw that the last apprentice lay in a pool of his own blood. She couldn't believe it as she looked around. No one was seriously hurt, her burn appearing to be the worst of it. Her thankfulness was short lived though as she realized it could have been so much different if Sergh hadn't fled. Spinning, she started for the far side of the cave, saying, "Sergh went this way. There must be another tunnel."

"Wait," Deavon called. "Let's regroup and let Kailyn take a look at your arm."

Gripping her sleeve as she spun around, Tesania said, "It's nothing." Turning her head back to the far side of the cavern she cried, "He's getting away!"

"We'll get him, Tes," Deavon assured her as the others came toward them. "But he knows we're here now. We can't just rush down the tunnel after him."

"We can't let him escape either."

"We won't," Deavon replied before looking around at the others. "Is everyone alright?" When they all replied that they were, apart from minor burns and scratches, he said, "Kailyn, light your staff. Raim and Aldan, light some torches."

"I couldn't fight him," Kailyn said softly, eyes planted firmly on her feet. "He's too strong . . . I . . . I."

"It's alright, Kailyn," Tesania said, stepping to her friend and placing her arm around her shoulder.

Looking up, Kailyn stared into Tesania's eyes sadly. "I didn't help you . . . Sergh was . . . I—"

"But you did," Tesania cut her off, pointing across the cavern to the crumpled apprentice.

"I suppose," Kailyn conceded, brightening a little. "He didn't see me . . . ." Looking at Tesania, eyes saddening again, she said, "But he was only an apprentice. Sergh is a master . . . ." Pausing, she swallowed hard another tear running down her cheek.

"You did well," Tesania assured her, gripping Kailyn's shoulders. "We never expected you to be able to beat him. But we all survived . . . all of us . . . You killed one of his apprentices. Without you, I'd probably be dead." It pained Tesania to see the torment in her friend's eyes, but she knew now wasn't the time to console her. Smiling disarmingly at her, she released her shoulders, returning her attention to Deavon, concern filling her voice as she held her lifeless sword out and then motioned to the far side of the cave, saying, "He's getting away. We can't let him escape."

Nodding his understanding, Deavon said to Raim, "Take point, the rest of us will follow."

With no apparent fear, the little soldier winked at Giddy and said, "Coming?" before moving toward the darkness, eventually calling back, "There's definitely another tunnel here."

Following the two soldiers, the light from their flickering torches shrinking in upon them as they entered the tunnel, Tesania relived the short battle in her head. She couldn't understand why Sergh would leave his apprentices to die. Did he truly think they were that powerful, that they could withstand the attack without him? "Why would he run?" she eventually asked Deavon's back.

"I've no idea," Deavon said over his shoulder.

"He knew me," she went on. "It was like . . . like he had seen a ghost . . . ."

"Careful," Deavon said, ducking under a low hanging rock only barely visible in the gloom. "You did shatter his spell outside your house," he reminded her.

"But would he know me?"

Shrugging in the darkness, Deavon replied, "We know his mist can see what it's doing. I assume he can see what it sees."

Nodding to herself as she digested his words, Tesania finally frowned in confusion and said, "But why would he run from me. I'm not a mage . . . I have no staff . . . I don't even know the first thing about the ways."

"You obviously hurt him," Aldan's voice drifted back from the shadows ahead. "When your sword destroyed his mist," he added.

"It makes sense," Deavon agreed. "Your sword has magic that he'd never have felt before. It obviously did something to him."

Falling silent, Tesania recalled Sergh's hand shooting to his temple, the fear and pain in his face obvious as he stared at her in horror. What the others said was the only thing that made any sense, the only thing that explained why a mage with the knowledge and power of Sergh would possibly flee when faced by an adversary armed with only a sword. She felt exhausted as the possibilities raced through her head. What if he had stayed and fought? With his power supporting his apprentices the outcome could have been very different. Shaking at the thought, she looked back at her young friend, head whipping back around as Raim's distant voice echoed through the tunnel.

"There's light ahead," the soldier called back. "Looks like it might be the exit."

Adrenaline burst forth in Tesania's veins, driving the exhaustion out as she pushed forward, hurrying Deavon along. Light grew in the distance, slowly illuminating the tunnel as she grew closer to the outside world, causing her to throw her hand over her eyes and cringe away from the brightness as she rushed into sunshine. Blinking, she peered left and right. They appeared to be on the same path that they had climbed before, only higher up the mountain side from where they had first entered the tunnel. The winding path allowed her to see only a short distance either way, disappointment flooding through her when Sergh was nowhere in sight. "Which way?" she asked to no one in particular.

"Down, I'd say," Aldan said.

"Agreed," Deavon said as he looked up the mountain's side. "He wouldn't go up."

"What if he did?" Tesania asked following his gaze.

"I can't see it," Deavon replied, shaking his head.

"He definitely went down," Rhys interjected. As Tesania turned to him, he added, "He's running." Pointing upwards, he said, "He wouldn't go up where he'd be exposed."

"He's right," Baird agreed. "Down is the logical choice."

Adjusting her impassive sword in her hand, Tesania looked up the mountain, eyes following the path until it disappeared. What if they were wrong? What if he had gone up to escape them? Weighing it up in her mind, she conceded that going down made more sense. Besides, even if he had gone up, he would eventually have to come down. That decided, she spun and started down the path, calling back, "Hurry, we can't let him get away."

49 - Elusion

Searing pain shot through Sergh's side as he slipped and stumbled on the loose rubble of the mountain path. Cursing, he clutched at his ribs in a futile attempt to drive the stitch away while sucking hot, dry air into his tortured lungs. Unused to anything more strenuous than a brisk walk, the flight through the tunnels and down the mountainside had taxed his body cruelly; his legs firing excruciating spears of pain through his nerves, demanding he stop his headlong descent while his heart burned and hammered against his chest like it was about to explode. Still, he stumbled on, desperate to get away from the woman in the cave.

He knew his apprentices would more than likely have eliminated the rest of the intruders that had entered the cave. After all, they seemed to only be soldiers and their ilk along with a young girl who thought to play at being a mage. But the woman . . . . Images flashed through his head as his hand snapped from his ribs to his temple, the pain he thought he had banished months earlier now returning with a vengeance, biting and stabbing at his brain. Surely his apprentices would have the power to overcome her he hoped, wishfully rather than with any conviction. He had felt her, knew the power of her magic. Confused, he recalled her clothing between ragged breaths. She did not wear the robes of a mage . . . nor did she wield a staff.

Instead, she dressed in plain clothes and brandished a sword. How then could she call upon the power of the ways with such potency; potency he himself could only dream of possessing?

Casting the thoughts from his mind, Sergh concentrated on the path as his shoes slapped, one after another, on the rough stone, sweat soaked robes clinging to his body. He knew he couldn't go on much longer as cramps clawed at his legs, agony manifesting itself throughout his entire body, screaming at him to stop. But he didn't dare to. He knew he wouldn't be able to flee all the way to Adena, knew he would have to face her, that he would need to call upon all of his power to overcome her magic and destroy her. But not out in the open, not on this bare, narrow path. Steeling himself, he pushed on, a faint smile managing to break through his misery and exhaustion as he glanced ahead and spied the barely visible thatched roofs of a little village through the trees.

50 - Affray

Fire exploded along Tesania's sword, the familiar pulse of power, the urgent shiver in the grip warning, demanding her attention. Halting her march down the mountain, she held her hand up to the others while staring down at the sword, mesmerized for a moment as the fire ebbed and flowed within the blade. "He's close," she muttered almost inaudibly before looking down the rocky path ahead.

"What is it, Tes?" Deavon asked stepping up beside her. "Did you see him?"

Shaking her head, Tesania slowly lifted the sword into his view, saying nothing as she scanned the swaying foliage of the trees below. She recognized where they were immediately, having stood in this very spot earlier in the day and looked back down at the thatched roofs of the little village at the foot of the mountain.

"Where is he?" Giddy asked shouldering eagerly past Deavon and peering down the track.

"That village, maybe," Tesania replied, looking around the barren landscape of the mountain before turning her attention back to her sword. "Wherever he is. He's close."

Scanning the mountain himself, Deavon nodded as the rest of their companions gathered around. Turning to them, he motioned to Tesania's agitated sword and said, "Sergh is close." Glancing around again, he added, "It's too open up here, so he's probably down in that village."

"Would he stop there?" Rhys asked. "Wouldn't he head straight for Adena . . . ? Where his own people could help him?"

"That would be the sensible thing to do," Aldan agreed with the thief. "Or straight to Hinos and get on a ship where we wouldn't be able to reach him."

"No," Tesania said holding her sword up as proof. "He's in that village. Or near it at least."

"He could be hiding," Giddy said. "Waiting for us to rush by before making his way to Hinos?"

"But we wouldn't," Lee said pointing at the glowing sword. "We know where he is, or at least that he's nearby."

"He doesn't know that," Kailyn replied. "Don't you see?" she asked the young lieutenant. "Tesania's sword is not like anything he would have seen before. That we know of anyway," she conceded as Lee frowned at her, unconvinced.

"She's right," Deavon said. "He can't know that Tesania's sword warns her of danger, that it's telling us he's nearby."

"Is Sergh the danger it's warning of?" Baird asked as he inspected the thatched roofs of the village.

"Who else?" Tesania asked unconvinced as the sword continued to tremble in her hand.

"The villagers?"

"No," Tesania said, "The sword didn't react when we passed here earlier."

"Sergh may have instructed them to stop us," Baird suggested. "We don't know if they are allied to him, or what power he has over them."

Wiping sweat from her brow, Tesania glanced down at the village and considered his words. It didn't make sense to her. The sword only reacts when someone or something meaning her harm is nearby. Would villagers commanded to stop a group of strangers on the side of a mountain be enough to set the sword off? Surely not, surely they would have no idea who was coming down the mountain and would not hold the animosity required to wake the sword's senses. Shaking her head, she said, "No. It's him. He's in that village somewhere."

"We can't be sure," Baird said.

"I'm positive," Tesania assured him, her eyes fixed on the village below. "Trust me," she said, holding the excited sword up, the light of its fire playing across the spies' face. "Sergh is somewhere in that village."

"Either way," Raim cut in. "We can't just rush down there."

"Baird could be right too," Giddy suggested, holding her hand up to Tesania's protest. "What I'm saying is, if Sergh does have power over the villagers, we could be facing them all at once."

"They're right, Tes," Deavon said his voice low as he stared down at the village, his eyes flicking from thatched roof to thatched roof. "We have to approach the village as if they're all our enemies."

"And if they're not?" Tesania challenged. "If they're just innocent villagers caught up in the middle of it?"

"Then we'll do our best to ensure their safety."

"I don't want any of them hurt," Tesania said, turning to the ranger and looking up at him. "Too many people have been hurt already."

Taking her free hand in his own, Deavon looked down at her somberly. "We'll do our best, Tes," he assured her. "But, if he's there . . . ." he faded off as he attempted a lopsided, apologetic smile.

"And if they do help him?" Baird asked.

Shrugging, Deavon released Tesania's hand and turned away from her before replying, "If they attack us, or hinder us in any way, deal with them appropriately."

Tesania stared at the big ranger's back. She knew he was right and that they would need to be prepared for anything. After all, they were deep within Sergh's homeland, deep within his territory. Still, it bothered her that innocents might be hurt in the upcoming fight. But what choice did they have? If they didn't enter the village and confront Sergh then he could well escape and be left free to attack Eldanal, to kill hundreds, even thousands of equally innocent people. Scowling, she vowed to do what she could for the villagers and then cast the thoughts from her head before turning her attention to Deavon as he instructed the others.

"He's either in the village itself," he said, pointing before sweeping his arm in an arc. "Or, he's in the trees nearby."

"Waiting to attack us?" Lee asked in a concerned voice, looking at Kailyn.

"Probably," Aldan replied.

"Can we face him?" Still looking at Kailyn, the lieutenant frowned. "He's powerful."

"You can stay up here if you want," Giddy suggested. "You'll be safe up here."

"I . . . I didn't mean that," Lee sputtered, face reddening as he looked at the soldier and then back to Kailyn. "I'll go where Kailyn goes."

"Good to hear," Giddy said, clapping the young sailor on the back.

"But," Lee went on, looking apologetically at Kailyn as he said, "I don't think Kailyn can match him . . . I mea—"

"He's right," Kailyn interrupted, voice small as she looked guiltily around the others. "His knowledge of the ways is beyond what I can counter."

"We don't expect you to," Tesania assured her friend, moving closer and draping her arm around her shoulder.

"Tes is right," Deavon said. "We just need to distract him . . . Give her the time and opportunity to get close enough to him."

"You don't understand," Kailyn muttered eyes darting from Deavon to Tesania. "His defensive spells are beyond anything I have. I won't be able to engage him for long enough. He'll destroy us before—"

"You won't need to engage him for long," Tesania pointed out, pulling the girl close to her side. "Just long enough—"

"I can't . . . ." Kailyn said pulling away, eyes wide, tears trembling in her lashes threatening to cascade down her face. "You can't expect me t—"

"It's alright, Kailyn," Giddy interrupted stepping to the distraught mage. "Just skirmish him. Hit and run if you like. Cast a spell and get behind cover, wait for your chance and cast again . . . Understand?" When Kailyn nodded slowly, wiping escaped tears from her cheeks as she attempted a reassuring smile at the soldier, Giddy said. "You'll do fine. Raim and I will stay with you if you like?" As she noticed the lieutenant's face beside them, she laughed and added, "And Lee too."

Wiping once more at her face, Kailyn muttered, "I suppose that'll be alright."

Draping her arm once more around her friend, Tesania drew her close whispering in her ear, "Naisa wouldn't have allowed you to come along if she didn't think you could do it."

Brightening, Kailyn looked up at her and briefly smiled. "I won't let her down."

"Good girl," Tesania said, smiling.

"Alright," Deavon began, pointing. "We go down to where the path opens out into trees there." Pausing, he waited for any questions. When none came, he went on, "Giddy, you and Raim take Kailyn and Lee," he indicated the sailor, "to the left into the trees. Don't go too far—"

"Should we split up?" Baird asked. "There's safety in numbers."

"And a large target," Giddy replied before Deavon could speak.

"Exactly," Deavon said nodding at the soldier. "If Sergh is as powerful as we think he is."

"He is," Kailyn said, voice soft.

"Fine," Deavon conceded, smiling briefly at the girl. "Sergh is powerful. The danger," he said pointedly to the spy, "is in numbers. We can't let him target all of us at the same time."

"And," Aldan added, "Tesania needs to get around him, approach him from his blind side. She won't be able to do that if we're all in a tight group."

Nodding, Deavon went on, "We need to split up, but not too far from each other." Looking around them all somberly, he said, "We need to be able to move quickly to aid each other if we contact him."

"When we contact him," Tesania corrected him.

"When we contact him," Deavon repeated.

"I'll go with Rhys," Baird suggested, continuing as the little thief looked at him dubiously. "We can head into the village along the path," he suggested pointing. "And then slip between the houses."

Nodding as he followed the spy's gaze to the village, Deavon said, "Aldan, you come with Tes and myself."

"To the right?" the ranger asked, silently accepting his allotted task.

"Yes," Deavon replied looking around the group. "As Kailyn has pointed out," he said. "This is not an apprentice we face." As the others looked back at him calmly, he went on, "He's a fully fledged Tiadath mage . . . A mage that can cast spells across oceans and control mists from thousands of miles away." Pausing, he looked around their faces once more. "Do not take him lightly . . . ." Looking now pointedly at Giddy and Raim, he said, "Don't be a hero . . . Your job is to find him and distract him so Tes can get close to him . . . Understand?"

"Yes boss," Giddy replied, excitement tingeing her voice as she glanced impatiently down the path.

Shaking his head, Deavon turned to Tesania. "You'll need to wait for your chance. Don't rush in too early."

"Or too late," Aldan said almost to himself before looking at Tesania apologetically.

Breathing in deeply, Tesania glanced at Kailyn, smiling briefly before turning back to Deavon, saying, "I know what to do."

Reaching out, Deavon took her hand searched her eyes with his. She couldn't quite read them, worry and concern mixed with what . . . ? "Let's go," he said spinning away from her, hand slipping from her fingers before she could decide. Pausing, she watched him walk away as the others began to move after him. Glancing from his back to Kailyn and then Giddy, Raim, Aldan and the others as they willingly walked toward danger, she looked down at her glowing sword, muttering to herself, "Why? Why me . . . ? Why couldn't someone else's ancestors have forged you?" Sighing deeply, she looked back to her friends. "Why do the people I cherish have to walk constantly into danger because of me." Moments passed as she looked down at the sword once more, feeling its power ebb along her arm as she contemplated her own question. "Because," she growled as she started down the path, "My forefather faced a Tiadath mage centuries ago, and, like him, I refuse to let them destroy everything I love."

Immediately, as she stepped beneath the shade of the trees and followed Deavon to the right side of the village, Tesania felt the air around her cool, a light wind bringing some comfort from the hot, sweaty descent down the mountain. Pulling her wet shirt away from her body, she savored the coolness for a moment as the air rushed over her clammy skin before quickly turning her attention to the village barely visible through the low hanging branches of the trees. She had no idea about the layout of the village or its inhabitants, having skirted around it on their journey up so as not to draw attention. Peering now through the rustling leaves as they danced and played on the breeze, she could make out at least a dozen buildings, a few with smoke rising from what appeared to be mud brick chimneys. She couldn't see any villagers moving about, in fact, apart from the smoke, the village looked to be deserted. "I can't see anyone," she said quietly to Deavon.

"No," Deavon replied, crouching down and pushing a branch aside as he continued to study the village. "Wait. There," he said pointing toward a worn, wooden verandah attached to the second house back.

Following his finger, Tesania took in the verandah not seeing anyone on the silvered old wood planks. "Where?"

"Against the wall," Deavon said. Sitting in a chair.

Confused, Tesania looked again and then adjusted her position behind the ranger, bending down to his level as she studied the verandah again. "Oh," she said. "I see him now. It doesn't look like Sergh?"

"No," Deavon agreed. "Not by his clothes anyway."

"A villager," Aldan suggested.

"Unless Sergh changed clothes," Tesania said suspiciously as she watched the motionless man.

"I doubt it," Aldan replied. "He doesn't have a staff. Sergh wouldn't leave himself exposed like that."

"Probably not," Tesania agreed.

"He may know where Sergh is though," Aldan suggested. "We could ask him."

Turning his head up to Aldan, Deavon asked, "Just walk up and ask him?"

"Why not?"

"We don't know if Sergh holds sway over these people. It could be dangerous."

"There's another one . . . look," Tesania interrupted, motioning to the verandah where a woman carried a tray with two mugs and a wooden pitcher. Running her tongue over her parched lips, Tesania could almost taste the cool liquid it must hold.

"They look relaxed enough," Aldan said.

Shaking his head slowly, Deavon stood. "It could be a ruse?"

"Possibly," Aldan replied. "No way of knowing from here."

"They may have seen him?" Tesania suggested.

"And they may be aiding him? Drawing us in to a trap?"

"Maybe," Tesania conceded. "But what else do we do? Sneak around in the trees until Sergh gets bored and walks out in the open?"

"Assuming he's here," Deavon said.

Lifting her sword, Tesania let the light rippling in the blade speak for her. Eventually, she said, "He's here . . . somewhere."

Deavon considered her words for a few moments, his attention moving from the flickering sword to the verandah visible through the trees. "They don't appear on edge," he said as he watched the two villagers chatting and sipping their drinks.

"Exactly," Aldan said. "They'd be nervous . . . looking about and searching the trees if they were aiding him in a trap."

"They look like innocent villagers to me," Tesania said.

"Either way," Aldan said. "We need to draw him out. If that means springing a trap, then so be it."

Turning to his friend, Deavon studied him for some time weighing up his words before turning to Tesania. "You'll need to stay back. If it is a trap you'll need to work your way around and come in from his blind side."

"I understand," Tesania said nodding as she adjusted the humming sword in her hand.

"Right," Deavon said smiling briefly at her before sheathing his sword and motioning to Aldan to follow. "We're just looking for Sergh to give him a message from our master," he instructed as they pushed branches aside and made their way toward the verandah.

Tesania remained still for a moment watching them go and then started making her way to the right so as she could have a better angle to come in from behind if Sergh did appear and engage the two rangers. It was a risk, she knew. What if it was a trap and Sergh attacked? They would have no defense against him, no protective wards, no way of deflecting his spell. Shaking her head as she stepped lightly through the leaf litter on the ground, she drove the thoughts from her mind and prepared herself to do whatever was necessary to help them.

It wasn't long before she heard Deavon's voice travel through the trees as he hailed the two villagers. Stopping, Tesania crouched and peered through the branches, able to make the rangers out as they approached the verandah and halted. She could see the villagers talking, but their voices didn't carry to her as she looked nervously about, expecting Sergh's spells to burst forth at any moment. But they never came. Instead, Deavon turned toward her after a few minutes of conversation and waved for her to come forward. Looking down at her glowing sword in confusion, she stood and searched the trees about her before slipping it into its scabbard and stepping tentatively into the village clearing and walking towards the others.

"He's not here," Aldan said. "Walcot," he added motioning to the man, "saw a mage come through here a half hour or so ago."

"He was heading toward Adena," the man on the verandah said gesturing to the trees on his left before suggesting to the woman she should get three more mugs from the house.

Looking into the trees, Tesania felt her sword vibrating against her hip. Shaking her head, she turned back to the villager and said, as the woman disappeared through a doorway with the wooden pitcher, "Half an hour ago?"

"About that," Walcot confirmed nodding. "In quite a hurry too."

"Was it Sergh?" Tesania asked.

"No idea," the villager said. "I have never met him before."

"It must have been. Who else would it be?" Aldan said as Giddy, Kailyn and the others appeared around the corner of the house and walked toward them.

"More of you," Walcot said easily, smiling at the two newcomers before calling into the house, "You'd better bring a few more mugs, Joayla"

"That's all of us," Deavon advised as Rhys and Baird appeared from the other side of the building.

"The more the merrier," Walcot said laughing aloud before calling to the woman, "Quite a few more it seems."

With the mirth still playing across his face, Walcot's eyes flicked from one of the travelers to the next as the woman arrived back with a fresh pitcher of water and a tray full of mugs. "A mixed bunch," he said eyes lingering on Kailyn's staff.

"Indeed," Deavon replied accepting a mug before saying. "Safety in numbers."

Slowly, the villager drew his eyes away from Kailyn's staff. "Around here?" he asked a little surprised. "There's not much to fear in these parts."

"So it seems," Deavon replied as he looked about the serene trees surrounding them. "But we have travelled a long way."

Once more, Walcot's eyes studied them only this time paying attention to their clothes and weapons. "That, I can see," he said eventually.

Tesania listened to their conversation as she drank thirstily from the mug the woman handed her. Sighing deeply as the cool water slid down her throat, she smiled thanks at the woman and then nudged Deavon, motioning with her head toward the trees. "We should be moving along. Our master's message is very urgent . . . remember?"

"You're quite right," Deavon replied, handing his mug back to the woman and thanking her. "We should be on our way. Thank you for the hospitality."

Dismissing it with a wave, Walcot said, "Any time my friend. Stop by again if you are ever in the area."

"I might just do that," Deavon replied before turning and starting toward Adena calling back to the woman, "Thank you again."

Nodding to the man and then the woman, Tesania turned and followed him, stopping next to him when he halted a hundred or so feet into the trees. As the others caught up and gathered around, he said, "We'll need to hurry. We can't let him get reinforcements." Looking at the two soldiers, he said, "You two take point." As they nodded and headed out he called, "Run! He mustn't reach Adena." As the two soldiers broke into a jog Rhys and Baird started off after them followed by Aldan, Lee and then Kailyn. Looking at Tesania, Deavon said apologetically, "This is not going to be fun," and started off after the others.

Tesania watched him go and then moved off after him, immediately deciding she would not be able to run all the way to Adena. Staring down at the ground, she jogged along, one foot pounding down after the other as she steeled herself to do the best she could and keep up, knowing that Kailyn would be struggling even worse in the hot, sticky conditions. Breath coming ragged, throat burning once more, she cast her mind back to the pitcher of water and the cool liquid contained within. As she imagined guzzling down another mug, something tapped at her senses, insisting there was something amiss. Running it all through her head, she recalled their entrance to the village and the conversation they'd had. The more she thought about it, the less it made sense. Why was her sword so excited near the village if he'd passed a half an hour ago? Why wouldn't the villagers question nine people arriving at once to give the mage a simple message? Why was the village virtually deserted except for the two villagers they had spoken to? Why would Walcot say he had never met Sergh before? After all, Sergh came through here to his altar in the cave on a regular basis. "It isn't right," she muttered to herself, looking back through the trees. "They must know who he is." Sliding to halt, dust billowing up from the path, she called out to Deavon. "He's behind us!" Not waiting for his answer she turned and started back up the path drawing her lifeless sword as she went.

"Wait!" Deavon called. "Tesania! We need to catch up with the others."

Not responding to him, Tesania marched back toward the village. She knew she was right . . . the sword wouldn't lie . . . Sergh was in that village and Walcot was covering for him.

"Tesania!" Deavon's voice came again. "Wait, I'm coming with you."

Knowing the ranger would catch her, Tesania didn't slow down. Instead she marched on, a satisfied smile spreading over her face as the sword burst back to life, shivering insistently once more as she drew closer to the village.

"Tes," Deavon called, closer now so he didn't need to yell.

Looking back at him, Tesania said, "He's in the village."

"How do you know?"

"It didn't make sense,' she said as he drew up next to her. "Walcot would know who Sergh is," she said.

"That doesn't mean he's in the village," Deavon replied looking back along the path. "The others have gone ahead," he said. "We need to catch them."

"I won't let him escape," Tesania said, eyes fixed firmly ahead as the village came into view. "He's up here, I know it."

"How can you be so sure?"

Thrusting her sword out, she said while motioning down the path, "It was dead down there. When I turned back it burst back to life."

Obviously knowing better than to argue against the sword's sense of danger, Deavon grasped her arm pulling her to a stop at the edge of the clearing surrounding the village. "Fine. But we have to get the others."

"He'll get away."

"You're back already?" Walcot's voice came from the verandah. "I thought your message was urgent?"

"It is," Tesania replied shrugging off Deavon's hand and striding forward. "That's why we came back to deliver it."

Walcot's eyes studied her sword as she approached. Eventually, he said, "With weapon drawn, after we showed you hospitality?"

"You lied to us."

"How so?"

"Sergh is here. You're protecting him."

"Protecting him!?" Walcot said laughing uproariously. "I did you a favor."

"You lied!"

"Yes. But for you, not for him."

"For me?" Tesania asked in a confused tone as Deavon stepped up beside her, sword drawn

"Do you know who he is?"

"I know exactly who he is!" Tesania almost screamed at the villager.

"Then you have no idea what he can do."

"I'm here because of what he can do . . . because of what he has done!"

"Get out of here . . . Run!"

"No! He's killing my peopl—" Stopping mid speech, Tesania looked about wildly, the air around her crackled and sizzled as it crushed down upon her, driving her to the ground. Struggling to remain standing, she caught movement from the doorway of the house as she fell to her knees. Fighting against it, she tried to stand to no avail, the air around her crushing her chest, restricting her breathing. Gasping, she turned to Deavon who was on his knees fighting his own battle against the spell constricting their bodies. Desperately, she tried to lift her sword, but the weight of the air was too much, it didn't move. Dropping the sword, she fought to reach out to Deavon, aware they were about to suffocate . . . that their plight was hopeless. But her hand remained by her side. Staring into his eyes, knowing it was all her fault, she whispered "I'm sorry."

"No," Deavon screamed face reddening as he drew upon all his remaining strength and drove himself against her, knocking her sideways.

Suddenly, she could breath. Sucking in breaths she writhed on the ground, coughing and spluttering as her tortured lungs fed greedily on the fresh air.

"You shouldn't have come," a voice came from the verandah.

Groaning, Tesania rolled over. She could see Deavon had been released from the spell and was struggling to regain his feet, pushing himself up on one knee as the air crackled once more and exploded, the shock wave smashing into Tesania driving her back to the earth as Deavon flew backward through the air, cannoning into the trunk of a tree, the sickly smell of burning hair and flesh filling the air, drifting over Tesania making her gag and retch as she spun her head around. Smoke rose from Deavon's inert body, drifting up into the leaves above his head. She couldn't see if he was breathing, if he was even alive. "Deavon," she moaned, reaching out to him as she struggled onto her knees.

"Another death to add to your list," Sergh sneered.

"My list?," Tesania growled as she heard the rustle of his robes drawing closer. "My list!?" she shrieked spinning on her knees looking for her sword. It lay out of reach a few feet away. Desperately, she scrambled toward it as the air crackled once more. Reaching out, she almost had the grip when once more she was enveloped in a crushing field of air. Not as heavy this time, at least she could still breathe, but it dropped her to the ground, pinning her with the tips of her fingers caressing the pommel of the sword.

"Now, now," Sergh said bending down on one knee and slipping her sword away from her fingers. "You have no need for a sword," he went on, smiling victoriously down at her as he lifted the inert, lifeless blade and studied it for a moment before tossing it a few yards away. "Surely you brought something more than a sword?" he asked as he picked Deavon's sword up and similarly tossed it aside.

"It's all I'll need," Tesania growled grimacing as Sergh squeezed his spell in on her.

Sergh's laughter rang out into the clearing. "Perhaps it would have been more prudent to bring your staff," he suggested happily as he walked toward Deavon and kicked his leg.

Relief flooded Tesania as Deavon groaned. She knew he was hurt badly, but at least he was alive. Struggling, she managed to turn her face up to Sergh and sneer, "I'm no mage."

"No mage," Sergh repeated her words his hand rising to his temple. "I have felt your power," he said voice low. "I have felt the pain—"

"Good!"

Approaching her, Sergh reached down, grasping her chin, pulling it up until her eyes met his. "You do have magic . . ." he said searching her eyes as if he were studying a book of lore. "Powerful magic . . . More powerful than I have ever seen." Confusion creased his face as he studied her.

"I have no magic," Tesania said through gritted teeth. She was powerless under his spell, couldn't move, couldn't lift her own fingers.

"Lies," Sergh roared shoving her face sideways as he stood and walked behind her. "Admittedly, you hide it well."

"If I had this power you speak of, would I be lying here?" Sergh considered her words as he walked around behind her out of her sight. Managing to turn her head, she caught sight of Walcot who looked back at her sadly. "Help me," she mouthed. Walcot's eyes flicked to Sergh for a moment before returning to her. Shaking his head, he turned and walked away, entering his house and closing the door behind him. Anger shot through Tesania. Why would people not stand up to these tyrants . . . why would they let them rule their lives? Sadly, she knew the answer only too well. Calming herself, she eventually decided she needed to try a new tack and said to Sergh, "Why, if you're so powerful, do you do the bidding of fools like Dalgliesh and his daughter.?"

Pacing out of her view, Sergh considered his answer for some time, eventually answering simply, "Money . . . Gold."

"Gold?. Surely you have enough?"

"No . . . not enough. Not when I want to rise to be the emperor of the entire world."

"Emperor," Tesania gasped. "You want to buy the world?"

"Buy . . . ." Sergh said, shrugging. "Conquer . . . Bend to my will . . . ." Walking around in front of her, he squatted down and said, "But enough about me. Let's talk about you."

"You're a madman," Tesania exploded. "A murdering madman."

"Now, now," Sergh said, "And here I was about to offer you a partnership."

"A partnership," Tesania said incredulously.

"With your power . . . and mine."

"I have no power, I told you that."

Slowly Sergh raised his hand to his temple once more while scowling down at her. "I know what I felt, what I saw," he said, rising and stepping away, he stared into the trees.

"If you're so sure I have magic, let me up so you can find out."

Sergh chuckled at her suggestion. "I'm not a fool. No, there is something about you," he said, back still to her. "Something powerful . . . something dangerous."

"I'm just a village girl. I can't hurt you. Let me up."

Just a village girl," Sergh scoffed. "No, you're dangerous. I can't feel the magic within you," he said touching his temple once more. "But I know it's there."

"Yes," Tesania said shifting tack once more. "I have power. Power that can destroy you . . . you know it . . . you said yourself you have felt it." Pausing, she let her words sink in before saying. "If you let us go, stop attacking my people, then I'll spare your life."

Sergh's laughter rang out once more. "Spare my life? You're hardly in a position to make threats."

"And you're insane," Tesania screamed.

"Insane!?" Sergh shrieked, spinning, staff rising as he crushed his spell down on her, driving the breath from her lungs as she felt her bones flex and bow under the pressure. "First, you will die, and then your friend over there and then every person you have ever known or loved!"

Tesania wanted to cry out, wanted to scream "No!" But her body wouldn't let her as the lack of oxygen drained her strength and the mage's spell robbed her of movement. Slowly as unconsciousness crept up to take her, she closed her eyes certain it was the end. As the darkness grew her body still struggled to breathe, its desire to cling to life overriding what her mind knew to be true. Sucking against her flattened lungs her mind joined her body in revolt, refusing to give up, refusing to let this mage destroy everything she loved. But it was hopeless, the spell pushing down on her was too strong, too powerful. Suddenly, as she neared defeat, air rushed in, her lungs filling with acrid, sulfur filled air. Gasping, she sucked the foul air in, eyes flashing open. Desperately she breathed in and out, feeding her oxygen starved cells as she rolled over. Sergh clambered to his feet some ten feet away his robes singed and smoldering. Turning her head, Tesania blinked against a bright light. Pulling her hand from underneath herself, she shielded her eyes. Amongst the glowing light were robes fluttering as if they were in a stiff breeze, hair flying about wildly as another spell shot forth, smashed into Sergh, driving him back into the trees. "Kailyn!" Tesania gasped.

"You dare to cast at me?" Sergh raged storming back into the clearing, robes smoking as he raised his staff and shot a spell at Kailyn.

Flicking her staff, Kailyn knocked the mage's spell aside. "I dare," she answered voice lacking her previous doubts as she raised the staff and shot a scorching spell at Sergh.

Tesania felt the blistering heat of the spell as it hissed past, but Sergh slapped it aside as easily as Kailyn had his. Knowing that Kailyn, even with her new found confidence, wouldn't be able to hold Sergh for long, she began to creep toward her sword, her body protesting at every movement.

"I thought Eldanal mages were weak," Sergh said. "Or so Dalgliesh would have had me believe."

"Dalgliesh is a fool," Kailyn said her eyes darting down to Tesania for a moment before locking back onto Sergh. "He is a lord. He knows nothing of magic or mages."

"Obviously," Sergh replied. "But even so, you cannot match me."

"I have so far."

Sergh looked down at his chest and laughed. "Yes, you have managed to destroy my robes." Looking back up at her, he raised his staff and sneered, "But sadly for you, I think that is the best you have got." The spell that fizzed toward Kailyn burnt the grass as it passed, turning it instantly brown as the heat radiated out. Kailyn dove sideways managing to evade the spell as it flew by her and exploded against a house, shattering its walls, burning debris careening into the air.

Rolling, Kailyn regained her feet and cast another spell at the mage that he easily knocked aside. Glancing once more at Tesania as she neared her sword, the young mage drew a deep breath and walked out into the open clearing. "The ways are a gift," she said as she walked away from Tesania to the opposite side of the clearing. "A gift that is to be used for good."

"You're going to preach to me about how I should use the ways?" Sergh said scowling at her as he turned to keep her in front of him.

"I'm not preaching. It's the law!"

"Your law," Sergh sneered.

Reaching out, Tesania held back a groan as she grasped the pommel of her sword, dragged it closer before wrapping her fingers around the hilt, the familiar burst of magic cascading through her body. Struggling to her knees, she used the cross guard as a crutch and pushed herself up, turning toward the Tiadath Mage.

Kailyn glanced at her for a split second and then raised her staff.

"I tire of this," Sergh growled. "You and your feeble magic cannot stop me from taking over the world."

"No," Kailyn agreed shrugging as she nodded toward Tesania, "But hers can." As Sergh spun his head, fear erupting across his face, Kailyn speared a spell at his temple, not much of a spell, not a fireball, more a bolt of pure energy that shot at the mage like a dart, shattering against his defensive spells, blinding him for an instant as he stumbled backwards.

Tesania lunged. It felt an eternity to her as the point of her sword drew closer and then finally contacted the mage, shuddering to a stop a fraction of an inch from his skin.

Spinning, Sergh stared down at the sword and then looked up at her face. "It seems your magic isn't as powerful as you thought," he gloated a sadistic grin spreading across his face as he raised his staff.

Muscles trembling with fatigue, legs threatening to give way, Tesania drew on her last reserves, driving forward. The sword trembled for a moment the fire in the blade pulsing wildly as its ancient magic burrowed through Sergh's defenses. Stumbling as the resistance suddenly gave way, Tesania felt the sword slide through and pierce the mage's body.

Snatching at the blade tearing at his organs, Sergh's eye grew wide as he stared at Tesania. "How?" he gasped, the words gurgling as crimson blood frothed in his mouth.

"The sword holds the magic . . . not me," Tesania explained to him matter-of-factly as he groaned, eyes flaring as she spoke. "In fact; it was forged by my forefather . . ." she went on. ". . . Centuries ago, to defeat a filthy, murdering mage . . . ." Sergh groaned once more his legs giving way and he crumpled to the ground, eyes vacant, body motionless on the smoking, singed grass. Tesania stared down at his body for a few moments murmuring almost inaudibly, "Just like you," as she slowly withdrew the now lifeless blade.

51 - Aftermath

Staring down at the mage's bloody body, Tesania felt no elation. Instead she felt cold, dirty even at having taken another's life.

Obviously reading her thoughts, Kailyn said quietly, "It had to be done."

Dragging her eyes up, Tesania looked sadly at the young mage. "He had such power . . . power that could have achieved so much . . . . and yet he chose the path of evil."

"When the ways run through you with that much intensity, dark magic can be very tempting," Kailyn said, shuddering as she glanced down at the mage.

"Are you tempted?" Tesania asked pointedly.

Shaking her head as she looked back up, Kailyn said, "I don't have his power."

"That's not what I just saw," Tesania said. "I'd be dead if it wasn't for you."

Sniffing dismissively, Kailyn said, "I was lucky. I couldn't have held him much longer."

"I saw your spells, felt your power," Tesania insisted. "You—" Spinning as a groan reverberated across the clearing, Tesania threw the sword aside crying out, "Deavon." Ignoring her body's protests, she rushed to the ranger lying on the ground at the edge of the trees admonishing herself for being so self centered when he was in desperate need of her help. Kneeling, she leant over him, looking into his face, cringing as she saw scorched face, blisters covering his exposed skin, hair singed away to mere stubble across his scalp. "Deavon," she whispered touching the charred cloth on his shoulder and shaking gently, fearing the worst as she shook him again and wailed, "Deavon!.

"Is he . . . .?"

Passing her hand close to his face, Tesania felt the faint movement of air as he almost imperceptibly exhaled. "He's alive," she announced, concern replaced by relieved excitement as she looked up at Kailyn.

"You must leave," Walcot's voice carried to them from where he stood over Sergh's body.

"We can't," Tesania growled. "He's badly hurt," before adding. "No thanks to you!"

"You don't understand," Walcot said. "The others will be back soon."

"Who?"

"The other villagers."

"Why would they care?"

"You killed him," Walcot said incredulously staring down at the blood covered mage.

"Yes," Tesania snapped.

"They won't be happy," he said as his wife stepped from the door and walked toward him. "They killed him, Joayla" he muttered to her as she approached. "What are we going to tell them?"

"He's right," Joayla said grasping her husband's hand. "You must leave before they return."

Standing, Tesania turned on her, "Can't you see . . . he's badly hurt. We can't leave."

Disentangling her hand, Joayla walked toward Deavon and knelt down. "The burns aren't too deep," she informed Tesania. Turning, she motioned to her husband, "Walcot, go to the house and get me some of the Eastoft leaves and some oil." As he hurried off to carry out her errand, she called after him, "And the pestle and mortar." Turning back to Deavon, she reached out and loosened his collar, inspecting his chest. "his clothes protected most of his skin," she informed Tesania. "Just his face and hands."

"Will he be alright?" Tesania asked voice small.

"I should think so," Joayla replied smiling up at her. "It will take some time for his skin to regenerate though." Feeling below the base of his skull with her fingers, Joayla pulled them away sticky blood staining them red. "He's taken quite a knock," she said.

"Get away from them," Giddy's voice echoed through the clearing.

Twisting about, Tesania stepped in front of the charging soldier, holding her hand up and saying, "It's alright, Giddy. She's helping us."

Halting as Raim came into the clearing behind her, Giddy lowered her sword while peering around her. "Helping?" she questioned.

"Sergh hit him with a spell. He's hurt badly," Tesania explained. "Joayla is going to help him."

Appearing unconvinced, Giddy scowled at the village woman as she walked up beside her and knelt beside Deavon.

"He hit his head badly," Joayla informed her holding up her stained fingers. "And he's burned."

"I can see that," Giddy said as she studied the ranger's face. "And Sergh?" she asked looking up at Tesania.

Turning and stepping out of the soldier's way, Tesania motioned to the pile of blackened robes. "Dead," she said simply.

Glancing at the mage, Giddy looked back to Tesania. "Well done."

"It was Kailyn," Tesania informed her.

"Me! It was you," Kailyn insisted.

"No," Tesania said quietly. "If you hadn't turned back to find us, Deavon and I would both be dead."

"And without you, I would be dead," Kailyn said shaking her head.

"It sounds like you did it together," Raim said as he walked up to them and peered down at Deavon.

Tesania thought about what he said for a moment and then smiled tiredly at Kailyn before walking to her and taking her into her arms and drawing her into her chest. "We did it," she said.

"Together," Kailyn's muffled voice agreed as Aldan and the others came into the clearing and took in the scene, bewildered.

"Where's Deavon?" Aldan asked as he looked from Sergh's body to Tesania.

Removing her arms from Kailyn, Tesania motioned to where Joayla ground leaves with the pestle and mortar Walcot had delivered to her. "He's hurt," she explained to Aldan as he hurried to his friend's side.

"How bad?" he asked, kneeling opposite Joayla.

"Some burns," Joayla replied continuing to grind the herbs and oil. "They'll heal in time," she went on.

"Why is he unconscious?"

"He hit his head during the fight," Tesania informed him. "Sergh hit him hard, threw him across the clearing into the tree there," she said indicating his path with her arm.

"Are you alright?" the ranger asked her.

"Yes," Tesania replied. "Kailyn came in time."

"You should have told us you were coming back," Aldan accused.

"I know," Tesania replied hanging her head guiltily as she used to do in front of her father when he admonished her. "There was no time," she said voice low. He would have escaped."

"And you and Deavon could have died." Staring at her for some seconds, he then demanded, "What then?"

Glancing up at Aldan, Tesania said, "I thought we . . . ." Her voice betrayed her as she saw the disappointment flooding his face as he shook his head.

"It was my fault," Deavon's faint voice floated between them. "Leave her be," he said, groaning as his eyes opened.

"Deavon," Tesania gasped, rushing to him and sinking down beside his head. She wanted to throw her arms around him, but knew his burns wouldn't allow it. Instead, she smiled down at him, the relief of hearing his voice once more flooding through her. "Welcome back."

A smile played at the corners of Deavon's lips quickly subsiding as he groaned once more, the pain evident as his body clenched.

Turning to Kailyn, who stood with Lee close to her side talking quietly to her, Tesania asked, "Have you got anything?"

"Only fermented lungis berries," Kailyn informed her, stepping away from the lieutenant and slipping her pack from her shoulders.

"That will have to do," Tesania said, holding her hand out for the vial as Deavon groaned once more.

Unstopping the vial, Kailyn handed it to her. Tesania leant over Deavon once more. "Open your mouth a little," she instructed, depositing a few drops on his tongue. "The pain will be gone in a few moments," she assured him, smiling once more.

"Thank you," Deavon whispered, relaxing and closing his eyes.

"Your face and hands have been burned," Joayla said as she leant over the ranger. "I'm going to apply some salve. I'll try to be gentle." As Deavon nodded almost imperceptibly, she scooped some salve from the mortar and began to apply it to his face. "You will need to repeat this over the next week or so," she explained to Tesania. "Until the skin looks like it's healing well enough to be left open."

"I understand," Tesania said, glad that the fermented lungis berries seemed to have taken effect on Deavon as he lay impassive under the village woman's ministrations.

"You must leave," Walcot repeated his earlier warning from beside his wife. "The others mustn't find you here."

"He's right," Joayla said as she moved on to Deavon's hands and applied the salve. "It will not bode well if they find you here with . . . ." looking toward the dead mage, she didn't finish.

"We can handle them," Giddy said tapping her sword hilt.

Turning sharply, Walcot glared at the soldier, "You people have done enough killing here," he growled.

"Easy," Giddy said holding her hand up.

"You will need to leave," Walcot said calming himself. "I want no more bloodshed here today."

"Will they care if Sergh is dead?" Tesania asked. "He's from Adena, not here."

"They'll care," Walcot replied ominously as he looked toward the far side of the village as if they might appear at any moment.

"Sergh pays them for herbs and other ingredients," Joayla informed her before glancing back at the body. "At least, he did."

"I see," Tesania said realizing they had robbed the village of some of its livelihood. "I'm sorry," she said looking to both of them.

"They'll survive," Joayla replied grimly as she nudged Deavon and motioned him to sit up. "There will be other mages, other crops," she said as she supported the ranger as Aldan helped him up.

Nodding her head, Tesania didn't doubt for a moment that the village would survive. "And you?" she asked Walcot. "Won't they blame you?"

"No doubt" the villager replied. "But Joayla and I were out collecting Eastoft leaves," he explained shrugging. "When we came back we found . . ." Motioning to the dead mage, he went on, ". . . that."

"Will they believe you?"

"They will have no choice," he replied shrugging.

"I'm sorry," Tesania said to both of them. "We have put you in danger."

"No," Joayla said. "Sergh is the one who came here and hid from you . . . demanded we lie to you and move you along. With all his power, he hid, behind us, like a coward, putting us in harm's way to protect his own worthless skin. No," she said shaking her head. "You didn't put us in danger, it was him."

"Did he tell you why we were chasing him?" Tesania asked curiously.

"No," Walcot replied. "He muttered something about the woman from Eldanal."

"That would be me," Tesania admitted. "You see, he was attac—"

Holding his hand up to cut her off, Walcot said, "The less we know, the more convincing our story will be."

Nodding understanding, Tesania turned her attention to Deavon as Joayla applied salve to his injured scalp. "Will you be able to walk?" she asked.

"No," Joayla replied for him. "He's had a bad knock, not to mention the burns." Speaking to her husband, she said, "They'll need a stretcher. The poles drying in the stable should do." As Walcot moved away, she added, "And some blankets from the house."

"Thank you," Tesania said.

Shaking her head, Joayla said, "Don't thank me. I'm only doing this to avoid more bloodshed."

Tesania studied the woman's face as she busied herself once more with the back of Deavon's head. "Still," she said. "Thank you."

A brief smile slipped over Joayla's face and was gone almost as quickly. "Take the extra Eastoft leaves," she instructed motioning to the bushel of dried herb on the ground. "And the oil."

"Thank you," Tesania said softly as Raim retrieved the items and put them in the pack on Giddy's back.

Walcot returned shortly after. Giddy and Raim busied themselves constructing a makeshift stretcher, eventually standing proudly over their effort before moving it beside Deavon and helping him shuffle on. With Aldan, Lee, Raim and Giddy on one corner each, they counted to three and lifted before starting down the path.

Tesania walked to her sword and picked it up. It was lifeless in her hand, the previous insistent glow of fire now gone. Wiping the blood off on Sergh's robes, she then turned to the two villagers and mouthed thank you as Giddy's voice floated back to her as she demanded to know of Deavon, "How much do you weigh?" Rolling her eyes, Tesania smiled and said, "Goodbye," before starting gingerly after them.

***

Two days had now passed since they had faced Sergh and defeated him. Transporting Deavon to the Caravel hidden outside Hinos had been an arduous task, the poles on his stretcher rubbing mercilessly on the bearers' hands. Tesania and Kailyn had tried to help, but the weight was too much for them and so they had left it to the six others to share between them. Skirting the outskirts of Adena, they travelled cautiously along the road to Hinos, Raim scouting ahead and warning of oncoming travelers so they could slip into the surrounding trees until they had passed. At Hinos, they cut inland making their way across country to the waiting ship, rejoicing at the sight of the caravel's masts swaying behind the coastal trees. Getting Deavon aboard took all of their effort, Lee eventually rigging a harness to the boat's tackle and hauling his stretcher up. As Tesania settled Deavon into a cabin and treated his burns once more with fresh salve, Lee's voice carried to them as he called to the others to unfurl the sails, Giddy telling Raim he was doing it all wrong.

Managing a small smile, Deavon said, "They suit each other."

"They do," Tesania agreed, gently smoothing the salve on his face.

"I wonder why they've taken this long to admit it?" he wondered aloud.

"Maybe they were afraid to fully commit to a relationship . . . ? Just like you."

"Like m-me . . . ?" Deavon stumbled over the words as he swallowed hard. "I . . . I . . . ."

Reaching out, Tesania touched his arm, "It's alright," she said disarmingly. "I'm sorry I said anything."

Averting his gaze Deavon looked down at her hand. "You're right," he said after a long pause. Drawing his breath, he looked into her eyes.

"I'm not the naive village girl you met so long ago, Deavon," Tesania assured him as she took his hand and began applying the salve once more. "You don't need to be my protector anymore."

Frowning, Deavon shook his head, doubt clouding his eyes as he said, "I took on the role of your protector the day I met you in the forest."

"I know you did," Tesania replied. "And I'm grateful. But I'm grown up now. I'm a woman."

"Still—"

"I thought I'd lost you up there," Tesania said looking imploringly into his eyes, willing him to understand what she meant. "I never want to feel that way again."

"I'm sorry," Deavon replied. "I should have seen him, I should have—"

"Deavon," Tesania interrupted in frustration. "I do not need a protector . . . . If I ever do; I will hire one."

"But—"

"I do not need a protector." Tesania insisted. "I need you."

"Need me?"

"I want you," she said shyly, moving her attention to his other hand. "I want what they have found . . ." she said nodding in the direction of Giddy's voice. ". . . with you." As Deavon stared at her fingers massaging his hand, Tesania said, "It's time we stopped being companions and submitted to our true feelings."

"Feelings . . . ?"

Exasperated, Tesania asked, "Do you love me, Deavon?"

"I d-do . . . ."

"I love you too," she said. "I always have . . . ."

"I felt it too," Deavon said sheepishly. "But you were young—"

Placing her finger to his lips, Tesania shook her head to silence him. "I was young," she replied. "But I'm not that girl anymore. I'm a woman." As he looked up at her, taking in her words, she added, "A woman that wants you."

Reaching out, Deavon cupped her face with his uninjured palm, "And I want you," he whispered.

A cough came from the doorway, breaking the moment. "Lee wants to know what heading he should set." Kailyn said.

Wiping her hands, Tesania replied. "I'll go and talk to him now." As the young mage rushed off, Tesania looked down at Deavon once more, grinning at the boyish look on his face as she said, "Get some sleep." Standing, she started for the door.

52 - Dalgliesh's lament

The rush of waves under the Swan's hull sang to Tesania like a lullaby as she stood at the bow of the ship, wind fluttering her hair as she looked out to sea. It had been more than a month now since they set sail from Hinos and sailed along the Tiadath coast in search of the Swan, lurking offshore from the fishing village where they had landed nearly two weeks ago. At dusk, the Swan appeared hull down on the horizon. It was no easy task contacting them as they turned away and set a heading to make distance on the unknown caravel. But Lee had kept after them, constantly adjusting the sails on the wind until they were close enough for him to flash a signal to them using a candle in a box with a sliding door. Tesania watched the flurry of flashes but had no idea what he was saying. Once aboard the Swan, they set the caravel adrift, Lieutenant Lee Nylor watching with sadness as his first command drifted off to stern while the others excitedly recounted their mission to the captain who listened politely but was more interested in sailing his ship out of Tiadath waters toward Eldanal and home.

Breathing in deeply, Tesania savored the salty air. It seemed to her to be the best smell she had ever smelt as the worries and anxieties of finding Sergh had now lifted. Deavon was healing well. Her people were safe, Eldanal was safe. Sighing contently, she breathed in once more, her enjoyment of the sea air suddenly fading as a realization shattered upon her. They could never be safe. Not while Lord Dalgliesh and Caitriona were still out there. Not while they could hire another mage, maybe even an army to send after them once more. Frowning as the anxiety crashed back onto her shoulders, she turned and strode along the deck toward Deavon. "We can't go home yet. We need to go get off the ship with Baird and Rhys in Aliaga," she told him as she approached.

"Why?" Deavon asked, his pink, healing skin glistening.

"Lord Dalgliesh," Tesania said simply.

"We don't need to worry about him," Deavon assured her. "The king will take care of him."

"No," Tesania said shaking her head. "We'll never be safe with him out there." Remembering his daughter, she corrected herself, "With them out there."

"Sergh is dead; they aren't dangerous anymore," Deavon said shrugging.

"Aren't dangerous?" Tesania gasped, eyes wide as she stared at him. "People are dead because of them . . . crops destroyed." Softening, she added quietly, "I almost lost you."

"But you didn't."

"Only because of luck," Tesania insisted pacing in front of him. "If Kailyn hadn't come back."

"She did though."

Exasperated, Tesania spun on him. "We wouldn't have even been there but for them and their petty revenge."

Nodding Deavon conceded her point. "But Sergh is dead now," he repeated.

"She won't rest," Tesania said. "You know it as well as I do. Caitriona will come up with another scheme to get at me. She's insane."

"Dalgliesh isn't."

Scoffing, Tesania looked at Deavon incredulously. "He'll do whatever his precious brat wants him to do."

Swaying with the movement of the ship, Deavon looked out at the ocean as he considered her words. Obviously accepting that her mind was set and he would stand no chance in changing it, he sighed in defeat and turned back to her. "What do you want to do?"

"Take them back to Eldanal . . . make them stand trial for the murderers they are."

"It isn't that easy, Tes," Deavon said shaking his head. "We have no jurisdiction in Aliaga. We can't just walk in and take their citizens into custody and drag them onto a ship."

"I'm not leaving her," Tesania vowed, her mind recalling Caitriona's crazed cackling on her bed. "She . . . they, have to be stopped."

"I'll talk the others," Deavon sighed.

***

The lookout's cry of "Land ho!" sent a cheer rippling along the decks of the King's Ship Swan as she ran before a stiff southerly breeze, the sailors rushing to the rails and cheering once more as the Aliagan coast appeared like a smudge across the distant horizon as the captain's angry voice boomed along the wind, demanding they return to their duties.

Captain Eades kept the coast off the port side for the next three days as the Swan ran up the Aliagan coast, eventually calling for the sails to be furled as they rounded the Estel headland in the late afternoon and made for the docks.

"Here's where I leave you," Rhys said as the party gathered at the bottom of the gangplank leading to shore.

"I've been away from my . . ." Pausing, he glanced at Baird. "Err, shall we say, business for too long."

"Business," Baird scoffed, grinning at the little thief before stepping forward and taking his hand, shaking warmly as he said, "We couldn't have done it without you."

"Does that mean you're my friend now?" Rhys asked his eyes calculating what that could mean.

"I wouldn't say we're friends," Baird replied, laughing aloud. "Let's just say we have an understanding."

"An understanding," Rhys repeated nodding as he weighed up what that might mean to his future business.

Laughing once more, Baird released his hand. "I'm sure I'll see you around."

"If I allow it," Rhys replied, winking.

"Even if you don't," Baird assured him, winking back.

"Thank you, my friend," Deavon said stepping forward and taking the thief's hand. "As Baird said, we couldn't have done it without you."

"It was nothing," the little thief said. "Besides," he added grinning at Giddy. "I will be reimbursed handsomely for my time."

"I'll remind General Legana when I get back," Giddy replied grinning back at him. "Perhaps, when he calms down, he'll let Raim and I bring it to you personally."

"You know where to find me."

One by one the others said goodbye, Tesania waiting until last and taking him into an embrace. "I'm glad Giddy found you," she said.

"As am I," Rhys replied disentangling himself and picking up his pack.

"I'm sorry you didn't find what you were after," Tesania said.

Shrugging, Rhys replied over his shoulder as he turned and walked away, "It was worth a shot. At least now I know what I'll be up against if I do decide to open shop in Tiadath."

"Farewell," Tesania called after him, watching him walk into the shadows of an alleyway. It saddened her to see him go. He had been integral in their mission and its success.

"We'd better go," Deavon said beside her, his face now all but healed, just a slight pinkness suggesting he had ever been hurt.

"Will we have to wait to see the king again?" Kailyn asked. "Like last time?"

"Leave that to me," Baird replied before asking, "Are you going to stay at the Vine Inn again?"

"I should think so," Tesania replied.

"I'll send you a message there."

Nodding, Tesania agreed, calling after him, "We need to see him as soon as possible."

"I'll see what I can do," he called back before disappearing into a throng of people.

"The Vine Inn it is," Tesania said, looking around at the others.

"And a bath," Kailyn sighed.

***

"Good morning, Miriam," Tesania said cheerfully to the woman who had tried to deny them entry to the King's Palace on their previous visit months before. "I trust you are well?"

Frowning as she looked at Tesania and then took in the others, Miriam's face slipped into a scowl as she obviously remembered them.

"Be a dear and run along to the page over there, will you? Let him know Lady Tesania and her entourage are here to see the king. In half an hour I believe."

"Tes," Deavon warned.

"Run along now," Tesania said to Miriam ignoring him as she waved the woman toward the page. "You wouldn't want us to miss our appointment, would you?" As the woman scowled at her and then turned and walked slowly to the page, Tesania said to Deavon. "She's a horrible woman."

"Still."

"I'm with Tes," Giddy said. "She deserves it after the way she spoke to us last time."

Shaking his head, Deavon said, "You've had your fun," as the woman walked back to them.

"If you would take a seat," she said feigning a smile. "The king will see you shortly."

"You have been very helpful, Miriam," Tesania said beaming after the woman as she hurried away. Glancing at Giddy, she smiled as the soldier winked at her before walking to a row of seats and sitting down to wait. It wasn't long however before the page called her name and directed them into the king's chamber. The room he ushered them into was the same one they had had their audience in before. Dragging a chair out noisily from the table running nearly the entire length of the room, Tesania sat, folding her hands together on the table as she nodded to Baird sitting to the king's right, the same people who had attended their previous meeting also sat at the table busily reading parchments in their hands.

"Baird," the king said motioning to the spy, "has brought me up to date with your mission."

"His help was invaluable," Tesania said, nodding as she smiled briefly at Baird.

"I'm sure," King Asden replied, dismissing it with a wave of his hand as if it were a given that Baird would perform well on the mission. "And now," he went on his eyes boring into her. "You wish to arrest Lord Dalgliesh and his daughter?" he asked eyes still intently watching her. "To take them back to Eldanal to stand trial?"

"Yes," Tesania replied

"On what grounds?"

"Treason . . . Murder . . . ."

"Lord Dalgliesh is not a member of your King's Court anymore."

"He was."

"He is not anymore. He cannot be accused of treason."

Leaning forward, Tesania returned the king's steely gaze. "Lord Dalgliesh and his daughter brought a mage from another land, a land that before now was uncharted and only spoken of in ancient scrolls. They brought him here for a specific reason . . . . They brought him here to employ him to murder and destroy across the breadth of Eldanal."

"What this mage did to Eldanal is not my concern."

Slamming her palm on the table, Tesania stood, her chair falling backward clattering on the flagstones as she said angrily, "He murdered countless people . . . destroyed acres of crops."

King Asden glowered at Tesania. "You dare raise your voice to me?"

Frowning as Deavon recovered her chair, Tesania muttered "Thank you," and sat back down staring at the table. "Forgive me," she said quietly. "But people have suffered at the hands of the mage, many have died."

"I understand your passion," the king said his voice now lowered. "But the mage is dead now, is he not? That is what Baird has led me to believe."

"He is," Tesania replied nodding slowly before looking back at the king. "That mage anyway."

"There are more?"

"Many more," Baird cut in. "There was a large guild in Tuscam."

"The ways are very strong in Tiadath," Kailyn added, shrinking back in her chair as the king turned his gaze to her.

"Nothing Aliaga's mages can't handle, I'm sure."

"Oh, much more than your mages can handle." Kailyn assured him, her voice small.

"Nonsense," the king scoffed. "Aliaga has some very skilled mages."

"Not skilled enough," Kailyn assured him. "The potency of the spells he cast at us was beyond anything we have."

"You have," the king replied, smiling at the girl. "Eldanal's mages are not of the standard of Aliaga's."

"You're wrong," Kailyn said. "I have studied the ways of Aliaga. I assure you, they would not be able to defeat a Tiadath mage."

"Yet you did," the king replied mirth in his voice, laughter in his eyes.

"No . . . I didn't," Kailyn replied. "Tesania did."

Turning to Tesania, the king studied her for a moment, taking in her clothes. "You don't strike me as a mage," he said eventually.

"I'm not," Tesania replied.

"So this mighty mage from Tiadath was beaten by a woman . . . A woman that isn't even a trained soldier."

"A woman that has courage you could only dream of," Giddy interjected.

"Giddy," Tesania said frowning at the soldier before turning back to the king. "You are correct. I am no mage, or indeed soldier. But my sword carries all the magic I need."

"Your sword?"

"The one we spoke of in our last meeting with these people," one of the women beside him said. "Remember, the Tenule chronicles where Aliaga was attacked and—"

"Yes, quite," the king said waving her to silence. Considering Tesania for some time, he eventually turned his attention to Kailyn, causing her to squirm under the scrutiny. "Their magic is that strong?" he asked.

"I'm afraid so," Kailyn replied. "It is beyond what we can deal with."

"Why? What exactly makes them so strong."

"Potency for a start," Kailyn replied. "Sergh's spells were so powerful that they scorched the earth as they passed."

"And?"

"The most dangerous thing is their protective spells. They encase themselves in a magic armor that cannot be penetrated by our spells . . . not even swords."

"Except yours?" the king asked Tesania.

"Except mine," Tesania said quietly.

"And we cannot forge more of these swords?"

'No," Tesania replied simply. "We don't know the spells that were used when it was forged."

Frowning, the king asked, "How far away is this land of Tiadath?"

"A little over three months."

"Three months!" the king exclaimed. "They are that close?"

"Yes," Tesania replied.

Shaking his head, he turned to the woman beside him. "Why don't we know of this land, Orissa?"

Nonplussed, Orissa shook her head. "We trade with Eldanal. Our ships don't venture out more than that."

Frustrated that the conversation had gone away from their original reason for the meeting, Tesania said, "They are close enough for Lord Dalgliesh to bring another one over and have them attacking us within six months."

"So we are back to Eldanal's problem again?" the king scowled.

"It's your problem as well as Eldanal's," Tesania assured him. "Agreed, right now you and Aliaga are safe. But what about when Lord Dalgliesh is offended by you or one of your lords? Or when his daughter thinks she has been insulted by some lady and begs her father to exact revenge?"

"I will deal with him then," the king replied.

"And the Tiadath mage he has attacking your palace? Destroying your farms and killing your people?"

Resting his elbows on the table, the king lowered his chin onto his forefingers and contemplated her words, his eyes never leaving her.

"He will do it," Tesania assured him. "He thinks nothing of ordering the death of hundreds of people, nothing of destroying farms and towns." As the king continued to look at her in silence, she added, "He's a murderer, if not by his own hand, then by his actions. He'll bring another mage to Aliaga, maybe more than one. It is up to us to stop him . . . to bring him to justice before he brings destruction upon us all." Pausing she pleaded with her eyes as the king considered her words before adding, "If we don't stop him before he floods these lands with Tiadath Mages . . . who will?"

Turning his gaze away from Tesania, the king sat back before looking at Orissa, seeming to have come to a decision, "I want a meeting with the archmage immediately." As Orissa started to write his command onto a parchment, he added, "Send a dispatch to King Eldine of Eldanal and extend an invitation for his archmage—"

"Naisa," Kailyn informed him.

"Invite Naisa," the king went on, smiling briefly at Kailyn, "To visit upon us and discuss these mages from Tiadath and the threat they pose." As the woman wrote frantically, he added, "Have the admiral come in tomorrow. I want to know more about Tiadath, exactly where it is, its coastline . . . we can't have a potential enemy only three months away and have no intelligence on them."

"We can send you a copy of the captain's sea charts," Deavon offered.

"Thank you," the king said. "That would be advantageous." Turning his attention back to Orissa, he said, "I want a meeting with the senior staff from all our forces tomorrow afternoon." Turning his attention to Baird, he said, "You will lead a detachment of soldiers and accompany these people to Lord Dalgliesh's estate and arrest him."

"And his daughter?" Tesania asked quickly.

"And his daughter too."

"We can take them back to Eldanal to answer for their crimes?"

Nodding his head, the king said, "Obviously Lord Dalgliesh does not know his place." Turning to Orissa, he instructed, "Have a warrant written up denouncing his title and clearing the arrest and removal from Aliaga of Lord Dalgliesh and his daughter. I will sign it in the morning." Turning back to Tesania and then looking around the others, he said, "Aliaga thanks you for bringing this to our attention. I trust you will have a safe journey back to Eldanal." With that, he looked down at the pile of parchments in front of him, leaving no doubt they had been dismissed.

***

The gates to Lord Dalgliesh's estate creaked open, his guards standing aside and offering no resistance as they nervously watched the two columns of soldiers march past them and into the compound. Baird had led the columns, stopping a few yards short and unrolling the king's warrant, reading it aloud before demanding the guards step aside and allow entry. Tesania and the others followed the thirty Aliagan soldiers in as they made their way to the whitewashed manor house glistening in the afternoon sunshine. As the soldiers formed up on the stairs, Tesania followed Baird up to the carved wooden entry doors. Turning, she looked at the others, asking, "Ready?" as she reached out and grasped the iron knocker, lifting it and striking the door three times, the sharp, staccato sound echoing through the compound.

It seemed an eternity to Tesania as they waited for the door to open. She stood nervously, knowing that Lord Dalgliesh would not readily surrender. And Caitriona? How would she react when Deavon, the man she loved, entered her home and arrested her and her father? "Be ready," she said. "This isn't going to be easy." Turning back to the door, she reached for the knocker once more, jumping back in fright as the door swung suddenly open.

"May I help you," Dalgliesh's butler asked, his eyes flicking across the travelers and then down the lines of soldiers. "My master isn't expecting anybody today," he said beginning to close the door. "You will need to make an appointment."

Stepping forward, Tesania placed her foot in the jamb and pushed the door back open, having to shove to overcome the butler's resistance. "We are on the King's business," she informed him as she stepped past. "I would appreciate you letting your lord know we are here."

"He will not be pleased," the butler said, watching the soldiers file past him and line up along the foyer walls.

"Whether he is pleased or not is not our concern," Tesania replied, smiling demurely at him. "Perhaps you could go now and inform him?"

Glancing at the soldiers, the butler asked, "Whom shall I say is calling?"

"Lady Tesania."

"Very well," the butler said, pulling down his jacket to smooth it out before turning and walking slowly toward a doorway at the back of the foyer.

"Who?" she heard a deep, commanding voice demand. A few moments passed before he spoke again, fear now tingeing his voice. "Call the guards. Have her taken to the guardhouse immediately." Moments passed before he demanded, "Then call all the guards."

Frowning up at Deavon, Tesania said, "This is getting us nowhere." As he nodded, she started forward, motioning to Baird to follow as Lord Dalgliesh's voice carried to them once more.

"The king's soldiers? In my home? He dares to threaten me!?"

"Oh," Tesania said stepping into what appeared to be the study. "He dares." As Lord Dalgliesh spun on her, rage contorting his face, her sword burst to life, jangling insistently on her hip. Ignoring it, she spoke to the butler. "Please locate Caitriona and have her attend us here."

"You will not," Dalgliesh ordered the butler furiously before demanding, "Remove these people from my home."

"It's alright," Tesania said to the confused butler. "He is no longer your master."

"No longer his master!" Lord Dalgliesh exploded. "You dare come into my home and undermine my authority with my own staff?"

"I do."

"By what authority!?"

"By King Asden's," Tesania replied smiling disdainfully at the outraged lord. As he glared back at her, jaw clenching, she addressed the butler once more. "Please ask Caitriona to attend us immediately." Turning to Baird, she said, "Perhaps a few soldiers will help convince her to come along quietly." Nodding his agreement, Baird left for the foyer to give the orders.

Shaking his head, Lord Dalgliesh laughed aloud, "You have no authority here."

"But I do."

"King Asden has given you," he said sneering as he looked her up and down, "a filthy village girl from Eldanal, jurisdiction over his own people . . . one of his most loyal lords."

"Loyal?" Tesania questioned, eyebrow raised as a shrill voice shrieked at her from the doorway.

"You!"

"Hello, Caitriona," Tesania said, adjusting her sword as it grew more insistent. "Thank you for joining us."

"I hardly had a choice," the indignant woman said, ripping her elbow from the hands of a soldier and adjusting her gown as she glared at him.

"Thank you," Tesania said, dismissing the soldier before turning her attention to Caitriona. "Please stand with your father."

"You can't tell me what to do," Caitriona said rising to her full height and jutting her chin forward defiantly.

Sighing, Tesania said, "Fine. Baird, call the soldiers back please."

"Alright, alright," Caitriona said quickly eyes darting to the doorway as she hurried to her father's side. "What is happening, Father?" she demanded before turning to

Tesania. "Why is this filthy village girl in our ho—" Stopping abruptly, she turned her attention to Tesania's side as she recognized Deavon. "Deavon," she said demurely, her demeanor changing instantly as she said to Lord Dalgliesh, "I told you father. Didn't I? I said he would come for me once Sergh destroyed her."

"Sergh is dead," Tesania informed her flatly. "And, as you can plainly see, I am still here . . . with Deavon nonetheless."

"Sergh . . . Dead," Caitriona repeated her words slowly confusion clouding her face.

Shaking her head, Tesania addressed Lord Dalgliesh. "You must know she's quite insane?" When he didn't answer her, she said sadly, "You have destroyed your standing, been banished from Eldanal, for what? For her petty grievances." Pointing to Deavon she went on. "For her deluded dream that he will one day come to her, take her away?"

"Do not talk of my daughter in such a way," Lord Dalgliesh bellowed his deep voice echoing through the room.

"You don't see it, do you?"

"What I see is an upstart village girl that stole my lands in Eldanal!"

"Lands you forfeited because of her! Because she's spoilt . . . because she wanted something she couldn't have!"

"Deavon loves me!" Caitriona screamed at her. "He always has."

"I have not," Deavon said incredulously. "I have never—"

"She's insane," Tesania proclaimed shaking her head in dismay as she said to Lord Dalgliesh, "Can't you see it?"

"You come into my house and call my daughter insane?" Lord Dalgliesh exploded. "Get out . . . Get out all of you," he bawled waving his arms toward the door. "Leave this house now!"

"I see it now," Tesania said sadly to Deavon. "He's as insane as she is."

"Insane!?" Dalgliesh questioned loudly.

"Deranged . . . self absorbed . . . insane."

"Leave my home now," Lord Dalgliesh demanded, finger quivering as he pointed at the door. "Run while you can," he added gloating at her, "Because I will not rest . . . will not spare a penny of my fortune hunting you down."

"You have no fortune," Tesania informed him. "Not anymore."

"What?"

"Baird," Tesania said, "Read it to him."

As Baird rolled out the parchment and read the king's warrant, Lord Dalgliesh's face paled turning whiter and whiter as Baird's words tumbled out, his jowls quivering as his anger rose. Stepping back a few paces, Tesania rested her hand on the pommel of her chattering sword and looked to Caitriona. She sat, picking at her nails, lips pouting as she swung her legs back and forth like a spoilt little girl who wasn't getting her own way. She almost felt sorry for her, knowing that she lived in her own, insane little world, but it was fleeting as images of dead servants and destroyed crops slipped into her mind. Shaking her head sadly, she looked back to Lord Dalgliesh as he exploded.

"He cannot do this to me!"

"He can, and he has," Baird replied. "You have been stripped of your title of Lord. You and your daughter are to be taken into custody immediately and taken to Eldanal to stand trial for your crimes."

"Crimes?" Dalgliesh spluttered. "What crimes."

"What crimes," Tesania repeated in disbelief. "Murder! Destruction!"

"Mur-murder," Dalgliesh stuttered. "I have murdered no one."

"Yes you have."

"No. I have never hurt anyone."

Scoffing, Tesania didn't know whether to scream at him or feel sorry for his madness. "You acquired Sergh's services," she said simply, shaking her head and scowling at the denial she could see in his face.

"What Sergh did is for him to answer for."

"No!" Tesania snapped. "It is for you . . . and for her. You paid him . . . instructed him . . . drew him maps and gave him directions. It is you who are responsible for the death and suffering, for the destruction of land and crops, people starving . . . . It is you that must stand before the King of Eldanal and beg his forgiveness."

"Beg," Dalgliesh spluttered. "I beg to no one."

"That's the word you heard," Tesania screamed at him. "You didn't hear death and suffering? Didn't hear that people are starving? Because of you? Because of her? Because she wanted her petty revenge on me?"

Eyes wide, Dalgliesh looked about the room. "You wronged her," he exclaimed. "She's a Dalgliesh . . . I had no choice."

"She tripped me on the dance floor in Wyvern. She," she said, "Not me. All I did was dance with Deavon."

"She wanted him."

"Wanted him! He didn't want her!"

"She is a Dalgliesh, if she wants him, no one else can have him."

"At any cost?"

"You stole him from her," Dalgliesh insisted eyes wild. "You deserved everything Sergh threw at you."

Tesania stared at him incredulously. Eventually, she looked up at Deavon and said, "They're both beyond insane."

"I am not insane!"

"This is going nowhere," Tesania said morosely. She felt exhausted from the conversation. Turning to Baird, she said, "Please formally arrest them. Have your soldier's escort them out." Without looking at the Dalglieshs' again, she motioned to Deavon and walked out of the front door and down the stairs wanting to scream in frustration.

53 - Home

"He's quite insane," Tesania explained to King Eldine, her voice echoing in the stateroom inside Wyvern Palace. "Caitriona is even worse I fear."

"It was wise of you to petition King Asden and secure their arrest."

"It made sense," Tesania replied. "Sergh was just the tip of the weapon. It was the Dalglieshs' that wielded it."

Nodding, the king asked, "And we won't be seeing any more of Sergh's attacks?"

"No," Tesania replied quietly looking down at her hands and reliving the final battle with the Tiadath Mage for a few moments before going on. "Sergh is dead."

"What about revenge?"

"I don't think so," Deavon answered. "His apprentices are dead."

"The villagers we saw didn't appear to hold much love for him, apart from trade." Aldan said.

"Tiadath seems to have a thriving society," Kailyn added. "The mages academy in Tuscam seemed very advanced."

"So they have many more mages?" the king asked, eyebrow lifting.

"Many," Kailyn replied.

"But without Dalgliesh to employ them they would have no reason to attack us," Deavon said.

"But they could," Naisa said from beside the king. "And they have magic we cannot match."

"Indeed," the king murmured.

"King Asden thought much the same thing," Tesania said. "He's sending a dispatch to ask for Naisa to travel to Aliaga and begin talks about what can be done with the ways to counter them."

"That sounds reasonable," the king replied, nodding as he turned to Naisa. "Arrange to travel to Aliaga at your earliest convenience. Take Kailyn here," he said motioning to the young mage, "with you. She knows firsthand what these Tiadaths can do."

"We could sail there on Lee's ship," Kailyn suggested beaming at Naisa happily. "The Swan."

Nodding affirmation, Naisa said, "We will leave in the next few days."

"And Dalgliesh?" Tesania asked.

Scowling, King Eldine said. "I offered him freedom last time; but banishment was not enough for him. Rebuilding his life with the money and assets he had spirited away couldn't appease his daughter's vain jealousies"

"They are insane," Tesania repeated her earlier words.

"Quite," the king replied. "They will grow to see the dungeons as home," he assured her. "They will not see freedom again."

"And their assets in Aliaga?" Tesania asked. "What will happen to them."

"I will speak to King Asden in due course."

"May I suggest," Tesania said. "The farm holders who have lost everything in the attacks, the pages and maids maimed and injured . . . couldn't they be compensated? Allowed to rebuild their lives with Dalgliesh's ill gotten gains?"

Nodding, King Eldine considered her words, eventually saying, "I will correspond with King Asden. I'm sure he will agree to release at least some of Dalgliesh's assets to them."

Knowing there was little chance of the two kings not keeping the lions share, Tesania smiled at her king and said, "Thank you."

Looking around the gathered travelers, the king said, "It seems you have once again saved Eldanal."

"It was nothing," Giddy said dismissing it with a wave.

"Nonetheless," the king said. "A reward is in order."

"The safety of my people is reward enough," Tesania assured him. "I need no reward."

"Nor I," Deavon agreed.

"You are heroes," the king insisted. "I must give you something."

"We're not heroes," Raim said. "We did what needed to be done. Nothing more."

The king stared at the little soldier for some time eyebrows knitting together when he eventually frowned and said, "You are indeed a hero Raim . . . All of you are. But," he went on holding his hand up to the chorus of denial. "What if I add your reward to the confiscated funds to help the people affected by Dalgliesh and his pet mage?"

"That would be fine," Raim said nodding.

"Very well," the king said, rising and looking around the table. "Eldanal thanks you for your efforts in stopping this threat from across the seas. We are indeed fortunate to have people of your caliber amongst our ranks."

"Thank you," Tesania said. "Anyone could have done it though."

"You are quite incorrect," King Eldine assured her. "You, and your party are amongst the finest Eldanal has ever produced."

"Thank you," Tesania said once more feeling the hotness of her blush flooding her face.

Starting for the door, King Eldine said, "I trust you will be at the ball in your honor tomorrow night?" Stopping, he held his hand up before they could protest. "Let me make it simpler for you," he said. "You shall be at the ball in your honor tomorrow night." Starting for the door once more he said over his shoulder, "That is an order."

54 - Peace

Ripples fled across the water of the Wyvern River as the bow of a small boat pushed against the current, the rhythmical splash of its oars biting the water echoing lightly off the clover covered river banks on either side. Tesania twirled her parasol in her hand, watching as it spun above her head. "It's over," she said to Deavon as he pulled at the oars. "Peace is so beautiful," she added happily gesturing to two swans gliding peacefully along the slow flowing water as the soft morning breeze played wistfully among the lush green grass on the banks drifting by.

Nodding, Deavon dug an oar into the water, pulling the boat around. "We'd better head back," he said. "We'll be late for the ball."

Tesania laughed. "So," she said lightly as she leaned on the rail and dipped her hand in the cool water. "It's so peaceful here. Let's stay forever."

"We can't," Deavon replied, "Duty calls."

"Duty . . . . Don't remind me," Tesania said flicking water at the ranger.

"Well, it does," Deavon insisted.

Crawling forward in the little boat as Deavon desperately tried to stop it rocking, Tesania murmured, "Hush," before cupping the back of his head and pulling him to her kiss.

~ The end ~

Author's Note

Greetings.

I hope you enjoyed Tiadath Mage. Thanks for reading!

Best regards
Grant E Brazell

Homepage: www.grantebrazell.wordpress.com
Facebook: www.facebook.com/grant.e.brazell
Twitter: www.twitter.com/GrantEBrazell#

ABOUT THE AUTHOR

Grant E Brazell was born in Sydney Australia in 1966 to parents of English heritage. He has been a reading buff for decades and spends most of his life wide awake in dreamland. He currently lives in Australia, with his wife, son and two cats.

Grant E. Brazell